BOOK 1

MONEY
MURDER
MAYHEM

BOOK 2

ART
WINE
and
CRIME

A LORD & LADY CROSSWICK
Mystery Bundle

Tana L.H. Boerger

A Lord and Lady Crosswick Mystery

MONEY MURDER MAYHEM

Tana L.H. Boerger

ONE

"**W**HAT WOULD YOU change about your life if you could pick anything?" Michael Findley asked, looking around the lavish dining table at his ten dinner guests.

"I want to go first! I want to go first!" A well-maintained, sixty-something woman fluttered her hand in the air, light bouncing off her ten-carat diamond.

"Tell us, Madeline, what would you change?"

She dabbed her napkin on either side of her mouth, then said, "I'd marry my second husband first!" She beamed at an attractive, much younger man sitting across from her, and blew him a kiss.

The table erupted in howls of laughter.

Conrad Reston, founder of the most successful law firm in the state, tapped his spoon on his wine goblet. The pretty tinkling caught everyone's attention.

"Okay, Conrad. The floor's yours."

"That's easy." The elegant septuagenarian arched a white brow. "Instead of working a hundred hours a week for the last thirty years to build a law firm that sucks the life out of me, I'd inherit my wealth!"

That drew a round of applause from the group of hard-working, successful diners.

Michael pointed to the other end of the table. "Go on, Philip, tell us, what would you change about your life?

Philip Warwick thought for several seconds, shrugged, and said, "Absolutely nothing."

The other guests hooted and booed; several threw their wadded napkins across the table at Philip's head.

Looking at her husband, Genevieve, his wife of forty years, blushed like a bride and grinned with pleasure.

"I can't imagine a better life than I live." He tilted his head. "Genevieve and I have a terrific son, a smart, loving daughter-in-law, and two hilarious grandkids. As entrepreneurs, we've worked our butts off and had our share of struggles, but that's been half the fun. We laugh a lot, rarely argue anymore, and we're still crazy about each other." His eyes caught Genevieve's. "Does it get any better than that?"

"If I had your life, I wouldn't change anything either," said James Wallard, one of Philip's oldest friends. James' stunning trophy wife, Lauren, sat next to Philip. She was thirty-two, more than three decades younger than Philip's wife, but with none of Genevieve's elegance. After forty years of marriage, Philip was still in awe of 'G,' as he had called her from the night they'd met at university. She was a second-year law student, he was about to complete his master's degree in art history. As he loved to say, "I married my trophy wife first!"

Now, seven hours later, Genevieve squinted, eyes reduced to slits. Having drunk her fair share of Champagne the night before, the reflection of the sun glancing off countless tiny waves on the lake was brutal. She leaned her thumping head back on the chaise and tilted her face toward the rising sun's warmth. The breeze coming off the water ruffled her hair, and a wisp tickled her nose. 7:30 a.m. It would be an hour before Philip stirred, too long to wait for coffee. Where was the butler when you needed him? Even as she mused about how difficult her life was without a manservant, her ears caught the sound of grinding coffee beans. She pried open her left eye. Through the window from the deck, she saw a lanky shadow moving about the kitchen. Grateful that her prayers had been answered, she hummed softly. She still thrilled at the sight of her husband. Though he wasn't a proper butler, he certainly was a handsome houseboy.

Genevieve teetered on the edge of a shallow dream in which Philip floated from the kitchen, took her hand, and handed her a steaming mug. The aroma of the brew was enticing, and it was only when Philip's lips brushed her forehead that she realized the coffee in her dream was on the glass table next to her. She sensed Philip lowering himself into the chair beside her.

"Good morning, pretty girl."

With effort, she opened her eyes to see Philip's lopsided smile. She chuckled and reached for her mug. "The service here is pretty good".

"Happy to take care of all your needs, Ma'am." He winked and fluttered his eyebrows.

Their deck was the perfect place to enjoy the early-morning

quiet. A heron strutted along the water's edge, stopping to look for a fishy breakfast. The home they had created suited them. Warm and inviting, it overlooked water and the endless green of a golf course.

Ceiling fans stirred the air, rustling geraniums in their yellow pots.

Philip stretched his long legs onto the ottoman and angled his face to the morning sun. "What did you think of Leslie's new face?" he asked without a trace of humor.

"Wow!" Genevieve said. "She got her money's worth! Who does she remind you of now?"

Philip knitted his brow. "Joan Rivers in a wind tunnel?"

Genevieve struggled to keep coffee from spraying out of her nose. She gulped then coughed before snorting out a laugh. As she pulled a tissue from her pocket to wipe her eyes, Philip's phone rang. He glanced at his watch. Eight o'clock on a Sunday morning. He pressed 'accept,' answering the unknown number.

"Philip Warwick. Yes. Yes." Silence.

Genevieve tensed. A call so early on a Sunday screamed "emergency," but Philip showed no signs of concern, just interest.

After a few minutes he said, "Let me talk to my wife, make a couple of calls...Of course."

She studied Philip's face for any sign of what the call might be, but it gave nothing away.

Philip listened; his forehead furrowed. "Yes. Yes. I understand, but it's critical to confirm all this.

Genevieve strained to hear but couldn't make out any words.

Should she be worried about their son, Duncan, his wife, Julia, their grandchildren Alexander, and Ella?

"Sure, as soon as the package arrives."

What package? Genevieve shoved herself from the chaise and began to pace back and forth on the deck, becoming more agitated by the second.

Minutes ticked by, punctuated by Philip's mumbles and nods. "Of course. Of course. I can verify all this with your New York office."

Genevieve tried to make eye contact with Philip, raising her eyebrows in a question. He ignored her. "This is quite a lot to take in."

Genevieve suppressed a groan of frustration. *What* is a lot to take in?!

At last, Philip said, "Let me make sure I have this right. You say he died ten months ago?"

Genevieve gasped. Who died? She couldn't believe Philip's detached expression.

"And you've been looking for the heir since then?"

Genevieve stood frozen, listening to the clues, trying to piece it all together.

"It sounds like a fantasy or more like a scam. Is the estate significant enough to warrant such a search?"

She crossed the deck to Philip's side, signaling for him to tell her what was going on.

At last, he looked at her. Surprise crossed his face as he suddenly remembered she was there. "I see. I see. Really?...

Hmmm. Really? Just a minute. Let me put you on speaker phone. My wife will want to hear this."

Philip pressed the speaker icon and put the phone on the table between them. "Genevieve, this is David Weatherington. He's calling from England, and he works for a law firm. Mr. Weatherington, tell Genevieve what you just told me."

"Good morning, Ms. Warwick. Or I should say, Lady Crosswick."

Genevieve's eyes widened. "What do you mean, Lady Crosswick? Why would you call me that?"

"Give Mr. Weatherington a chance to explain, G." Philip put his hand on her knee.

"Lady Crosswick, last November Jonathon Laney died. He was the 12TH Earl of Crosswick, and also your husband's distant cousin on his mother's side." Genevieve gave Philip a quizzical look, shaking her head as she listened to David Weatherington's posh accent. She stood and as Weatherington told his story, she wandered to a pot of geraniums, and started deadheading the old blossoms.

"He had no children and, it turns out, your husband is his closest living relative. Jonathon Laney was one of the richest men in England. Since his death, executors at Holmes Fitch Smythson Morrow have been confirming Mr. Warwick's identity and legal right to this inheritance."

"Inheritance?" Genevieve's attention whipped from the spent geraniums to the voice on the phone.

"More than £990,000,000, plus several properties."

Genevieve's look of shock met Philip's perplexed grin.

"You'll receive a DHL package shortly. It will confirm all this information. Did I leave anything out, my lord?"

Philip made a funny face at Genevieve and mouthed 'my lord.' "I think that about sums it up, Mr. Weatherington."

Genevieve started at the sound of the doorbell then bolted into the house.

"I think the package just arrived. Genevieve's checking. Yes, I'll do that. Thank you, Mr. Weatherington. Of course, David." Philip ended the call and walked into the kitchen where Genevieve met him with a thick DHL envelope in hand.

"What a way to start a Sunday!" Philip searched Genevieve's eyes. "What in the world? Do you think this could possibly be true?"

"I have no idea, but I bet the information in the package will be interesting at the very least." She handed the envelope to him, her excitement growing. "Open it, Philip! Open it! I want to see where it says we're billionaires!"

He tossed the envelope onto the kitchen table and sauntered to the Nespresso coffee maker. He placed a pod in the head, put his empty cup under the spigot and pressed the button. While the machine poured out fresh coffee with a topper of thick foam, he turned around and leaned against the cabinet. He folded his arms. "You seem to be pretty excited, G."

"What is wrong with you?" Shaking her head at her annoying husband, Genevieve laughed as she threw a dishtowel at Philip. "Open the damn envelope!"

"Whoa! Lady Crosswick's getting bossy. The potential of becoming absurdly rich is making her drunk with aggression!"

"If you won't open it, I will." Willing to wait no longer, Genevieve reached for the DHL pouch but before she could snatch it, Philip grabbed her wrist.

"Not so fast, my lady," he said. "Look at the name on this envelope. Philip James Warwick. Do you see Genevieve Hayden Warwick written anywhere? It would be a federal offense for you to open my mail. In fact, it's probably a violation of international law since it came from England." Philip pulled Genevieve into his arms and tickled her showing no mercy. She squirmed and wiggled trying to escape his grasp, gasping for air between snorts of laughter. "I bet Interpol will knock down the door any minute!"

"Stop! Stop it, you beast!" Tears streamed down her cheeks.

"I'll stop if you say, 'Please stop tickling me, my lord.'" Philip found a new spot on her ribs to attack. "Go on. Say it, my little wench."

"Lady…Crosswick…is…not…a…a…wench!" Genevieve managed to wheeze out the words. "Please, Philip. Stop!"

"All right, all right. I've tortured you enough." He eased his hold on her and stepped back, gripping her shoulders until she was stable.

"I can't remember the last time you tickled me like that." She wiped her streaming eyes with a tissue. "You're terrible. Now would you please open the envelope?"

"My God, the woman is single-minded." Philip picked up the packet and his coffee and carried them to the massive kitchen island. He pulled out a stool and sat, nodding to Genevieve to do the same. "Okay. Let's see what's in this Pandora's box, my darling Lady Crosswick. Hand me the scissors, please."

"When you put it that way, it sounds a little ominous. You don't think this is going to open a flood of problems, do you?" Genevieve pulled the scissors out of the knife block and gave them to Philip.

"I was just trying to dazzle you with my command of literary references. Did it work?"

"Actually, it gives me pause. If we're trading literary references, how about 'Heavy is the head that wears the crown?' I bet there are a few burdens that come with a billion pounds. Can you imagine the scammers who'll come out of the woodwork?" Genevieve took Philip's hand, cradling it in both of hers. Holding his gaze, she said, "Until we know something different, Let's just take it step by step and enjoy every minute."

"Great plan, oh wise one." Philip held up the envelope and the scissors. "Shall we?"

"Oh yes!" Genevieve said, her enthusiasm bubbling over.

Careful not to cut the contents, Philip slid the scissors along the edge of the heavy plastic pouch. Genevieve was off her stool and hanging on his shoulder, stretching to see what was inside.

"G, could you please give me a little breathing space? I promise I won't hide anything from you." Though he smiled, Genevieve heard an edge in his voice that made her sit back down.

Philip pulled two inches of thick, cream-colored bond from the sleeve. On top was a letter of introduction with the name of one of London's oldest and most prestigious law firms: Holmes Fitch Smythson Morrow.

"Here we go," he said clearing his throat before he read.

Holmes Fitch Smythson Morrow
26 Upper Brook Street
London
W1K 7QE,
United Kingdom

Dear Lord Crosswick,

It is with pleasure Holmes Fitch Smythson Morrow write to confirm you are the sole legal heir to the estate of Jonathon William Wallace Laney, 12TH Earl of Crosswick, who, on November 18TH, died of natural causes at Margrave House, his townhouse in Kensington, in London.

The enclosed documents verify the information Sir David Weatherington provided via telephone. Sir David will be your principal contact going forward and will arrange your trip to New York to begin the transfer of your inheritance as soon as is practicable. In the meantime, enclosed for your review is general information about the estate and its holdings.

We will continue to serve you as we served your cousin, the late 12TH Earl of Crosswick and the five preceding generations of the House of Crosswick.

I have the honour to be Your Lordship's obedient servant,

Sir Mark James Holmes

Sir Mark James Holmes
Managing Partner
Holmes Fitch Smythson Morrow

"So much for perfunctory ass-kissing. Where is the list of assets?" Genevieve was anxious to see an inventory of the estate's wealth. She stood, reaching for the papers.

Philip scooped them out of her reach. "I've known you for forty-three years and I had no idea you were such a greedy girl." He gave Genevieve a sharp look and held the stack high above his head.

She plopped back onto her stool. "I'm surprised myself. This isn't like me, is it?"

Philip's eyes softened. "It's okay, G. This situation is unreal. I think we can give ourselves a little slack. We should give ourselves permission to feel however we feel for, let's say…" he looked at the ceiling then back at his wife. "Let's say we give ourselves until we get to Wilmingrove Hall. Until then we can feel greedy, excited, suspicious, happy, unhappy, miserable, thrilled—whatever we feel. But when we get to Wilmingrove Hall, you and I will have a serious conversation about what this all means and how we're going to handle it. Until then, we just enjoy the ride. Deal?"

Genevieve extended her hand, and they shook. "Deal," she said. "Now, show me the big fat list of stuff we're about to own!"

Philip flipped through page after page of the will until he got to the exhibits. "Aha. Here we go. This is what you want." He handed Genevieve several pages with the heading 'Property Inventory.' "Start with that." He continued scanning the pages. "Here are a few more." He put a dozen sheets with 'Art Inventory' next to the first stack.

"Wow. Just wow, Philip! Listen to this."

He dropped the papers on the counter and leaned back.

"We own a thirteen-room apartment in New York on Central Park West. We own the townhouse in London, Margrave House, where the Earl died. Evidently, Jonathon enjoyed living the good life. Thank you for that, Jonathon. We own Wilmingrove Hall, the family seat since 1882. There is an apartment in Paris on Avenue Foch, one of my favorite streets in Paris."

"Well, aren't you the lucky girl!" Philip smiled with pure joy as he listened to Genevieve, watching her excitement mount. To him, none of this would be real until they met with the lawyers in New York, but he was enjoying that Genevieve was embracing their possible good fortune.

"And we have a vineyard in St. Emilion. Do you remember when we visited several wineries there a couple of years ago? Wouldn't it have been funny if we'd toured Chateau Beaulieu, our vineyard?"

"That would be pretty amazing." Philip couldn't take his eyes off his wife's face. She looked twenty, cheeks flushed, eyes sparkling.

"And last but certainly not least, we own a horse farm in Lexington, Kentucky."

"A horse farm?" Philip began to absorb some of Genevieve's infectious excitement. "I wonder if we own any racehorses. I'd love that."

Genevieve stood up, put her hands over her head and stretched like an elegant cat. "Before I read any more, I need to go take a shower and let this sink in." She walked toward their bedroom, stopped and, over her shoulder said, "Care to join me?"

"I'll be there in a minute," Philip said, absorbed in a spread-sheet.

Genevieve walked through their bedroom into their spacious bathroom. She turned on the faucet and slid her silk nightgown off her shoulders.

Though she was sixty-four, a lifetime of exercise and great genes gave her a body defined by long, taught muscles and lovely skin. She was grateful how kind Mother Nature had been.

She stepped into the steaming stream, letting the water pound over her head. She heard the bathroom door open and felt Philip's presence.

He stepped into the shower and fitted his body against her back. He cupped a breast in each hand and leaned down, kissing her ear. "Darling girl." His voice was husky. "If this inheritance proves to be what it seems, our lives have just changed forever."

Genevieve turned in his arms and looked into his eyes, her lips just a breath away from his. "Last night you said you wouldn't change a thing about our lives."

"That was last night. This is today," Philip said, a smile on his lips and mischief in his eyes.

TWO

THROUGH THE WINDOW of the Bombardier Global 6000, Genevieve stared into a gray, wet wall, rain streaking across the glass. Forty-eight hours ago, she and Philip were nursing the after-effects of the previous night's party. Now, they were hurtling toward New York City in their private jet to claim a king's ransom.

Yesterday's call from their long-time attorney, Michael Findley, confirmed everything David Weatherington had said. Philip was the heir to Jonathon William Wallace Laney, the 12TH Earl of Crosswick's immense fortune.

"Champagne, Lady Crosswick?"

Genevieve looked up into the hazel eyes of a leggy flight attendant, holding a crystal glass filled to the brim with pretty bubbles.

"Yes please." Genevieve accepted the flute, licking the side of the glass where a small stream of Champagne had escaped over the rim. She grinned, looking up at the flight attendant. "We don't want any of this to go to waste."

The young woman gave Genevieve a wide smile. "Certainly

not!" she said in a posh English accent and extended a silver tray of hors d'oeuvres. "The salmon caviar bites are wonderful. In fact, everything is quite spectacular. Your chef is outstanding."

"My chef is outstanding... I have a chef," Genevieve thought to herself. Her lips turned up as she mouthed, "I have a chef." In her mind, fireworks exploded, and James Brown bellowed, "I Feel Good!"

Across the cabin Philip and Michael faced each other, their laptops open on a mahogany table between them. They had been talking non-stop since yesterday. In just a few hours, Michael had become the Warwicks' expert on the 12TH Earl of Crosswick. Philip and Genevieve wanted to have as much background as they could before meeting with the Estate's lawyers. The more they learned, the more interesting it became.

The Laneys' extraordinary family history unveiled generations of entrepreneurs and philanthropists. Now, Philip James Warwick, the 13TH Earl of Crosswick, and his wife, Genevieve Hayden Warwick, Countess of Crosswick, were the next link in the House of Crosswick chain.

Philip scowled at the sheaf of papers in his hand. He sat slumped in his dove gray leather seat, glasses perched midway down his nose. "The more I study these papers, the more complicated this inheritance seems to be. You have no idea how grateful I am you're here, Michael," Philip said.

"I just want you to remember that I knew you when!" Michael joked. The three of them had been friends since he and Genevieve were in law school, long before Michael became their attorney.

"It's exciting but mind blowing," Philip said. "I mean this guy is—well, was—seriously rich!"

Her Champagne glass in hand, Genevieve crossed the aisle to sit next to Philip. "And now, it appears, so are you. Tell me again what David Weatherington told you about your cousin."

"David wasn't at all surprised that my family didn't know about Jonathon Laney." Philip flipped through his notes and began to tick off entries. "He was ninety-eight when he died last November. He was an only child. He graduated from Cambridge, barely. His parents were killed in a car accident when he was twenty-three, at which time he inherited the Crosswick title and all the wealth that went with it."

Genevieve drank the last of her Champagne and hoped the flight attendant would take note of her empty glass. "Go on."

"At that point, he embarked on an earnest career as a jet-setting playboy, acquiring the Paris and New York apartments. When he was thirty-seven, he became engaged to an American heiress he met in New York."

Genevieve leaned forward, elbows on the table, chin cradled in her hands. "I love that he fell in love with an American."

"You're such a romantic." Philip brushed Genevieve's cheek with his knuckle and continued. "About a year and a half after they met, they were skiing in Sun Valley, Idaho, where he had an accident that left him paralyzed. He broke off his engagement and lived the rest of his life as a recluse in his townhouse in London, seeing only his small staff and few visitors."

"I'd prefer a happy ending." Genevieve looked at Philip and

Michael, eyes shiny with tears. "Please don't tell me that was the end of his love life?" Genevieve's said.

"I think David said something about an affair." Philip looked at his notes, flipping back a page. "Here it is. He engaged a young art historian to help him catalogue his art collection. She was doing a practicum with the Laney Museum of Art. According to the gossip, the professional relationship turned into an affair, but in the end, Jonathon encouraged her to find love elsewhere."

Genevieve sniffed then blew her nose. "Cad," she said.

Philip looked up from his notes. "David said unless someone in our family did a genealogy, no one would have any idea we were related to this very wealthy earl. I know my mother's ancestors were Laneys, a land grant family. They received land in the eighteenth century, but the information pretty much stopped there, at least as far as I was concerned. Believe me, If I'd known my cousin, Jonathon Laney, was holed up in a posh townhouse in London for sixty-one years, sitting on a billion pounds, I would have shown more interest in the family tree!" Philip grinned and looked over his glasses that had slipped to the tip of his nose. "I have to admit, this is getting interesting. As you know, I've never inherited a billion dollars…err…pounds before."

Genevieve's eyes sparkled. "It's been so exciting the last couple of days, talking about the great things we're going to do with this wealth. Believe me, darling boy, I'll be right by your side to help. I'm going to stick to you like glue." Laughing, Genevieve gave Philip a noisy kiss on the cheek. "I'm not going anywhere!"

When their plane touched down at Teterboro, the closest general aviation airport to Manhattan, the rainy day had turned sizzling and sultry, unusual for mid-September. At the bottom of the stairs a black Maybach limousine waited, motor running. When they saw the car, Philip caught Genevieve's eye. With a wry smile, he raised one eyebrow and said, "Of course there's a Maybach waiting for us."

Genevieve's shiny brown bob swished over her shoulders as she did a little jig ending with a bump into Philip's hip. "I think I'm going to like being outrageously wealthy!"

"Try to show some decorum, would you?" Philip said trying to hide his excitement.

Nestled in the luxury of the Maybach, they headed directly to the New York offices of Holmes Fitch Smythson Morrow on 6TH Avenue and West 49TH Street, where they would meet Sir David Weatherington for the first time. Though it was only thirteen miles from Teterboro Airport to mid-town Manhattan, it took almost an hour to navigate New York City's mid-morning traffic.

Except for classical music wafting from the Burmester sound system, and the low murmur of Philip and Michael talking, the car was quiet. Genevieve stared out of the window at the crowded sidewalks, lost in her own thoughts until the car stopped in front of a stone building with massive, carved wooden doors.

Their driver opened the car door and the three alit from the limousine. They jostled their way across the crowded sidewalk and pushed through the doorway into the imposing lobby.

An attractive, athletic man, about six feet tall, stood by the reception desk. His chestnut hair, graying at the temples, was fashionably long, curling just over the collar of his starched, pin-striped shirt. The moment he saw Philip and Genevieve, he burst into a broad smile as if seeing old friends. "Lord and Lady Crosswick, I'm David, David Weatherington. It's wonderful to see you." Striding forward to meet them, he extended his hand. "We're so pleased you could come to New York so quickly. I hope the flight was all right?" His English public-school accent seemed appropriate, given the baronial atmosphere of the foyer.

"When you're flying in your own jet, things seem to go pretty well." Returning his smile, Philip took David's outstretched hand, shook it warmly, then introduced Genevieve.

To her surprise, David grasped her shoulders and, in a much more Continental than English fashion, kissed Genevieve on both cheeks. "Welcome, welcome," he said.

"And, David, this is Michael Findley. Michael has been our attorney for twenty years and is a long-time friend as well. He'll be working with your group."

"I look forward to that, Michael. You'll find plenty of interesting estate law for all of us to share." Turning back to Philip and Genevieve, David said, "I can't tell you how splendid it is to meet you both at long last. After months searching for you, verifying your existence and your lineage, I feel as if I've known you forever."

"I'm glad you were so persistent," Genevieve chuckled.

"It's not every day I get a call saying I've inherited a billion pounds." Philip said. "In fact, I can't remember the last time that happened."

Their laughter bounced around the marble lobby.

"Shall we go up?" David gestured toward the bank of elevators.

Philip took Genevieve's elbow and guided her into the waiting car. "I have the distinct feeling once these doors close, our lives will never be the same."

"There's a significant chance of that," said David, punching the button marked P. "I hope you don't find the next few hours too dry or boring. There's a lot of legal ground to cover."

Philip scowled. "I can't imagine how anything about this situation could be dry or boring. What has just happened to us is not only shocking and overwhelming, but life changing."

"And thrilling," Genevieve added, her smile crinkling the corners of her eyes.

David looked apologetic. "Of course, you're right. As you said, this doesn't happen every day."

"It does not," Philip confirmed.

"Though Jonathon Laney was an invalid and recluse for the last sixty years of his life, I'm happy to tell you he managed his estate brilliantly." The elevator stopped. The doors slid open revealing a paneled reception room that looked more like an exclusive London club than a New York law office.

David ushered the Warwicks into the lobby. "So, while you are not taking on any financial terrors, there are hundreds of details to address: creating new wills, making decisions on charitable giving, overseeing a foundation, managing multiple homes, a vineyard and numerous other business interests, and getting a grasp on millions of pounds of artwork and antiquities: those owned personally and those held by The Laney Museum of Art, and the more recent Laney Musée des Beaux Arts, Paris. And, of course, security."

As David spoke, Genevieve looked around the genteel chamber they had entered. Wingback leather chairs were flanked by mahogany tables that Genevieve was quite sure were original Queen Anne pieces. At the far end of the room stood a large fireplace, its realistic gas logs awaiting a chilly day. She scanned the art hanging on every wall and smiled at the contemporary works of David Hockney, Georgia O'Keeffe, a crazy, rhythmic canvas by Anselm Kiefer and a massive Franz Kline, all a wonderful contrast to the staid elegance of the Georgian room.

"Wow, this is quite a surprise. Who's the collector?" Genevieve asked.

"Well… um, actually, the partners are great supporters of the arts." David looked down at his shoes then back at Philip and Genevieve.

"They have excellent taste," Philip said his voice full of admiration.

"They do, Lord Crosswick." David abruptly changed the subject.

"I understand that when you're finished here in New York, you're going to London to finish some legal work, then to Wilmingrove Hall. Is that correct?"

"That's the plan, right, G?"

"Yes. We're anxious to see this glorious family seat we've heard so much about. We can hardly wait to immerse ourselves in Laney history. Why do you ask, David?"

"If you don't mind, I would very much like to join you there for a couple of days." Lowering his voice, David continued, "I have several…uh…several concerns I want to share with you about the current relationship between Holmes Fitch Smythson Morrow and your estate."

Cocking her head to one side, Genevieve raised an eyebrow. "David, are these concerns things we need to know about sooner rather than later?"

"No. No." David said, but he looked unsure. "They can wait until the end of the week. It's fine. I shouldn't have mentioned anything until I came to Wilmingrove Hall. For now, just forget I said anything."

Philip narrowed his eyes. "Of course, now we won't be able to think about anything else!" He gave David a light punch on the shoulder just as a patrician man with a shock of white hair strode across reception.

"Lord and Lady Crosswick, what a pleasure to meet you at last. I'm Sir Mark Holmes, Managing Partner of Holmes Fitch Smythson Morrow." His voice dripped with arrogance when he emphasized *Sir* Mark. "Everyone in the firm has been looking forward to this occasion since David located you. Quite a story, isn't it? We had almost given up hope that we'd find an heir, and then…." He trailed off, leaving the sentence hanging in the air.

"Yes. As I'm sure you can imagine, it came as quite a surprise to us," Philip said. "A lot has happened in a short time. We understand we have a full agenda today."

"You do, indeed. This afternoon and tomorrow you have many documents to sign, then we will get into the interesting part of the estate: properties, inventory, investments, that sort of thing. I understand you plan to go to London and stay at Margrave House on Friday, before going on to Wilmingrove Hall. I don't think you will be disappointed in either property, but the Hall is particularly special."

With David's cautionary words still echoing, Philip said, "That's what we understand. We're anxious to confirm the family estate has been well managed and is in good shape." There was steel in his voice.

Sir Mark arched an eyebrow and drilled into Philip's eyes. "I assure you, Lord Crosswick, everything has been managed to perfection." His defensive tone confirmed Philip had made his point.

They made their way into a large conference room where floor to ceiling bookshelves were brimming with leather-bound volumes. Though the room was large, the low, coffered ceiling created a coziness. As they entered, twelve men of varying ages and shapes rose. Introductions were made one by one around the table. In addition to David and Sir Mark, Henry Fitch was the other partner who had flown from London to New York for the meeting. Henry was the son of now retired Winston Fitch, one of the name partners, and nineth in an unbroken line of Fitches in the law firm. Henry was cute in a Paul McCartney sense. He was a bit fleshy, his buttons straining the buttonholes of his shirt, his belly bulging over his waistband a bit. No women were among the brain trust, Genevieve noted with disappointment. She was the only woman in the room. Even the attendant responsible for the comfort of the meeting participants was a man.

After a few minutes of pleasantries, Sir Mark urged everyone to be seated. "Lord and Lady Crosswick, please sit here." He gestured to chairs on either side of his place at the head of the massive conference table. For the next three hours a steady flow of documents was presented, discussed, and signed. Questions were asked. Questions were answered. Estate taxes and how, over the years, the estate had been structured to pay the least amount of tax was presented at length. The partners' pride was evident as they explained to Philip and Genevieve how the firm had used every legal strategy available to estates as large as the Laney inheritance and how, through years of careful planning, they had minimized the taxes that must now be paid.

After hours of tedium, there was little energy left in the room. "There's one last subject we need to cover before we adjourn," Sir Mark said, fatigue obvious in his voice. "David, I believe you're going to address the issue of security."

Most of the day David had remained quiet, deferring to the two name partners who wanted very much to dazzle the new Earl and Countess. But at this point, he stood up, walked to a credenza, and picked up a remote control. "Lord and Lady Crosswick, the greatest and perhaps the only downside of your inheritance is that you also inherit the need for security. Because the previous Earl was a recluse, security was easy and minimal. For you and your family, however, that will not be the case."

Philip held up his hand. "David, let me stop you there. We appreciate that the estate is significant," he stopped himself and chuckled. "Well, enormous. But does it really put our family in jeopardy?"

Without hesitation, David said, "Trust me, my lord. It does, both physically and online. The moment we confirmed your identity as the heir to the Laney fortune, an entire world knew who you were and how wealthy you were about to become. Have you or the countess ever been scammed or had your credit cards hacked?"

"Multiple times, of course," Philip said.

Genevieve nodded. "It's part of life these days, isn't it?"

"It is, but this is quite different than finding an unauthorized charge on your American Express card. Just as there are elite athletes, there are elite criminals who spend every waking moment analyzing extraordinary fortunes and figuring out how to take as much money as they can from people with great wealth, even if they have to do harm."

"David, I appreciate what you're saying, but, unless Genevieve objects, I'd rather save this conversation until later. First give us a minute to embrace the idea of being billionaires. Then give us another thirty seconds to process the reality that everyone wants to take our fortune. Do you agree, G?"

"I do," she said. After the grueling day they had just had, the only thing she could think about was the glass of wine and dinner she hoped was waiting for them at their apartment on Central Park West.

THREE

"I'M EXHAUSTED." GENEVIEVE slumped against the marble wall in the lobby of the grand, pre-war building.

The Warwicks arrived at their apartment after seven hours with their team of lawyers. During the marathon meeting, they covered the list of domestic staff in their properties, most of whom had been in the estate's employment for years, a comforting fact. Now, Philip and Genevieve were about to meet the first of that staff.

They entered the elevator and Philip fumbled with a small brass key as he tried to coax it into the slot next to 43E. He turned the key and Genevieve's stomach filled with butterflies as the elevator sailed upward.

"Are you nervous?" Genevieve asked Philip as the floor numbers sped by.

"Very. I mean, Mrs. Proctor has taken care of this apartment since 1974. I'm sure as far as she's concerned, it's her apartment. What if she doesn't like us? If she doesn't let us in, I guess we can afford to spend the night at a Hampton Inn."

Genevieve chuckled, grateful for the comic relief.

The reality of the huge roles they were assuming caused her breath to quicken.

"Do we really want to do this?" Genevieve sagged from her head to her toes, overwhelmed by fatigue. "Last week, our lives were our own. We were only responsible for our family. Today, we're shouldering the responsibility of hundreds of *other* people's lives."

Philip kissed the top of Genevieve's head. "I have to say, there were several times today when I thought we should just donate everything to MOMA and go home."

"My feelings exactly. But I was thinking the Guggenheim." Genevieve looked at him, relief in her eyes.

Philip offered a resigned smile. "But the thing I kept thinking all day is, we never wanted to spend our retirement watching the world go by. This inheritance gives us the opportunity to bring extraordinary resources to our passions, to the things you and I have been working on for years. The Laney Museum of Art is going to give us a huge platform to affect the art world. That alone will make this worthwhile."

"That, and the fact that we have our own private jet!" Genevieve couldn't contain her laughter.

For almost forty years at the Warwick's thirteen-room New York City apartment, Mrs. Proctor the housekeeper and Mr. Emory the houseman had worked as a team. They kept the apartment in immaculate condition, updating as necessary, answering only to the financial team that scrutinized every penny spent on the estate's multi-country holdings. It was hard to imagine the two would welcome the new heir with open arms.

The elevator slid to a stop. "Oh boy. Here we go," Philip said under his breath.

The doors opened and there, through a forty-foot wall of windows, lay a panoramic view of Central Park in all its glory, a green, lush canopy stretching before them. Neither Philip nor Genevieve understood where they were. It appeared, perhaps, they had arrived at a sophisticated lobby.

"Are we in the right place?" Genevieve whispered.

The doors began to close, and Philip stuck his arm out to stop them. He gave Genevieve a quizzical look and a slight shove in the back, nudging her out of the elevator car. They walked across the foyer's classic black and white checkerboard floor, looking for someone who could help them.

"Oh my! I am so sorry I wasn't downstairs to greet you," called an energetic voice with the polish of a slight English accent.

A willowy woman strode through the archway at the far end of the room. She was medium height with short, spikey, white hair. Her close-fitting pants accentuated her narrow hips. Genevieve recognized the woman's crisp, white linen shirt as designer quality and the gold cuff on her wrist as the work of one of Genevieve's favorite jewelry designers.

"We must be paying her well," Genevieve thought, suspicion overtaking her appreciation of the woman's style.

When she reached Philip and Genevieve, she stopped and bobbed a slight curtsy.

"I'm Harriet Proctor," she said. "You are, I presume, Lord and

Lady Crosswick. I can't tell you how thrilled we are to have you here! It's very exciting, the prospect of life and activity in the apartment." Her eyes sparkled.

Philip and Genevieve were speechless, so surprised were they by the warm greeting. In addition to expecting a chilly reception, they each had a mental image of their housekeeper as an elderly, austere woman.

The first to recover, Philip said, "As you can imagine, we're a bit overwhelmed."

"Who wouldn't be?" Mrs. Proctor rolled her eyes. "But trust me when I tell you: it will all be fine. You have many excellent people to help you along the way. Most of us have been with the estate for years and now that we have an active Lord and Lady, things will be much easier and much more exciting!" She clapped her hands. "Mr. Emory will be with us shortly. He's selecting wines for dinner, which can be served any time. I imagine you are exhausted after travelling so early and sitting in meetings all day. May I show you to your rooms?"

"That would be perfect. I'm dying to have a shower and change," Genevieve said, almost pleading.

"That can be arranged," Mrs. Proctor said, turning on her heel. "Right this way."

As they entered the living room, Genevieve's jaw drop. The view stretched from where they stood just off the foyer, across the acres of thick camel carpet, out onto a wide slate terrace, and across Central Park. Sounds of a jazz piano filtering through ceiling speakers filled the apartment. She grabbed Philip's hand and squeezed.

"Mrs. Proctor, this is magnificent." Genevieve breathed in the delicate fragrance of roses then spied a huge bouquet of vivid coral blossoms sitting on a carved credenza to the left.

"Lord and Lady Crosswick, if there is anything you would like redecorated, changed in any way, you must let me know." Mrs. Proctor stopped in front of a dynamic painting hanging over the fireplace. "I understand you two are art lovers."

"My God, is that a Motherwell?" Philip stared at a canvas dancing with burnt sienna, crimson, yellow and black. He leaned close to the signature and whistled under his breath. "It is. It's a Robert Motherwell. Does this belong to the Earl?"

"It does, my lord, it belongs to you." Mrs. Proctor smiled and continued across the living room. "Shall we?"

Speechless, Philip and Genevieve looked at each other, turned and followed Mrs. Proctor down a hall flanked on the right by a bank of French doors flung wide to the terrace, lined with pots overflowing with scarlet geraniums and periwinkle blue plumbago. At the end of the hall, double doors stood open to a large, sumptuous bedroom. The room reminded Genevieve of something out of a Kathryn Hepburn movie: understated old money. Every surface was polished to a sheen or luxuriously upholstered. Like the living room, soft grays, camels, and creamy whites worked together to create an irresistible retreat.

Mrs. Proctor stood to the side and spread her arms, encouraging Philip and Genevieve to enter. "Your clothes have been put away in the closet and drawers, and your toiletries are in the bathroom. I hope we have anticipated your needs, but if we have overlooked anything, please let me know. We want you to be very comfortable. Would you like a cocktail or glass of wine while you change?"

"I would love a glass of Champagne," said Genevieve. "It seems appropriate, doesn't it?"

"It does," Mrs. Proctor grinned. "And you, my lord?"

"I'll have the same, please. Is it necessary to call me 'my lord,' Mrs. Proctor?" Philip asked. "It makes me feel uncomfortable."

With a reserved smile and a twinkle in her eye, Mrs. Proctor said, "I'm sure you'll get used to it soon enough. Is there anything else, my lord? My lady?"

"No, thank you," Philip and Genevieve said in unison.

With that, Mrs. Proctor backed out of the doorway, pulling the double doors closed.

Within the hour, the Warwicks were refreshed, relaxed, and seated at a small table on the terrace. The evening had evolved from a sultry late-summer day into a balmy twilight. Candles flickered, their soft glow bouncing off cut crystal goblets filled with a delicate pink Bordeaux rosé.

Just as Mrs. Proctor brought plates of cold salmon with a peach coulis and crispy grilled vegetables, Philip raised his glass gesturing to his beautiful surroundings. Locking his eyes on Genevieve he said, "Here's to a great adventure and the only woman with whom I would ever want to share it." They clinked glasses and sipped the rosé.

"Mrs. Proctor, this wine is magnificent!" Genevieve said. "I love it! Where is it from?

"I'm so glad you like it, my lady. It's from your vineyard in St. Emilion."

Philip and Genevieve looked at each other, then at Mrs. Proctor. They raised their glasses toward her. "This is going to be a lot of fun," Philip said, and he took a rather large gulp.

FOUR

Sitting at an eighteenth-century mahogany secretary, Genevieve tapped on her laptop, organizing, making lists, evaluating. Just as she thought how wonderful a cup of tea and a cookie would be, Mrs. Proctor walked through the study door carrying a silver tray laden with a china tea service.

"You read my mind, Mrs. Proctor. How did you know I was longing for tea and treats?"

"That's my job, my lady, to anticipate your needs."

"Well, you do it brilliantly. If you have a minute, I'd love for you to join me. I have a million questions that only you can answer."

"Of course, my lady. It would be my pleasure to be of help any way I can."

Genevieve rose from her desk, moved to the sofa, and sat down, pulling her legs under her. She motioned for the housekeeper to sit.

"My first question is does the staff from each of the Earl's properties know each other?"

"No, though I speak with Bertie MacIntosh often. She's the

head housekeeper at Wilmingrove Hall. She's wonderful… and so very Scottish. I think you and Lord Crosswick will like her. She calls just to gossip now and then, or we chat about what's going on in the village, about all the events they're doing at Wilmingrove Hall."

"Events at Wilmingrove Hall?" Genevieve was surprised. "Why would they be doing events? No one lives there."

"Ah, of course. That must sound strange."

Genevieve detected a small note of condescension in Mrs. Proctor's voice and, for the first time since they assumed the earldom, she felt slightly out of her depth.

"Let me explain. As you know, Wilmingrove Hall is the manor house and family seat of the Earl of Crosswick. As such, there are many obligations the estate assumes regarding the county and the village of Wilmingrove, which grew, over the years, as a support village for the Hall. Year after year, the Lord of the Manor grants permission to hold certain events on the estate. Noblesse oblige, you understand."

Genevieve nodded, trying to grasp their future obligations. "So, what kind of events are we talking about?"

"There are fetes, gymkhanas —"

"What's a gymkhana?" Genevieve interrupted.

"A gymkhana is a local Pony Club event with competitive games on horseback. The Pony Club nurtures young riders, and their gymkhanas are always very well attended." Mrs. Proctor nodded, smiled, and carried on. The Hall also hosts charity balls, flower shows and all manner of fundraising efforts for the village and county. In addition, there are shoots, and *many,*

many, many country weekends for the partners of Holmes Fitch Smythson Morrow." As she repeated 'many,' Mrs. Proctor's voice dripped with disapproval. "Considering there has been no earl in residence at Wilmingrove Hall for well over sixty years, it's been a very busy place indeed." With that pronouncement, Mrs. Proctor tilted her head to one side and sat even more erect, waiting for Genevieve to reply.

"Hmmm," Genevieve said, not quite knowing what Mrs. Proctor wanted her to say. After a moment, she said, "Are you suggesting some people—the law firm or perhaps the village—have taken advantage of the fact there's been no one in a position of authority at Wilmingrove Hall to say 'No?'"

"Well, I'm not one to gossip."

Genevieve tried to hide her amusement. "Of course not, Mrs. Proctor." She leaned in, encouraging the housekeeper to continue.

"I'm just suggesting that it will be a very welcome change to have you and Lord Crosswick managing the estate. That is, for some." She left her final two words hanging in the air.

"Needless to say, Philip—um, Lord Crosswick and I appreciate your clear-eyed perspective on all these matters." Genevieve had no idea what 'these matters' might be, but whatever they were, she wanted Mrs. Proctor's viewpoint, even if it were only tittle-tattle between two housekeepers. Genevieve was sure that, as she and Philip delved deeper and became more involved, they would learn many unsettling things about the estate and who was doing what to whom. If a few people had taken advantage of the opportunity to enjoy Wilmingrove Hall or use it for charity or events traditionally hosted by the Lord of the Manor, they would sort it out in time.

Hearing the elevator door open, Mrs. Proctor said, "If there is nothing else, my lady, I need to check on lunch."

"Thank you, Mrs. Proctor. You've given me a lot to think about. Please don't ever hesitate to share your concerns with me." Genevieve looked over Mrs. Proctor's retreating shoulder to see Philip, sweat plastering his running clothes to his lean frame.

"Hi, you disgusting creature." Genevieve wrinkled her nose and scrunched her face in a look of revulsion. "Eeeuuu! Stay away," she giggled, as Philip strode towards her, holding out his arms for a massive hug.

"Come here, my dahling," Philip said in his best Bella Lugosi. "I vant to press my sweaty body against you."

Just in time, Genevieve stuck her foot into Philip's firm abdomen, holding him at bay. They laughed like kids as Philip grabbed Genevieve's foot in his two hands and proceeded to do "this little piggy."

Genevieve squealed, wrenching her foot from Philip's hands. "Would you please go take a shower? You're revolting!"

"Come in with me?" Philip leered.

Genevieve giggled as he leaned forward and licked the tip of her nose.

"Is that a yes?" he asked.

"Ugh! Absolutely not!" She pushed him away and grimaced as she touched his soaked t-shirt. "As tempting as it is, 'No' has to be my answer. Really, Philip. Go. Go take a shower and when you're clean, I'll tell you what I did while you loped around Central Park." Admiring his lean frame, Genevieve watched as he dragged his dripping body toward the bedroom.

Their apartment offered several wonderful places to dine, and Philip and Genevieve were having lunch in Genevieve's current favorite: a small room just off the kitchen, where floor-to-ceiling paned windows overlooked the south end of Central Park. Across the park's vast green expanse, one could see the upper floors of the Plaza Hotel. Though the apartment's interior was perfection, the view beyond the windows was the real star.

"Can you imagine sitting here in the winter during a snowstorm?" said Genevieve.

"Hmm?" Philip looked up from a sheaf of papers he was reviewing. "Sorry, G. What did you say?"

"I said, 'Can you imagine sitting here during a snowstorm?' What are you reading?'"

"Just more legal papers. A courier brought them while I was running. David's coming over this afternoon to talk about them." He flapped the pages at her. "You need to look at these. It's information about the foundation: its mission, finances, and the biographies of the people running it. It's interesting."

"Does it look as if it's well run?" Genevieve rose and walked to the sideboard where a bottle of white Bordeaux sat in a silver wine cooler.

"I haven't done a deep dive, but its endowments are growing at a respectable rate and the expenditures are pretty consistent from year to year. Why was that your first question?" Philip held up his glass for a refill.

"Mrs. Proctor seems to think the law firm is using Wilmingrove Hall as its own personal playground! Maybe they're diddling the foundation as well. So, what do you think of that, Lord Crosswick?" Looking smug, Genevieve plopped back into her chair.

"When you say the law firm is enjoying the use of the Hall, I assume you really mean the partners."

Genevieve nodded.

Philip picked up his glass and took a generous gulp.

"I know, I know." Genevieve rolled her eyes and bobbed her head side to side. "It probably was an arrangement Jonathon Laney made years ago with the firm and when I said it out loud, it sounded a tiny bit petty, but…."

"But you're new to this being-a-billionaire thing so you decided a few Londoners playing country squire, shooting a few of our squab and drinking a few bottles of our claret would put a dent in our finances. Is that about it?" Philip chuckled.

"Honestly, Philip, the way Ms. Proctor told me, in such confidence…" Genevieve twisted the yellow linen napkin in her lap. She looked across the table at Philip. "So, you think this is nothing?"

Still smiling, Philip put his elbows on the table, leaned forward and whispered, "I think, as lovely as she is, Mrs. Proctor wants to ingratiate herself. By offering juicy tidbits of insider information, she thinks she'll gain value in your eyes."

"Whoa! Look at you, getting all psychological, Lord Fancy

Pants! I think she has reservations about what's going on across the pond and she doesn't want us to be blindsided. So there!"

"Okay. We'll keep that in mind. In the meantime, David will be here any minute. I'm assuming we have some dessert we can offer him." Philip began clearing the table.

"Only what you made." Genevieve smacked Philip's butt as he walked by.

Walking in on the conversation, Mrs. Proctor said, "Did I hear something about dessert? How about chocolate souffles with fresh raspberries?"

With a dazzling smile Philip said, "Mrs. Proctor, you are, without a doubt, my favorite housekeeper!"

FIVE

At 7:05 P.M. the Warwick's plane was wheels up. It hadn't taken long for Philip and Genevieve to decide they couldn't live without their private jet. After drinks and a four-course dinner, there were still a few hours for sleep during the seven-and-a-half-hour flight from Teterboro to London City Airport.

Quickly adjusting to their new life, Philip and Genevieve were unsurprised by the dark emerald Rolls Royce Phantom waiting on the tarmac to motor them through the Saturday morning traffic, into London, to their solicitors. Today's meetings would deal with issues that must be addressed on English soil.

As they passed the Tower of London, Genevieve watched rowers slide across the waters of the Thames in perfect rhythm. Across the river, the Eye gave visitors a bird's-eye view of the city. She loved London and all things English and had since she was a child. She pinched her palm just to make sure she wasn't dreaming. It was hard to believe she and Philip had abruptly become a part of English history. The Rolls threaded its way through the traffic until the Palace of Westminster loomed before them.

"Philip." Genevieve turned away from the window. "Do I remember correctly from our conversations with David that, because you're foreign-born, you can't vote in Parliament?"

"Exactly. So, in essence, my peerage is all play, no work. Not a bad gig." He beamed. "I think, however, from what we've learned so far, fulfilling my responsibilities as Earl of Crosswick is going to be a full-time job."

"There's no question you have big shoes to fill to keep the estate on a sound financial course, but you know, my darling, you're more than up to the task."

Philip touched Genevieve's cheek then took her hand. "I'm counting on you to widen the influence of the Foundation. I know you're excited about what we can accomplish with this new-found wealth and influence and you're just the girl to do it. Granted, it's not Bill Gates' or Jeff Bezos' money," they both laughed, "but there's plenty we can do with what we have. I can't wait to develop a plan and get moving."

They had no idea how to proceed, but they had plenty of clever people at their disposal who could help them figure it out and they had confidence David Weatherington would be at the head of that team.

An hour after they landed, the Rolls glided to the curb at 26 Upper Brook Street and stopped in front of an Edwardian building of white stone where window boxes overflowed with creeping jenny and wave petunias and fat pillars announced the entrance. Since 1864, the London offices of Holmes Fitch Smythson Morrow had been ensconced here.

Less than a week ago, Philip and Genevieve walked into the firm's offices in New York City unnerved by the mystery of what lay ahead. Today, they were collected and self-assured as they entered the elegant building. They were ready to assume their new roles. It was amazing what a difference a few days could make, and how quickly they had become comfortable in their new shoes.

"Hi there, you two." David Weatherington emerged from the elevator just as Philip and Genevieve entered the paneled lobby. "Have you got into any mischief since I left you in New York?"

"We've hardly had time. This estate assumption thing has kept us too busy, David." Genevieve beamed at their new friend. "And you're not helping. Forms, forms, forms, sign, sign, sign, fly here, fly there on our private jet, visit our posh properties, make sure everyone bows and scrapes when we enter a room. I mean, David, it's exhausting!" Genevieve flopped down on a sofa, flung out her arms, and threw back her head. "Simply exhausting! I don't know how long we can keep up this pace without buckets of Champagne!"

David rolled his eyes. A chuckle started in his throat, turning into a full-blown laugh. "My God! You've gone mad under the strain of becoming obscenely wealthy! Champagne, please, Mrs. Connley." He nodded to the receptionist as he ushered Philip and Genevieve into the elevator car.

"Are you ready for some fun?" David pressed the button for the fifth floor. "The partners who weren't in New York are all here to make sure everything goes smoothly. You're about to enjoy some major arse-kissing from some very pompous arses!"

Philip's eyebrows shot up, he said, "Isn't that rather risky talk?" Though their relationship had grown quickly to an "old mate" closeness since their first telephone exchange less than a week ago, David's cheeky candor was still a bit shocking.

Noting Philip's look of surprise, David quickly said, "Though some pompous men are waiting for you, a fine firm represents your interests. And you have some of the UK's sharpest estate law minds protecting your inheritance and minimizing your tax liability. And, best of all, you have me as your loyal dogsbody! As you can tell, I'm comfortable with you both, and I already feel a strong loyalty to you. I suppose it's because of all those months I spent chasing you down. I think of you two as friends. I hope the feeling is mutual and our relationship will last well into the years to come because, if that's not the case, I've just flushed my professional future in the loo."

Philip patted David on the back. "Now that you've called the senior partners a bunch of arses, I'm pretty sure you have to do our bidding forever! What do you think, G?"

"No question. Benedict Arnold had nothing on this guy. He's very lucky we already consider him an asset. Otherwise, we'd turn him over to the redcoats in a heartbeat!" Genevieve snickered.

"You two better be nice to me. I'm your inside man, your secret weapon." David sobered the conversation. "If it's still all right, I'm planning to come to Wilmingrove Hall this weekend. As I said in New York, I have a few things I need to discuss with you."

"We're planning on it, David. We can send the helicopter back for you." Philip scrunched his face into a crazy grin. "I can't believe I just said that!"

"Amazing how quickly you're adjusting to having obscene wealth. Now remember. Don't let on what I said about the other partners."

The elevator slowed to a stop, the doors opened and there stood Sir Mark, smiling like a Cheshire cat.

SIX

"**A**ʟʟ ɪ ᴡᴀɴᴛ is a long soak in a hot bath with bubbles up to my chin." Genevieve lay her head back on the buttery leather of the Rolls' headrest. She closed her eyes against the evening London traffic.

"We'll be at the townhouse in just a few minutes." Philip covered Genevieve's hand with his and squeezed. "I'm ready for a scotch by the fire and dinner. There's no rush in the morning to get to Wilmingrove Hall."

Genevieve opened her eyes and looked at Philip. "You're right. The helicopter isn't going to leave without us, is it?"

"And that's why it's good to be us." Philip pulled Genevieve's hand to his lips and kissed her palm.

"After I get out of the tub, I want to wander through the house. From all the photos we've seen, it's quite beautiful, don't you think?"

"If you like old money elegance, it's alright I guess." Philip's smile was relaxed. "G, what would you expect after New York? Jonathon knew how to do it right."

The Rolls turned off Kensington Road onto Victoria Road.

Two blocks down, their driver stopped in front of the white, stately townhouse.

Walking through the black lacquered front door, they smelled the aroma of warm pastry and spices.

"Oh my," Genevieve sighed as she walked through the foyer into the quiet lounge. Sitting on the sideboard was an ice bucket chilling a bottle of something delicious, no doubt. On a silver tray, just begging to be eaten, were little pastry shells piled with cheese and bits of sausage still warm from the oven. Genevieve held out her hands, palms forward as she walked to the fire blazing on the hearth. She turned to warm her back and faced the living room. "Two weeks ago, we thought our lives were perfect," she said to Philip who slouched in the doorway watching her. "Boy, was I wrong. I had no idea how wonderful it would be to have people anticipate our every need. Jeeze, Philip! How did we manage?"

"Good evening, my lord, my lady. What a pleasure to have you here. I'm Mrs. Baker, your housekeeper." Short and sturdy, Mrs. Baker looked every inch the part of an English housekeeper. From her fuzzy halo of hair to her white starched shirt, from her cable knit cardigan to her tweed skirt, right down to her sensible brogues she was a character straight out of a cozy crime novel. "Cook thought you might enjoy a drink and hearty dinner after your busy day."

Genevieve beamed. "Philip and I have been looking forward to meeting you. What a treat to come home to a cozy fire and dinner waiting." Genevieve walked toward the chilling bottle.

"Allow me, Lady Crosswick." Mrs. Baker hastened across the

room to the sideboard. "Lord Crosswick, would you care for a glass of wine, or can I get you something a bit stronger?"

"Something stronger, please. For the last hour I've been thinking of nothing else but a scotch in front of the fire. Neat, please, Mrs. Baker."

Mrs. Baker delivered the drinks then passed the hors d'oeuvres. "Will there be anything else?" she asked.

"I can't imagine what it might be." Genevieve put her nose in her wine glass sampling the bouquet then drank. "This is wonderful," she said. "Is it ours?" It amused her how quickly she had adapted to owning a world-class vineyard.

"Yes, my lady. It's a blend from Chateau Beaulieu, your vineyard. I'm glad you like it. Please let me know when you're ready for dinner."

"I was going to bathe, but all of a sudden I'm ravenous."

Philip nodded. "I'm ready to eat any time."

"Shall we say fifteen minutes?" Mrs. Baker raised her eyebrows.

"Perfect."

"Well, this is pretty wonderful." Genevieve wiggled her shoulders deeper into the overstuffed sofa. She rolled her head trying to work out a kink in her neck. "I need a good massage. I'm wondering if Mrs. Baker does that as well. She seems to take care of everything." Genevieve looked at Philip, who was staring into the fire. "Philip, are you okay?"

"Listen, G. Something's been plaguing me this entire day. Sitting in the meetings, I got this overwhelming sense of being out of my depth."

"I don't understand." She saw a look on Philip's face she didn't recognize. "What do you mean?"

"I mean this is a vast, complicated estate and I don't know that I—that *we*—have the skills to navigate it."

"I think we've done very well over the years, don't you?"

"We have, in a big fish, little pond way. We've done very well. But this is swimming-with-the-sharks territory and, while we both have the capability, I don't think we have the experience for this."

"But Philip, we have this massive team of attorneys and accountants managing every aspect of the estate."

"And that's one of my concerns. The partners didn't miss any opportunity to point out how invaluable they are and how we can't negotiate this complex estate without them. They took great pains to impress upon us how we should leave everything in their hands and not worry our pretty little heads about anything but having a good time. Isn't that the fox guarding the henhouse? I'm sure you noticed Sir Mark's reaction when I told him I was going to have our lawyers in the states review the powers of attorney. I keep thinking about what Mrs. Proctor intimated about the firm using Wilmingrove Hall as their own playground. If they're doing something so obvious, why wouldn't we think they're taking money from the estate in more surreptitious ways?" He took a deep drink, lamp light bouncing off his facetted glass. "You're the first one who was suspicious. What happened to that?"

"I guess I felt a little silly when you made fun of me. And, as you just said, everyone at the law firm makes me feel that they know what they're doing. You're the one who convinced me to enjoy what we have and see where it takes us. Can't you just do that?"

"I don't know. After today, I don't I feel comfortable being blissfully ignorant. Before he left us in New York, Michael cautioned me to look at everything that's being done, supposedly on our behalf. I kept thinking about that today. That's why I'm sending him the POA's. We'll see what he says.

Genevieve sighed. "What do you think about David?"

"I like him, don't you?"

"Very much. Do you trust him?"

"Oddly, yes."

"That is odd given what you just said about the other members of the firm."

Philip put his empty glass on the coffee table and turned to look at Genevieve. "Look, G. I'm just trying to share my concerns with you. You're always asking me to tell you what I'm thinking. I just did. All I'm saying is let's not be complacent or captivated. Let's listen to our gut and yes, enjoy our good fortune, but we need to stay in control. We'll make some judgements and, if we have to make any changes, we will."

Genevieve opened her mouth to respond just as Mrs. Baker entered the room. "My lord, my lady, dinner is served."

SEVEN

GENEVIEVE'S PINK TOES peaked through the mounds of bubbles filling the claw-footed bath. Resting her head against the porcelain tub, she breathed in the woodsy, floral fragrance of her bath gel, her lids drooping until they closed. When at last she opened her eyes, her mind began to wander, wondering if Jonathon had ever made love to his fiancée in this bathtub. She imagined him with a white towel wrapped around his waist, lathering his face to shave, and looking at Katherine in the gilt-framed mirror above the sink.

Genevieve's mind floated from Jonathon to Philip and their earlier conversation. Philip was right. Since she had known him, the one thing she found most annoying about him was how taciturn he was when she most wanted to hear his thoughts. In their early married years, it was the source of more than one heated argument, always one-sided since he refused to jump into the verbal fray. Why did he choose now to be so forthcoming, just when she had shoved her earlier concerns about the law firm misusing the estate to the back of her mind?

"Life can be impossibly difficult when you're filthy rich," Genevieve giggled.

Goosebumps rose on her arms and she realized the water was no longer warm. As she stood, bubbles slid down her legs into the water. Wrapping herself in the warmth of thick terrycloth, she smiled. She loved that the English didn't like cold towels or dinner plates and always warmed both.

Cozy in a gray cashmere bathrobe and slippers, Genevieve brushed her hair back from her face and proceeded with her evening ritual. She leaned close to the mirror looking at the lines around her eye. "Can't you just stay away," she said to the crow's feet and dabbed elixir at the corner of each eye. Surveying her face, she tugged with her fingertips, coaxing the edges of her jaw up . "Hmmm, maybe just a little tuck wouldn't hurt." She opened a jar that smelled of lavender and marjoram.

Hearing the door open in the next room she called, "Philip, is that you?" Moisturizer covering her fingertips, her hand stopped mid-circle on her forehead as she listened.

"Philip?" she said again. She patted the remaining cream on her cheekbones as she walked into the bedroom.

The door stood wide. Genevieve shivered, startled at the cold air. "How strange," she said, crossing her arms for warmth as she stepped into the hall. Seeing no one, she came back into the room, latching the door behind her. Her nose caught the distinct fragrance of roses. She scanned the room, looking for a bouquet but saw none.

At last, she said to herself, "What is the matter with you? You think someone who wears old-fashioned rosewater came into your bedroom then turned around and left? Get a grip, girl. You have lots of things to think about and someone creeping into your room isn't one of them." She chuckled at her pep talk and headed back to the bathroom.

Finished with her regimen, she went in search of Philip who was still in the living room. Since dinner, he had been sitting by the fire with his briefcase open, surrounded by papers.

Genevieve kissed the top of his head. "Do you know if Mrs. Baker came upstairs while I was in the tub?"

"No, she was here talking to me most of the time. She has some great stories about Jonathon. Why do you ask?"

"I just had the strangest experience," she said. Eyes bright with excitement, she told Philip what had happened. "Do you think it was anything?"

"I don't know what you mean by, 'anything.' Do you mean was it something other than the bedroom door of a two-hundred-year-old house not closing properly and opening because of air movement from the furnace? Probably not."

"But what about the smell of roses?"

"Furniture polish?"

"Boy! You have an answer for everything, don't you?"

"Pretty much," Philip said, smiling a superior smile.

Feeling silly that she had been unnerved by a cold room and a pretty fragrance, Genevieve appreciated the logical explanations. She grabbed Philip's hand, trying to tug him out of his chair. "Come on. Take a break and explore the house with me, Mr. Smarty Pants?"

"You go ahead. I want to finish going over this stock portfolio.

At least this is something I understand." Philip looked up at Genevieve's scrubbed face. Marveling at her enduring beauty, he touched her velvet cheek. "Bring back something interesting to tell me," he said. "Do you want to take a glass of Port with you?"

"Great idea." Genevieve looked around. "Do you know where the Port might be?"

"Watch this." Philip moved his foot and pressed a button under the carpet with the toe of his shoe. Within seconds, Mrs. Baker appeared. He looked at Genevieve with a serious face but laughing eyes. "Mrs. Baker, could you please get Lady Crosswick a Port? She's going to explore the townhouse and thought it would be nice to take it with her."

"Tawny or Ruby Port, my lady?"

"Tawny, please. That would be perfect." She leaned over and whispered to Philip, "Great party trick."

Mrs. Baker returned with a Scotch refill for Philip and a small, stemmed glass containing amber liquid, which swished as she walked. "Your Port, my lady. Would you like me to come with you to explore the house? I'd love to share some of its stories. There is a lot of interesting history here at Margrave House."

"I would love that." Genevieve delighted at the idea of having a docent guide her through the historic home. "Shall we?"

Philip watched the two women as they left the room, one tall, willowy, gliding, the other short, stout, waddling. When they were gone, he brought the Scotch glass to his nose and sniffed at the smokey bite of the peat. He took a sip and wondered what tales Genevieve would have when she returned.

Mrs. Baker led the way down the hall to a double doorway. She flipped a light switch and the ash-paneling of the study glowed with lamp light.

"What a wonderful room," Genevieve said. Looking at the double-sided partners desk and floor-to-ceiling bookcases, it was easy to conclude this was the 12TH Earl's sanctuary.

"It is special, isn't it?" Mrs. Baker's eyes misted. "His last few years, Lord Crosswick spent most of his time here or in his bedroom. It's dark now so you can't see it, but there's a lovely view of the garden."

"You were with him for a long time, weren't you?"

"Thirty-seven years, my lady, every year a pleasure."

As they spoke, Genevieve wandered around the 12TH Earl's study. She stopped in front of a full-length painting, hanging above the green marble fireplace. A stunning young matron beamed from the canvas, surrounded by three children: a solemn boy with his hand protectively on his mother's shoulder and two girls, both with their mother's smile and mischief in their eyes. "Oh my," Genevieve was struck by the woman's radiance. "Who is this beauty?"

"Ah." Mrs. Baker's wistful smile promised a tender story. "This is the spectacular Charlotte Camille Chaubert, Countess of Crosswick, wife of Philip George Winston Laney, the 9TH Earl of Crosswick. She was French and brought a great deal of style to this house and Wilmingrove Hall, as you will see when you're there. She and the Earl were the forces behind the Laney Museum of Fine Arts here in London. Charlotte was also an animal lover; she and

Lord Crosswick were major donors to many animal rights groups."

"If she was half as magical as she looks, she must have been spectacular. Look how radiant she is. Please tell me she and the Earl were mad about each other?"

"They adored each other, and London adored them." Mrs. Baker pulled a tissue from her cardigan pocket and blew her nose. Her eyes clouded with tears.

"What is it, Mrs. Baker? Have I said something to upset you?"

"Indeed not, my lady." Mrs. Baker sniffed and dabbed at her eyes. "I'm so sorry, but their story ends so tragically. It always makes me sad."

"What do you mean? What happened? Tell me, please." Holding Mrs. Baker's gaze, Genevieve sat on the corner of the desk.

"On the evening of the Earl and Countess' fortieth wedding anniversary, they invited thirty friends for dinner, men in white tie and women in satin and feathers and jewels. The guests gathered in the foyer with Champagne, waiting to toast the countess when she made her grand entrance."

Genevieve leaned forward, not wanting to miss a word.

"When Charlotte appeared, beaming at the top of the stairs in a silver gown, all the guests fell silent. She was still breathtaking at sixty-four, with her hair piled high and diamonds flashing at her ears. The gown's train swept to her side. At the foot of the stairs, the Earl raised his glass to toast her, and said," Mrs. Baker cleared her throat before she said in a tearful voice, "'To my magnificent bride of forty years. No one else has ever walked the earth, whom I could love as I love you.'"

"What a romantic toast. I can see why you get a bit misty when you tell this story." With the back of her hand, Genevieve wiped a tear from her cheek.

"At the end of the toast, the band struck up Charlotte's favorite song 'Oh You Beautiful Doll' and Charlotte blew a kiss to the Earl. When she started down the stairs, the toe of her shoe hooked on her gown's silver train. She tried to grab the banister, but missed and tumbled head over heels, smashing her head over and over on the stairs. By the time she reached the bottom, her neck had snapped." Mrs. Baker's voice broke as she finished the story. "To this day, we feel her presence. We smell her perfume wafting through the house."

The blood drained from Genevieve's face. For an instant she felt an icy hand on her shoulder then it was gone. Eyes wide, breath shallow, Genevieve asked, "Was her fragrance a rose scent?" She held her breath waiting for the answer.

Mrs. Baker's eyebrows shot up and her mouth formed a perfect 'O.' "How did you guess? She wore Otto of Roses, an elegant scent made from a very special Bulgarian rose."

"Mrs. Baker." Genevieve felt faint.

"What is it, my lady? Are you all right?" The housekeeper took Genevieve by the arm and helped her to a chair next to the desk. She handed Genevieve the Port. "Drink this," she ordered.

The heat of the wine slid down her throat as Genevieve drained the glass. Looking into the face of the woman who had cared for this house for nearly four decades, her eyes burned with tears. "Mrs. Baker, Charlotte came to my bedroom tonight."

EIGHT

EYES WILD, ROBE flapping, Genevieve burst into the living room. "Philip, come with me!"

Philip saw the sweat on Genevieve's brow as she tugged him to stand. "What's going on? Did something happen?"

She pulled Philip toward the door. "It did, but it was more than a hundred years ago." A hand on each shoulder, Genevieve pushed Philip in front of the painting of Charlotte Chaubert.

He threw a concerned glance at Mrs. Baker.

"It wasn't the furnace that opened the bedroom door, and it wasn't furniture polish I smelled," Genevieve said, defiance emphasizing each word. "You see the woman in this painting?"

"I do," Philip said, caution edging his voice. "She's beautiful. Who is she?"

"Mrs. Baker, please tell Philip, er, Lord Crosswick, the story you told me."

Mrs. Baker shared the tale again while Genevieve sniffed and whimpered until Mrs. Baker finished.

From her place on the loveseat next to the fireplace, Genevieve said, "That's who came into the bedroom tonight. That's whose perfume I smelled."

Philip rubbed his face with both hands, before looking at Mrs. Baker and then Genevieve, his brows arched. "Mrs. Baker, do you think that's the case?"

Mrs. Baker twisted the tissue in her hand, her voice quivering. "Well, people have spoken for a century of the countess having a presence in Margrave House. I never met Charlotte directly, but I did witness an event. In fact, a young woman who was here for about a year helping the Earl, had several encounters with Lady Charlotte. It was in this very room they met for the first time."

The hall clock bonged, and Philip jumped, hairs prickling on the back of his neck. "Wow, that startled me," he laughed.

"Spooky, isn't it?" Genevieve met his laughter with hers.

Humoring Genevieve, Philip said, "Sure, G. Maybe just a little. But what about this girl who encountered Charlotte? How was she helping my cousin?"

"Do you mean professionally or personally?" Posing the question as delicately as she could, the color rose in Mrs. Baker's cheeks.

"I'm not sure how to answer that." Philip shrugged. "Uh, both I guess."

"The young lady was here from America for a year on a Laney Museum of Art Fellowship. Lord Crosswick was cataloging his collection at Margrave House and requested an intern from the LMFA program to help him."

"And this young American showed up at the door?" Philip asked.

"Lord Crosswick seems to have been drawn to American women," Genevieve said, a note of pride in her voice.

"He was. American women have a lively spirit. I think he was drawn to that. Though he was in his seventies and bound to his wheelchair, Lord Crosswick was handsome, charming, and filled with youthful energy." The housekeeper's eyes sparkled as she talked. "I must admit, even I had a bit of a crush on him." Smiling sweetly, she looked up at Philip and Genevieve through her lashes, seeming much younger than her fifty-seven years. "The young lady, Revy Harris was her name, came three afternoons a week and sometimes on Saturday as well. She and the Earl quickly formed a good working relationship. Midway through the summer, she started staying for dinner, then after a while, she would linger late into the evening. When I served dinner, I began to notice flirtatious glances between the two of them."

"Of course!" With a flash of recognition, Genevieve realized Mrs. Baker had been a witness to history. "You were here at that time!"

"Yes, I was, and, though the Earl and Revy were discrete during their time together, I knew Lord Crosswick was smitten and the relationship was developing into something more than work. My first thought was that she would break his heart. She was very young and seemed… I don't know. She seemed very aggressive. I guess she frightened me a little. But it was wonderful to see Lord Crosswick greet each day with an enthusiasm I'd not seen before. He was always kind and such a gentleman, but after Ms. Harris started coming to the house, he was full of joy."

"Were you jealous at all?" Genevieve surprised herself. Though she had been wondering how Mrs. Baker felt about a young woman sparking life into Jonathon, she hadn't intended to ask the question so directly.

"Oh, my lady." Ms. Baker's laughter filled the room. "You must remember I have been in service since I was eighteen and, except for my first two years as a housemaid in a country house near Woburn, I've been here at Margrave House. I know my place and my feelings for Lord Crosswick were not passion, but admiration."

Genevieve felt heat in the tops of her ears. "Mrs. Baker, I'm so sorry. I didn't mean to insult you."

"You just have to chalk it up to us being spirited Americans," Philip said, his comment bringing smiles all around. "Please tell us about Ms. Harris' encounter with Charlotte. Why in the world would she be the one to cross paths with this aristocratic ghost?"

"Aah. That's a good story, indeed," Mrs. Baker regained her rhythm. "During her first week here, I helped her find records to do her research on the works of art. Those first few days, she would come to the kitchen at teatime, and we'd have a cuppa. I got to know her a bit and found her interesting. Though they had different coloring, she reminded me of pictures I'd seen of Katherine Robeson, the Earl's fiancée. Revy was fair and Katherine had dark hair and olive skin. Maybe it was their eyes. But, as I said, there was something unsettling about her."

Genevieve tucked her legs under her and pulled the edge of her robe over her bare feet. "Can you describe what was unsettling?"

"I've thought a lot about it, but I've never been able to pinpoint why she made me uncomfortable. One day we were looking for a file in the Earl's study and Revy asked about Charlotte's painting. I told her Lady Crosswick's fatal story and the rumors of her lingering presence at Margrave."

"Did that make her run screaming from the house?" Genevieve was only half kidding.

"Quite the contrary, my lady. Revy got very excited. She said she was born en caul, that's when a baby is born with the amniotic sac intact. But that's all I knew."

"We're familiar with a caulbearer." Philip had been sitting in an overstuffed chair for the last few minutes, fatigue overtaking him, but the conversation was so compelling, he didn't want to interrupt it. Stifling a yawn, he said, "Our granddaughter Ella was born en caul. It's very rare and, if Ella is any indication, everything they say about these special babies is true."

"Do you know that people born en caul can be clairvoyant and sensitive to spirts?" Genevieve chimed in.

"Yes, I do now." Eager to share the rest of the tale, Mrs. Baker picked up the pace. "Revy said from the time she was a child, she was able to feel the presence of spirits and she often knew something was about to happen before it did."

"So, she thought she might be able to communicate with Lady Crosswick?" Genevieve asked.

"She did. She was certain of it. And she proved to be right."

"Really?" Philip and Genevieve said in unison.

"How so?" Philip was anxious for facts.

Mrs. Baker walked to the garden window and looked out into the night. The black panes reflected the warmth of the glowing room behind her. Mrs. Baker's husky voice was barely audible as she began. "The first night Revy stayed for dinner, she and the Earl were working here in the study. For the previous two days they had been cataloging the works in this room. That particular day, they spent the afternoon confirming the provenance of Charlotte's portrait."

Genevieve pulled a thick throw from the back of the loveseat and dragged it across her lap.

"When I came into the room to announce dinner, Revy asked if Lord Crosswick and I smelled roses. I smelled nothing. She said the fragrance was overwhelming. As I was about to leave the room a cold wind swirled around Revy, like a tiny tornado. Her long hair stood straight up in the column of wind. Nothing outside of the funnel moved. It only lasted a matter of seconds. The wind stopped as abruptly as it started, leaving no evidence that it had ever happened. If all three of us hadn't witnessed it, we wouldn't have believed that it happened."

Eyes wide, Genevieve was rigid in her chair.

"This really happened?" Philip said. "Right here in this room?"

"Right here where I'm standing." Mrs. Baker pointed at her feet. "It happened right here."

Philip blew out a puff of air, shook his head and said, "Wow. Just wow." He shook his head, then asked, "After that first incident, there were more?"

"Yes, several." Mrs. Baker's eyes danced. "Nothing as dramatic as that first encounter, but small things: a cold hand on Revy's shoulder, a page magically turned in a research book she was using, papers moved on the desk. All things that could be explained away or brushed off. But just before Revy walked out of the door for the last time, she said she felt a frigid kiss on her cheek."

Genevieve walked across the room to the gas logs burning on the hearth. She shivered and tugged the throw around her shoulders. "Why did she leave?"

"Ah, like so many things concerning the 12TH Earl, the parting was sad, and it broke his heart to insist she go."

Genevieve pulled a tissue from her pocket, prepared to dab her tears again.

"Revy was young and beautiful and had her entire life ahead of her. Lord Crosswick didn't want her to wither, spending her years caring for an invalid. I overheard their arguments. She pleaded her love, she begged him to let her stay. He insisted she could not. In the end, he told her she was no longer welcome at Margrave House. And she left, apparently with Charlotte's blessing. I can attest to the fact that was the last romance Lord Crosswick had in his life and he lived many years after that. "He was too beautiful a man to have suffered such tragedy in his life." Mrs. Baker wept quietly for a moment, then dabbed her eyes, sniffed, and walked to the desk. She picked up a small photograph of Revy and handed it to Genevieve. Staring at her was an enchanting sprite, her violet eyes filled with love. Her chin rested on her right hand and on her finger was a massive square ruby surrounded by diamonds.

"What a beauty," Genevieve said. "And what a stunning ruby."

Philip joined her in front of the fire and took the photograph Genevieve handed him. "I see why Jonathon fell in love. I can't imagine how difficult it was to let her go."

"I assure you, he was devastated." The energy had drained from the room. "My lord, my lady, if there's nothing else, I believe I'll retire."

"I think that's a very good idea." Philip's shoulders slumped. "I'm desperate to go to bed, but, Mrs. Baker, this evening has been worth missing a lot of sleep."

Rather than fatigued, Genevieve was energized. Her earlier encounter with Charlotte promised future contact with the spectacular spirit. "I think it's exciting. Thank you, Mrs. Baker for sharing this with us. I look forward to lots of exchanges with the magnificent Charlotte Chaubert."

"Come on, G. Let's go to bed. This is just the beginning of our new life. I have a feeling we're going to need all the rest we can get if we're going to keep up with our adventure." Genevieve massaged the back of her neck as Philip led her out into the hall. "Good night, Mrs. Baker. Sleep well"

"And you, my lord. You don't need to stop and smell the roses tonight." Mrs. Baker chuckled at her joke. She flipped the light switch off and pulled the double doors closed. As she walked away from the study, an icy tingle slid down her spine and she wondered if Charlotte had been watching them.

NINE

To Genevieve, few adventures were more exhilarating than flying in a helicopter. The physics of going straight up and down was more than a little mystifying. It was better than a rollercoaster and harrowing enough to send a shock of excitement through her. She and Philip had taken a helicopter to a glacier in Alaska once, where they were the middle craft in a parade of three. Following the lead chopper through an icy canyon at high speeds was thrilling. That was twenty years ago and now, here they were in an AgustaWestland AS609, an aircraft with the speed, range and altitude of a fixed-wing turboprop airplane and the vertical take-off and landing versatility of a helicopter—and it belonged to them. On opposite sides of the cabin, Philip and Genevieve had their noses pressed against the window, watching the London Heliport on the south bank of the River Thames as it diminished in size. They shot to a thousand feet.

Their pilot, Captain Bruni, greeted them over the intercom. In a lilting Italian accent, he described the sites. "If you look down, you'll see we're following the Thames past Westminster and Big Ben, past St. Paul's. Just after the Tower Bridge we'll turn north and head across the Yorkshire moors to Wilmingrove Hall."

"I assume the coffee I smell brewing is coming our way soon." Philip's arms were folded over his chest and his voice was curt.

"What's the matter with you?" Genevieve pulled her attention from the view to her sulking husband.

"Honestly, G, I'm exhausted. After days of monumental changes in our lives, and last night's ghost fest, I just need time to process everything. Don't you?"

"I think we're looking at this from two very different perspectives." Genevieve changed seats so she faced Philip. "I've gone full circle. I was beyond excited when we heard you inherited your title and all that comes with it." Genevieve leaned forward, her elbows on her knees. "Then, when Mrs. Proctor told me her concerns about Wilmingrove Hall, I was sure the law firm was using the estate as a cash machine. But after you pointed out that Mrs. Proctor was probably just gossiping to ingratiate herself, I decided to stop seeing problems around every corner. I decided to just enjoy our good fortune." She sat back and folded her hands in her lap. "And, as for Charlotte, our beautiful ghost, I'm thrilled. Never in my life did I think we'd own a house with a ghost as a resident. I love it!"

Philip couldn't help smiling at Genevieve's wide eyes and flushed cheeks. He cradled her hands in his and brought them to his lips. His smile faded as he said, "I hate to burst your bubble, but last night when I finished going over the stock portfolios, I studied some of the other files."

"From the look on your face, I assume whatever you found wasn't good."

"Well, for one thing, there have been a lot of huge expenditures over the last eighteen months, one of which is this helicopter. Why do we own a twenty-five-million-dollar helicopter?" In response to Genevieve's look of surprise, Philip said, "That's what was expensed. I mean, don't you think it's unlikely Jonathon, the recluse, bought a helicopter on his deathbed? This fabulous aircraft isn't more than a couple of years old! Who bought it?"

"That's a good question." Genevieve leaned forward again, scooting to the edge of her seat.

Philip continued, "The last two years, while Jonathon was in failing health, Holmes Fitch Smythson Morrow, as trustees, have had free rein over the estate. If they chose to—" Philip stopped mid-sentence.

An enthusiastic young steward brought a tray of coffee and chocolate-covered biscuits through to the passenger cabin. "Excuse me, my lord. May I serve coffee?"

Genevieve looked at the young man's name badge. "Thank you, William." She smiled up at him as he stooped to avoid the cabin's low ceiling. "My husband was just saying he would kill for a cup of coffee, so you may have saved both our lives."

"My pleasure, my lady." William grinned, showing a gap in his front teeth.

"So, William, do you always crew this craft?" Philip was anxious to know more about their pricey asset.

"Yes, until recently, my lord. But I'm about to join your Bombardier crew. I also staff at Wilmingrove Hall when they need me." William's face radiated the enthusiasm of a young man on the brink of a big adventure.

Genevieve couldn't help but smile. "Well, we're delighted you're with us. There are a lot of exciting things ahead for all of us."

"How often does this helicopter fly?" asked Philip, still wanting to know more about the chopper.

"A couple of times a month. A few of the partners from the law firm go between Wilmingrove Hall and London pretty often." Eager to endear himself to his new employer, William continued. "They do know how to enjoy themselves." As the words came out of his mouth, William seemed to know he had overstepped his bounds. "I beg your pardon. That was most inappropriate," he back peddled. "I look forward to serving you any way I can, my lady, my lord. Please never hesitate to call on me, even for the smallest thing."

Amused by his embarrassment, Philip said, "Thank you, William. I hope you don't live to regret that!"

William offered an uncomfortable nod as he poured coffee from the Laney-crested china pot into mugs.

"Will there be anything else, my lord?"

"I think we're good for now. Thank you, William," Philip said.

"My lord." Nodding, William backed out of the cabin.

Genevieve waited for William to exit. As soon as he was back in his forward seat, she turned to Philip, sloshing her coffee, a few drops landing on her jeans.

"Well!" She said in a loud whisper as she set her mug on the console beside her. "How about that? If you need one, you have a spy already in place! You two can play sleuth and I'll just enjoy myself. How's that for a plan?" Genevieve vibrated with excitement and Philip couldn't help chuckling, captivated by his bride of many years. Though Genevieve was a beauty in jeans or a ball gown, working at her computer or pulling weeds in the garden, at this moment, she was breathtaking. Philip reached out and pulled her head towards him until her face was within inches of his. Staring deep into her green eyes he said, "You're a mad woman and I love you for it!" He kissed her lightly on her lips then deepened the kiss until there was heat. "If we had any privacy, I would be on top of you right now."

"Coward," Genevieve said. "Where's your sense of adventure?" She unlatched her seatbelt. Before he realized what she was doing, Genevieve had straddled him and was returning his kiss, hers even more urgent than his. Philip grabbed Genevieve's bottom, a cheek in each hand and squeezed. Pulling back, she said, "The minute we're alone, you're on!"

"Oh, you think? I'm not sure I can wait that long. I may jump you when you least expect it!"

"Jump me?" Genevieve laughed, sitting back in her seat, and refastening her seatbelt. "I don't think I've ever heard you use that phrase before."

Philip laughed, "I've never been an outrageously wealthy nobleman before."

Before Genevieve could reply, the intercom crackled. "Lord and Lady Crosswick, this is Captain Bruni. We are twenty-five miles from Wilmingrove Hall and have begun our decent so please make certain your seatbelts are secure. We'll be on the ground in about ten minutes."

Genevieve leaned toward the window, her knees pressed

against Philip's. They looked at each other, linked fingers, then looked back at the view below. Dotted with curly-horned sheep, rolling hills rose and fell. Then, on the horizon, they saw the hazy outline of a huge building nestled in the mist. Second by second the Laney family seat came into sharper focus until Genevieve gasped.

"Are you kidding me?" Philip couldn't believe his eyes.

The Warwicks had seen hundreds of photographs of Wilmingrove Hall and had viewed a drone video of the property. They had read an article in *Britain Magazine* from years ago, featuring Wilmingrove Hall as a "Jacobean Treasure." People repeatedly told them how magnificent the Hall was, but nothing had prepared them for what was coming into focus. Buff-colored Yorkshire stone glowed in the light of the afternoon sun. The helicopter followed the long lane, which was flanked on either side by silver birch and ended with a circular driveway at the front façade. The chopper swooped to the left of the vast building, hovered above the helipad, then set down gently.

Genevieve squeezed Philip's hand. "Oh my," she said. "Just, oh my."

"Here we go." Philip handed Genevieve her sweater.

William came from the galley to open the door. "Lord and Lady Crosswick, welcome home."

The Warwicks ducked through the helicopter door and down the steps. Before them was an imposing sight. Wilmingrove Hall sat on the edge of a manicured bluff overlooking the river. From the front, there was no hint of the exquisite terracing in the back or the acres of parterres.

A fireplug of a woman stood just off the edge of the landing pad, dressed in a tartan skirt, starched white shirt and sensible cordovan oxfords. Her ramrod posture made the most of her stocky five feet. There was no question, this was Bertie MacIntosh, the Scottish head housekeeper.

Though there was plenty of room between the chopper blades and their heads, Philip and Genevieve bent over as they walked toward Mrs. MacIntosh.

"Mrs. MacIntosh?" Philip said holding out his right hand in greeting. "I'm Lord Crosswick and this is, as you may have guessed, Lady Crosswick."

She ignored Philip's hand, which he yanked back. "My lord, my lady, I'm pleased to meet you both and relieved you're here. We've been without a lord of the manor for much too long." Mrs. MacIntosh's sober expression softened only slightly as she offered a small curtsy.

"We're anxious to learn everything about being a proper earl and countess. I'm sure you have a manual that can tell us all we need to know, and we'll be up to speed in no time." Oozing charm, Philip smiled and chuckled, but Mrs. MacIntosh was unamused.

Genevieve gave Philip a discrete elbow in the side and stepped in to smooth things over. "Mrs. MacIntosh, Lord Crosswick and I are grateful for your loyalty to the Laney family and for your years of service here at Wilmingrove Hall. From everything we've been told, you've been an excellent captain on a rudderless ship. We look forward to learning about the estate from you.

As custodians, we'll work to preserve and protect this historic property."

Philip couldn't help but roll his eyes while Genevieve waxed a bit too rhapsodic trying to win over the somber Scot. But it worked.

At Genevieve's words of appreciation and praise, Mrs. MacIntosh's face eased into a soft smile. "Lady Crosswick, I vow to do my best for you and Lord Crosswick. There are many things I know you'll wish to address, and I am at the ready. Shall we go to the Hall? Tea will be served, and the staff is anxious to meet the new Earl and Countess. Wallace had to go to Glasgow yesterday, but he'll be back late this afternoon. He asked me to express his apologies, but it was unavoidable. His sister had to go into hospital, and he is her only sibling."

"I'm sure we should know, but who is Wallace, Mrs. MacIntosh?" Philip asked.

Mrs. MacIntosh looked up at Philip, rolled her eyes and said, "My lord, Wallace has been the butler of Wilmingrove Hall for the last thirty-five years." With that, they got into a stretch golf cart and began the short journey from the landing pad up the hill to embark on the most revealing part of their adventure yet.

TEN

MRS. MACINTOSH SLOWED the golf cart to a stop in front of the Hall's massive front door. Above the oak portal, set into Yorkshire stone, was a weathered Laney crest with its family motto, "Garde Le Roi."

Mrs. MacIntosh smiled with pride as she explained, "The motto, 'Guard the King,' comes from the Laney family's role saving King Charles II. Your ancestor, Colonel John Laney, was a supporter of the king. After the Battle of Worcester, where Cromwell's army defeated the Royalists, Charles fled for his life. Colonel Laney hid the future king at his mansion in Staffordshire. From there the fugitive prince was taken, in disguise, by the Colonel's eldest sister, Jane, to her cousin's residence in Bristol."

"It sounds dangerous." Genevieve was riveted.

"It was. If it had been discovered they were helping Charles, they could have lost everything, including their lives." Mrs. MacIntosh's admiration was obvious. "After the restoration of Charles to the throne," Mrs. MacIntosh continued, "the Crown demonstrated its gratitude to the Laney family. Jane received an annual Royal pension of £1,000 for life. Her brother, John, was granted the Arms of England, the three lions on a red field and the Royal Crown. As you can see," Mrs. MacIntosh pointed to the crest, "the Arms of England were combined with the motto, 'Garde Le Roi,' to create the Laney coat of arms."

Looking up at the crest, Philip was overcome with the reality that he was the next link in an unbroken chain of rich, important history. His eyes stung. He cleared his throat. "I, um, I'm a bit overwhelmed," he said. "I didn't expect this to be such an emotional experience. Being here at Wilmingrove Hall makes it all real. Until now, it's been about balance sheets, big numbers, and a lot of fun, but being here, where my ancestors built a legacy over hundreds of years…well, I feel it. It hadn't occurred to me that I would experience such a connection."

Genevieve squeezed Philip's hand.

Mrs. MacIntosh smiled, pleased. "It doesn't surprise me, my lord. It doesn't surprise me at all. The Laneys are a compelling family with great strengths passed from generation to generation. It's no wonder you are beginning to feel the Laney blood coursing through your veins. And I would venture to say this is only the beginning. You and Lady Crosswick are going to be glorious standard bearers."

Philip tucked Genevieve's hand under his arm. "I'm going to need all the encouragement I can get," he said, offering the two women a sheepish smile.

"I will be your biggest cheerleader," Mrs. MacIntosh said. "Now, would you like to see where your cousin lived as a child?"

"Yes, please," Philip answered.

Mrs. MacIntosh stood aside for Philip and Genevieve to

precede her through the door, but Philip motioned her to go ahead. "Please, Mrs. MacIntosh, lead the way."

"As you wish, my lord." She stepped through the door and into the grand salon.

Walking into the imposing hall, Genevieve was assaulted by the strong fragrance of roses pouring from a large blue and white ginger jar sitting on a sideboard. She inhaled recalling Charlotte Chaubert's perfume and shivered.

"Are you chilly, Lady Crosswick?" Mrs. MacIntosh was quick to ask.

"Oh, no. I'm fine," Genevieve said. "But I do have a crazy question. Do you know about Charlotte Camille Chaubert, the 9TH Earl of Crosswicks' wife?"

"Oh, the beautiful Charlotte." Mrs. MacIntosh raised her clasped hands to her chin. "Isn't the Countess's story tragic? I spoke to Mrs. Baker this morning and she told me you met Charlotte last night, in a manner of speaking."

Genevieve opened her mouth, closed it, opened it again before she spoke. "Well, I, um," Genevieve stammered. "Um, as you said, what a tragedy. I cried when Mrs. Baker told me how she died."

"Yes, Mrs. Baker said you were moved to tears."

Genevieve shouldn't have been uncomfortable that the two housekeepers had been gossiping about their new lord and lady, but she was.

"So, what did you think of our resident ghost?" Mrs. MacIntosh asked.

"When you say resident ghost, do you mean the ghost who lives at Margrave House?"

Mrs. MacIntosh leaned close to Genevieve and dropped her voice to a whisper. "Occasionally, she spends time here, at Wilmingrove Hall."

"Are you serious?"

"I'm quite serious, my lady. For the last few years, she's been coming once or twice a year. Usually around the holidays or during an event. She was last here in the winter when Sir Mark brought clients for a shoot."

"How did you know she was here?" Genevieve realized she had lowered her voice to meet the housekeeper's whisper and bent over so she and Mrs. MacIntosh almost touched foreheads.

"The shotgun shells are kept in the estate office under lock and key. On the morning of the shoot, every single shell had been replaced with a rose. The shooting party couldn't find a shell anywhere." Mrs. MacIntosh beamed. It was obvious she loved telling this story. She raised her hand before Genevieve could comment. "I know. You're going to say anyone could have been playing a prank. But the stable girl, Missy Overton, swears she saw a woman in a shimmery, silver dress sweep through the barn the night before, carrying a basket. When Harrington checked the security cameras, he saw what looked like whisps of smoke wafting through the stable hall. The next day, he found the basket in the tack room. Full of shells."

Genevieve said nothing for a moment, then she threw back her head, howling with laughter. Still giggling, she said, "This is great. I guess our ghost has quite a sense of humor. She's going to be a lot of fun to have around. Mrs. Baker mentioned Charlotte was quite an animal activist. Think of all the pheasants who lived another day thanks to Charlotte exchanging roses for shells."

Wandering from room to room, engrossed in one spectacular painting after another, Philip heard Genevieve's roar of laughter. "What's going on? What did I miss?" he said as he returned to the grand salon.

"Mrs. MacIntosh just told me that Charlotte is in residence with us from time to time here, at the Hall."

"Oh, is she?" Philip's eyes sparkled. "Well, that's exciting. Another beautiful woman at the Hall! Is she here now?" Philip smirked.

"Scoff if you will." Mrs. MacIntosh looked at him over the wire rims of her glasses. "When you're awakened by an icy touch on your cheek and the smell of Otto Rose perfume in your room, don't expect me to come running," she said, with surprising cheek.

"Mrs. MacIntosh," Genevieve soothed. "As I told Philip this morning, I love Charlotte's presence. What could be better than her enchanting spirit hovering around us? If she's a kind ghost, that is."

"She has always been funny and charming, and she loves playing tricks. So be on your toes. Especially you, Lord Crosswick. She adores handsome men."

Philip blushed.

"I see no reason for her to change," Mrs. MacIntosh said. "Lady Crosswick, what made you think about Charlotte?"

"A few minutes ago, when we walked into the foyer, I smelled roses. The fragrance reminded me of my encounter with Charlotte yesterday, and I did wonder if she ever comes here. Apparently, the answer is yes. Where do you get these gorgeous blossoms?" Genevieve asked, burying her nose in a fuchsia floret.

"They're grown right here. Your gardens and greenhouse are designed for year-round blossoms, herbs, cold-weather vegetables and, of course, we have our own chickens, eggs, lambs and plenty of fish and game. Do you shoot, my lord?"

"Not yet," Philip said. "But I could be persuaded to learn. I like the clothes."

Philip's infectious grin coaxed a giggle from Mrs. MacIntosh and the color rose in her cheeks.

"You would cut a fine figure in a tweed shooting jacket and breeks, my lord," she gushed.

Genevieve leaned into Philip and whispered in his ear. "I believe Mrs. MacIntosh just batted her eyelashes at you."

Mrs. MacIntosh scurried ahead of the Warwicks. "Come, let me show you to your room. You can freshen up before tea." She led Philip and Genevieve through the grand salon to the grand staircase.

Looking up to the landing, Genevieve struggled for words. At last she said, "This is like something from a movie set. It's stunning. And everything is perfect. I don't see any cracks in the plaster, any peeling paint. It must take a lot to keep everything so beautifully preserved."

"I'm glad you're pleased, my lady." Mrs. MacIntosh fidgeted. "Sir Mark is fastidious about the maintenance of the Hall. He spares…" Mrs. MacIntosh caught herself. "He's a fine custodian of the estate," she finished.

Climbing the stairs, Philip stopped midway. He looked up twenty feet at the paneled walls covered with portraits painted over several centuries. "Mrs. MacIntosh, are all these portraits my ancestors?"

"They are." Mrs. MacIntosh paused on the landing at the top of the stairs. "There is a book in the library by Kenneth Baron. I'm sure you'll find it interesting. It chronicles all the artwork in the Hall. Not just the paintings, but every piece of art including bronzes, fountains, and any historic architectural elements of note. It's a comprehensive reference work and will be helpful when you have questions about any of the works: their history, their provenance, the artist… anything, really. I'll make certain it's on the library table for you."

"Sorry, I got sidetracked by this stunning landscape," Genevieve called from the bottom of the stairs. "The signature looks like it says 'Gainsborough'."

"It does," said Mrs. MacIntosh. "It was one of his last landscapes."

"I see." Genevieve started up the stairs, shaking her head in disbelief. "So, the Hall has quite a collection?"

"Yes, my lady. You and Lord Crosswick have quite a collection, as you will see when you look at Kenneth Baron's book."

Following Mrs. MacIntosh down the broad hall, Philip and Genevieve glanced at each other, silently making faces of awe, surprise and disbelief. They walked by several closed doors until they saw light spilling from an open doorway ahead on the left.

"Lord and Lady Crosswick, I chose the Green and Gold Room

for you because it has a lovely south-facing view of the gardens and river," said Mrs. MacIntosh as they arrived at the bedroom. She stepped aside and ushered the Warwicks into an emerald jewel box.

Genevieve gasped as her eyes swept around the room. Walls covered in jade leather and striped with burnished-gold molding served as the backdrop to a massive four-poster bed. Each fluted bedpost was brushed in gold leaf and pushed ten feet towards a coffered ceiling. A pale green silk duvet covered the bed. Pillows of gold and verdant hues were layered several deep, obscuring the headboard.

Polished mahogany floors peeked out from under the edge of a massive green needlepoint Aubusson rug, which stretched the width and breath of the room. Though the bedroom was large and the ceilings high, the colors and textures created a cozy chamber. An overstuffed sofa sat in front of a fireplace ready and waiting for the first chilly night.

"Mrs. MacIntosh, I'm speechless," said Genevieve. "I've never seen such a beautiful room." Genevieve walked around the chamber, trailing a finger over smooth silks and running her palm over woodwork gilded with gold leaf. She breathed in the sweet fragrance of lilies and daphne, which rested in a green and white Wedgewood vase.

Her circuit around the bedroom ended at the green-veined marble fireplace.

Hanging above the mantle was a portrait of an elegant young woman with dark hair and porcelain skin. She leaned forward, as if listening to an unseen companion. Her cornflower blue dress matched her eyes. Velvet sleeves slid off pale shoulders, just enough to offer a glimpse of delicate bones. Her left hand lay in her lap while the right cradled her heart-shaped face, her elbow resting on the arm of the tapestry-covered chair. Genevieve moved closer to the painting, then closer still. She blinked. She rubbed her eyes.

Philip and Mrs. MacIntosh had been talking about the history of the Green and Gold Room while Genevieve moved from piece to piece, appreciating each treasure. Now she froze in front of this exquisite portrait, eyes riveted on the woman's right hand. Her long, slender finger was encircled by a wide gold band on which perched a stupendous, square-cut ruby, surrounded by two rows of diamonds. A magnificent ring, and one Genevieve had seen before, just last night. Her heart pounded in her ears as she realized this priceless family heirloom had been stolen.

ELEVEN

T HE THREE OF them sat together on the down-stuffed sofa opposite the fireplace, looking at the portrait hanging over the mantle. Wedged between Philip and Genevieve, Mrs. MacIntosh balanced Kenneth Baron's book about the treasures of Wilmingrove Hall on her knees. It was opened to page seventy-four where a reproduction of the painting filled the glossy sheet. Mrs. MacIntosh read the description aloud.

"Victoria Catherine Winston Laney, only daughter of James and Imogene Gilcrest, the Duke and Duchess of Wallingford and wife of James Charles Philip Laney, the 8TH Earl of Crosswick.

The portrait was painted by Andres Gilbert in 1849 and given by Lady Crosswick to the Earl on their first anniversary. The ruby and diamond ring worn by Lady Crosswick was a gift from Lord Crosswick to his wife on the birth of their first son. Gilbert added the ring a year after the painting was completed.

Andres Gilbert became a favorite of Lady Crosswick, and subsequently painted each of the Laney's four children. It was widely rumored that Lady Crosswick admired more than Gilbert's skills on canvas. In correspondence found after her death, one of Lady Crosswick's closest friends commented that William, the Countess's youngest son, had black hair and brown eyes so similar to the coloring of Gilbert rather than the fair hair and blue eyes of his father. The confident also wrote that the 8TH Earl was, perhaps, too busy securing the financial future of the Laney dynasty to notice his wife's new-found passion for art and artists."

As she finished reading, Mrs. MacIntosh closed the book and looked up at the likeness of Victoria Catherine Winston Laney. "It's been years since I read about Lady Crosswick's portrait. She was certainly bonnie and a most interesting woman."

"She was beautiful, I have to agree. And a bit of a vixen, it would seem." Genevieve eyed the countess with a wry smile. "Can you tell us anything else about the ruby ring? Does it show up in any other portraits of the Laney ladies?"

"We can look through the book. Or better yet, let's walk around and look at the original works." Philip rose to his feet, took the book from Mrs. MacIntosh and put it on the coffee table then helped her off the sofa.

"Before you do anything else, I must insist you meet the staff and have tea." Mrs. MacIntosh spoke with surprising authority. "You have to be starving."

"What a good idea, Mrs. MacIntosh." Taking her elbow, Philip guided Mrs. MacIntosh toward the door. "There will be plenty of time to investigate the mystery of the ruby ring," he chuckled. "That sounds like a Poirot title. Mrs. MacIntosh, give us ten minutes and we'll be downstairs."

"Of course, my lord. The staff will be waiting in the grand salon," Mrs. MacIntosh said over her shoulder as she walked out of the room.

Half an hour later, Philip and Genevieve had met their twenty-person staff. Their head cook was jolly, round Elsie Lomax, and their estate manager, Sean Harrington, exuded presence and natural authority, qualities perfect for his role. They also met Andrew Frazier, windswept from the Scottish Highlands where he learned his skills as a falconer.

Now they sat at a round table in the charming, cozy conservatory. French doors stood wide, allowing the balmy afternoon air to waft in. Blue and yellow jacquard linens covered the table ladened with a bowl of perfect, red strawberries, and tiered trays of tea sandwiches, petit fours, and scones. Everywhere she looked, Genevieve marveled how meticulously everything at Wilmingrove Hall was appointed and preserved. In an age when venerable estates scrambled to keep the rain from pouring through the roof and stately homes had turned shabby chic into an art form, no cost had been spared to maintain the Hall to a high standard.

"Philip, don't you love that everything at Wilmingrove hall is perfect? Nothing is run down or fraying or tired," she said, shoving a rather-too-large bite of scone, clotted cream, and jam into her mouth.

Philip looked up from spreading preserves on his scone. "I'm not surprised you're falling in love with this place. It's wonderful we haven't inherited a big house with termites and a sieve for a roof, but I keep wondering who's writing the checks to maintain everything? If there's anything unscrupulous going on, we'll figure it out, but in the meantime…" Philip reached across the table to catch a jammy crumb at the corner of Genevieve's mouth. "I think my favorite thing about being an earl other than having a billion pounds and owning this grand estate is that I can have scones, clotted cream and jam anytime I want."

"You know, Philip, you don't need all this to have scones, right?" Genevieve gestured to their surroundings. "Even commoners can get a scone whenever they want, anywhere they are," Genevieve said.

"I know, but somehow, they're so much better when you're very, very, very wealthy. He took a bite, closed his eyes, and sighed a blissful sigh. At last, he opened his eyes. "Okay. Let's talk about the estate. I've been thinking a lot about what might be going on here and I'm sorry to say, my list of concerns is piling up."

"So, you've been making a list of your suspicions? What a sleuth!" Genevieve teased. "Don't forget David will be here tomorrow with issues to talk about. Can we wait until he gets here? Oh, did you remember to send the chopper back for him?"

"Of course, I did," Philip shot back, his cheerful mood replaced by exasperation.

Genevieve's eyebrows arched.

"I don't want to wait until tomorrow. I've been hinting at this since we left New York and you keep putting me off. I want to talk now, so we're both on the same page when David comes," Philip finished with a barbed tone.

"Okay," Genevieve snapped. "But I don't know if that's going to happen, Philip."

"Why not?"

"I'm so excited about sharing our good fortune with the kids that I don't want to imagine there are any problems. You, on the other hand, seem to see bad omens everywhere you look." She ran her hands through her hair and puffed air from her cheeks. "Why can't we just enjoy this moment? Everything in life has ups and downs." Her eyes softened. "Look, Philip, I'm sure there are going to be challenges ahead. But for now, let's enjoy our extraordinary fortune."

"That's how people get conned. It's how people lose money. We can't both be Pollyannas unless we want to lose everything as quickly as we gained it."

"I'm not being a Pollyanna." Genevieve leaned forward. "I just want a moment to enjoy myself. Shame on me." Sarcasm dripped from each word.

"G, I understand. I do." Philip's voice softened and he reached across the table for Genevieve's hand. "You know misery loves company. I don't want to be the only one with reservations. Will you at least listen to my worries?"

Genevieve kissed Philip's knuckles, one at a time. "I'll promise to start looking around every corner for bad guys if you'll promise to enjoy our windfall just a little bit."

Philip turned his hand palm to palm in Genevieve's and shook it. "It's a deal," he said.

"I'll go first." Philip pulled a small notebook out of the pocket of his sweater and flipped it open.

"You're kidding me," Genevieve said, barking a laugh. "You really have written a list?"

"I didn't want to forget anything, so I made a few notes." Philip leafed through several pages. "Okay. The first thing was the law firm using Wilmingrove Hall as a corporate retreat."

Genevieve shrugged. "I'm sure they were here often enough, keeping an eye on things. It's logical that Jonathon would have said, 'Use the Hall, guys.'"

Philip looked up from his notebook. "That's reasonable. But why didn't they mention it? We've spent a lot of time with the senior partners this week. They could have filled us in on their side deals."

"I'll give you that." Genevieve played with a sandwich on her plate. "What's next?"

"Why do we have a Bombardier jet? Why do we have an AugustWest 604, the newest of the new, twenty-five million pound, very fancy helicopter?"

"It's actually an AgustaWestland."

"Whatever," he snapped." Very strange for a man who was a recluse for more than sixty years." Philip began to tick off entries as he spoke. "Who's responsible for all of Jonathon's properties, well, now *our* properties, being maintained to an impeccable standard? Who authorizes all these expenditures? And one last, but very big revelation."

Genevieve sat a bit straighter waiting for the reveal.

Philip pulled the Kenneth Baron book of Laney art from

under his chair and plopped it on the table. He flipped to page eleven then swirled the book toward Genevieve. "Does that look familiar?" He challenged.

Genevieve's forehead furrowed. "I don't understand. What am I looking at?'

"That painting you're looking at is attributed to the Laney collection, but we saw it hanging in the New York City law offices of Holmes Fitch Smythson Morrow, our illustrious team of attorneys."

"When…wha…I…uh…I don't even know what to ask."

"Leaf through the book. You'll find the other paintings we saw in the offices. Looks to me like they've, uh, *borrowed* a few of our priceless works of art. Odd David didn't mention the paintings were ours when we asked who the collector was."

'Oh, Philip." Genevieve wrung her hands. "You don't think David knows about this do you?"

"I have no idea, but remember, he did say he has concerns about his firm's relationship to our estate. When he gets here, we'll see what he has to say. I wouldn't be surprised if this is just the tip of the iceberg." Philip slapped his notebook closed and pointed his finger at Genevieve. "What do you say to that, Watson?"

She puffed out a noisy breath and slumped back in her chair. "You're way ahead of me in 'the game is afoot' department. I'll give you one thing, Sherlock: we need to find out who has access to the Laney money. In all our meetings we have never discussed the mechanics of how money flows in and out of the estate. Who has access to our accounts? What checks and balances are in place? Other than the various brokerages and investment banks where a substantial part of the estate is managed, how and where is money invested? We've spent most of our time getting through the legalities of transferring the holdings from your cousin to you. Gosh, I hope David turns out to be one of the good guys.

"I'm counting on it," Philip said. "It's going to be an interesting visit."

"Yup." Genevieve stared at her plate. "Worrying about David is going to keep me up tonight, but I guess there's nothing we can do about it until he gets here." She looked back at Philip. "What are you up to this afternoon?

Leaning back in his chair, Philip scratched his chin. "I'm going to spend time with Sean Harrington." Philip glanced at his watch. "In fact, I need to get a move on. Harrington and I have an appointment with the police."

"The police?" Genevieve's eyebrows shot up. "You've already broken the law?"

"Very funny, G. They're coming to interview me."

"As the new lord of the manor? Ooo." She fluttered her eyelashes and patted her heart. "Will there be TV cameras and a dashing reporter?"

"Don't get excited. It's one cop coming to make sure I'm not a crazy person so they can transfer the gun licenses to me. Apparently we have a sizable collection. Then Harrington's going to show me around the estate. Can you come, or do you have something better to do?"

"I'd love to join you." Genevieve thrust her lower lip into a pout. "That would be such fun, but I'm going to spend the rest of the afternoon with Mrs. MacIntosh and Wallace, who should be back from Glasgow by now. We're going to tour the house from top to bottom, go over household budgets, and discuss events on the calendar. You know, all the usual things one does as lady of the manor." Genevieve offered a dismissive wave of her hand.

"Can you get through the entire house in one afternoon? That's a lot of ground to cover." Philip looked at his watch. "It's 4:30 already."

"We'll get started today." Genevieve stifled a yawn. "I'm sure it will take a week or so to get a feel for how all of this works. I want to learn as much as possible before David comes tomorrow. The more we know, the more he can help."

"That's exactly why I want to spend time with Harrington," Philip said. "He's going to be a wealth of information and, you know, everybody loves to gossip. I bet I come away with a lot more than just facts about annual yields and forest management."

"I also need to choose bedrooms for the kids for next week." As she mentioned the children, Genevieve's face glowed. "I'm so excited they'll be here soon. FaceTime doesn't do justice to the reality of what's happened over the last couple of weeks. Even Julia will be blown away!"

"I think you're right. Even she might be the tiniest bit dazzled. It's going to be fun doing a big show and tell. Alex will love the horses and Andrew Frazier can put on quite a falcon show for the kids. He's impressive, isn't he?"

"He's drop-dead gorgeous and seriously charming, that's what he is!"

"I thought you'd say that." Philip looked amused. "Ella will think she's a princess, Wilmingrove Hall's her castle, and Andrew Frazier is her Prince Charming."

"If I don't call dibs on him first. You know, I outrank our granddaughter." Genevieve picked up the last strawberry and brought it to her lips.

"I'd say you outrank everyone in the county. Except for me, of course." Philip crossed his arms, jutted out his chin, and pursed his lips. "Please do remember your place, my dear woman."

"You arrogant aristocrat!" Genevieve giggled. Instead of popping the juicy berry into her mouth, she tossed it, hitting Philip on his chest, leaving a red stain on his pullover. He looked down at his lap where the berry landed.

Eyes wide, Genevieve gasped. "Oh my God, Philip! I'm so sorry. I shouldn't have done that! I was just kidding around."

Philip plucked the piece of fruit clinging to his sweater and tossed the strawberry into his mouth. Leaning on the table and trying to keep a smile from his eyes, he loomed over her. "Madam, when you least expect it, I shall exact my revenge," he said, with as much ice in his voice as he could muster.

Genevieve stood and walked around the table. She looked into Philip's handsome face, slipped her hands around his waist, and drew him close. "Lord Crosswick, I hope your revenge is as exhilarating as everything else in our lives." Her lips brushed his. "I'm having the most exciting adventure. When we made our wedding vows, you promised our marriage would never be dull and by God, you've kept your word."

Philip kissed her. He could feel her smile beneath his lips. He pulled back just enough to say, "Upstairs?"

"I'll race you."

TWELVE

H ALF AN HOUR later, Genevieve descended the grand staircase, buttoning the cuffs of her blouse and running her fingers through her hair.

Mrs. MacIntosh was waiting in her small office near the kitchen.

"I hope I haven't delayed us too long," Genevieve said. "Philip and I, uh… had to take care of something." To her surprise, heat flushed her cheeks.

Mrs. MacIntosh rose from her chair, seemingly unaware of Genevieve's embarrassment. "My lady, your timing is perfect. Wallace is waiting for us in the cellars. We thought we'd start at the bottom and carry on upward floor by floor. There are one hundred and thirty-seven rooms in the Hall, so we'll get our steps in today. She smiled and tapped her Fitbit, then gestured for Genevieve to precede her through the door.

They passed the servants' dining room and the kitchen, then headed down a small passageway and through a large wooden door.

"Be careful, please," Mrs. MacIntosh cautioned as they started down a curved stone staircase. The temperature dropped with each tread until they stepped off the last stair into a cool, stone room lined with racks of bottles. The overhead lighting was soft and indirect.

In the middle of the room, a man of about sixty sat in front of a laptop, with a green-shaded lamp casting a circle of light across the small desk.

When he saw Genevieve, the butler popped to his feet. Wallace was exactly as Genevieve had pictured him. A fastidious fringe circled the bald crown of his head, and his black suit and starched white shirt were immaculate.

"My lady, welcome to your wine cellar. What a pleasure to meet you at last." Wallace gave a quick bow of his head. "We are thrilled that you and the Earl have arrived."

Genevieve offered a warm smile. "The Earl and I are excited to be here, Wallace. I trust your sister is better?"

"Very kind of you to ask, my lady. She is. She's well on the mend."

Genevieve turned slowly where she stood. "Wow," she whispered under her breath. "Wallace, I have to say, I didn't expect this. I anticipated a nice collection, but this! There must be several thousand bottles here."

Wallace gestured around the cavernous space. "Actually, my lady, there are eight thousand and fifty-four reds, seven thousand and twelve whites, three hundred and twenty-two bottles of Champagne and two hundred and four bottles of Port. Would you like a tour?"

Genevieve clapped her hands at the prospect of wandering through the cellar. "Oh, yes, please."

The three of them sauntered down an aisle stocked with high-shouldered, straight-sided bottles filled with Bordeaux wines. "What a stupefying collection! We're going to have to drink frequently and heavily, Wallace."

"My lady, you'll be interested to know, this row in particular has many bottles from your vineyard in St. Emilion. I have no doubt you will fall in love with Chateau Beaulieu. It's a beautiful property producing exceptional wines; one of the best boutique vineyards in Bordeaux.

Genevieve couldn't stop grinning.

"In addition to Chateau Beaulieu bottles, we cellar fine wines from other regions of France, many from Spain, Italy, and the U.S," the butler paused to wipe dust from a bottle's edge with his cuff then continued, "some from Germany, South Africa, Australia, New Zealand, and, of course, Argentina is well represented."

"It sounds as if no self-respecting wine producing country has been left out."

"Indeed, my lady." Wallace's chest swelled.

"And what are we doing with all these wines? It's been years since Wilmingrove Hall hosted grand parties that would warrant such a lavish wine collection. Talk to me, Wallace. Who's drinking all this fine grape?"

Though the cellar was cool, tiny beads of perspiration popped out on the butler's forehead. He glanced at Mrs. MacIntosh, whose nod was almost imperceptible, gulped then looked back at Genevieve. "As you know, my lady, we here at Wilmingrove

Hall have been fulfilling our duties at the direction of the trustees of the estate, Holmes Fitch Smythson Morrow. Everything at Wilmingrove Hall is directed by Sir Mark Holmes."

Genevieve nodded, encouraging Wallace to continue.

"Often, he emails a list of wines to be sent to various locations, including his London residence and to the homes of the other partners. I always include a shipping copy in the case, so Sir Mark knows I keep track of every bottle that leaves the wine cellar. I don't know if he reimburses the estate…" Wallace paused, "…but I rather doubt it."

Mrs. MacIntosh pulled the corners of her mouth down and gave Wallace a subtle shake of her head.

Ignoring Mrs. MacIntosh's look of caution, Wallace went on. "Of course, my lady, I have maintained scrupulous records of every bottle that has come in to or gone out of this cellar for the last forty years."

Genevieve was not shocked at Wallace's revelations. The firm's free-wheeling access to the Hall's wine collection was in keeping with Philip's suspicions. "I have no doubt you could tell us where every drop has gone, Wallace," Genevieve reassured him. "Sixteen thousand bottles of top-quality wines and spirits… hmm…Wallace, what's the value of the collection?"

"The market price of the cellar fluctuates, but it's safe to say that the average value is around three."

"Three hundred thousand pounds?" Genevieve gulped.

"No, my lady. That's three *million* pounds. The collection is insured for three and a half million, which allows for substantial additions without increasing the insurance."

"I see," Genevieve said, but she didn't. She couldn't imagine anyone owning three million pounds of wine. Yet another surprise to share with Philip. The hits just kept on coming.

Wallace invited them to sit at the table in the tasting room.

Mrs. MacIntosh pulled a lace-edged handkerchief from her sleeve. "My lady, it is a great relief to have you and the Earl here."

Genevieve smiled at the compliment.

Mrs. MacIntosh looked down at her fidgeting hands, avoiding Genevieve's gaze.

Wallace nodded his encouragement.

Mrs. MacIntosh cleared her throat. "For some time, Wallace and I have shared misgivings with some heads of your other households. We all feel uncomfortable with some things that have occurred at Wilmingrove Hall, Chateau Beaulieu and your horse farm in Kentucky.

Genevieve's smile faded. "What do you mean, uncomfortable?"

Mrs. MacIntosh faltered. "It's not really my place…"

Genevieve touched the housekeeper's sleeve. "Mrs. MacIntosh, you can tell me anything. You already had the courage to tell me we have a ghost at Wilmingrove Hall. After that, anything else should be easy," Genevieve teased.

Mrs. MacIntosh couldn't help but smile. "You make a fair point," she chuckled. "Lady Crosswick, you have wonderful people running your properties, but we are subject to the directions and whims of the trustees. We're not always confident their actions are in the best interest of the estate, but it's not our place to question them. It's a great relief to be able to share our concerns with you."

Much to Mrs. Macintosh's surprise, Genevieve squeezed her hand.

"Our loyalty has always been to the Earl and the estate rather than to the trustees."

Genevieve rose from her chair, put both hands on the burnished oak table and leaned forward. She looked into the earnest faces of the two long-serving loyalists. "I promise I'll share everything you've told me today with Lord Crosswick. The Earl already has suspicions about the law firm's ethics, and I promise, this is not our last conversation about the questionable practices of Holmes Fitch Smythson Morrow." She stepped away from the table. "But for now, let's get three glasses, open a bottle of Chateau Margaux, which I'm sure we have, and continue our tour."

With their burden shed, Mrs. MacIntosh had a spring in her step and Wallace actually smiled. Glasses in hand, the three climbed the stone staircase from the cellar to the lower-level floor. Their first stop was the servants' dining room, which, though renovated to a modern standard, retained the aura of another century. A long, oak table was alive with the spirit of years of below-stairs life.

Genevieve pulled out a wooden chair and sat. "I can just imagine the servants gathering around the table, with the butler at the head, of course," she nodded at Wallace. "Taking their meals, darning socks, gossiping about the gentry upstairs and sharing the daily trials of their lives. Lives devoted to providing comfort to those in the grand rooms above."

Mrs. MacIntosh and Wallace exchanged smiles.

Genevieve rose and moved on to the kitchen. "This space is massive," she said, awe in her voice.

"It has been refitted with a number of upgrades in the last two years. The old icebox was replaced with large stainless-steel refrigerators, including a walk-in freezer." Mrs. MacIntosh walked to the back wall of the kitchen and heaved open a thick door.

Genevieve's breath formed little puffs as she stepped into the freezing room. Bundles were stacked on wire stainless steel racks five feet high, running the length and width of the room. The contents of each package was handwritten in black marker on the white butcher's paper. "What in the world are we doing with all this meat?" Before Wallace or Mrs. MacIntosh could speak, she said, "Don't tell me…the partners."

Wallace nodded. "The partners like to have certain cuts of meat when they come to the Hall." Wallace looked at Mrs. MacIntosh for support.

"They like to live well," she confirmed.

Genevieve shivered from the cold and hugged herself as she left the freezer. "Another arrow in Philip's quiver," she muttered. "Or another 'steak' through the partners' hearts." She chuckled at her joke. "Brrrrrr. Remind me to put on a winter coat before I go in there again."

Mrs. MacIntosh opened a cupboard and pulled out a square linen tablecloth the yellow of the kitchen walls. Folding it into a triangle, she draped it across Genevieve's shoulders. "There, my lady. This should warm you."

"Why, thank you. That's very sweet."

"We can't have the lady of the manor catching cold." Wallace handed her a refilled glass of wine.

'Ooo, thank you, Wallace." Genevieve cradled the glass between her hands as if it were warm. "Now, tell me more. What other improvements have there been in the last few months?"

Under the fourteen-foot trough sink was a bank of four commercial dishwashers. "The sink has been here for years, but the dishwashers are new." Mrs. MacIntosh confirmed.

"I love the blue and white Delft tiles. They're so cheerful with the yellow walls."

"The paint is new, but the tiles are original to the house." Mrs. MacIntosh took a sip of her wine.

"That is without a doubt the largest Aga I have ever seen," Genevieve exclaimed. "And right next to a twelve-burner La Cornue, my dream stove! Are these both new?"

"Yes, my lady."

Genevieve scratched her forehead. "This is confusing. Why are the partners spending all this money to upgrade the kitchen? When was the last big party at the Hall?"

Mrs. MacIntosh's face clouded. "I wouldn't call it a party, but there was a large gathering after the Earl's funeral at the local church. At least five hundred people came to pay their respects over the course of three hours. That was the last time there were so many people to feed."

"But what about—," Wallace froze, silenced by a steely glance from Mrs. MacIntosh. "But, Bertie," he insisted, "Lady Crosswick wants us to tell her anything we think is dubious. I think feeding thousands of visitors every year falls into that category."

Genevieve's jaw dropped. "What do you mean, 'thousands of visitors?'"

"Two years ago, Sir Mark told us the house would open to visitors to supplement the income of the estate." Wallace looked skeptical. "I'm sure you know that many stately homes have opened to the public to defray some of the maintenance costs."

Genevieve nodded. "The Earl and I have visited numerous great houses that welcome visitors. But I thought Wilmingrove Hall, and the estate are on solid financial ground." Genevieve closed her eyes and shook her head. She felt more confused with every revelation.

Wallace scowled. "Mrs. MacIntosh and I were most concerned with the arrangements. People toured the main floor and the ballroom on the first floor before they went through the stable and the gardens for one ticket price. For an additional fee, they could have tea at the stable cafe and see Andrew Frazier's falconry show."

"I think Philip's meeting with Andrew this afternoon." Warmer now, Genevieve pulled the makeshift shawl from her shoulders and put it on the counter.

"Lord Crosswick will love seeing our birds of prey in action. It's a magnificent sight," said Wallace.

"I can't wait to see the falcons and hawks, too. Working birds are so exciting. I love that the public can see the birds in action, but I'm not wild about them coming into the house. Are we still doing tours?"

"We are not," said Mrs. MacIntosh. "Sir Mark announced we

would no longer open the house a couple of months after Lord Crosswick died."

"Hmmm." Genevieve chewed her lip. "Was that around the time they tracked down Philip—uh, Lord Crosswick?"

"It seems a bit too coincidental, don't you think, my lady?" Disdain dripped from Wallace's words.

"Mrs. MacIntosh, do you have any idea how many people toured the Hall? Are we talking about a few tourists, or a lot?" Genevieve pressed.

"Over the course of the two years, I believe we had about sixty thousand people visit the Hall. I can check my records for an exact number."

"Good lord! Sixty thousand people!" Genevieve was stunned.

"That's how many people who paid an average of fifty-four pounds per ticket. Then there were additional sales from high tea in the stable cafe."

"Good lord," Genevieve said again. "That's over three million pounds. Where did that money go?"

Wallace shrugged his shoulders and looked at Mrs. MacIntosh, who shook her head.

Genevieve tugged a heavy stool from under the kitchen's center island and sat on the edge. She drained her wineglass. It tinkled as she put it down on the marble counter. "My head is spinning from all this information." Genevieve put her elbows on the counter and rested her chin on her clasped hands. For a moment, silence filled the room, then she said, "I have a huge question for both of you. Do you think Sir Mark has managed the estate well or has he taken advantage of having no earl heading the family fortunes?"

Mrs. MacIntosh and Wallace looked at each other.

Wallace studied his black wool jacket and picked invisible lint from his lapel. Looking back at Genevieve, he said, "My lady, there is no question in our minds that Holmes Fitch Smythson Morrow, and in particular Sir Mark Holmes, took liberties as trustees of the Laney estate." Relieved of the burden of carrying this dark secret for years, Wallace let out a mighty sigh.

"You two!" Moved by a rush of fondness for her housekeeper and butler, Genevieve blinked back tears. "Lord Crosswick and I owe you both an enormous debt of gratitude for your years of stewardship under the most challenging circumstances. You two are spectacular. Wallace, why don't you open another bottle of this Chateau Margaux? Catch up to Mrs. MacIntosh and me in the…where are we going next, Mrs. MacIntosh?"

"The grand salon, then the music room."

"Onward and upward. Wallace, we'll see you upstairs."

Genevieve didn't know if it was the wine or the adrenaline rush from being an amateur sleuth, but she felt a distinct buzz of exhilaration. She set a brisk pace up the back staircase to the main floor. Mrs. MacIntosh followed behind, keeping up as best she could, huffing her way up the stairs.

They popped out into a small stairwell brightened by yellow plaster walls, hung with photographs of Wilmingrove Hall over the years. "Aren't these wonderful?" Genevieve thrilled at the history in front of her. "Look at this picture of all the staff. There must be almost a hundred servants in this photograph!"

Mrs. MacIntosh tilted her head. "Actually, there were one hundred seven people in service at the Hall in 1884 when this was taken. In its heyday, this house required a huge staff to maintain the lifestyle of a landed family."

"Hard to imagine. This aristocracy thing was big business, wasn't it?" Genevieve stopped in front of a picture of elegant people. "The upstairs crowd," she said under her breath. She leaned forward until her nose was six inches from the photograph. She squinted, trying to bring the image into sharper focus. "Is this Charlotte?" Genevieve pressed her finger on the glass. Pointing to a beautiful woman of about forty.

"It is, my lady."

"She looks so much like the portrait I saw at Margrave House. The artist was very good." Genevieve's breath coated the glass. She pulled back a few inches and ran her sleeve over the fog, leaving little damp streaks.

Moving to Genevieve's side, Mrs. MacIntosh stood on her toes to get a closer look at the family gathering. "You're looking at three generations of Laneys. This was taken two years after Wilmingrove Hall was completed. You can see how vivid the coat of arms is. This is James Charles Philip Laney, the 8TH Earl." She pointed to a man with a gray moustache trailing down his cheeks into mutton chops. His top hat shaded his eyes so only the bottom of his face was visible. "He's the earl who secured the Laney fortunes."

"Who is this?" Genevieve pointed to a clean-shaven man.

"That, my lady, is Philip George Winston Laney, the 9TH Earl and Charlotte's husband." Mrs. MacIntosh pointed to a lanky blond boy with regal bearing. "This is George William Morris Laney, the 10TH Earl."

"I don't know how you keep all the earls and their names straight," Genevieve said with admiration.

"I've lived with them for a long time. You'll get the hang of it. Shall we continue?"

"I guess we should. We have a lot of ground to cover, don't we?"

"We do, my lady, and I plan to give you the full fifty-four-pound tour." She gave Genevieve a sly smile. "So, we'd better get on our way." Mrs. MacIntosh moved ahead and began her docent tour in the salon.

In her poshest Yorkshire accent, the housekeeper began her lecture. "Wilmingrove Hall was built as a country retreat by the 8TH Earl of Crosswick. By the mid-1850s, many great British family fortunes were on the wane. But the 8TH Earl was a clever man. Through several decades of shrewd business moves, the generations of earls significantly altered the Laney fortunes and ensured the family would remain financially sound well into the future." She cleared her throat and went on. "With that sense of security, the 8TH Earl felt comfortable spending thirty-four million pounds to create Wilmingrove Hall for his family and future heirs. He began constructing Wilmingrove Hall in 1874. After numerous delays, the Hall was completed in 1882."

Genevieve suppressed a smile, both impressed and amused by Mrs. MacIntosh's formal presentation.

Mrs. MacIntosh reached into her skirt pocket. To Genevieve's surprise, she pulled out a laser pointer and flicked on the light. She pointed toward the ornamental moldings twenty feet above.

"Though premade crown molding and cornices were available, the 8ᵀᴴ Earl insisted all decorative elements for the Hall be hand crafted. No expense was spared. The estimated value of the Hall in today's currency is two hundred and fifty million pounds." Mrs. MacIntosh walked regally to the center of the salon. It was obvious she took great pride in Wilmingrove Hall and its illustrious history.

"Very impressive, Mrs. MacIntosh. You should be giving tours at The Tate."

Mrs. MacIntosh surprised Genevieve with a wink. "They couldn't afford me, my lady,"

Genevieve's jeans pocket vibrated. She pulled out her phone to see Philip's face fill the screen. She held up one finger. "Mrs. MacIntosh, just a moment, please."

"Hi, cute boy," she answered with a smile.

His voice business-like, Philip got straight to the point. "G, I know you're in the middle of your tour, but we need you here for a few minutes."

Genevieve looked up at the ceiling, impatient to get back to Mrs. MacIntosh. "Why?"

"The policewoman is here to interview us for the gun license transfer. I didn't know she'd want you here, too, but she does."

"I don't want to interrupt my time with Mrs. MacIntosh and Wallace. I'm learning a lot. You really need me?

"Kafritz, the police officer, wants you here."

"All right." Genevieve blew out an annoyed huff. "I'll be right there." Turning to her tour guide she asked, "Which way is the estate office?"

THIRTEEN

Genevieve hiked down the terraced hill and arrived at the estate office ten minutes later. The small room had floor-to-ceiling pine shelves fitted on two walls, each packed with binders. A boot jack caked with mud sat just inside the door, and a Labrador Retriever lay dozing by a wood-burning stove, which warmed the room.

Sean Harrington sat at his desk with Philip looking over his shoulder at a computer screen. Across the desk, a policewoman faced them with her back to the door, her uniform a bit too large for her small frame.

As Genevieve walked in, Philip looked up and smiled.

The chocolate Lab raised his head to see who was disturbing his nap. Finding Genevieve of little interest, he rolled onto his side, stretched his legs in front of him and was softly snoring again within seconds.

Harrington stood up. "Lady Crosswick, thank you for coming. I know you were in the middle of something, but Sergeant Kafritz wanted to meet you and explain the importance of transferring the ownership of the gun collection."

The officer stood and turned.

Genevieve blinked, trying not to show her surprise. She couldn't remember ever seeing anyone quite so homely. It was hard to tell her age. She could be in her twenties; she could be close to forty. Her mousy brown hair was parted in the middle and pulled back into a severe bun, which accentuated her coarse features. Her eyes, magnified behind thick rimless glasses, had no distinguishable color and her nose was too large for her face. The whole image made Genevieve think of the funny nose and glasses she loved to wear as a child. The officer's complexion was pasty, but her mouth was startling. Her lower lip was as full and ripe as a cherry, and her upper lip was a perfect cupid's bow. It was a beautiful, perfect mouth on an achingly plain face.

Genevieve pulled her attention from the sergeant's appearance. She started to extend her hand then, remembering herself, dropped it back at her side. "Sergeant Kafritz. Thank you for including me. It might be hard for you to imagine because we're Americans, but Philip and I are not used to owning guns. This is all new to us."

"Lady Crosswick." The sergeant gave a deferential nod. "I'm glad you joined us. I was just about to do an inventory of the gun safe and cross reference the paperwork." Kafritz had a lisp and a Yorkshire accent. "But before I do that, why don't I give you an overview of the procedure." She looked around at her audience of three. "Then you can all get back to what you were doing. I'll take the inventory and leave the keys wherever you like."

For fifteen minutes, Sergeant Kafritz rambled on about the UK's strict gun laws until Genevieve was numb with boredom.

When at last the sergeant finished her lecture, Genevieve couldn't leave fast enough. She loped from the estate office up the path and the stairs, until she stood in the doorway of the housekeeper's office, panting, her face glistening with sweat.

Looking up from her paperwork, Mrs. MacIntosh chuckled. "Ran all the way, did you?"

Genevieve smiled. "I think we're becoming friends," she said to herself. And they resumed the tour.

FOURTEEN

THE MUSIC ROOM was one of Genevieve's favorite spaces. Tucked into the southwest corner of the house, it had a beautiful afternoon glow. Fourteen-foot windows offered stunning views over the gardens and out to the river. Genevieve, a life-long pianist, couldn't resist sitting at the Bosendorfer grand, running scales up and down the keyboard. It was one of the most elegant pianos she had ever played; it was in perfect tune and the action of the keys was agile and responsive.

"Oh, my lady, you play the piano." Mrs. MacIntosh clapped her hands with delight. "How wonderful it will be to hear music in the house!"

"I've played since I was a child, but like most kids, I hated practicing. I just started playing again a few years ago. And I've never played a Bosendorfer! I'm sure all of this is a dream and I'll wake up any moment." Surveying the room, everywhere she looked was perfection. British elm paneling and floors gave the room a magical radiance. As she sat on the toile-covered piano bench, she could almost hear string quartets, piano recitals, operatic concerts, and jazz combos.

"Was the music room used a lot?" she asked.

"Before his accident, the 12TH Earl was in residence at the Hall for months at a time. He loved music, all kinds. According to our Wilmingrove Hall historian…"

"We have an historian?" Genevieve interrupted.

"Yes, my lady. His name is Fenton Morrissey. I've asked him to join us." Mrs. MacIntosh shoved her sleeve past her Fitbit to glance at the time. "He should be here any minute."

As if on cue, an Ichabod Crane-lookalike bumbled through the door and across the room, juggling a stack of thick volumes in his skinny arms. His mop of ginger hair bounced with every step he took. He failed to watch where he was going, tripped over a small footstool, and staggered to keep upright.

"Lady Crosswick!" A tome toppled from his tower of books, crashing to the floor.

Genevieve stooped to pick up the volume as another book fell, thumping her on the head. She smashed to the floor, thunking her nose on the hardwood.

"What's going on here?" Wallace bellowed as he strode through the door, a bottle of Chateau Margaux in each hand. Then he saw his mistress lying face down on the floor. "What's happened? Lady Crosswick, are you all right?"

Mrs. Macintosh squatted beside Genevieve as she pushed herself to her knees and twisted to sit on her bottom. She wiggled her nose to assure it wasn't broken, then touched her fingers to her nostrils. No blood. She began to giggle. The giggle rolled from her throat, exploding into a belly laugh.

Mrs. MacIntosh stared open-mouthed while Wallace grabbed Genevieve's arm and tugged. "Let me help you up, my lady," Wallace said.

The more Genevieve tried to stop laughing, the more she gasped for air.

Fenton Morrissey had not moved, still clutching his books. He was frozen in place, eyes popping out of his head, his face the color of his starched, white shirt.

Genevieve remained sitting on the floor, resisting Wallace's efforts to pull her to her feet. At last, her laughter subsided. She gazed up at the trio towering over her. "Please don't look so worried. That was hilarious. I'm sorry we don't have a video of the fiasco!" Finally, she stuck out her hand and allowed Wallace to help her up.

Without ceremony, Genevieve rearranged her sweater and pulled her jeans up by the belt loops. "So, Mr. Morrissey, this has been quite an auspicious introduction."

Her genuine smile was such a relief to Morrissey that his breath, which he'd been holding for the last minute, whooshed out.

"Wallace, shall we open those bottles and find another glass for Fenton?" She pointed to the wine Wallace had plunked on the piano.

Turning back to the historian, Genevieve pointed to a sideboard. "Mr. Morrissey, why don't you put your books over there."

Grateful for the suggestion, he laid the pile on the dark-green marble top.

"I was just asking Mrs. MacIntosh to tell me about the history of the music room. She said you are the authority." Genevieve touched Morrissey on the arm, hoping to put him at ease.

As he began sharing the room's history, a transition came over the gawky man and he began to sparkle. "Oh, my lady, we have historic confirmation that many notable musicians graced Wilmingrove Hall: Billie Holiday, Ella Fitzgerald, and Aaron Copeland." He moved to the curve in the piano, struck the pose of a model and clasped his hands at his chest. "Photos show Leontyne Price standing right here on this spot singing arias." He headed back to the credenza. "I brought several books from the library, one of which I used to bludgeon you." He smiled sheepishly, hoping Genevieve would enjoy the joke. "I know you're in a bit of a hurry this afternoon, so I'll put them on the library table for you and Lord Crosswick."

"Please do! And I'd love to spend time with you next week familiarizing myself with the library. But I want to get a helmet and pads before we meet again." Genevieve returned his joke.

"Just one last thing. I did want to ask if by any chance you put this on the library table?" Morrissey handed Genevieve a book with a glossy, black dust cover, bright red ink splashed across the front. In jagged letters it said *How I Killed My Daddy*, a novel by Olivia H. Conway. "It appeared this morning. I thought perhaps you brought it with you."

"No, Fenton. I haven't seen this before. Interesting title." The hall clock chimed five, and Genevieve turned to Mrs. MacIntosh. "I suppose we should pick up the pace or we'll still be touring the house at midnight. Fenton, I look forward to spending time together soon." She put her hand on his tweedy shoulder. "And thank you for today."

"It's been my pleasure, Lady Crosswick."

"I thought we would just cover the main floor this afternoon. We can resume the tour at your convenience." Mrs. MacIntosh led the way to their next stop. "I know Sir David is coming tomorrow, so you will be busy while he's here. Perhaps early next week would be a good time to carry on."

"That sounds like a good plan, Mrs. MacIntosh. I'll count on you to organize it. Where to next?" Not used to drinking wine in the afternoon, Genevieve felt a bit woozy. She would have loved a nap before dinner but didn't have the heart to cut the exploration short. Mrs. MacIntosh and Wallace were anxious to share the glories of the Hall, and perhaps they would tell her more about Sir Mark's shenanigans. She also didn't want to break the spell of new camaraderie developing between them, so on they pressed into the drawing room.

The moment they entered the grand chamber, Genevieve was enveloped in a sweet, delicate fragrance. She looked around the room searching for bouquets of cut flowers. She saw none.

"Mrs. MacIntosh, I smell roses."

"Do you? It's Charlotte, I suppose." The housekeeper sniffed the air. "I don't smell a thing, but that's not unusual. Often Charlotte reveals herself to just one person in the room."

"Charlotte? Are you serious?" Genevieve rolled her eyes. "Well, I smell roses, so I guess I should feel honored. But why me?"

"Perhaps she's reaching out to you because you are now the matriarch of the Laney clan, and she wants you to know you have her support. This was always her favorite room, so it makes sense she would greet you here. She finished redecorating it just before her accident."

A warmth spread through Genevieve at the suggestion that Charlotte had chosen to embrace her. She did a slow turn, admiring the soft colors and light playing off polished wood and faceted chandeliers. She could imagine elegant Edwardian women draped across the chase lounges and divans, laughter and chatter filling the room. "She did a splendid job," Genevieve said.

"Shall we, my lady?" Wallace motioned for Genevieve to go through to the next room.

The thirty-six-foot-long dining room was grand and opulent, with one wall lined with the same soaring French doors found in the music and drawing rooms. Cherry floors gleamed, and imposing sideboards anchored each end of the room. Eager to miss no detail, Genevieve took in color and texture, fabric, wood, and metal until her gaze stopped on a painting above the fireplace.

"Wallace, Mrs. MacIntosh, who is that?" Genevieve pointed to a modern portrait of a very handsome man in formal attire.

"That, my lady, is the 12ᵀᴴ Earl of Crosswick, the current Earl's cousin. He was quite a figure, wasn't he? Do you see the resemblance to the current Earl?"

"Oh, my. I do." There was no question. Philip was Jonathon's doppelganger. "He's magnificent. He looks exactly like Philip twenty years ago. How old was the Earl when this was painted?"

"The portrait was painted when he was thirty-six, six months before his skiing accident. He had just become engaged to

Katherine Robeson, the daughter of an American media mogul."

"Lord Crosswick and I learned the story when we were in London. It's tragic. He gave up the love of his life because he was paralyzed, and then he met Revy Harris and it happened all over again." A tear slipped down Genevieve's cheek and she swiped it away with her knuckle. "There's no end to sad Laney family stories, is there?"

The tour had lost its energetic sparkle. Maybe it was the sobering story about the Earl's sad love affairs or perhaps the giddy effect of the Chateau Margaux was fading. It was hard to tell.

Genevieve looked away from the 12TH Earl's portrait and refocused her attention on the enormous dining table. "How many can we seat around the table when it's fully extended?"

"Forty with the table as-is and fifty-two with all the leaves in place," Mrs. MacIntosh said. "When the table is formally set and the dining room is ready for a dinner party, it's quite grand!"

Genevieve stood with her hands on her hips, imagining the beautiful room filled with women in stylish gowns and men in black tie, glasses clinking, candles flickering, the sound of music wafting in the air. "I have an idea," she said, her energy sparking again. "Don't you think we should plan a big dinner party, or at least a whopper of a cocktail party? I don't know who we would invite, but I'm sure with some thought we could come up with a wonderful group."

"Oh, yes!" Mrs. MacIntosh grinned.

"We could celebrate the new Earl and Countess of Crosswick taking their place at the helm of Wilmingrove Hall." Genevieve leaned close to Mrs. MacIntosh and Wallace. "And maybe we could set a trap for our crafty Sir Mark. What do you two think?"

"That's a wonderful idea, my lady," Mrs. MacIntosh agreed.

Wallace's smile nearly gave him away, but he mustered his composure just in time. "Splendid. Simply splendid, my lady. Wilmingrove Hall will be radiant. You and the Earl will bring this grand house back to life! Mrs. MacIntosh and I will be proud to be a part of it. An elegant party is the perfect trap to ensnare Sir Mark. But, perhaps more important, you need fine cheese to catch a posh rat."

"To the beginning of a new era," Genevieve raised her goblet and with only a splash of wine left, she clinked glasses with her co-conspirators.

Philip and Genevieve shared a cozy table in the study by a crackling fire, dining on salmon from their own river, late-season tomatoes, and home-grown brussels sprouts.

"Charlotte's here," said Genevieve, before sipping a soft white Bordeaux from their St. Emilion vineyard.

Philip stopped, his fork midway to his mouth. "You're kidding!" he said, eyes crinkling from his broad smile. "How do you know?"

"I smelled her." Genevieve tilted her chin and blinked. "Mrs. MacIntosh says I'm special."

"I wouldn't argue with that." Philip gathered more food on his fork.

"I'll let you know the next time Charlotte and I get together." She laughed. "Thanks for stealing half an hour of my time with that gun transfer business. I certainly didn't need to be there. Sergeant Kafritz is unusual, wouldn't you say?

"She was. She was extremely…" Philip paused, searching for the right word. "…competent."

Genevieve held her breath and stared at her plate. She knew if she looked at Philip, she would burst out laughing. "Competent. That's the right word." She giggled.

"Can you believe this?" Philip closed his lips around a forkful of salmon. Butter oozed from the corner of his mouth and a groan of pleasure hummed in his throat.

Genevieve sat back in her chair, amused as she watched her husband wallow in the pleasure of his meal. "You're hilarious. You'd think you'd never had a good meal before."

"Maybe everything is so delicious because it all came from our estate." His smile reached his eyes. "Those are words I never thought I'd say."

Genevieve nodded. "All day I've felt I'm in a fairytale. Everything is perfect… maybe too perfect." Small lines of concern feathered the corners of her eyes.

"I didn't expect to hear that. At lunch you were falling in love with the house and thrilled that it's not shabby." Philip crossed his eyes. "I'm getting whiplash. You're like a yoyo. 'I'm happy. I'm worried. I'm happy. I'm worried.'"

"Really, Philip, it's hard for a yoyo to give you whiplash." Genevieve put her elbows on the table and rested her chin on her fisted hands. "You're right. I changed my mind after my tour with Mrs. MacIntosh, but for good reason. But first, I want to hear about your tour. Do you like Mr. Harrington?" Genevieve asked.

"A better question is, does Mr. Harrington like *me*," Philip said.

Genevieve looked puzzled.

"We met at the stables before Sargent Kafritz arrived and, as I walked through the door, Harrington started bombarding me with complaints about Sir Mark."

Philip went on, corroborating everything Mrs. MacIntosh and Wallace had told Genevieve earlier that day. "Get this: there was even a visitor who took cuttings of several types of ivy and snipped a huge bouquet from the rose garden. Harrington said she thought the price of the tour entitled her to flowers and ivy! He was steaming, but once he realized I was not in favor of Wilmingrove Hall functioning as an amusement park, we became mates pretty fast."

Genevieve leaned back in her chair. She grinned, enjoying Philip's rendition of similar stories she had heard earlier from their housekeeper and butler. She took a slow drink of her wine and nodded at her husband. "Go on."

"That's just the beginning." Philip emptied his glass and refilled Genevieve's goblet then his own. "Harrington told me during the past two years, Mark Holmes has run at least fifty thousand people through our home."

Genevieve enjoyed Philip's use of our home.

"And Mrs. MacIntosh has been serving as docent for the tours."

Genevieve nodded, the faintest smile on her lips. "I had Mrs. MacIntosh's tour today. She's very good."

"So, you know all of this?"

"I do."

"Okay, Miss Smarty Pants. Did you know Sir Mark ran high ticket events here during shooting season?"

"I did not."

"Groups from all over the world have been paying thousands of pounds to shoot pheasant and grouse. When I asked where the money goes—and it's a hell of a lot of money—Harrington said he hasn't seen…." Philip paused as Lottie, a petite young lady from the kitchen staff, appeared in the doorway.

"My lord, may I serve the pudding?" she asked.

"That would be great." He waited until she retreated, then leaned on his forearms across the table. "Should we worry about any of the staff spying on us for Sir Mark?" he whispered.

Genevieve grinned at him, thinking he was joking. But his brow furrowed, and a genuine look of concern clouded his eyes.

She snorted a laugh. "You're serious," she said with disbelief.

Philip sat back in his chair as the door opened again.

Lottie entered, carrying two raspberry souffles puffed two inches above the ramekin rims. She poured steaming coffee into their Limoges cups.

Philip watched her every move until she disappeared through the door when he spoke again. "I don't know. It just occurred to me when Lottie came in. But you don't think it's something we need to worry about, so never mind. Anyway, it's your turn. How did your day go and what do you think about my revelations? Inquiring minds want to know."

Genevieve took a luxurious bite of her warm raspberry souffle. The tartness of the berries played perfectly with the sweetness of the fluffy egg cloud. She sighed a note of pleasure. "Philip, you and I have spent the day getting the same information from three reliable sources. I think it's safe to say, we have a trap to set and a rat to catch."

FIFTEEN

Y ESTERDAY'S BEAUTIFUL DAY had turned chilly and wet, and the rain sheeted down. Though it was midday, lamps lit every corner of the house. As he descended the stairs, Philip couldn't help wondering what their electric bill must be. He often found himself turning off lights he felt were unnecessary, although he knew Genevieve would roll her eyes and call him ridiculous if she saw him.

Just as Philip passed through the foyer, the front door burst open. "David!" Philip said. "I didn't realize you had arrived. Whoa, are you drenched!"

David stood dripping on the marble floor, wet hair plastered to his head. "Rather! It's bucketing down out there, and the flight wasn't brilliant, I can tell you."

With perfect timing, Wallace appeared, towel in hand. "Sir David, may I take your coat?"

"Wallace, how wonderful to see you! It's been ages. I don't think I've seen you since the last Pony Club gymkhana here at the Hall. Remember? The Duchess of Margress was so squiffy she drove the pony trap into the reservoir. Wasn't Sir Henry with her when they went in? God, they were a funny sight."

"I'm sure I don't know to what you refer, Sir David." Wallace took David's coat, handed him the fluffy white towel and winked at him. "Drinks will be served in the library when you're ready, my lord."

"Wallace, could you please tell Lady Crosswick Sir David is here? I'm not sure where she is," Philip said.

"Of course, my lord," Wallace said over his shoulder. He left with the dripping coat and damp towel.

Philip and David moved into the library, where a fire threw welcoming warmth into the room.

"Have a seat, David," Philip said, motioning to over-stuffed chairs near the hearth. "Man, am I glad you're here. We've only been here twenty-four hours, and we have mysteries popping up everywhere. I'm sure you can shed light on most of them."

"Your lordship, I—"

Philip cut him off. "Will you stop with the 'lordship' crap! This is starting to get on my nerves."

David grinned. "In the twenty-first century it really is absolute bollocks, isn't it?"

"God, yes! As an American, I've always been seduced by your class system. I thought it would be great fun to be a peer, but after a couple of weeks in the thick of it, it's rubbish, as you say."

Philip pulled a chunky log from the wood box and tossed it into the fireplace. Flames snapped, gobbling the dry timber. "David, wouldn't you say the important thing about having wealth and privilege is noblesse oblige? Genevieve and I've been talking a lot about this. Both of us want to do extraordinary work with the massive inheritance that's fallen into our laps. We're going to need your help to figure out how to do the greatest good with what we have." Philip ran his hands over his face, then blew air from his puffed-out cheeks. "God, David, I'm sorry. I should at least wait until you have a drink in your hand before I start bombarding you!"

"David!" Genevieve's warm greeting reached across the library as she entered the room.

Both men smiled, watching her stride to where they were seated.

"Please don't get up! You two look very cozy sitting here." She flashed a grin, looking every inch the part of a lady to the manor born. A short, purple cashmere sweater hit just at the waistband of a purple, green, and black wool tartan skirt that swished around the tops of Genevieve's cordovan ankle boots. She had pulled her hair up and clipped it into a messy bun with a silver fastener.

With his butler's intuition, Wallace was at her side. "My lady, what would you like to drink?"

"Wallace. I think a glass of the Margaux we had yesterday would hit the spot," Genevieve leaned into Wallace and dropped her voice, "or did we drink it all?"

"I'm sure I can find a drop for you, my lady."

"Ooo, super. Thank you. You know, Wallace, I think of all the marvelous things about being the Countess of Crosswick, you are one of my favorites. If you're not already, you should be a national treasure."

As color rose in Wallace's cheeks, the butler offered Genevieve a silver tray with delicious-looking morsels. "My lady, it is a genuine pleasure to be in your service. Will there be anything else?"

"Thank you, Wallace. I think we have everything we need at the moment. Lunch in about an hour will be perfect," Genevieve said.

"As you wish, my lady." Wallace retreated and the threesome was alone.

Genevieve scooched forward in her chair. "Okay, boys. What did I miss?"

"Lord Cr…"

Philip shot David a sharp look. David raised both hands, palms out. "All right, all right."

'What's that about?" Genevieve screwed up her face.

"I've insisted David ditch our titles and call us by our first names, but it may take a while before he gets the hang of it. Feel free to wrap his knuckles until he gets it right, G."

Genevieve threw David a wicked look. "It will be my pleasure," she said, rubbing her hands together.

The threesome spent the next hour talking about the various characters at Holmes Fitch Smythson Morrow.

"I've been with HFSM for twenty years. I've always been proud to be part of a firm that had the highest standards, but in the past four or five years, things have changed." David rolled his wine glass between his palms then took a long, slow swallow. "As long as I have been with the firm, the partners have used Wilmingrove Hall as a retreat, but I believed it was with the full knowledge of Lord Crosswick. They were respectful and, as far as I know, never abused the privilege of being here. But a while ago, even before Lord Crosswick began his decline, it seemed the partners began to take advantage of the Earl's generosity. I'd say it started when they brought the art into their offices."

"We were going to ask you about that." Philip's eyebrows arched, waiting for further explanation.

"I didn't want to tell you when we were in the New York office. I was hoping Sir Mark would explain why they have millions of pounds of your art collection on the firm's walls. But he didn't. When did you figure it out?"

"We saw the works in a book by Kenneth Baron that lists all our art and antiques." Philip's mouth tightened to a thin line."

"Please believe me. I intended to tell you from the beginning." Little beads of perspiration dotted David's upper lip.

Genevieve and Philip looked at each other then back at David. "If you say that's one of the things you're concerned about, we believe you. What else do you have to tell us?"

David's right knee pistoned up and down. "Well, Sir Mark began the tours, and the shoots, and then they bought the jet and the helicopter. And there was some scuttlebutt about Sir Mark freely availing himself of the offerings of the wine cellar." As David spoke, Philip and Genevieve exchanged knowing glances. "It seemed to start slowly then accelerate to warp speed." As David spoke, it was clear his concerns were the same as the Warwick's.

"Do you know anything about Revy Harris and a ruby ring?" Genevieve walked to the fireplace, pulled a small log from the wood holder, and tossed it onto the pile glowing on the hearth. It caught, crackling, and spitting sparks.

"Revy Harris?" David's face was blank.

"Yes. When we were at Margrave House, we saw a photograph of a beautiful young woman named Revy Harris, on the Earl's desk." Genevieve wielded an iron poker, pushing the logs further back into the firebox. "I guess you'd have no reason to know who she is. Over twenty years ago, she was a Fellow with the Laney Museum of Fine Arts. As part of her internship, she helped the 12TH Earl catalogue the Margrave House collection." Genevieve replaced the poker and turned away from the fireplace, flushed from the heat. "According to Mrs. Baker, she went from intern to inamorata in just a few short months. But, David, the reason I'm interested in her is not because of that salacious story. It's because I was dazzled by the ruby ring she was wearing in the photo."

Philip, who had been absorbed answering a text, glanced up from his phone. "Don't let her kid you, David. She wants all the details about the hot sex between the cute American and my cousin."

"Okay, you got me. I probably wouldn't cover my ears if you have any of those tidbits." Genevieve wiggled her eyebrows up and down and twisted her lips to a lascivious smile. "But seriously, boys," she said tapping a fake cigar, "I want to know about the ring."

Vibrating with excitement, Genevieve told David of seeing the same ring on Revy's finger in the photograph that she later saw in the portrait of Victoria Catherine Winston Laney, the 8TH Earl's wife. "I want to know how this pipsqueak American wedeled her way into Jonathon Laney's life and ended up with an extraordinary Crosswick treasure."

"You believe this girl has illegal possession of a Laney family heirloom?" David looked skeptical.

"Yes, but she's not a girl anymore. She'd have to be about your age, or maybe a bit younger. You know, quite long in the tooth." Genevieve slapped her thigh, cackling.

David ignored her joke. "Genevieve, if Lord Crosswick was having an affair with this beauty, he might well have given her a piece of jewelry." He shrugged his shoulders. "An old, crippled man may need more than charm to keep a beautiful young lover. I've never had to use it myself, but I understand jewelry is a hell of an aphrodisiac."

Genevieve rolled her eyes. "I suppose you're right. I just thought she might have conned him out of it. That's a lot more interesting than Jonathon giving it to her in exchange for, you know…" she hugged herself, pooched her lips out and made kissing sounds. She glanced at Philip, who was punching send on his phone. "Philip what are you doing on your phone?" she asked, annoyed.

Philip put his phone back in his pants pocket. "I was just answering a text from Sir Mark."

Genevieve leaned forward on high alert. "What did he want?"

"He asked if David got here all right." He threw David a questioning look. "Is he always so concerned about your whereabouts and wellbeing?"

"Absolutely not. That's strange." David bit his lower lip. "I didn't realize he even knew I was coming to Wilmingrove Hall."

"Reeeally?" Genevieve stretched out the word. "Do you think he's worried you'll tell us things he doesn't want you to share?"

"Hmmm." The corners of David's mouth drew down. "There's a chance he's wondering why I'm here. But as far as I know, he doesn't suspect I think he's a miscreant."

"If indeed he's been dipping his toes into the Laney Pond, 'miscreant' is a much-too-elegant name to call him." Philip's eyes were flinty, and his voice edged with steel. "I can forgive a lot of things, but I pity anyone who exploits my family. If we confirm Sir Mark has misused his position as my cousins' trusted guardian, I don't envy him."

The smoldering logs hissed in the fireplace. Genevieve sat still as a mannequin, eyes wide, lips taut. There was no question in her mind that with every new revelation about the House of Crosswick, Philip felt more a part of the illustrious bloodline and more protective of his ancestry.

After several minutes, David broke the heavy silence. "I guess this is as good a time as any," he said looking solemn. "I have something to tell you."

"Oh boy," Genevieve said and bit her lower lip. "This can't be good."

David set his wine glass on the table beside him and folded his hands in his lap. He felt his heart accelerate and took a deep breath to calm himself. "One of the reasons I wanted to come to the Hall this weekend, in addition to talking to you about these fiduciary concerns, was to let you know that I've decided to leave the firm. Of course, that means I will no longer be your solicitor."

"No, it doesn't," Philip said immediately. "You can be our attorney and we will be your sole client. Genevieve and I have talked about this, and we're convinced Sir Mark is an embezzler." He spat out the word. "His behavior's blatant. He's arrogant, and he thinks I'm too naïve to see what he's doing. Hubris will bite him in the ass every time." Philip rose and walked to the sideboard.

"David, we're about to do battle with Sir Mark and his mighty law firm," Genevieve said. "We need you for that. After we destroy them, there's plenty of work with the Laney estate, the museums, and the Foundation.

"You know we can afford to pay you what you're worth. Well, we'll need to pay you *more* than you're worth. You couldn't possibly live on what you're worth." Philip grinned as he refilled David's glass.

David returned the smile with a rude gesture. "You can stop beating me up anytime."

Genevieve held out her glass for Philip and piled on. "David, we need a brilliant legal mind to help us, but in this case, we'll settle for yours." She threw her head back in mock hilarity.

"Whoa! I'm being brutalized here!" David held up both hands. He looked at Philip and Genevieve, his gaze shifting from one to the other. "Are you serious? Work for the Laney Estate as my sole client? I swear, I'm not here to solicit your employment."

"Don't be absurd," Genevieve said. "You can't leave us in the lurch. We might be on the verge of taking down Holmes Fitch Smythson Morrow." Genevieve pumped her fist. "You don't want to miss that!

David looked at Genevieve, then Philip, then back at Genevieve. "Listen, you two. I've been a slave to the firm since my wife died four years ago. An extremely well-paid slave, but a slave, nonetheless. The idea of working with you is very appealing, even though you're Yanks."

"Good. I'm glad you won't let the fact that we're ugly Americans get in the way. For some crazy reason, David, Genevieve and I trust you. We need you. Don't we, G? Bring on some smart, young talent if you need help; it would be a wonderful opportunity for any newly minted lawyer to work with you. We'll hammer out a compensation package. We're paying the law firm a fortune so whatever we work out, we'll most likely save money."

"I don't have to think about it. There's nothing I'd like better than working with you. I can't think of a more interesting way to spend my time. All that is to say, I accept your proposal, but with a slight alteration." He leaned forward, a grave look on his face. "Having said all this, I think for the time being, I need to stay at the firm."

Genevieve looked crestfallen. "Why is that? I want you away from those horrible people immediately. If Sir Mark is suspicious of you, could he do you harm?"

David almost sprayed wine from his nose. He swallowed and spat out a harsh laugh. "My God, Genevieve! In the twenty years I've known Sir Mark, I've never seen him do anything more violent than dress down the club steward for skimping on the olives in his martini. Mark's a pompous old man, but he wouldn't harm a fly. I'm sure he thinks anything he's taken from your estate is deserved and complimentary."

Genevieve let out a sigh of relief.

"They might fire my arse." David made a gravely sound in the back of his throat. "But they won't cross the street to punch my lights out."

"I'll ask you again. Why can't you leave them right now, today?"

"I like our plan. And I need to stay at the firm to gather forensic evidence. Because I'm one of the partners assigned to the Laney Estate, I can access more than two hundred years of information without arousing suspicion."

"Is there a confidentiality issue or conflict of interest here? Would you be in trouble if you're caught sharing information that will incriminate the firm?"

"I could, but if I uncover evidence of his wrongdoing, Sir Mark certainly isn't going to press charges. If this doesn't go our way, however, I could be disbarred. I'll be useless to you then. But I've always wanted to attend clown college."

"Well then," Philip raised his glass. "Here's to having our very own jester."

With her ear pressed to the slim crack in the paneling, she could hear their every word. The secret passageway was narrow, but she was a sylph and able to float easily through the corridor. She couldn't believe her luck. The people she had targeted for over a year were beginning to gather under one roof. How very convenient. She felt a tickle in her nostrils from the dust in the hidden hall and brought her rose-scented handkerchief to her nose. Scrunching her face, she willed the sneeze to evaporate.

SIXTEEN

SUNDAY MORNING AFTER breakfast, the threesome set out to explore the estate before David returned to London. They drove down lanes, bumped through fields and across streams. The old Land Rover Defender had seen many years of service and had the nicks and dents to prove it. Philip loved its worn, rugged appearance: a vehicle born to work and happy to do so.

Philip lumbered across a rutted field, which merged into a stand of trees. He eased the Defender to a stop. "Look over there," he whispered, pointing.

In the back, Genevieve squinted and leaned forward through the seats. "What are we looking for?"

"There's a deer in that stand of birch," Philip said.

"That's a red deer." David pulled his sunglasses to the bridge of his nose and looked over the top of them. "You often see them in the Highlands."

"Wow!" Philip grabbed his phone and snapped several pictures. "That's quite a pair of antlers."

"He's magnificent." Genevieve gaped in awe.

They watched in silence until the buck wandered deeper into the trees, then the Defender lumbered back across the field until they reached the lane.

"I have no idea where we are." Philip looked at David for an indication of which way to go.

David looked at his GPS. "I think you need to turn around to return to the Hall. It looks like we're four or five miles west of the manor."

Philip looped back into the field. As he drove back onto the narrow gravel road, a loud explosion pierced the air, and the glass shattered on the passenger's side.

Philip slammed the car to a stop. "What the fuck!"

David slumped forward, held in place only by his seat belt.

"David! David!" Genevieve shrieked. Blood streamed down the left side of David's head. Stunned, she reached forward to touch the sticky warmth oozing from a five-inch-long rut across his skull. "Philip, David's bleeding!

Philip pivoted in his seat toward his limp friend. "David." He shook the lifeless body. "David!" he yelled again, pulling up one of David's eyelids. To his relief, David's pupil reacted to the light.

Genevieve yanked the cardigan from her shoulders, wrapped it around her hand and pressed hard against David's wound. Philip punched the screen on his phone. Almost instantly they heard Mrs. MacIntosh's voice on the speaker. "Mrs. Mac, call 999. David's been shot and we need an ambulance. We'll be back to the Hall as fast as we can get there."

Philip gunned the engine, gravel spraying. He accelerated on the winding lane, taking the turns at breakneck speed. Genevieve swayed drunkenly in the back, trying to keep pressure on David's wound.

Eight minutes later the Defender screeched to a stop in front of Wilmingrove Hall. Harrington and Wallace stood at the ready. Harrington held a shotgun, Wallace a decanter of brandy. Sirens wailed in the distance, quickly gaining volume.

Mrs. MacIntosh flew out of the front door, waving her cell phone. "The ambulance is on its way," she cried.

The terrified group huddled in the driveway, watching with relief as a police car and a lemon-yellow ambulance screamed toward them along the allee with a "nee-naw, nee-naw". Moments later the cavalcade arrived in a flurry of noise and flashing lights. Three paramedics jumped out of the transport almost before it stopped.

"He's over here!" Philip stood next to the open passenger door, his eyes on David's lifeless body.

"Excuse me, sir. Please step back." Carrying an oxygen tank the paramedic stepped in front of Philip. He put two fingers on the inside of David's wrist. "Faint pulse," He said to his partners.

Afraid to let go, Genevieve was still applying pressure to David's skull. The EMT put his hand over Genevieve's and gently pulled it away from the wound. "Thank you, Ma'am. I'll take over from here." He probed David's bleeding skull. "No entry wound," he said. "A bullet appears to have grazed his skull. The wound looks shallow." He put the oxygen mask over David's mouth and nose, securing the elastic behind his head. Two medics eased him from the car and onto a stretcher.

"Where are you taking him?" Philip began focusing on next steps.

"We'll take him to LGI. Leeds General," said the red-haired paramedic with 'P. Jamison' embroidered on his jacket. "That's the nearest trauma center."

Two paramedics were already in the back of the ambulance with David. They inserted an IV and attached electrodes to David's chest, all while talking through their wireless earbuds to the LGI trauma surgeons. The third tech slammed the rear double doors, sprinted to the driver's side, hopped in, and gunned the engine. The ambulance retreated until it turned onto the main road, when the siren split the air once more.

Unable to move, everyone watched until the ambulance was out of sight. Twenty-four minutes had elapsed since the crack of the gun shot. It seemed like a nanosecond. It seemed like forever.

"Philip, I'm going to the hospital while you deal with the police." Genevieve turned to the house to get her purse.

Philip grabbed her arm. "Harrington should take you. You don't know the roads and it will be faster if he drives. And, G." Philip lifted Genevieve's hands in his. "You'll want to wash your hands and change." They looked down to see the brown stains on her wool skirt and palms, all smeared with David's blood.

Genevieve's pulse quickened. Tears stung her eyes. "Oh, Philip." Her voice was raspy. "What if…"

"Don't." Philip put a finger on her mouth and stopped her before she could finish her thought. He kissed her forehead, then her lips. "Go get changed. Harrington and I will have things ready for you to leave when you come back."

Genevieve kissed Philip on the cheek then raced into the Hall, still clutching her bloody sweater.

"Actually, my lord, it would be faster to take the helicopter." Harrington was standing at Philip's side. "Captain Bruni was waiting to take Sir David back to London this morning. He's in the chopper, ready to go. I'll go tell him they're flying to the hospital rather than London."

When Genevieve returned twenty minutes later, Mrs. MacIntosh was waiting with the golf cart. The chopper blades were already circling in a rhythmic slap, slap, slap by the time they reached the helipad. Genevieve ducked to climb the helicopter's stairs, walked to the back, and took her seat.

"My Lady. May I get you anything?" asked William.

"Thank you, but no, William." She pulled a tissue from her pocket to dab her eyes and blow her nose. She snapped her seatbelt. The door closed with a "thunk," and they were ready for takeoff.

On the ground, Philip saw the chopper rise, pause, then shoot forward. He watched until it disappeared over the horizon, and willed everything to be all right.

"Excuse me, Lord Crosswick." Buried in his thoughts, Philip was startled by a husky voice. "Sorry. Thought you heard me come up. I'm DCI Fields." The rumpled man scratched his head, tousling his thinning hair, leaving several strands sticking straight up. "We have an interesting situation here, don't we?" Cigarette smoke escaped from the policeman's mouth with each word. He took a last drag, flicked his cigarette butt to the ground, and toed it into the gravel driveway.

Philip gave Fields a withering look and pointed to the stub. "Do you mind?"

Confused, the copper gazed at his shoe before realizing Philip's meaning. He squatted with a grunt, picked up the butt and put it into his pocket with no apology.

"Shall we go into the Hall, Lord Crosswick? Somewhere we can talk."

"Follow me," Philip snarled, and headed toward the main house.

The detective tried to keep up with Philip's long strides, wheezing with each step. Just inside the Hall, Fields stopped. He bent over, his hands on his knees to catch his breath.

"Are you all right, Detective?" Philip turned to see Fields's bright-red face.

The policeman held up one hand and said nothing for a moment. "I'm fine," he gasped. "Just a bit winded. You're a fast walker." At last, he stood, his breath less labored. "Where to?"

"We'll go to my office." Philip led the way through the grand salon, where several uniformed men and women milled around, some on phones, some waiting to be given a task.

"You might want to give up those cigarettes. And more fruits and vegetables wouldn't hurt you." Philip couldn't resist chiding this tubby, frowsy man.

Arriving at his study, Philip motioned for Fields to sit in a green leather wing-back chair.

Mrs. MacIntosh was right behind them, carrying a tray with coffee service. Without asking, she poured Philip's coffee then handed a cup to Fields. She placed a plate of chocolate biscuits on Philip's desk in front of the detective and scurried out, closing the door behind her.

DCI Fields leaned forward, eyeing the wafers, a drop of saliva at the corner of his mouth. "These are my favorite fruits and vegetables." A chuckle rolled from the back of his throat, and he plucked two biscuits from the plate. He took a gulp of his coffee then a bite of cookie. Crumbs sprayed the front of his shirt and the lapels of his rumpled suit.

Philip walked to the study windows, needing a moment to tamp down his disgust for this man. He was stunned at the number of officers already outside combing every inch of the terrace, each wearing latex gloves and blue paper booties. A policewoman picked up a cigarette butt, no doubt another one of Fields's, and placed it in an evidence bag.

"What's going on out there?" Philip turned back to the detective. "Why are there cops all over the terrace? Why aren't they in the field where David was shot?" Philip grew angrier with each question he asked. He stood in front of Fields, menacing the detective "Do your people know what the hell they're doing?"

"I assure you they do, my lord," Fields shot back, all of a sudden looking less like a fool, more like a detective. "We have police everywhere, including the field and woods near the shooting. They are combing the area for shells, footprints, fibers, anything that will shed light on who tried to kill Sir David, you, and your wife."

"Me? My wife?" The blood drained from Philip's face. He froze, his eyes locked with the detectives. He paced back to the window, looked out, and then strode back across the room to stand in front of Fields.

"Lord Crosswick please sit down," Fields directed. "Please, my lord, sit."

"Tried to kill…" Philip half sat against the edge of his desk, his arms stiff at his sides, his knuckles white, gripping the curved, mahogany top. His armpits felt clammy. "Wasn't it an accident? Someone hunting. Maybe a couple of guys were drunk and thought…."

"My forensics team dug four bullets out of the car. Two embedded in the back seat, two in the passenger door. This rules out hunters accidently firing at your vehicle."

"Tell me, Fields, who would want me dead?" His voice cracked as he asked the unthinkable.

"You tell me." Fields turned the question back to Philip. "Has anything out of the ordinary happened to you in the last few months that would make you a target?"

"I barely know anyone in this country. That makes no sense." Philip ran his hands through his hair then rubbed his face with his palms. He studied his shoes and chewed his lower lip. "You're talking about the inheritance."

"Money is a powerful motivator." Fields's gaze lasered into Philip.

"So, you're suggesting David wasn't the target." The silence in the room waited for someone to speak. "Only my family stands to gain by my death. That's my wife, son, daughter-in-law and their two young children."

"Have you already altered your will to reflect the inheritance?"

"It's in the works, but no. The estate is complicated. As you might imagine, it will take some time to complete the will and make all the transfers."

"Is there somebody who would benefit if the will *isn't* changed?"

For the first time, Philip noticed the keen intelligence in the detective's eyes. He shoved himself to stand and walked back to the window. Deep in thought, he stared out at the terrace without seeing. The entertaining mystery of whether Sir Mark was embezzling or not had turned into a potentially deadly whodunit. If he was in danger, Genevieve and the rest of his family would be targets as well, wouldn't they? With that jarring thought, Philip spun away from the window.

"Fields!" His eyes were wild. "Genevieve needs protection. You need to make a call and get somebody to the hospital."

The detective tilted his head and stopped his fingers from drumming on the arm of his chair. "A security team has already been dispatched."

Philip looked at him, with relief and new admiration. "I guess this isn't your first rodeo," he said with a sheepish smile.

"Or as we Brits would say, 'I didn't come down with the last shower.'" Fields looked at Philip with genuine sympathy. "I don't suppose this is what you expected when you learned you'd just inherited a title and a fortune, is it?"

"It is not. Quite the contrary."

Fields didn't hear the vibrating hum, but Philip lunged to grab his phone from where it sat on his desk, knocking over a small vase. Genevieve's grinning photo filled his screen as he jabbed 'accept' and looked around for a cloth to sop up the water trickling its way across the desktop.

"G," he shouted into the phone. "I've been waiting for you to call. How is David?" Philip held his breath, waiting for Genevieve to answer.

"I don't know," she sobbed into the phone. "They won't tell me how he is. They won't tell me anything, not even if he is still alive."

DCI Fields righted the vase, plopped the flowers back in haphazardly, and dabbed up the little bit of water with a linen napkin. He leaned towards Philip, straining to hear Genevieve's words. "Put her on speaker," he whispered.

Philip laid the phone on the desk and the detective bent forward, aiming his voice at the speaker. "Lady Crosswick, this is Detective Chief Inspector Fields. I'm here with the investigative team. I'm not surprised the hospital staff won't release Sir David's information to you. Our Data Protection Act safeguards the privacy of patients. While you're talking to your husband, I'll phone and find out Sir David's status. I'll be right back."

"Thank you, DCI Fields. I knew someone could help."

Philip could hear Genevieve's annoyance. He waited until Fields was well out of earshot. "G, are you okay? I'm so sorry I'm not there with you."

"You're right where you should be. Sorry about the tears. They're frustration more than anything else. I was about to pop somebody in the nose, I was so exasperated. Does DCI Fields know what he's doing?"

"An hour ago, I would have said he's a joke, but I stand corrected." Philip sat in his leather desk chair and leaned back.

His temples throbbed with tension. He rolled his head in slow circles hoping to relieve the ache in his neck.

"What made you change your mind?" Genevieve's voice was full of warmth.

Philip relaxed, comforted hearing his wife. The throbbing in his head begin to ease.

Just as he was about to respond, Fields walked back in. His chubby cheeks bloomed at each side of his smile. "Put me on speaker. Lady Crosswick, I just had a word with Michael Murton, the hospital head."

"Believe me, I know who he is. I had *several* words with him just a few minutes ago, none of them pleasant," Genevieve's voice dripped sarcasm. "I'm sorry, DCI Fields. What did you find out? Is David all right? My fingers are crossed."

"Uncross your fingers, my lady. Has Mr. Singh joined you in the lounge? He is Sir David's surgeon."

Philip and Fields could hear Genevieve talking to someone at her end of the phone. Introductions were exchanged and Mr. Singh began. "When he arrived, though Sir David was conscious and stable, it appeared he had lost a great deal of blood. Head injuries generally bleed profusely. Until they are thoroughly assessed, it is difficult to determine their severity.

"Sir David was most lucky. The bullet grazed the left side of the skull, creating a shallow, ten-centimeter channel from the left temple to just above the ear, more like an abrasion, really. The incident was sufficient to make him lose consciousness, due more to shock than injury. Blood loss was not as substantial as originally thought, so it was not necessary to transfuse the patient. Sir David is alive because of a matter of millimeters. A few millimeters to the right and you would be planning a funeral. As it turns out, he didn't even need sutures, just a bandage. We don't often see such good fortune."

At one end of the phone Genevieve couldn't breathe. At the other, Philip had no words.

DCI Fields broke the silence. "How is Sir David now?"

"Aided by the morphine, he has been sleeping, but he was waking just before I came to the lounge. Lady Crosswick, anytime you want to see him, you may. I'd like to keep him here a day or two to insure we have missed nothing. If he progresses as I expect, we will discharge him on Tuesday. He should rest for about a week, resuming his usual activities after that. As I said, he was extremely lucky. Now, if you'll excuse me, I'll get back to my other patients."

"DCI Fields, give me a few minutes to talk to my wife, then we can resume our conversation. Why don't you go to the kitchen and have Mrs. Lomax get you a sandwich or something?" The detective's eyes lit up at the mention of food and he went off in search of the kitchen.

"Tell me what's happening there," Genevieve said. Philip could hear the longing in her voice to be at Wilmingrove Hall and with him.

"Police are swarming everywhere and they're interrogating every person on our staff. They dug two bullets out of the back seat of the Defender, where you were sitting. They believe one was the bullet that grazed David." Philip went silent.

"Philip, did I lose you?"

"No, no. I'm still here." His voice was husky. "The bullet missed you by inches." He cleared his throat. Cleared it again. "G, I can't stand to think about what might have happened."

"Philip, nothing happened to me." The terrifying implications of Philip's words didn't immediately register. "I'm here, safe and sound. It's David we have to worry about."

"Nonetheless, the York police are sending two plainclothes officers to the hospital. They'll be with you until you come back to the Hall. Then we'll figure out what we should do going forward. I guess we should have done something about security when David suggested it in New York."

"Do you really think I need protection here at the hospital?"

"I do." Philip left no room for argument. "DCI Fields believes this was attempted murder. He also believes David may not have been the target." His voice cracked. Silence reclaimed the air between them.

Blood rushed to Genevieve's head. "Do you think they're right?"

"I have no idea, but I can't think of any other reason our car would be peppered with bullets, can you?"

Genevieve tried to hold on to her thread of calm, but it was quickly dissolving.

A firm knock at the door startled her.

"I heard a knock. Is that the security detail?" Philip snapped.

She looked up as a man pushed open the door just enough to stick his head in. "Lady Crosswick?"

"Philip, hold on. I think the police are here."

"I'm going nowhere," Philip said at the other end of the line.

The men moved into the lounge, scanning the room as they walked toward her.

"Lady Crosswick, I'm DCI Marcum and this is DS Cromwell. Did anyone inform you that you would be assigned a protection detail?"

"My husband and I were just talking about that. Is it absolutely necessary?"

DCI Marcum shifted from one foot to the other and cleared his throat. "Given the circumstances, it seems prudent to take such precautions until we have determined what's going on here."

Genevieve put the phone back to her ear. "Did you hear that, Philip?"

"I did and I agree. As soon as you've seen David, get into the chopper, and get home. Until then, do exactly as the police advise. Please, G. You have two jobs: see David, then get back here safely. I love you."

Tears sprang to Genevieve's eyes. Philip's love was always evident, but he seldom said the words. He preferred to tell Genevieve in deeds: a pat on the bottom, a kiss on the back of the neck, a cup of coffee delivered to her in bed. Hearing the words out loud pricked her emotions, which were already raw.

"Philip, I love you, too.

She couldn't keep the smile from her face. What a bunch of fools. She was throwing them into chaos, and it was so easy. This was going to be fun. A lot of fun.

She waited until the mighty Lord Crosswick and the buffoon detective left the study before drifting back through the dark corridor, careful to move silently, until at last, she came to the stairs that took her to just behind the wine cellar, then out the door near the stables. She had to get back before she was missed.

SEVENTEEN

A FEW DAYS AFTER David was shot, the police swarmed the estate, finding a lead, tracking it to a dead end, finding another lead, tracking it to another dead end. There was a frenzy of activity when forensics experts confirmed the bullets came from a 1994 Purdey rifle, which was part of the Laney gun collection. The rifle was always kept under lock and key in the gun safe in the estate manager's office. The only people with keys to the safe were Sean Harrington, the estate manager, and Andrew Frazier, the estate falconer. All guns were accounted for when Sergeant Kafritz took inventory the Friday before the shooting.

The morning of the shooting, Harrington had taken a shotgun into the woods to check a fox trap. When he returned, he replaced the shotgun and noted all the guns were in the safe. He insisted to the police the keys were in the lockbox. When the police retrieved the Purdey rifle from the safe, it was wiped to a spectacular sheen, just like the other forty-seven guns in the collection.

DCI Fields was convinced either Harrington or Frazier was the culprit. He couldn't imagine how anyone else could have accessed the Purdey rifle. However, after hours of interviews, Fields confirmed alibis for both men: when David was shot, Frazier was forty miles away in York meeting with a conservation specialist, and security footage confirmed Harrington was working in the stables.

When that lead fizzled, all the coppers agreed the whole thing was a hell of a magic trick. What the police couldn't agree on was how this magic trick was done, who did it, and what the motive was.

It was four weeks since the shooting and still little was resolved. During David's recuperation at the Hall, he, Philip, and Genevieve spent endless hours reviewing, hypothesizing, and speculating.

"The only thing that makes sense is that Charlotte's ghost took the rifle, floated out into the field and shot at David," Philip offered one rainy afternoon as they threw around ideas.

"And why would she want to shoot me?" David asked.

Proud of his theory, Philip grinned. "Because, of course, you don't believe in ghosts and that pisses her off!"

They debunked each other's theories. They went down one rabbit hole after another, each one more preposterous than the previous.

One evening after dinner, the three sat in the library before a crackling fire. After several glasses of wine, Genevieve was sure she had the answer. "I've got it! I've got it!' She bounced on the edge of the love seat where she sat with Philip.

"Oh, do tell," David said with an overly posh accent.

"Remember Revy Harris, the American girl Jonathon Laney fell in love with, then sent away?

"No." David shook his head. "But go on."

Genevieve stopped bouncing and sat still on the edge of her cushion, eyes wide and intense. "I bet Revy Harris heard about Philip's inheritance and went berserk, thinking it should be hers, since Jonathon had been her lover. She came here intending to kill Philip so she could get her hands on the estate, but she wasn't a very good shot and hit David instead. What do you think of that?"

The room was dead silent for a moment, then David threw a toss pillow at her. "Hisssss! Boooooo!"

The men rained down a chorus of jeers until she put her palms up in surrender. "No, huh?"

"Of all the crazy theories we've conjured, that's maybe the craziest. But you're still pretty cute." Philip leaned forward and planted a kiss on her cheek.

With each deflated speculation, they returned to the facts they knew, facts that pointed to Sir Mark Holmes: Sir Mark had created numerous revenue streams at the Hall, extracting large sums of money from the estate, and he had used the Laney wine collection as his personal never-ending cellar. And then there was the recent, extravagant upgrade of the kitchen, and the flawless maintenance of the Hall—though those were hardly capital offenses.

In the end, David suggested that when Philip became the heir to the Laney fortune, Sir Mark feared his schemes would soon be discovered. Genevieve believed that Sir Mark panicked at being found out and hired someone to shoot at the Defender, thinking this would frighten the Warwicks back to the States. There were many holes in their plotline, and they had not addressed the mystery of the Purdey, but the three amateur sleuths bolstered each other with high fives as they advanced their scheme to ensnare their villain.

"So, we're all in agreement: we'll host a fabulous party. We'll invite the partners from Holmes Fitch Smythson Morrow, some of the peers we've met, people from our museum and the Foundation, our neighbors, and any other fancy people who come to mind." Genevieve gathered steam as she talked about the gala that she'd already planned in her head.

"David, your job is to spend the evening with Sir Mark. Ply him with alcohol and draw him out about how he used the estate to line his pockets."

"Yes, ma'am. Whatever you say, ma'am." David gave a smart salute.

"Philip, your job is to charm the other partners into telling you anything that might support our theory that Sir Mark is the villain in all of this."

Philip narrowed his eyes and raked his hands through his thick hair. "I'm sure they'll spill their guts the moment I spin my web of charisma. They won't be able to resist my suavity."

"Suavity?" Genevieve and David said together.

"Ha! Where did you get that word?" David scoffed.

"I think it's a word. But if it's not, it should be." Philip's grin lit his eyes. "Either way, it describes me to a tee, don't you think?"

"Sure, Philip." Genevieve gave him a sidelong stare then looked back at David, who shrugged his shoulders. She raised her goblet and they all stood to toast for good luck.

"I guess we're ready, then!" she said, and drained her glass.

EIGHTEEN

I T H A D B E E N years since the Hall felt so vibrant. Mrs. MacIntosh and Wallace were in their full glory supervising, arranging, rearranging. Genevieve directed caterers to the kitchen, musicians to the landing on the grand staircase and the last of the flowers to the bar. Wilmingrove Hall pulsed with energy. Staff bustled. Florists had filled every room with aroma and brilliant color. Extended to its full length, the dining table glittered with silver, crystal, china—all polished to a spectacular sheen. Six towering candelabras adorned the center of the table, swathed in coral roses. On every hearth, fires awaited a match.

"Tutu!" Cheeks pink from the chilly wind, nine-year-old Alex rushed into the great hall, anxious to tell his grandmother about the morning's explorations. Hot on his heels, seven-year-old Ella clutched a bag of oats with a hole in it, leaking its treasure onto the sparkling marble floor.

Much to Philip and Genevieve's delight, their son, daughter-in-law and grandchildren had arrived two days before. Because of the unresolved shooting, Philip suggested the family remain within the estate: the house, stables, gardens, and the mews.

Happy to oblige, they had spent every moment exploring the many nooks and crannies of Wilmingrove Hall, still overwhelmed by the grandeur.

"Yes, my darlings!" Genevieve beamed. "What exciting adventure have you been on?" For Philip and Genevieve, the joy of having their family with them was overwhelming. Genevieve had not stopped smiling since they arrived. The couple loved watching their family discover excitement and delight at every turn. Alexander and Ella had already experienced a falconry lesson. Alex was in love with the Harris hawk he had flown. Ella was in love with dashing "Hawk Man," as the children were now calling Andrew Frazier. For Alex and Ella, this was their own personal fairytale.

"We fed the horses!" Ella flaunted her punctured sack. "Uh-oh," she said, watching the oats stream to the floor.

Swooping in, Mrs. MacIntosh snatched the bag and closed her hand around the hole.

"Never mind, Lady Ella. It's nothing. We'll take care of this quick as a flash and everything will be tickety-boo. Come on, you two. Let's go to the conservatory and have a tea party." Mrs. MacIntosh turned to Julia, raised an eyebrow to ask permission.

"Have fun!" said Julia.

And off they went.

Genevieve gathered her clipboard, cell phone, sweater, and glasses. "Are you two ready for some lunch?" she asked Duncan and Julia. "Your dad and David are meeting us in the conservatory."

"What's he been doing?" Duncan asked. Since Philip was confirmed heir to the Laney title and fortune two months ago, he and Duncan had talked often about the vastness of the estate, but Duncan couldn't fully appreciate what it all meant until he experienced it in person. The magnitude of wealth and responsibility was hard to comprehend. As his parents had told him, it was life changing for all of them. There were many decisions to be made, but none that had to be made today. So, for the moment, he and Julia would enjoy the pleasure of this unfolding adventure.

"He's been supervising the caterers. You know your dad. Any chance to hang out with people who know what they're doing in the kitchen is too tempting. Duncan, it's your responsibility tonight to make sure he stays where the party is, not where the party is being prepared." Philip loved all things culinary. He loved learning about food. He loved experimenting with food. He loved the process as much as the product. Perhaps in another life, he would have been a master chef, but at this point, dabbling was satisfying enough.

Though a lavish evening was mere hours away, Elsie Lomax had crafted a picture-perfect luncheon for the four Warwicks and Sir David.

"I could get used to this," Julia said.

Genevieve motioned for her daughter-in-law to take a seat next to David, looking out over the vast gardens. Duncan held the chair opposite for his mother.

"Look at that, G. We did something right! What a gentleman." Philip loved having their son with them.

"Do you need help with your chair, old man?" Duncan grinned at his dad.

"Be careful, little boy." Philip looked up at his handsome six-foot-three son. "You're not a spring chicken anymore, you know. It won't be long before we're the same age."

Duncan straightened, adding another quarter inch to his frame. Looking down at his father, he said, "No matter how old we are, neither one of us will ever dunk a basketball!"

"Yup, one of our great failures, for sure," Philip agreed. The banter continued as they ate and drank their way through a jolly lunch until Philip raised the subject of the evening's event. "This party we're throwing tonight, we need to tell you about some of the people. Most of the partners from the law firm will be here tonight, including Sir Mark Holmes."

Julia's dark curls bounced as she looked from Philip to David then back to Philip. "Does this have anything to do with David being shot?"

"Sir Mark was in London at the time, but he could have an accomplice or have hired someone to do his dirty work. The police aren't keen on us investigating on our own."

"Mom, Dad, I think I have to be the voice of reason here," said Duncan. "Don't you think the intelligent thing to do is to come home with us after the party?"

"What?" Genevieve's response was more forceful than she had intended. "Why would we do that?"

Duncan looked at David. "David, help me out here. Hell, you're the one who was shot. Don't you think it's too dangerous for my parents to stay here? And what about you? You could come back to the States with them until the police figure out what's going on here."

David rolled his dessert fork between his fingers. "I, um…" he began, unsure what to say. He placed the fork back by his plate.

"Duncan, don't drag David into this." Philip's heart warmed at his son's concerns. "I can't say the idea hasn't occurred to me, but your mother and I think we should stay and help the police."

"We just don't want anything to happen to you," Julia chimed in.

"Okay, everybody." Genevieve stood, ready to get back to work. "Let's see what happens tonight. Maybe Sir Mark will stand at the top of the grand staircase, make a dramatic confession then throw himself on our mercy."

"Any bets?" Duncan said.

NINETEEN

AT THE STROKE of half six, the parade began. Rolls after Jag after Bentley after Porsche rolled down the long driveway to Wilmingrove Hall, depositing their tony passengers at the stately home's grand entrance. Lights blazed in every window, spilling onto lawns and terraces. Furs, that hadn't seen an outing for years, draped over bare shoulders.

She was lying on her stomach in a grove of silver birch, fifty yards from the manor's façade. Looking through high-powered night vision binoculars, she could see diamonds glittering on ears and sparkling around necks as guests moved into the great hall. The chill of the ground crept its way through her black, lycra bodysuit until it reached the flesh of her prone torso. It was time to steal into Wilmingrove Hall and melt into the bustle of the party.

It was time to let them know she meant business. She felt her excitement rise and willed her breathing to slow.

Philip and Genevieve greeted their guests in the grand hall alongside Duncan and Julia, introducing the future Earl and Countess of Crosswick. Philip and Duncan made a handsome father and son duo, resembling a Ralph Lauren advertisement in their classic tuxedos, pleated-front shirts, and black hand tied bowties.

Standing between them, Genevieve was the picture of easy grace in a long-sleeved gown with a burgundy velvet off-the-shoulder top and full tapestry floor-length skirt, her waist cinched by a wide burgundy belt. Her radiant smile greeted each guest.

To Duncan's left, Julia completed the elegant family picture in a flesh-colored figure-hugging gown with a black lace overlay. It was easy to see she was a runner. A mass of curly mahogany hair sat loosely piled on her head, tendrils dancing around her cheeks. She grasped each person's hand as they made their way down the line to her and welcomed them with her warm smile.

Next to Julia at the end of the receiving line, a liveried server offered each guest a glass of Champagne, at which point everyone could move into the party.

Most of the invitees hadn't entered Wilmingrove Hall for years, if ever. If they had attended a town or county event—a fete, a town celebration, perhaps sheep dog trials—they would only have roamed the grounds. The house would have been off-limits. But now, invited by Lord and Lady Crosswick, guests moved through the grand hall, eyes wide with awe. They drifted into the drawing room, dining room and music room, drawn by the sound of a jazz pianist at the Bosendorfer. Wilmingrove Hall was dressed to dazzle.

By ten minutes of seven, the contingent from Holmes Fitch Smythson Morrow began to arrive. First through the door was the youngest partner, Henry Fitch and his wife, Gillian. Henry looked less disheveled than when Genevieve met him in New York at the law offices. Perhaps he had shed a couple of pounds, was sporting a fresh haircut, or maybe it was his well-cut tuxedo. Whatever it was, Genevieve thought he looked quite sweet. At the other end of the spectrum, his wife Gillian was breathtaking, her wippet-thin frame draped in layers of flowing crimson silk, each tier edged in fuchsia. She had pulled her blond hair into a severe chignon, which gave her a slightly feral look.

"Who's that?" Philip said under his breath.

"I think it's Henry Fitch's wife, Gillian. Brace yourself."

Genevieve felt Philip tense. "She looks scary."

"Lord Crosswick, Philip! I'm Gillian Fitch," she gushed, rushing toward Philip, hands outstretched. "How marvelous to meet you at last." She kissed Philip on both cheeks, leaving a streak of red lipstick. She wiped his cheek with her thumb as she held his gaze.

"Gillian," Genevieve cut in. "We're delighted you and Henry could join us this evening. And Henry." Genevieve thrust her hand across Philip to grab Henry's hand, breaking Gillian's hold on Philip. "We couldn't be happier to see you!"

Philip threw Genevieve an amused sidelong glance. Duncan looked down at his mother, tickled at how she was protecting her territory.

To Genevieve's relief, other partygoers from the firm began to pour through the door, prompting the Fitches to move down the line.

And so it went for the next half hour until most guests had arrived.

"Why don't you two go have some fun," Philip said, relieving Duncan and Julia of their co-hosting duties. "That was quite a maneuver, my beautiful little blocker," Philip chuckled into Genevieve's ear.

Genevieve gave him a kiss on the cheek. "A girl's gotta do what a girl's gotta do to protect her husband from vultures in evening gowns!" She winked and floated off into the boisterous crowd.

TWENTY

FOR THE LAST hour, Philip had been holding court in the music room, talking to a group of foundation staff and Lillie Langdon, the Executive Director of the Laney Museum of Fine Arts Foundation. They were young, creative, energetic, and full of fun. The pianist was playing Miles Davis, the mood in the music room was full of life, and Philip was having a wonderful time.

He saw Genevieve across the salon, caught her eye, and waved her over. It took her several minutes to make her way through the crowd. Everyone wanted a piece of Lady Crosswick, the Lady of the manor and architect of this dazzling evening. At last, she reached Philip's side and slid her hand into his, squeezing it. The exuberant cluster of artsy guests greeted her with toasts and *la bise*, the French double-cheek kiss. It always amused Philip and Genevieve how the English loved everything *from* France but loathed the French.

Genevieve whispered in Philip's ear. "Have you seen David? Do you have any idea how he's doing?"

"When I saw him last, he was in the library with Mark. I've been shirking my hosting duties far too long, talking to this group, but I've been having a terrific time. These kids are brimming with ideas for the Foundation, and I've picked up some interesting tidbits that might explain where some of the money from the Hall has gone."

"That's exciting and more than you bargained for. I can't wait to hear. Have you seen Duncan and Julia? I hope they're having a good time."

"They always do," Philip said. "I'm sure they're busy charming all our guests."

"Of course, they are. It's impossible not to be charmed by those two. Why don't you go find David and Mark while I spend some time with the Foundation crew? You're well on your way to establishing a good relationship with these youngsters, old man. I'd like to do the same." Genevieve threw Philip a wicked grin.

He returned the favor by squeezing her bottom and hoping no one had noticed.

She watched as he wove his way through the crowd, navigating the flood of merrymakers. She felt a little giddy and couldn't help but smile as he turned from the far side of the room to look at her, and she threw him a kiss. "Lucky girl," she thought, then turned back to the energetic, young group.

Philip made his way through the grand salon where a noisy group crowded around the bar. Cheers and claps erupted every few seconds. As he watched, a bottle flew up high above the heads of the crowd, followed by a roar of appreciation.

"What's going on?" he asked a guest as another whoop exploded from the crowd.

"The barmaid's putting on quite a show."

Philip edged into the middle of the swarm of guests until he could see the main attraction, a young, sprite of a girl. Black, spikey hair surrounded a heart-shaped face, highlighted by enormous brown eyes and a full crimson mouth. Her clever banter accompanied the deft preparation of drink after drink. She was a circus act with a stand-up comic's patter. Philip marveled at her skill and antics, wondering if she worked for the caterer.

He finally backed out of the crowd and continued his search for David and Sir Mark. He found them in the library in front of the fireplace, which sparked and crackled with new logs. Compared to the other rooms, the library was an oasis of calm.

Deep in conversation, the two men didn't notice Philip until he was directly in front of them. The moment they felt his presence, they stopped speaking and looked up.

"So, what am I missing?"

Sir Mark motioned to the chair across from him. "Lord Crosswick, please join us,"

"Thank you, Sir Mark. But please call me Philip."

"If you call me Mark."

"I can do that, Mark. I hope you both have been having a good time. Have you had anything to eat? And where are your drinks?"

"We have drinks coming." said David. "Philip, the food is scrummy. Were you in the kitchen all day cooking?" David teased.

"Of course, I did it all. Not bad, eh?"

"Not bad at all. Ah, great. Drinks." David rubbed his hands as a server arrived carrying a silver tray with two tumblers, one with two fingers of what appeared to be whisky, the other filled close to the brim with a golden liquid, a wisp of warmth rising from the glass.

David looked at the server apologetically. "I know I asked for a mead, but I changed my mind. Would you please bring me a whisky, neat?"

"But, sir, the barmaid told me to be sure I gave you the mead."

"And so you have." David plucked the glass from the tray. "Now, would you please bring me a tumbler of scotch?"

"David, take my whisky," Sir Mark said. "I quite fancy a mead."

The two exchanged glasses and Mark took a sip. "This is brilliant." He inhaled the honeyed aroma. "Philip, is this made on the estate?" He took a longer draw this time. "If it is, you should bottle it. It would be a spectacular revenue stream."

"I have no idea where the mead is from." Philip raised an eyebrow at Sir Mark's candor about creating cashflow from the Hall but decided not to comment. "What have I missed? Have you two solved the world's problems?"

"Not all of them. I've been telling David about opening Wilmingrove Hall to the public the last couple of years and how much revenue it generated for the Foundation."

Surprised at Mark's openness, Philip leaned forward.

Sir Mark continued, "In, oh, probably the last five years of his life, Lord Crosswick became concerned about the financial security of the estate. He wanted to insure the properties and the Foundation were sufficiently endowed. No matter how much I assured him of their fiscal health, the older he got, the more he worried. This is not unusual. Often aging brings on irrational financial fears. I've seen it over and over." Mark spoke with ease with no indication that he might be lying.

For the first time, Philip wondered if their conjecture about Sir Mark being the villain was unfounded.

Sir Mark took a long, slow drink of mead, closing his eyes in enjoyment. He licked the residue from his lips. "Delicious."

"I'm so glad you like it." Philip had not seen Sir Mark in a relaxed setting before and he liked this charming version.

Mark set his glass on his side table and went on. "It would be an understatement to say Jonathon Laney was in command of his empire until the end. Three years ago, he charged us with two massive projects. The first was to update all his transportation. He wanted a new plane, new helicopter, new cars. He intended to visit his holdings in France, America, and, of course, Wilmingrove Hall. To do that, he would need transportation that could accommodate his needs."

"This is fascinating." Philip thought Mark Holmes was either a masterful liar or he was telling the truth.

"The second was to make certain all his properties were in excellent repair and self-sustaining. His intention was to divest himself of any property that wasn't financially autonomous. He gave Winston Fitch and me eighteen months to accomplish the task, with instructions for strict confidentiality." Mark picked up his glass and the last of the golden mead was gone.

David's curiosity was piqued. "Why did he want it to be confidential? Why was that important?"

"The markets, David. The markets. He didn't want anyone to get wind of his plan to dump his unproductive holdings. He feared the markets would interpret that as financial vulnerability. At ninety-five, the old man was still sharp as a needle. Winston and I worked like demons, creating revenue streams, eking out every pound we could from the properties."

As Mark spoke, Genevieve wandered in and perched on the arm of Philip's chair. She and Mark exchanged smiles, and he continued.

"We could do nothing to create revenue with the apartments in Paris and New York. They were, however, appreciating at a fast clip. The vineyard in St. Emilion and horse farm in Kentucky had always done well, but Wilmingrove Hall was all outgo, no income, so that was the big challenge. And I just told you what plans we implemented here to correct that. Successfully, I might add."

Perhaps it was fatigue, perhaps an excess of drink, but Sir Mark began to slur his words, and his eyes glazed. But he carried on speaking:

"The properties were always maintained to a high standard, so needed no major upgrades, though we did refurbish the main kitchen here. And we quietly auctioned off some wine. I think Wallace was quite suspicious of that. By the time the eighteen months was up, and everything was in place, the Earl's health had declined, and he was unable to travel."

At the far end of the library, a regal case clock announced the time in bass chimes. Genevieve was stunned. "My goodness. I can't believe it's midnight."

"I dare say your guests are beginning to overstay their welcome. Me included." Sir Mark stood, weaving as he did so. "My goodness, I feel a bit dizzy. Good mead, I suppose." A sheepish smile fluttered across his face, and he steadied himself, putting his hand on David's shoulder.

Philip stood up as well and gripped Mark's elbow. "Are you okay? You look pale. Genevieve, why don't you go find Margot? David and I will stay with Mark."

"Of course. I'll be right back." Concern for Mark churned her stomach as she walked into the grand salon. Her eyes searched for a squat, gray-haired matron. Though Lady Margot Holmes lived on the frumpy side of sixty-five, she was a bundle of energy with a lusty wit. Genevieve heard the peal of her raucous laugh before she saw her.

"Lady Margot." Genevieve strode across the marble tiles, waving her hand.

Margot was chattering and giggling with a clutch of partner's wives. When she saw Genevieve, her grin widened. "We were just saying what a brilliant evening this has been. You are wonderful for having all of us."

The women talked over each other, thanking Genevieve, cooing about the fabulous food, and marveling about the beauty of Wilmingrove Hall.

"And the barmaid! Wherever did you find her?" asked Elizabeth Smythson. "She was simply fabulous!"

"It's been such fun for us to have all of you here." Genevieve hooked her arm into the crook of Margot's elbow, anxious to pull her away, but not wanting to alarm her. "We want to do it again very soon, maybe during the holidays. But for now, I'm going to have to borrow Margot," Genevieve said, finessing Lady Margot away from the cheery klatch. As they moved toward the library,

Genevieve's voice was gentle. "Margot, Mark doesn't seem to be feeling very well. He's in the Library with Sir David."

Margot looked up at her host, her eyes filed with alarm. "Oh, my lord, Genevieve, Mark has a serious heart condition. Just last week, his cardiologist warned him to be careful." Her short legs lengthened their stride.

When they walked into the library, Julia was holding Mark's wrist, looking at her watch as she took his pulse. Mark's head tilted back against the sofa cushion, his pale face bathed in sweat.

"Mark!" Margot's hands flew to her face, her eyes huge with fear. She bolted to Mark's side, plopping on the sofa. "Julia, what's wrong with him? Is it his heart?"

As she stroked her husband's damp forehead, he opened his eyes, peering through narrow slits. Attempting a reassuring grin, he croaked, "Maybe I had a bit too much mead. I feel terrible." He closed his eyes again.

Margot leaned over to kiss his cheek, startled at how cold his skin felt.

Julia opened her medical bag, which Duncan had collected from their room. Her stethoscope in her ears, she listened to the erratic rhythm of Mark's heart, checked his blood pressure, his pupils, his temperature.

"Genevieve," Julia nodded toward the door. The two women rose, and Genevieve slipped her arm around Margot's shoulders, pulling her with them. When the three were just outside the library, Julia took Margot by the arms. "Margot, I don't believe Mark had too much mead. His blood pressure is very low, and I'm not sure what the problem is but Philip has called an ambulance. I want him to go to the hospital immediately."

Margot's breathing turned jagged. She blinked hard, tears squeezing onto her lashes. "He looks like a ghost." Little choking noises stuck in her throat before a sob burst out.

"Margo, I've got to get back to Mark," Julia said as Genevieve gathered Margot into her arms. They stood hugging each other and weeping for several minutes until Genevieve saw her daughter-in-law standing in the doorway. Instinctively she tightened her arms around the weeping woman. In the distance, Genevieve heard the faint wail of a siren gaining volume as it approach.

Julia stood as still as a statue, clutching her hands in front of her. Her face was shattered with sadness and tears streamed down her cheeks, dripping off her chin onto her collarbone. Holding Genevieve's gaze, Julia bit hard on her lower lip and shook her head almost imperceptibly. "Mark is dead," she mouthed.

TWENTY-ONE

TWELVE HOURS EARLIER, Wilmingrove Hall had throbbed with energy, music, laughter. Now, it was like a tomb, ticking clocks haunting the main floor and a steady drizzle sheeting the windows. The gloom throughout the Hall was as thick as fog. Not even lamps glowing in every room could cheer the house.

Usually full of fun and life, Philip and Genevieve sat deflated, their mood at odds with the cheerful yellow and blue breakfast room. Philip drank his third cup of coffee while Genevieve nibbled at a piece of toast, dabbing her red eyes now and then. They looked up as David entered without a word and walked to the sideboard. He stared at the pastry offerings for several minutes without making a choice. At last, he poured a cup of coffee and dragged himself to the table, shoulders drooping.

"I can't believe it. I just can't believe it," he moaned.

Genevieve squeezed his shoulder. "They think it's a heart attack. Did you know Mark had heart issues?"

David gave her a wan smile. "I did. He had a pretty serious

heart attack about three years ago. My God. Poor Margot." Looking down at the table, he held his head in his hands and shaded his eyes. Droplets hit the linen tablecloth. Tears, Genevieve assumed.

"I was sure Mark was an embezzler. And probably behind the shooting." Philip stared into his coffee cup. "Boy, do I feel guilty."

Genevieve blew her nose, then sniffed. "I'd say there's plenty of guilt to go around. We all thought Mark was a bad guy, including Wallace and Mrs. MacIntosh. And all the time he was carrying out Jonathon's directives. We got it so wrong." She inhaled a shaky breath. "Now we're back to who shot at David. Or you, Philip."

David raised his head. His eyes were red-rimmed and glistening. "The shooting seems a thousand years ago, doesn't it?"

"Lord Crosswick." Wallace had slipped unnoticed into the breakfast room and stood near the door. All eyes turned to the butler. "I'm sorry, my lord, but Penelope Ballard, the Commissioner of Scotland Yard, is on the phone for you. She insists she must speak to you."

"The head of Scotland Yard? Why in the world is she calling me?" Philip strode to the sideboard and picked up the phone. "Philip Warwick here." He locked his gaze on David and Genevieve. "Yes, Commissioner Ballard. How can I help you?"

He took a sharp intake of air and his face paled. "When did you get the report?"

David and Genevieve could hear the caller's voice but couldn't make out the words.

Philip hesitated then asked, "Do you know what kind of poison?"

"What? Poison?" Genevieve whispered. She looked at David, whose eyebrows arched into the furrows on his forehead, his eyes as round as marbles. She shook her head in disbelief and mouthed "poison" again.

"Yes, Commissioner, I understand. Our son and his wife return with their children to the states in the morning and Sir David Weatherington was going back to London tomorrow. Do they need to change their plans?" Philip looked at his wife and friend.

They strained forward, trying to hear more.

"Of course, of course. We'll expect them." Philip was ready to end the conversation. "Yes, you're right, we have a helipad. Of course, we'll make sure it's available for your team. Ten o'clock. Yes, yes. I appreciate you making the call yourself. Goodbye, Commissioner."

As Philip hung up, he met David and Genevieve's fearful gazes with tears in his eyes. "Mark had a heart attack all right, but it was caused by poison. Poison in his mead."

TWENTY-TWO

"AAALLLLEEEEXXXX, EEEllllllaaa."

Engrossed in a cutthroat game of checkers, Alex and Ella didn't hear their whispered names.

"Ella! You can't move that way." Alex snatched her red piece off the board, closing it in his fist.

Incensed, Ella screamed, "Stop it, Alex! Put my checker man back on the board!" She grabbed his fist and pulled on it with both hands.

Scrunching his face and gritting his teeth, he held fast.

"Give it back! Give it back." She sobbed angry tears.

"Myyyyy daaarliiiings." Louder this time, the ethereal voice floated between the screeching of the children locked in sibling combat.

They stopped, mid-tug.

Alex looked at Ella. "Did you hear that?"

Ella waited, listening.

Again, the breathy voice purred, "AAAlllleeeexxxx, EEEllllllaaa."

"Who's that?" Alex looked right, then left.

"Where are you?" Still holding Alex's fist, Ella searched the room with suspicious eyes. "Where is she, Alex?"

"I'm here, children. I'm here in the wall."

Alex and Ella's fear mirrored each other, eyes wide, mouths agape.

"Don't be frightened. Come play with me. We can have so much fun."

Alex released his fist and the checker dropped to the floor.

"Alex, Ella," Julia called.

The children heard their mother's footsteps approaching.

"Lady, are you still there?" Alex asked the voice in the wall.

No response.

Julia stood in the doorway, an unnaturally bright smile lighting her face. She and Duncan intended to hide Mark's tragic death from their young children as best they could. There was no need to share the harsh realities of life with them yet. It would all come soon enough.

"What have you two been doing?" She kissed the top of Alex's head, scooped Ella onto her hip and squeezed her.

"Mommy, not so tight," Ella squealed.

"We were playing checkers until Ella cheated…"

"I did not!"

"You did, too!"

"Please stop, you two. You need to stop arguing over every little thing."

"And we were talking to a woman in the wall." Alex said, matter-of-factly.

"Oh, were you, indeed? What fun." Julia ruffled Alex's hair and tickled his neck. "How about some lunch?"

'I'm starving," they sang in unison.

She heard their steps retreat. What an unexpected gift. Two innocent children to play with. Things just kept getting better and better, except for Mark. Poor Mark… that was unfortunate. She hated it when things didn't go as planned.

TWENTY-THREE

"MOM, HAVE YOU seen my wax jacket?" Duncan called.

Genevieve was standing on the landing talking to Ms. MacIntosh. A sense of déjà vu welled in her. She rolled her eyes and chuckled. "As I've told you for forty years, it's exactly where you left it."

Duncan heaved an exhausted sigh.

She took pity on him. "Have you looked in the mud room? That's the logical place."

"I know. I was on my way. Just thought I'd ask."

Genevieve descended the stairs, keeping her eyes on her son. She knew him better than anyone and could tell by his slumped shoulders and worried eyes, that something was amiss. "What's wrong, darling boy?"

"What could possibly be wrong?" Sarcasm dripped off each word. "Since you've been here, someone shot at Dad, and now someone poisoned your attorney."

"Ah, yes, I see your point." A tender smile raised the corners of Genevieve's mouth. "Hardly a time to celebrate, is it?" She put her arms around Duncan and hugged the man she still thought of as her little boy.

Duncan's tone softened as his arms tightened around his mother. "Aren't you afraid someone tried to kill Dad? They could be trying to kill you as well. It makes a hell of a lot more sense they're after you two, rather than David. You have a lot more money than he does. When Julia, the kids and I leave tomorrow, I want you to come with us."

Genevieve gave Duncan a final squeeze. "Let's see what these people from Scotland Yard have to say. Then we can decide. Is that fair?"

"I can live with that. Let's hope we'll *all* live with that," he said, smiling down at her. "Now, I need to find my jacket. Harrington is taking Alex and Ella to an Angus farm. Another adventure with their pal and we won't have to worry about little ears hearing gruesome stories." Duncan headed to the mud room at the back of the house.

By ten thirty, eight people sat in the drawing room anxious to explore the details of Sir Mark Holmes' poisoning. The salon smelled of steaming coffee and pastries, fresh from the oven. The five civilians had no appetite. The three police officers ate heartily.

"Good morning," Chief Superintendent Francis Darlington commanded the room from his wingback chair. With his salt-and-pepper hair, Harris Tweed jacket, and polished brogues, the Chief Superintendent looked the part of a fictional Victorian detective. The two deep furrows etched between his eyes enhanced his ruggedness.

He began. "My team and I have assumed responsibility for this investigation. So far there has been an attempted murder," he nodded at David, "and as of Friday, the murder of one peer in the residence of another. As such, this case has been elevated to Scotland Yard. Though DCI Fields has done a fine job, the Met feels it necessary to bring greater resources to this investigation."

Darlington addressed Morris MacTavish, his subordinate. "Chief Inspector, the report," he said, his voice oozing authority.

Genevieve and Philip exchanged an impressed glance.

MacTavish placed a slim file in his superior's waiting hand and addressed the room. "Please be advised these proceedings are being recorded." His professional obligation completed, he resumed his position at the table in the corner.

Chief Superintendent Darlington sat with his elbows on the chair arms, hands tented. He looked around the room, his gaze lingering on each person. "I must say, this is a fascinating case," he said. "Very Agatha Christie. It appears that Sir Mark was murdered by poison in his mead." Darlington leaned forward. "We bagged Sir Mark's glass from Friday night at your party. There was a residue of mead left, enough to analyze, and that's where we found the poison. I understand, Sir David, you were with Sir Mark when he drank the mead."

"Yes, I was with Mark most of the evening." David stopped to clear his throat. "About an hour before everyone began to leave, one of the young servers asked me if I would like a mead. He said the barmaid had been told it's my favorite drink, and the caterers brought a special Polish mead just for me." David told the officers the story of switching drinks with Mark. As he finished, the blood drained from his face. "That means the poisoned mead was meant for me, doesn't it?"

Silence blanketed the room, all eyes riveted on Darlington.

The Chief Superintendent picked up his coffee cup and drained it. "Looks that way." He walked to the sideboard and refilled his cup. "Whoever did this went to a great deal of trouble and risk, and they had little control over the outcome. Here's something interesting. This mead was poisoned naturally. It was made from honey produced from rhododendron nectar. Most of the time this kind of honey wouldn't kill anyone. It would only make a person feel a bit ropey."

"I don't know what ropey is," Julia said, puzzled.

"Sorry, ma'am. It means unwell. I think you Americans might say 'sick.'" Darlington looked in his file folder, flipping through the pages. "The medical examiner said it can cause nausea, drooling, vomiting, slow pulse, low blood pressure, diarrhea, seizures, and coma. Sir Mark had a heart condition—arrhythmia—that made his ingestion of the poisoned mead fatal."

"I'm sure you know Sir David had an attempt on his life last month." Julia said. "You realize David may be a target of some crazed murderer?"

Darlington snorted his response. "Of course, we're aware of that. The confusion with the drinks makes sense when you consider the previous attempt on your life, Sir David. Sir Mark as the unfortunate bystander seems plausible."

"This means the person who's trying to kill me was here, in Wilmingrove Hall." David still looked stunned. "Have you talked to the barmaid?"

Darlington bit his bottom lip. "That's a bit of a problem. The caterer claims the barmaid was hired by Wilmingrove Hall. Your housekeeper insists she came with the caterers."

"This is crazy," Duncan said. "Is it even safe to be in this house, Chief Superintendent? Is it safe for our family and for David to be at the Hall?" Duncan paced the room, his anger on full display. "That's twice someone has attempted to kill David on my family's property. As far as we can tell, the local police aren't close to discovering who shot David last month and now that person seems to be moving freely around the estate. Officers from York and the National Crime Agency were here Friday night and still Sir Mark Holmes was served a drink that poisoned him. How in the hell did that happen?"

"Duncan, please." Genevieve was touched by her son's protective instincts. "This news is frightening, but we need to be calm and help the authorities. Perhaps now they'll approach this situation with more urgency. We certainly will."

"I appreciate your voice of reason, Lady Crosswick." Darlington nodded his thanks. "I understand how distressing this news is, and how it emphasizes the fact that Sir David's life is in danger."

"If I may interrupt," Philip's annoyance had built to near eruption. "David was shot in the head almost two months ago. That was a pretty good indication his life is in danger, don't you think?" Philip glared at Darlington, his nostrils flaring.

"I understand your frustration, Lord Crosswick."

"I don't think you do," Philip said, still seething.

Darlington continued as if Philip hadn't spoken. "I must say, however, in both attempts on your life, Sir David, perhaps the goal of the assailant was not to kill you, but to frighten you and Lord and Lady Crosswick. Think about it. When you were shot, it wasn't a fatal wound—"

"But it could have been," David interrupted.

"Yes, but it wasn't," Darlington acknowledged. "And Friday night if you had drunk the mead, you would have been wretched, but you would not have died… probably."

"Very comforting," David scoffed.

"Excuse me, my lord." Wallace stood at the door, holding a gold box tied with a navy-blue ribbon. "A courier just delivered this and said it was urgent that Chief Superintendent Darlington receive it immediately. I thought I should bring it right in."

"Of course, Wallace. Thank you." Philip motioned for Wallace to give the box to the Chief Superintendent.

"Put it over on that table." Darlington jerked his head towards an inlaid mahogany antique.

"You mean the Hepplewhite sideboard, sir?" The arrogance in Wallace's voice was hard to miss.

Darlington nodded, Wallace's disdain lost on him. "Franklin, put your gloves on. Assuming it's not a bomb, open it."

The lowest ranked of the three Scotland Yard officers opened his satchel, pulled on latex gloves and approached the package. "There's a card, sir."

"And?" Darlington barked.

Franklin eased the card from under the ribbon and read out loud:

Chief Superintendent Darlington,
Please share this lovely mead with Sir David.
I made it especially for him.
I was pretty annoyed the drinks got all mixed-up
Friday night.
Do tell Margot I'm sorry about Mark...oops.

"Open the box, Franklin."

Gingerly, Franklin tugged the end of the ribbon, pulling the bow loose.

"Step it up, man!" Darlington snapped.

Franklin lifted the box lid and peered inside.

"Well, what is it?" Darlington was out of his chair and striding towards the sideboard.

Cradled in a velvet nest was a small, lidded pewter tankard. Red sealing wax oozed from around the rim, keeping the lid secure.

"Lord Crosswick. Call your butler back in here," Darlington ordered.

"I'm still here, sir."

Surprised, the Chief spun around. "Tell me everything you can about the courier."

Wallace drew himself up to his full height. "The courier was a woman, about five feet, six inches and maybe eight and a half stone, very lean. She was dressed head to toe in black, wearing a Shoei helmet. The visor was down, and, I believe, she spoke with a slight accent, though it was difficult to hear her because of the visor. The motorcycle was a Ducati Superleggera V4, red with black trim. The reg was MI99 DVD."

Everyone in the room stared at Wallace with surprise and admiration.

"Wallace! Impressive, very impressive." Philip smiled at his butler.

"In my youth, I raced motorcycles, my lord. I never got over my love for a fast, open ride."

"You're an onion, Wallace." Genevieve grinned and shook her head. "We keep peeling you and finding new layers."

"Could we get back to the courier?" Chief Superintendent Darlington pressed the group to stay on topic. "Can you tell me anything else?"

"One other thing. As she handed me the package, she laughed."

Darlington rubbed his late-afternoon stubble. "Arrogant. Pretty damn arrogant. Assuming the assailant is the same person who dropped off the package, we know several things. We know that person is a woman, five feet, six inches tall, lean, a motorbike rider, egotistical, self-assured, no doubt a thrill seeker. If she is the same person who shot at you, Sir David, we know she is an expert marksman. If she was the barmaid, we know she is a chameleon easily changing her appearance to suit the role. And if she made the mead, she is someone who knows about brewing. And, as I said, she's arrogant. That could be her Achilles heel. I'd say we know quite a lot if we make a few assumptions."

Philip said. "That's a lot of information from a brief encounter."

Darlington relaxed into his chair and chuckled. "I dare say, she wanted us to know everything I just told you. She's a clever little minx. We're going to have to be at the top of our game to stay ahead of this one."

TWENTY-FOUR

Each nursing a glass of scotch, Philip, David, and Duncan recapped the day's events in Philip's study. It had been a long, brutal day.

On both sides, questions had been asked and answered. Tempers had flared, accusations had flown, competence had been challenged. The bartender was a key suspect and was nowhere to be found, with little prospect of tracking her down. Tomorrow promised to be another grueling session.

David looked at Philip and Duncan with exhausted eyes. "Before Mark died, it never occurred to me that this mystery might not be solved. Now I think it will be a miracle if it is, and maybe even more of a miracle if I live through it."

Philip took a swig of his drink then set his glass on his desk. "I know what you mean. As naive as it sounds, before last Friday, I kept thinking the police had it wrong and it was hunter's shots gone awry. But now..."

"I'm glad at last you both realize how serious this is." Lines etched their way between Duncan's eyebrows.

Philip's computer tweeted. He glanced at his screen and saw their London housekeeper, Anna Baker, was calling him on Messenger.

"Oh crap! What now?" Philip muttered to himself as he hit 'Accept'.

Mrs. Baker popped onto the screen.

"Mrs. Baker. Is everything okay at Margrave House?" Philip tried to keep any trace of concern out of his voice.

"Everything is fine, Lord Crosswick. I just have a question for you."

Philip noticed she was in the study. His mind flashed to the night she told them about Charlotte's tumble down the stairs to her death, becoming the Laney family ghost. "How's Charlotte doing?" he smiled.

Mrs. Baker gave a robust laugh. "Our favorite ghost mentioned she would be at Wilmingrove Hall with the family. Have you seen her?"

"Genevieve smelled her in the drawing room when we first got here, but I don't think she's made herself known since then." They smiled at each other.

Philip motioned to David to come to his side of the desk. "Mrs. Baker, I don't think you've met Sir David Weatherington, have you?"

"No, we've never met, though I certainly know you by repute, Sir David. You did a smashing job tracking down Lord and Lady Crosswick and we thank you for that. Though with all that's gone on at Wilmingrove Hall, I wonder if Lord Crosswick is happy he was found." Mrs. Baker's dimples pierced her cheeks as she grinned.

"I can't say it's been dull, that's for sure." Philip relaxed at the sight of Mrs. Baker's cheerful face.

"Lord Crosswick, the reason I called is that you and Lady Crosswick are receiving quite a few invitations. Would you like me to forward them or respond on your behalf?"

"We won't be back in London for some time. If you could send our regrets, I'm sure Lady Crosswick would appreciate it."

"Consider it done."

Philip could feel David hanging over his shoulder, leaning closer and closer. When he turned his head, his lips were almost on David's. Startled, Philip sat back, and David moved even closer to the monitor. "Mrs. Baker, that picture on the desk, could you please bring it closer to the screen so I can see it?"

"This photo?" Mrs. Baker turned the silver frame toward the computer.

"Who is she?"

Mrs. Baker blinked at David's sharp tone. "Why, she was a very close friend of the 12TH Earl. Her name was Revy Harris."

"When were she and the Earl, um, close?" David was hardly breathing.

Mrs. Baker ran her sleeve over the glass of the frame, wiping off non-existent dust. "It was twenty-one, maybe twenty-two years ago, after a brief affair, that Lord Crosswick insisted she return to America."

"She's American," David voice was flat.

Philip gripped David's arm. "Do you know her, David?"

"I do." In an instant, loathing, lust, and panic he hadn't felt for years raged through him. "I know her, and I now know who's trying to kill me."

TWENTY-FIVE

AFTER A SLEEPLESS night, of pacing, thinking, rethinking, and doubting, David gazed out the windows at the terrace, where huge pots overflowed with fall flowers of blues, reds, and oranges, still drenched from yesterday's showers. The overnight rains had moved on and now billowy clouds raced across the sky like sailboats on a blustery day.

This morning, everyone had gathered to hear his tale.

"It's hard to know where to start." His voice was flat and his shoulders sagged. "I guess the beginning is as good a place as any."

Genevieve wondered if he could muster the energy to tell his story.

"I grew up in Cornwall, in Falmouth. My family lived there for generations. My dad and his brother had a family business, Weatherington Bespoke Yachts. They designed and built custom-made boats. When I was eighteen, I went to Cambridge. During the summer before my last year at university, I stayed in Cambridge to work." His hands shoved deep in his pockets, he stood looking out of the library windows, seeing nothing.

"An American family was in Cambridge for the summer,

George and Katherine Conway and their three children: a seventeen-year-old daughter, Becca, who was starting at Harvard in the fall; and two boys, Conner and James. The dad asked me to coach the boys. He wanted them to spend most of their time on the water, honing their rowing skills. It was a smashing opportunity." Pausing, David took a long, slow drink from his water tumbler.

"After two weeks working with them every day, they were getting quite good. They loved learning everything and even loved maintaining the shell. Anything to hang around the club and the rowers. At the end of the second week, Mr. Conway asked if I could also work with Becca. She was already a decent sailor but wanted to make the Harvard team. He thought if I worked with her, she could sharpen her skills and become more competitive. In retrospect, I imagine Mrs. Conway said to him, 'You find something for Becca to do or I'm going to kill her!' It turns out Becca was precocious, whip-smart, desperate to be sophisticated, and a challenge for her parents."

"That's Ella in a few years," Philip said, drawing a laugh from the room.

"What do you mean, Dad, in a few years?" said Duncan.

Another round of laughter filled the library.

"I hope not," David said. "At seventeen she was stunning, one of those girls you can't take your eyes off. Though she was from Kentucky, she was every Brit's idea of the perfect California girl: tan, long limbs, blond hair. If I'd known what I was getting into, I would have told Mr. Conway my schedule was too busy. But it seemed like another amazing opportunity. I was making a ton of money and doing something I loved. It was a dream summer—until it turned into a nightmare." David ran his hands over his face as if to wipe away the memory. "That first day when I arrived at the marina, Becca was waiting for me in a bikini bottom and no top."

The men in the room looked more shocked than the women.

"What the hell did you do, David?" Philip asked.

"My first inclination was to turn around and walk away, but I quicky decided it would be an opportunity to teach this young girl a lesson in a safe environment. Very mature of me, wasn't it?"

The five men agreed. The two women rolled their eyes.

"So, how did you handle it?" Duncan asked.

"I stepped onto the Firefly, the dinghy we were using that day, picked up a life jacket, tossed it to her and said, 'You'll need to wear this. Let's go. We need to shove off.'"

Comments poured forth from David's audience:

"Absolutely brilliant!"

"How very clever."

"Good thinking, David!"

"Well done, Man."

David shook his head. "I was sweating buckets."

"So?" Darlington said. "What did she do?"

"I can honestly say if looks were daggers, I would have been dead on the spot. Seventeen-year-old girl-women are terrifying. I bruised her ego and I guess that's about the worst thing a person can do to a teenage girl. It was the beginning of years of Becca storming in and out of my life, always leaving chaos and trouble in her wake."

David ran his hands through his thick hair. He laced his fingers behind his neck and dropped his head back, trying to relieve the tension running across his shoulders.

Julia leaned forward on the edge of a loveseat cushion, her elbows on her knees. Vibrating with curiosity, she asked, "What in the world did this girl do to you?"

David smiled at Julia's lusty enthusiasm and went on. "The entire summer, Becca tried to entangle me in a romance. Well, romance is the wrong word. She tried to lure me into some pretty lurid sex games."

All eyes were wide, waiting for David's next revelation.

"She was seventeen. I was twenty-one." He shivered. "One night when I got home from the pub, I found Becca naked in my bed. She got into my flat by telling my landlady it was my birthday and she wanted to surprise me." He sighed and shook his head. "She surprised me alright. She threatened that if I didn't make love to her, she'd tell her father I raped her." Little beads of perspiration glistened on David's upper lip.

"Jeez, David. What the…! That's terrifying." Philip took a deep breath, unable to imagine what he would do in that situation. "How did you handle it?"

"The only thing I could think of was to call her bluff. I reached for the phone to ring her parents. With that threat, she grabbed her clothes and scrambled out the door. This kind of sexual blackmail went on the whole summer until British Airways took Becca and her family back to the U.S. at the end of August. God, that was a happy day." David swiped the back of his hand across his lips. "When she got home, she wrote daily letters, dripping with teenage despair, which I ignored. They trickled to weekly. Then, thank God, they stopped.

"After my final year at Cambridge, I headed to Boston for my next big adventure in Harvard's MBA program."

Duncan walked to the sideboard, put his cup under the spigot and filled it almost to overflowing. "Whoa! David, you have me so distracted I can't even pour a cup of coffee. This is quite a story."

"To paraphrase Al Jolson: 'You ain't heard nothin' yet'. My first week at Harvard, I was at a party thrown by Henry Fitch, the same Henry Fitch who is now part of your legal team. He was in his second year of the MBA program."

"Small world," Philip said.

"No question." David uncrossed his legs then eased his ankle onto his knee. "An hour and three beers into the party, I was in deep conversation about the EU with a couple of econ wonks who were dazzled by their own intellects. As I was about to pull the plug on their theory, I felt a hand on my shoulder. Lips pressed to my ear and said in a seductive voice, 'Hello, Darling,' followed by teeth tugging on my earlobe. A hand slid down my back and into the pocket of my jeans."

David interrupted his story to clear his throat. He looked around the library. Each person was leaning forward, eager for him to continue. Even the three seasoned Scotland Yard policemen were rapt.

"Who was it, David?" Genevieve's eyes were wide with excitement.

"It was Becca, of course," Julia said.

David resumed. "It *was* Becca, with her perfect heart face, bow mouth and intense, blue-violet eyes. She flashed a wicked smile and tugged my lower lip between her teeth. To say I was surprised to see her was an understatement. For the last year, I had thought about Becca once in a while, always with a sense of dread. But I hadn't worried much about running into her. It's a big campus. I was a grad student, and she was an undergrad. Maybe it was my pleasant, boozy buzz or Becca's breathtaking sensuality, but that evening I was excited to see her."

Julia narrowed her eyes. "Honestly, David. After all she did to you. How could you have even tolerated being in the same room with her?"

David put his hands up. "I know. I know. I have no defense. She looked amazing and knew her way around the room. She was a sophomore, but she knew most of the people at the party. She introduced me to the most interesting and influential students, and by the end of the evening I had met a lot of Harvard's movers and shakers. After the initial shock of seeing Becca, I was feeling pretty full of myself that she still had a thing for me. You know, I was twenty-two." He cocked one eyebrow and shrugged his shoulders.

David paused to take a long drink from his water glass.

Clouds had moved in again and the light in the library had faded to dusky shadows. Only the glow of the crackling fire brightened the room. David rose from his chair, stretching to release his muscles, tight from sitting. The day was intense, and fatigue was weaving its way among the people in the library.

As he settled back into his chair, David said, "I am not a

believer in regrets. but in this case, if I could change what happened next, I would." Remorse swept across David's face, his eyes glistening with emotion. "The decision I made that night was made by a twenty-two-year-old boy, so filled with hubris he thought he could have what he wanted, without consequence.

"Before I left with Becca, Henry warned me. He said Becca had a well-deserved reputation for exacting revenge against anyone she felt slighted her. I thought he must be drunk, or jealous. I was an idiot. It was just over a year since she spent the summer trying to lure me into bed. Every time I rejected her, she had threatened to ruin me. How soon one forgets when heavy drinking and the prospect of sex with a sensual woman are involved. That's all I wanted. What I got was a terrifying night with a wicked, beautiful sociopath."

Chief Superintendent Darlington cleared his throat to interrupt. "Sir David, are you suggesting you slept with a lass and, I assume, never called her back, so she attempted to kill you, twice, twenty years later? I'm sure you're irresistible to women, but…." His voice trailed off, leaving skepticism hanging in the air.

"I don't know why Becca was obsessed with me. Maybe we met when she was the perfect age to fall deeply in love and I was the one who was there." David's voice cracked. "Cambridge is a romantic place, and the summer was full of idyllic interludes." He looked beyond Darlington, his eyes glazed. "Sailing is a seductive sport: the sun, the breeze, long, tan legs, warm nights, Champagne to celebrate every race. I'm sure her infatuation had little to do with me and everything to do with the environment and circumstances."

David looked at his hands, folded in his lap. His words hung in the air for several seconds, the crackling fire and ticking clock the only sounds in the room.

"David!" Genevieve shook him with her voice. "David!"

When he looked up, David's eyes glistened with tears and exhaustion. For the last half hour, Darlington had been assessing David's fatigue and emotional state. He glanced at his watch. "I think we should call it an evening and resume in the morning. Sir David, we've been at this a long time and I'm sure you're tired."

David nodded.

"Whatever you say, Chief." Philip stifled a yawn and stretched his arms overhead. "I'm sure I speak for everyone when I say it's been a riveting day.

Darlington walked across the library to where he had draped his Harris tweed jacket across the arm of a chair hours ago. "Tomorrow the forensic team is coming back to go over everything one more time." He patted the elegant box that had arrived earlier. "This little gift of mead from the courier will, no doubt, be our best lead."

"Do you think they'll find any more evidence?" David asked.

Darlington tugged on his jacket and buttoned the middle button. He shot his cuffs, and said "In my experience, Sir David, there's always one more piece of evidence to find."

Philip smiled at the dry response. "What time will the forensic team arrive?"

"They'll be ready to start by half eight." Darlington motioned to his two subordinates to gather their equipment and files. "We appreciate your hospitality."

"Of course," Genevieve said. "Anything we can do to help, you just have to ask."

"Chief Superintendent, when do you think Julia, the children and I can leave?" Duncan slipped his arm around Julia's waist. "We're trying to talk my parents into coming with us, and David if he would. I think they'd be a lot safer in the States. Don't you agree?"

Darlington snapped his briefcase closed. "At this point, I'd like to think Lord and Lady Crosswick, and Sir David, are safe at Wilmingrove Hall. But since we don't know who the murderer is, whom they're trying to murder or why, I think you'd better make that decision on your own." He picked up his case and headed to the door, then stopped and turned back to Duncan. "We should be finished here tomorrow. You could probably plan to leave the day after, on Tuesday. We know how to get in touch with you if we need to speak while you're in the States, and you could come back, if needed, correct?"

"Of course. Thanks." Duncan shook Darlington's hand and nodded.

Philip escorted the Scotland Yard team to the door and returned to the library. There wasn't an ounce of energy in the room. No one had the strength to move.

Desperate to get into a hot bath, Genevieve stood. "I'd suggest anyone who's hungry should raid the kitchen. I'm sure there's plenty in the fridge. Mrs. Lomax and her staff are off on Sunday evening so you're on your own. David, you must be bone tired."

"I didn't realize it until Darlington suggested we stop for the day, but I am absolutely knackered."

Genevieve rolled her shoulders. "Julia, Duncan, kiss the kiddos for me, please. I'm outta here!"

"I'll be up in a minute." Philip kissed Genevieve's palm.

Genevieve threw kisses, leaving behind silence except for the ticking of the clock and the simmering of embers on the hearth.

"David, your story's unbelievable." Julia yawned as she spoke. "You're sure Becca's behind all this, aren't you?"

"When you hear the rest of the saga, I know you'll agree. Given her obsession with me and her history of threatening behavior, it's hard to think anything else." David heaved himself from his chair. "Shall we see what Mrs. Lomax left in the kitchen?"

"I need to go find our children. They were supposed to be having a picnic in front of the fire in the study, but who knows what that's evolved into. Duncan, could you make me a sandwich or whatever? I'll be upstairs in a minute."

"You bet, babe."

The three men headed to the kitchen to forage, while Julia went in search of two small picnickers.

Half an hour later with everyone tucked in their rooms upstairs, no one heard the house phone ring: four rings, five rings, six rings, until voicemail answered. It wasn't until the next morning anyone listened to the message.

TWENTY-SIX

"**S**IX, SEVEN, EIGHT, nine, ten. Ready or not here I come." Alex peeked between his fingers as he finished his count. "Ella, where are you?"

Lightening flashed as he looked around the music room, followed immediately by a crack of thunder.

Startled, he jumped and thought he saw the drapes move. He dashed to the rain-sluiced window and yanked back the silk curtains, sure he would find his sister. Nothing. He turned, his eyes riveted on a wide pedestal where a marble ballerina stood en pointe.

Stealthy as a cat, he crept across the room until he was close enough to hear Ella breathing on the other side of the column. He eased around the column's edge and peered directly into her gaze.

She screeched.

He shrieked in return.

Thrown off balance by surprise, he fell forward, clawing the air. As he tumbled toward the floor, his hand hit the ballerina.

Instead of falling off the pedestal, the dancer levered back, and a wall panel slowly, silently opened. Alex and Ella gawked at each other, eyes bugging and mouths open, stunned into silence, not knowing what to do next. Still on the floor, Alex crawled toward the opening in the wall while Ella sat cross-legged watching her brother.

The music room filed with another explosion of lightening and crash of thunder. "Alex, don't!" Ella shouted.

On all fours, Alex turned his head to look at his sister. "Come on. I want to see what's in there."

"But, what if there's a monster or a ghost?"

"Don't be silly. You know monsters aren't real."

"But what about a ghost?"

Alex sat back on his haunches considering the possibility. "I don't think there's a ghost in there." He chewed on his hoodie drawstrings, unsure. He hopped up, offered Ella his hand and pulled her to her feet. "Let's just peek in."

They clutched each other's hand and tiptoed to the black opening. Alex pulled her behind him. "Let me go first."

"Why?" Ella's chin jutted, eyes defiant.

"Because I'm older." Before Ella could object again, he stepped through the gap and into a dusty corridor, lit only by the gloomy light from the music room behind them.

"It's okay. It's just a hallway."

Ella was already at his side. "This isn't scary at all." She walked a few steps along the narrow passage then stopped as the light quickly faded. "Where's that flashlight you always carry on your belt?"

Alex's pocketknife jingled against his mini torch. He loosened the small carabiner from his belt loop and slid his flashlight off the fastener. He switched on the penlight and shot a small, bright shaft at the wall. A spider scurried into a narrow gap between two ancient beams. Unfazed, the two explorers crept on, Ella's hand on Alex's back. As they inched forward, he swiveled the column of light back and forth like a lighthouse beacon. They took step after cautious step until the torch shone on a thick door with two beveled panels, daring to be opened. Alex stopped and Ella smashed into his back, her nose taking the brunt of the crash.

"Ack!" she said with a sniff.

"Shhh! Be quiet!" He turned to see Ella's face scrunched, preparing to sneeze. He grabbed the bridge of her nose, pinching it tight. "Don't sneeze," he hissed.

Ella tugged his hand away and wiggled her nose. She looked over Alex's shoulder. Her eyes flew wide. "Are we going in there?" her little voice quivered.

Needing to be brave for his sister, Alex took a deep breath and turned the jiggly doorknob. The knob played on its spindle a quarter turn before it caught and unlatched.

They looked at each other. Her breathing was rapid and shallow. His eyes were wild with excitement. "Here we go." He held his breath and squeezed his eyes closed. As he pushed the door forward, he opened his eyes just enough to peer through slits.

A moaning sound filled the air.

Alex froze, holding his breath.

The moaning stopped.

Realizing it was just the sound of creaking hinges, he started again, pushing until the door was wide open. The room glowed with tiny green lights, some flashing, some emitting a steady gleam. Alex danced the flashlight beam around the curved walls of the small chamber, the light bouncing off one computer screen after another—three, four, five—a bank of six computers, all hibernating, waiting for someone to wake them.

"What the, what the…?" Alex moved further into the room, walking to the semicircular console. Ella stood in the doorway, ready to bolt at any second.

They heard a rumble in the distance; the storm's first wave. "Alex, we should go," Ella whimpered, teetering on the edge of tears.

"Don't be a scaredy-cat," he taunted. "I just want to see if these work." He wiggled a mouse, and the lower middle screen sprang to life. On the monitor, Elsie Lomax bustled in the kitchen, pulling trays of bread from the oven. The children watched as Lottie pushed through the swing door, picked up a china coffee pot and dashed back out.

Her curiosity overtaking her caution, Ella eased to Alex's side. She grabbed his arm, unable to take her eyes from the screen. "We should leave."

"It's okay. I just want to see what's on the other screens."

Ella sniffed, then sniffed again. "Hey, do you smell something? Something sweet? Like the roses Mommy and Daddy gave me on my birthday."

Alex glanced at her and then back at the screens, engrossed in all the tech. "Nah, I don't smell anything." He woke another monitor.

"Look! There's Mommy!" Ella's smile broke through her fear.

"Shhh," Alex warned. They watched Julia descend the staircase and walk out of the camera frame toward the grand salon. On the next screen, the library was empty. The fourth screen showed several people coming in and out of the reception hall. Some people stood talking to each other; some gawked at the grand environment. Some wore police uniforms; some were in civilian clothes.

Their mother strode into the picture and shook hands with a man they recognized from yesterday. She pointed, nodded, then walked out of the room.

Forgetting her fear, Ella sat in the desk chair, fascinated by the action. Alex stood behind her, like a commander on a starship's bridge watching his fleet's tactical maneuvers.

"What's on the other two screens?" Ella bounced her knees up and down, her excitement mounting.

Alex brought the next display to life. In the conservatory, Duncan, Philip, and David sat around a table eating breakfast. Duncan rested his elbows on the table, cradling a cup of coffee and listening to Philip. Talking and gesturing, Philip picked up a triangle of toast and poked the pointed end at David. Philip said something, David shook his head and both Duncan and Philip laughed.

"It looks like they're having a good time," Ella said. "What's on the last one?" She wiggled in her chair, wanting more.

"I guess you're not scared anymore." He smiled at her and moved the final mouse. An image of the stables filled the screen.

Ella stopped bouncing. "I was never scared," she snarled. "Hey look! It's Missy." She saw the girl who helped saddle her horse and guided her on a lunge line when she trotted around the ring.

"I like her."

Missy was hanging tack on the appropriate pegs, dressed in riding breeches and a long-sleeved green t-shirt. Her high ponytail swished back and forth as she hung the last bridle and looked around as if making sure no one was watching.

She shrugged into her barn jacket, pulled a small spray bottle from her pocket, held it up, checking the contents, then tucked it back into her coat as she walked out of the screen.

"Wonder what she has in the bottle?" Alex had been leaning into the screen to get a better look.

"Alex! Ella!" They could barely hear their mother's voice calling them.

He froze, his face still inches from the monitor. "We've gotta go!"

He grabbed Ella's hand, dragging her out of the chair and through the door. He stopped, spun around, and pulled the door until it latched. Pushing in front of Ella, Alex shone the flashlight down the hall to where the faint light seeped in from the music room. "Come on, Ella," he growled over his shoulder as they scuddled toward the opening.

Her ragged breath was hot on his neck. They didn't break their stride until they shot out of the secret passageway and into the comforting glow of the music room.

Alex ran to the ballerina, cradled her head in his palm and pulled the statue upright. For a moment, nothing happened.

Then, without a sound, the panel swung back into place, filling the gaping hole in the wall. As the panel latched with a soft click, Julia sailed into the room to find her two children panting and flushed.

"I've been calling you two. What have you been doing?"

Alex shot Ella a withering glance. "Just playing hide and seek." He affected an angelic smile, oozing innocence.

"Yeah, hide and seek," Ella mumbled, staring at her shoes.

"Well, come on and have some breakfast. You must be starving!" She took Ella's hand and leaned to kiss the top of her little girl's head. She draped her other arm over Alex's shoulders. "You kids should log some screen time this morning. You don't want to lose your computer skills while you're here." Alex and Ella exchanged funny faces behind Julia's back then ran ahead of their mother, hoping there would be chocolate chip pancakes waiting for them.

TWENTY-SEVEN

RAIN DRUMMED AGAINST the bedroom window. A low rumble of thunder encouraged Genevieve to pull the duvet over her head and burrow further into her pillow. She stretched her leg behind her, searching for Philip, but felt nothing but the cool of linen sheets.

She opened one eye and looked at her watch. Nine o'clock. Even though she had slept deeply for twelve hours, she felt herself floating back into a luscious twilight. Her mind wandered through the mist of the last three months, drifting to life before the phone call which heralded so many changes for the Warwick family. Before unimaginable wealth, before murder, and mayhem.

Just as she floated over the edge into sleep, the nutty fragrance of coffee brought her back. A hand caressed her face and lips tickled her ear. "Good morning, pretty girl," a voice whispered.

"Mmmm. Come back to bed, Philip. I'll make it worth your while," she murmured.

"Not possible." Philip swatted her backside through the covers. "The forensic team has been here over an hour. I let you sleep as long as I could, but you need to get up now. The Scotland Yard boys are on their way."

Eyes still closed, Genevieve enjoyed a luxurious stretch.

"Come on, kiddo, let's go. Do you want Mrs. Lomax to bring you a breakfast tray so you can eat while you get dressed?"

"I don't need a tray. I'll be down in fifteen minutes." She threw a pillow at Philip's retreating back. "You're brutal."

"And you love it, don't you?" He tossed the pillow back. "See you in a minute."

"Philip."

He stopped in the doorway and turned around.

"How is David this morning?"

"He's in great spirits. We had breakfast together and he told me that he feels some control over his life again, for the first time since the shooting. As he said last night, he's positive his old nemesis is somehow involved in this. He's also anxious to get the rest of his story on the record. It's going to be another busy day, so let's go." Philip clapped his hands, encouraging Genevieve to pick up her pace.

Twenty-four hours after they first gathered, the group reconvened in the library, except for Chief Superintendent Darlington. Everyone looked refreshed, but no one as much as David. Nattily dressed in a crisp white shirt, camel shawl-collar sweater, and tweed pants, he settled into a roomy down-cushioned chair, ready to resume his story.

"How was the Wilmingrove Inn?" Philip asked Chief Inspector MacTavish and Inspector Franklin.

"It's very nice, but we didn't have an opportunity to enjoy it."

MacTavish offered a sheepish grin. He was dressed in the same suit as the previous day but with a new shirt and tie. "I was hoping for a good meal and early night, but the Chief Superintendent had a different idea. We were on conference calls for two hours, first with the forensic team then with the Commander. That pretty much took care of the evening. By then, a sandwich was all we could get out of the kitchen."

Genevieve grinned at the two young officers and pointed to the sideboard, piled with pastries. "Please help yourself."

"Thank you, Lady Crosswick. All of you have been so hospitable," said Inspector Franklin, who had spoken little since arriving at the Hall yesterday.

Genevieve noted how chatty he was in the Chief's absence.

Chief Superintendent Darlington entered the room, rubbing his hands together in anticipation of the day's events. "All right, is everyone ready to get started?" He wore a black pinstripe suit, white shirt, and blue and black repp stripe tie, all pressed, starched, and knotted to perfection. Genevieve couldn't help smiling at how dashing he looked.

"I'd say we're all caffeined-up and anxious to hear the next installment of David's riveting tale." Duncan gave David a nod, then savored a sip of his steaming Sumatra.

"Let's see. Where was I?"

"You were about to leave the party with Becca." Julia prompted David.

"Ah, that's right. Henry was trying to warn me off getting involved with her and I was too barmy to heed his excellent advice."

"Yup, assuming barmy means crazy." Julia said. She leaned forward in anticipation.

"I needn't go into detail, but suffice it to say, the night was sleepless and filled with the most inventive and intense shagging I'd ever experienced." Even the Americans in the room understood what David was saying. "The next morning Becca started talking about setting a date for our wedding. She asked me how many children I wanted. At first, I thought she was taking the mickey out of me, but I realized pretty quickly, she was serious." David's eyes narrowed. "I remember I laughed and said that was a great joke, trying to lighten the mood. That was the wrong thing to do. Becca flew into a fury. She came at me like an animal, clawing and hissing. She scared the hell out of me. The night before, she had been wild, demanding, and aggressive, but under the circumstances, it was exciting. In the light of day, however, her behavior was terrifying. I finally got hold of her, sat her in a chair and warned her that if she got up, I would call her parents and tell them how she was behaving. That always seemed to work. She was either afraid of them or didn't want to disappoint them. Either way, it was effective.

"Desperate to leave, I told her there was no future for us. I assured her she would find a great love someday. She wasn't having it. In the end, she left me with a chilling warning. She said I should carefully consider my decision to push her away. She said if I chose not to love her, I would be sorry. Three days after that, Weatherington Bespoke Yachts, my family's boat building business, burned to the ground. The police confirmed arson. From the beginning of the investigation, there wasn't a doubt in my mind. Becca was behind it, and I told the police that's where they should look."

With no other sound in the room, the rain pounding against the windows was deafening.

"But, David, how could Becca have been involved in the fire?" Genevieve looked skeptical, furrows deep between her brows.

"I know it sounds like the ravings of a madman, but some things one simply knows. And, in the end, my gut feelings were born out."

"The police confirmed the fire was Becca's doing?" Philip uncrossed his legs and sat forward. "They found evidence she was guilty? Did she go to jail?"

David held up both hands, palms out. "Whoa! Hang on just a minute. Let me explain. Using CCTV and a thumb print left on the backdoor lock of the building, the police tracked the purchase of the accelerant, gasoline, to a petty crook and minor drug dealer from Cambridge, a guy named Michael Greyson. They verified he had met Becca the previous summer while she was in Cambridge. According to his mates, she bought marijuana from him throughout the summer. The trail came to a dead end, however, when he was killed in a car crash returning to Cambridge from Falmouth. His brakes failed and he crashed into a tree."

"Was there any foul play regarding his brakes?" Darlington asked.

"As far as I know, the police didn't check. They're not that concerned with how drug dealers die. The police found no money trail, and no correspondence between Becca and Greyson.

Greyson didn't have a computer, so any email communication between Becca and him would have been sent from someone else's computer."

"What about cell phone records?" Everyone was anxious to ask a question.

"The police never found a cell phone. At that time not everyone had a mobile. The police reached out to Interpol, hoping they would inquire about Becca on their behalf."

"Wow! Interpol!" Julia said. "Did they help?"

David shook his head. "They declined to investigate the daughter of a wealthy American businessman when there was no evidence of her involvement in a crime, just vague suspicions. The case was closed with Michael Greyson listed as the guilty party."

"You were right there on campus with Becca for another year. Did you ever accuse her of hiring Greyson?" Julia asked.

"Not then," David said. "While the case was open, the police insisted I have no contact with her. After the case closed, however, I did confront her."

Darlington's eyes flashed with surprise. "And what happened?"

"I saw her in one of the campus haunts the Friday night after the police closed the case. She was with a group. When I caught her eye, she walked over to me, put her arms around my neck and kissed me on the lips. I grabbed her wrists, drilled into her eyes, and asked if she had anything to do with my family's fire. She smiled an eerie smile and said, 'Remember, I told you to consider your decision carefully.' It was chilling. That was the last time I saw her. It was, however, not the last time I felt her presence."

Darlington had been pacing around the library as he listened to David. At this, he stopped. "Were you surprised by Becca's response?"

"I was not."

"Did you believe her?"

"I did."

"Did you tell the police about the exchange?"

"Of course."

"And what did they say?"

"They said the case was closed. They said there was no evidence that Michael Greyson had any accomplices. The thing they couldn't resolve was Greyson's motive, but with the physical evidence confirming him as the arsonist, they didn't need to look further. They felt they had done their job."

"Understandable, I suppose." Darlington massaged the bridge of his nose, then his forehead. "What do you mean by 'felt her presence'?"

David stood at the rain-streaked windows, watching the storm. After several minutes, he pulled his focus back to the room. "Seven years after the fire, Hannah Montgomery and I decided to get married. Hannah was a brilliant actor and quite the toast of the West End. I had been at Holmes Fitch Smythson Morrow for a couple of years. Our engagement party was brilliant, until it wasn't. About an hour into the party our host suggested we open our gifts. I remember Hannah's beautiful face, cheeks flushed with excitement. When we were about halfway through the pile, we chose an elegantly wrapped package which looked like artwork; ideal for our new flat. Hannah grinned like a kid as she began to read the card which came with it, but then, her voice trailed off and she looked up at me, confusion replacing joy. I took the card from her and read the calligraphy message." David paused to settle his racing pulse.

Genevieve couldn't stop herself from asking, "What did it say?"

"It said, 'David, darling, you will know what this means. Still loving you, B.' I could feel the blood drain from my head. When we first met, I told Hannah about Becca's obsession with me and how I believed she was responsible for the boat factory fire, so I didn't have to explain who she was."

"What did she send?" Duncan asked.

Looking down at his lap, David folded then unfolded his hands. He took a long breath before he spoke. "It was a skillfully replicated painting of Salome holding a platter with John the Baptist's head on it. But instead of John the Baptist's, the head was Hannah's, looking out from the canvas with dead eyes and blood dripping from her shredded neck. Holding the head, fingers entwined in Hannah's hair, instead of Salome, was Rebecca Conway, aka Revy Harris."

"Rebecca Conway?" Duncan and Julia cried in unison. "Rebecca Conway, the heiress to the Harris Distilleries?" Duncan asked.

"One and the same. When I think about it, I can't believe it took so long for the lightbulb to go on, but when I saw her photo on the desk at Margrave House, it hit me like a lightning bolt. For years Rebecca Conway has been mucking about with my life."

"Who the hell is Rebecca Conway?" Clueless, Philip waited for someone to fill him in.

Julia jumped in. "Maybe you've seen the ads on TV or in magazines for Harris Distilleries. Rebecca Conway is the beautiful blond who's not just the spokesperson for the company, but the owner as well. Third generation."

"Of course!" Genevieve said. "I know who she is."

"Could I have read about her in *Fast Company*?" Philip began to show signs of recognition. "Doesn't she have a lifestyle company?"

"She does." Duncan said. "I don't understand, David. She's the person who's trying to murder you? She's a pretty prominent businessperson."

"I actually said I believe she's the person *behind* the attempts on my life, and now Mark's murder. She would never get her hands dirty, but she has plenty of resources. I'm positive Rebecca Conway is somehow involved."

TWENTY-EIGHT

T HE LIBRARY EXPLODED with a bolt of lightning and deafening clap of thunder. Lamps flickered, dimmed, went out. Gloom crept into every corner of the room. No one spoke. No one could. The shock of David's revelation rendered everyone mute. The only sound was sleet tapping against the library windowpanes until a loud rap at the door startled everyone.

Chief Superintendent Darlington bolted from his chair and strode across the room. "Excuse me. I'll be back," he said, closing the door behind him.

Genevieve looked at David, his shoulders slumped, his head cradled in his hands. She ached for what he was going through. What a wrenching experience this must be for him. It was hideous enough someone had tried to murder him twice, but to relive Becca tormenting him for so many years must be agonizing.

"David, how are you holding up? This has to be excruciating for you." Philip seemed to read Genevieve's mind.

"I'm okay," David said, looking up. "It's exhausting, but quite therapeutic to share this saga." He flashed a sweet smile that made him look like a young boy.

Julia stood. Reaching her arms toward the ceiling, she stretched her angular frame. "What do you suppose Darlington's doing?" She bent to touch her toes. "All this sitting is making me creaky."

"I've noticed he's been texting a lot the last half hour," Duncan said. "Maybe the forensic team found something. Maybe the smoking gun." Duncan blew imaginary smoke from his index finger.

Another rumble of thunder and groaning gust of wind announced the storm was still very much alive. The electricity flashed back on, lamps again flooding the library with a welcome glow.

With the break in the morning's session, everyone snatched the opportunity to take care of waiting tasks. Duncan and Philip buried their noses in their phones, responding to messages received in the last few hours. David sat, fingers steepled, gazing into the fire. Julia dashed upstairs to check on the children, and Genevieve went to the kitchen to make sure lunch was organized.

After about ten minutes, Wallace entered the library. "Sir David, Chief Superintendent Darlington requests you join him in the study. The Chief Superintendent suggests the rest of the group adjourn for lunch."

David exchanged a bemused look with Philip and Duncan as he left, all three wondering what was coming next.

The storm continued. The temperature dropped. Rain turned to wet snow and began sticking to the library windows.

Philip and Duncan sauntered together into the conservatory,

where the table was set for lunch and a fire blazed on the hearth in cozy contrast to the howling tempest outside.

"This doesn't look promising for us leaving tomorrow, does it?" Duncan said to his dad. According to the UK's national weather service, the unusual weather system was going to sit over Yorkshire for the balance of the day and well into the night. Several inches of snow were expected by morning and winds gusting to forty miles an hour would continue throughout tomorrow. It didn't look as if anyone would go anywhere anytime soon.

"I know you're anxious to get back to D.C., but I'd say tomorrow is not going to happen." Though Philip knew Duncan and Julia had many things to do on the other side of the pond, he loved having them at Wilmingrove Hall and was in no hurry for them to go back to the States. "You know it's going to kill your mother when you leave." Philip examined the pattern in the carpet. "I…um… I might miss you guys a little bit, too."

Duncan rested his hand on Philip's shoulder. "Dad, we'll be back in a month for the holidays. You know I still think you and Mom should come back with us."

Philip frowned and started to speak, but Duncan held up his hand. "I know. I know. You're going to see what happens today, then decide."

Philip gripped Duncan's hand and squeezed. "Exactly. David's become like a member of our family. And we need to be here to help him through this.

"Of course, I get it but I'm still worried about you staying here."

From down the hall, children's giggles could be herd approaching the conservatory. "Brace yourself, Dad," Duncan said, with a note of joy.

Like two colts escaping their paddock, the children stampeded into the conservatory, Ella in hot pursuit of Alex.

"You're cheating!" Ella shrieked at her brother. "You got a head start!"

Alex stopped, causing Ella to slam into his back for the second time that day. Turning around, he towered over his sister. "I did not cheat. You were just slow off the starting line!"

"Well, I won in sardines!" Ella howled, now on the verge of tears.

"Okay. Okay, you two." Duncan snatched Ella by the waist just as she was about to shove Alex in the chest. He tucked her under his arm and her rage turned to delight, arms and legs flailing as her father tickled her, showing no mercy.

"Daddy, stop! Stop!" Ella gasped between giggling convulsions. Duncan turned his daughter upside down, holding her by her ankles. Her thick mane cascaded toward the floor.

"Is this better?" he asked the wriggling child.

"No! Daddy, put me down!"

Duncan lowered her until her hands touched the floor and he guided her into a gentle somersault. "Do it again," she said, still laughing.

"Absolutely not," he said. "What have you two been doing all morning?"

"We played hide and seek then we had chocolate chip pancakes then we played sardines," Alex said. "Do you know what that is?"

Duncan and Philip both shook their heads.

"Let me tell!" Ella was ready to take center stage.

"Hold on, Ella, I'd like to hear Alex's version." Philip pulled Ella into a hug.

"It's a cool game. It's like Hide and Seek, only in reverse," Alex began. "One person hides then everybody else tries to find them. When you find the person hiding, you hide with them, so everybody's packed in the hiding place like sardines. Get it? The last one still looking loses and is the one to hide in the next game. I don't understand why the last one is called the loser because the one to hide is the lucky one. It was hard to play with just two of us."

Ella wiggled from Philip's arms. "We found an awesome hiding place this morning nobody else knows about."

"Ella!" Alex shrieked, snatching an apple from a bowl on the sideboard and throwing it hard at Ella, smacking her in the stomach.

"Ugh!" Ella grunted, staggered backward and plopped to her bottom, the wind knocked out of her.

"Alex!" Duncan boomed. He crossed to Alex in two long strides and grabbed the little boy by the arm. "Why would you do that?" He loomed over his quaking son. "Why would you hurt your sister?"

"I...I...I was just kidding around." Alex's lower lip began to quiver, and his eyes welled up.

"That did not look like kidding around to me. Go upstairs to your room. I'll tell you when you can come down."

Wounded by his father's disappointment and embarrassed by

being scolded in front of his grandfather, Alex dragged himself across the room, head hanging. He turned back to face his dad, tears staining his flushed cheeks. "I was just playing, Dad. I'd never hurt Ella."

Duncan pointed at the door. "Go upstairs and think about what you did."

Alex sniffed, wiped his nose with the back of his hand, turned and shuffled out of the room.

Philip squatted beside his little girl, who remained on the floor. She was now breathing normally but was still shaken. "Are you okay, sweetheart?"

She wrapped her arms around her father's neck and squeezed. Her lips close to Duncan's ear, Ella whimpered, "Don't be mad at Alex, Daddy. He was just reminding me not to tell our secret."

"What secret?"

Releasing her grip on Duncan's neck, she leaned back and giggled. "Daddy, I can't tell you. It's a secret."

"Of course, darling. Good for you. It's important to know how to keep a secret." He gave her a noisy smooch on her perfect little cheek. She puckered her lips, kissed Duncan's nose, then jumped up, fully recovered, and skipped out of the conservatory.

Standing just outside the conservatory door, Wallace patted Ella on her bouncing curls as she flounced out. He walked into the room and cleared his throat. "My lord, Chief Superintendent Darlington and Sir David have returned, and the Chief has requested you join them as soon as it's convenient."

Pushing back their chairs, the diners stood and drifted away from the coziness of the fire.

"Is there coffee in the library?" Genevieve asked Wallace.

"Of course, my lady."

"Um, Wallace." She shifted her weight from one foot to the other then back again. "I know you don't eavesdrop, but have you heard anything?"

"Well, my lady, I have overheard a few things." He took a step closer to Genevieve and lowered his voice. "The house maids were furious this morning after the police went through all the rubbish bins outside the kitchen. The place is an absolute tip. And after crating all that mess, I don't imagine they found anything, do you? After all it's been three days since Sir Mark was…," Wallace pressed his lips together, "well, you know."

Genevieve leaned toward Wallace, her hand on his arm. "Not exactly information that's going to crack open the case is it, Wallace?"

"Are you saying, my lady, that's not what you were looking for?" he said, eyes twinkling.

"Wallace, you scoundrel. You did hear something." Genevieve buzzed with excitement. "Tell me. Tell me."

"I believe I heard the Chief and his men talking about mead residue on a server's shirt."

"Oh, Wallace, you are an excellent spy. What would we do without you?"

"It would be a struggle, my lady." He maintained his sober demeanor, though Genevieve detected a slight upturn of the corners of his mouth. "I imagine, however, you and Lord Crosswick would manage…somehow."

TWENTY-NINE

Chief Superintendent Darlington stood with his back to the newly stoked fire, hands clasped behind him. It was evident from the grim line of his mouth that he had significant news. To his left, David sat stone-still, staring at the floor, brow furrowed.

"We had several developments this morning," Darlington began. "We have been reviewing the findings with Sir David for the last couple of hours and are anxious to share them with the rest of you in the hope you can help us piece the puzzle together."

Genevieve glanced around the room. Philip, Duncan, and Julia all strained forward in their chairs, eyes riveted on Darlington. Genevieve willed her clamped jaw to relax. She caught Philip's eye and, together, they breathed in, then exhaled. Philip sat back in his chair, rotating his head in a gentle circle to relieve the taut muscles in his neck.

Darlington continued. "This morning the forensics team found two significant items when searching the rubbish bins. The first is a glass container with mead residue. The team was able to lift a near-perfect print off the jar. The second is a shirt similar to those worn by the catering staff on the night of your party. There is a small stain on the cuff which we believe is mead, indicating it was worn either by the person who made the drink or the person who brought the drink to Sir David. We may be able to pull some DNA off the shirt. The items have already been sent to our labs in London. They left this morning before the storm picked up."

Genevieve smiled to herself feeling smug that she heard about the shirt first.

"I'm thrilled they found evidence in the bins." Philip shook his head. "What was the killer thinking? It seems like a bonehead move to put anything in the garbage cans."

Darlington pressed on. "The other important development is a message on the house phone. It was left last night at 9:47."

"I wonder how we missed that," Philip said. "I guess we had all gone upstairs by about nine thirty."

"And, because it was Sunday night, the staff wasn't here," said Genevieve. "Who was it?"

"It was Rebecca Conway calling for Sir David," Darlington said.

"What?" Duncan gripped the arms of his chair, his knuckles turning white.

"Are you kidding?" Julia's voice cracked.

Philip looked from David to Darlington then back to David. "I don't understand. What in the hell did she want?"

David looked up from the carpet. He gazed around the room, looking dazed. "We don't know what she wanted."

"Franklin, play the message," Darlington directed.

A strong, polished voice filled the room. "This is Rebecca Conway. I'm trying to reach David Weatherington. I have reason to believe he is at this number. David, please call me as soon as you receive this message. It's critical I speak to you. I have important information that may save your life."

David looked at Philip, then Genevieve.

"I'm assuming you haven't returned the call yet." Genevieve walked to David and put a hand on his shoulder. "David," Genevieve squeezed his knotted muscles, "do you have any idea what this means?"

David looked up at Genevieve, eyes warm with gratitude. "I do not. I've heard nothing from her since we received that wretched, insane painting fifteen years ago at our engagement party. " He paused, looking at his clasped hands before continuing, "that's not exactly true. Three years ago, when Hannah died, Becca sent a card. It was a combination 'I'm sorry I made your life a living Hell, and condolence' card. I was stunned at the kind message."

"I bet," Julia scoffed.

"She said she could never apologize enough for her terrible behavior. With the card, she included a copy of a poem, 'The Hopi Prayer'. She said her heart broke for my loss and she hoped my years with Hannah had been as wonderful as I deserved. It brought me to tears."

"Did you believe what she said?" Like Julia, Duncan was skeptical.

"No, I did not. But as long as she left me alone, I didn't worry about it. A psychopath has the spectacular ability to bend the truth to suit his or her needs. When this chaos started, I was pretty sure her remorse was a smoke screen. I thought she was most likely lying low until she found the right moment to cause me the maximum amount of pain. That may be true. It may not. But what is true is the next step is ours. Chief Superintendent Darlington, would you like to tell our band of amateur detectives what happens next?"

While the snow deepened and the winds continued to howl, Chief Superintendent Darlington shared what they knew about Rebecca Conway's phone call.

"By using voice recognition, we verified the caller was indeed Conway. The call came from a land line at Harris Distillery in Lexington, Kentucky. Rebecca left a cell phone number for David. Nothing about the call appears to be threatening, but before he returns it, I want to be sure Sir David is well prepared.

"David, isn't talking to Rebecca going to be horrible for you?" Genevieve frowned and chewed her lower lip.

"It may sound crazy, but I'm anxious for the conversation, particularly if she can shed light on what's been happening the last few weeks." David drummed his fingers on the arm of his chair, the only sign of any nerves.

"Her message sounds as if that's why she's reaching out. My team is preparing for Sir David to call Ms. Conway three hours from now, at six o'clock, one o'clock in Kentucky." Darlington uncrossed and recrossed his legs. "We're setting up recording equipment, and Chief Inspector MacTavish and Inspector Franklin are creating a list of the information Sir David will try to extract from Ms. Conway."

"David, what do you think you'll get out of all of this?" Philip asked.

David straightened in his chair and took a deep breath as if to gain strength. "Perhaps Becca can lead us to whoever is playing this demented game. Or if she's responsible for all of this, she may tip her hand. I think that's what you're expecting, isn't it, Chief Superintendent?"

"I try not to have expectations. I find they can cloud my vision. It's best to keep an open mind and follow the trail of evidence to the end. And, as of this morning, we have some excellent evidence."

"Let's hope she has some relevant information, and this isn't just another effort to disrupt Sir David's life." Philip nodded at David.

"Regardless of the outcome, we'll be a step closer to a resolution." Darlington rose. "Do any of you have other questions before Sir David and I return to the study to prepare for the call? We just wanted to bring you up do date with this morning's revelations."

Julia, flushed from sitting near the fire, looked at David with laser focus. "David, do you want one of us to be in the room with you when you call Becca?"

Surprised and touched, David smiled. "Thank you, Julia, that's not necessary, but I appreciate the offer. It's sweet of you. Don't worry. I promise I won't fall apart." David rolled out of his chair sprawling onto the floor.

Laughter filled the library at David's antics, brightening the mood in the room.

"All right. All right. I get it. You're tough as nails."

"Just let us know if there's anything we can do to be of help." Philip stood, indicating they should let David and Darlington get on with their preparation. "We'll be waiting to hear, needless to say." Philip shook David's hand then pulled him in for a hug.

"Here we go," David said as he followed the Chief Superintendent to Philip's study.

David sat at the desk and listened to Chief Inspector MacTavish and Inspector Franklin.

"After you tell her how much you appreciate her call, you need to—"

"Wouldn't it be smart to let her play the first card?" David interrupted. "Couldn't I just treat her as an old friend and see what she has to say?" David raised his eyebrows.

"Our goal is to control the conversation. By the end of the call, we want two things. First, we want to discern if she's behind the attempts on your life and the death of Sir Mark. Second, if it sounds as if she's not directly responsible, we want any information she may have that will lead us to the assailant."

It may have been fatigue, it may have been stress, but David felt prickles of annoyance rising to the surface. "Why don't you blokes just piss off! You know I'm a barrister. I've led hundreds of witnesses through testimony to my desired end." David looked at the ceiling, let out a deep breath, then looked back at the three coppers. "Look, Inspector, I'm not demeaning your skills, but I know how to talk to Rebecca Conway, who, I'm assuming is a hostile witness." David rose and headed for the door. "I'm going to have a lie down. I'll be back by half five."

Franklin and MacTavish looked at each other, panic in their eyes. MacTavish rang Chief Superintendent Darlington who was with the forensic team.

"Don't worry about it. He'll be fine," Darlington said. And that was that.

THIRTY

T HE CLOCK IN the grand salon bonged six times. David cradled the house phone and punched in the international code for the U.S. followed by the number Rebecca left on her message. His hand tremored, and his breathing was shallow and rapid. After a long pause, the line connected and began to ring. David willed himself to slow his breathing. On the fourth ring, a refined voice said, "Hello, David."

"Becca? Is this Rebecca Conway?" David didn't recognize the voice. He struggled to steady his own. His heart pounded in his ears.

"Yes, David, this is Becca. Are you all right? You sound strange."

To his relief, David heard himself laugh. He wiped his sweaty palms on his woolen pants and took a drink of water. "I guess I'm a bit nervous talking to you after all these years. You must admit our relationship hasn't always been smooth."

Now it was Becca's turn to laugh. "That's an understatement. I cringe to think of my deplorable behavior for so many years. If it hadn't been for my parents having me committed so I could get psychological help, I would be dead. Or, at the very least, in prison." Becca sounded detached, as if she were talking about an acquaintance rather than herself. "I hated them for years after they placed me at Winthrop Hills, but it was a perfect place for me. It took a long time to forgive them and finally thank them for making the hard choice to place me there." She cleared her throat. "But, David, I didn't reach out to tell you my woeful tale. I called because I know about everything that's happened to you since you were shot, and I think I know who is responsible for the attempts on your life and for Mark Holmes' death."

"I don't understand." David's shoulders tensed. "How do you know what's been happening?"

"Henry Fitch and I have remained friends since Harvard. We speak every couple of weeks and knowing how you are has always been important to me. Please don't be angry with Henry. I promise, he only kept me apprised of your health and happiness. I was heartbroken when he told me you lost Hannah. You two seemed so in love and so happy. The year before she died, I was in London on business and saw her in *The Importance of Being Ernest*. She was spectacular. It was easy to understand why you fell in love with her."

At the mention of Hannah's name, David felt the sting of tears. He cleared his throat, careful not to break Becca's verbal stride. He barely breathed, afraid he would spook her and cause her to end the call. Softly and slowly, he inhaled as she continued.

"When Henry told me someone shot and almost killed you, I was shocked. But it didn't take long for me to realize who might be responsible. I would have called sooner, but I've been doing a lot of sleuthing. I didn't want to raise suspicions if my feelings had no basis in fact. And then when Sir Mark died from poisoned mead meant for you…" Becca couldn't finish the sentence.

"And what did your *sleuthing* reveal?"

"I checked on the whereabouts of the person I suspected and, I'm sorry to say, she wasn't where she was supposed to be."

Silence filled the line.

"Becca. Becca, did I lose you."

"No. I'm still here." Becca's voice cracked. "David, assuming you're still in Yorkshire, I think it's best if I come to Wilmingrove Hall to talk to you in person. I'm sure I can be of some help to the police. My pilot told me earlier today you're having a strange late-fall storm, but the weather looks good for the day after tomorrow. I could be there Wednesday morning. What do you think?"

Chief Superintendent Darlington handed David a notepad with a scribbled note written in black ink:

Yes! Ask her who she thinks is trying to kill you.

"Becca, there's no question it would be helpful if you came here. I'd be grateful for any information you can give the police. Do you really have an idea who might be behind all of this?"

"Yes. I'm quite sure I know who it is."

"It just seems strange that you would know anything about this. You're four thousand miles away and we haven't had any contact for almost twenty years. Why in the world would you have any idea who's trying to kill me?"

"When I tell you, you'll understand."

"You said 'she wasn't where she was supposed to be. It's a woman?"

"Yes. Her name is Olivia."

"I don't know anyone called Olivia."

"Olivia Conway."

David's eyes widened. "Is she related to you?"

David heard Inspector Franklin's rapid-fire keystrokes as he googled "Olivia Conway." Franklin scribbled a note and handed it to David.

She's 20 years old. Last known address, London

"Becca, Olivia Conway is only 20. I don't think I know anyone in their twenties. I'll ask you again. Is she related to you?

"She is. David. She's my daughter.

A drop of sweat hung from the tip of David's nose. He sent it flying with a flick of his finger. "I don't understand. I didn't know you had a daughter. Why in the world would she want to kill me?"

There was silence at the other end of the line. David held his breath. "Becca, are you still there?"

"I'm here, David." Becca's voice was husky with emotion.

"Becca, why would Olivia want to kill me?" He was angry now.

Because, David, she believes you're her father and she hates you for it."

THIRTY-ONE

WEDNESDAY MORNING DAWNED cloudless and calm, the storm finally over. Snow piled high, lining the runway edges at Yorkshire's Leeds Bradford Airport. As the wheels on Rebecca Conway's Airbus touched down, the House of Crosswick's Bombardier waited second in line for takeoff. Julia and the children were heading home, leaving Duncan behind. Duncan and Julia had decided he could not leave his parents and David alone with the woman who might be responsible for their recent nightmare arriving.

In their short week at Wilmingrove Hall, they had been engulfed by Philip and Genevieve's new world of great fortune. It was hard to comprehend until you stepped onto your family's luxurious private jet. Only then could you begin to grasp the reality of jaw-dropping wealth.

The plane rolled forward. "We are next in line for takeoff." Captain Bruni's sensual Italian accent came over the intercom. They would soon be on their way.

Julia glanced out of the window and saw the Harris Distillery logo on the side of the Airbus. She pressed Duncan's number on her cell.

One ring and he answered.

"She's here."

"How do you know?"

"I'm looking at her plane. She's taxiing to the terminal. Wow. I thought *we* had a fancy private jet!" Julia smirked. "Becca's plane makes us look like a poor relative." She broke into a full-throated laugh, amused at her ridiculous complaint.

As the Harris Distillery aircraft rolled toward the terminal, Rebecca Harris Conway breathed deeply, hands folded in her lap. She appeared serene, self-possessed. She turned her head to look out of the window and her beveled blond hair swung just above tense shoulders. She looked younger than her forty-two years, even with the small lines at the corners of her ice-blue eyes. Her olive skin and full mouth were gifts from her mother's Italian heritage.

Butterflies fluttered from her stomach into her throat at the thought of seeing David after so many years. She didn't really need to fly to England. She could have told David and the Met detectives when they had spoken on the phone why she suspected her daughter of terrorizing David. But she couldn't resist seeing him in person. So, she offered, and they agreed she should come to Wilmingrove Hall.

A woman used to making hundreds of decisions daily, Becca had labored over what to wear for her initial meeting with David and the Scotland Yard team. She had changed her clothes four times before settling on a black cashmere turtleneck, slim black jeans, and a camel and black herringbone tweed hacking jacket. She finished the classic look with black leather boots with a two-inch heel. She kept jewelry to a minimum, with large gold studs in her ears and on her right ring finger a square-cut ruby surrounded by two rows of diamonds.

Becca didn't doubt for a moment that she was doing the right thing. After her conversation with David, she had spent half an hour on the phone with Chief Superintendent Darlington. The Chief had been cordial, offering her the department's gratitude for coming forward with information, and traveling to York to help. Now, about to depart the safe haven of her plane, her temples throbbed, and her stomach continued to churn.

"You need to be here," she said to herself. "This is the only thing you could do. You owe David a great debt and you may be saving his life."

The plane slowed to a stop as her captain said over the intercom, "Ms. Conway we have arrived at Leeds Bradford Airport. The local time is 8:27 a.m. and the temperature is forty-two degrees Fahrenheit. The stairs will be in place shortly for your disembarkment."

Becca walked back to her sleeping cabin, slipped into her wool trench coat, gathered her handbag, and walked forward to the exit door. Captain Marshall had come from the cockpit to see her off and stood with Marion and Edward, the two flight attendants.

"Thank you all for an uneventful flight. It was most appreciated." Becca offered a genuine smile that crinkled her eyes. "I'll keep you posted regarding my schedule, but in the meantime, enjoy yourselves."

Edward eased open the exit door, allowing a blast of cold air to push into the cabin. Across the tarmac stood three men. There was no doubt these were the men from Scotland Yard. The officer standing in front was several inches taller than the other two. If appearances counted for anything, he was the alpha male. Becca ran her tongue over her lower lip as she admired the man's rugged good looks. Even at this distance, she could appreciate his chiseled jaw and full mouth. The sun glanced off his aviator shades.

Becca had not had a serious relationship since ending her engagement eight years ago. Her former fiancé was an attractive, kind, Lexington tax attorney who bored her to tears. After many years of tumult, she had been lured by the idea of stability and a life without drama. But one deadly dull year later, she realized she would be happier alone than in a colorless world filled with colorless people. However, she still appreciated an attractive, interesting man, and at a distance Chief Superintendent Darlington looked very interesting indeed.

Standing at the top of the stairs, Becca pulled on calfskin gloves and filled her lungs with chilly morning air. Descending the stairs, she, too, hid behind dark glasses.

"Chief Superintendent Darlington?" Alighting from the last step, Becca held out her hand. "It's good to meet you."

"Ms. Conway, as I told you when we spoke, we appreciate you coming across the pond to help."

"Chief Superintendent, as I told you, I'd prefer to deliver my information to David in person." Shoving her sunglasses to the top of her head, Becca turned her focus to the two other men standing with them. "And who are these fellows?"

"May I introduce the other two members of our Met team: Chief Inspector MacTavish and Inspector Franklin." They exchanged handshakes and cordial smiles. "Lord Crosswick's people are handling your luggage and paperwork. Unless you need something from your aircraft, we can go directly to Wilmingrove Hall."

"Thank you. If someone is taking care of my luggage, I'm ready to go. Is Wilmingrove Hall far?"

"It's about a twenty-five-minute drive." Darlington ushered Becca into the back seat of a black Range Rover, which had been left running. The warmth in the car was a welcome relief from the biting chill of the morning. Conversation was spirited during the drive from the airport to the Hall. A lover of bourbon, Darlington pelted Becca with questions about running a world-renowned distillery. He surprised her with his knowledge about her lifestyle program, *The Most Interesting Woman in The Room.*

"I haven't watched too many episodes, maybe four or five." He offered a sheepish smile. "But my favorite was the one about reinventing yourself."

"Aha," Becca nodded. She placed her gloved hand on the Chief's arm and leaned into him. "I assume you were doing research on me?"

"Guilty as charged. At least that was why I watched the first couple of episodes. When I saw the show about how people could change their lives, I realized it was personal for you." Darlington's eyes held Becca's. "Particularly the part about how even terrible people can take their lives down a very different path. Do you honestly think that's true?"

Becca's hand slipped from his arm. "Yes, Chief. It was a *very* personal show. And yes, I do believe people can transform their lives. But they have to be repentant." She broke his stare and slid back to her side of the car. "It's why I've come to help."

After passing through the charming village of Wilmingrove, the Range Rover turned off York Road onto Wilmingrove Lane to the Hall, stopping in front of a high iron gate. Inspector Franklin rolled down the driver's window, reached out to press the button on the intercom, and announced their arrival into a security camera perched atop the fence. The gates parted, and they proceeded down the allee toward the house.

Becca had spent a lifetime in elegant surroundings, but she had never experienced an entrance quite like that of Wilmingrove Hall. Silver birch lined the quarter-mile drive, autumnal gold leaves shimmering in the mid-morning breeze. At this time of year, the trees mirrored the color of the Hall's glowing Yorkshire stone. On either side of the lane, the fields overflowed with the brilliance of yellow tansy, purple-pink heather, and the vibrant lavender of spear thistle, all of which had survived the storm and were pushing their sturdy heads through the remnants of the melting snow. In late fall, much of the thistle was morphing into seed heads, blanketing the fields with a ghostly cast as the thistle seeds waited for a gust of wind to lift them onto the breeze and take them to parts unknown. At the lane's end the car emerged from the shelter of the birch, arriving at the circular drive and Wilmingrove Hall.

For the past half an hour, Becca had been deep in conversation then dazzled by the drive to Wilmingrove Hall. She hadn't been considering what was about to happen. But as the door to the Hall opened, blood rushed to her head. Her vision blurred and sweat popped out on her forehead.

As he stepped from the massive doorway into the sunlight, David looked just as Becca remembered. His build was still athletic, but a bit leaner now. His hair was gray at the temples and more styled, but he was as handsome now as he had been twenty-five years ago. Her heart raced and she noticed she was holding her breath.

"Are you all right, Ms. Conway?" Darlington turned in his seat to look at Becca.

"I, uh… I'm fine," she stammered. "Much to my surprise, I'm a bit overwhelmed seeing David. Who knew?" Trying to make light of her nervousness, she gave a laugh that came out as a snort, causing her to giggle. Realizing Franklin was holding her car door open, she pulled herself together and scooted out of the Range Rover.

"David!" Becca strode toward him, her hand outstretched.

"My God, Becca!" Desire, dread, anxiety, gratitude all overwhelmed David as he shook Becca's hand. "We can't thank you enough for coming forward with your ideas about this mess. This can't be easy for you. If your theory about your daughter is correct, this will be hellish for you."

"David, knowing what I know and believing what I believe, there is no way I could stay silent. I'm just grateful you don't think *I'm* behind these attempts on your life."

David said nothing.

Becca held his gaze as she continued. "As you well know, there was a time I would have been the logical suspect. In fact, there's a time I might have been the culprit. It doesn't surprise me at all I was the first person you thought of when you started wondering who's causing all this," she fluttered her hands, "all this trouble. I'm relieved you and the police are taking my suspicions seriously."

"Well, you're here and I'm grateful." Taking her elbow, David ushered Becca into the grand salon. Becca grinned, looking up at the coffered ceiling inset with frescos. "To coin a phrase from my youth, David, this is awesome. If Lord and Lady Crosswick are as wonderful as their home, I can hardly wait to meet them."

"You need wait no longer because here we are, the wonderful Philip and Genevieve Warwick." The couple crossed to where Becca stood with David.

Becca peeled off her right glove. Philip proffered his hand formally. "Welcome to Wilmingrove Hall, Ms. Conway?"

She flashed a warm smile. "Please call me Becca," she said, putting her hand on Philip's arm.

Genevieve blanched and swayed as the blood rushed from her head.

"G, are you all right?" Philip grabbed his wife's arm and led her to a chair. "Sit down?"

"Genevieve, I'll get you a glass of water." David dashed toward the kitchen.

"Darling, put your head between your knees."

Genevieve waved all the attention away. "It's the ring," she said. "Becca, you're wearing Victoria Laney's ring.

Becca stared at her hand, frozen in place. Seconds passed before she blinked and said, "It was stupid of me to wear this ring before I told you about my relationship with Jonathon. I'm so sorry."

No one knew what to say. Becca looked from Genevieve to Philip to David, then back to Genevieve. "Perhaps I should stay in the village," she said pulling her glove back on.

Genevieve collected herself "Don't be ridiculous. I'm the one who should apologize. It was just a shock seeing the ring in reality after seeing it in your photograph and in Victoria's portrait."

"My photograph? What portrait?"

"I'll tell you all about it later." Genevieve almost smiled. "Welcome. We're grateful you're here. We've been anxious to meet the infamous Rebecca Harris Conway!"

"Infamous indeed!" Becca exhaled, looking relieved. "From the moment I knew I had to reach out to David, I've been terrified how I'd be received—by David, by the police, by the two of you—apparently for good reason. I've been here five minutes and almost gotten myself thrown out!"

Becca stuck her gloves in her coat pockets and David held the collar of her coat as she slipped her arms out. "I'm sure David told you about my horrible, sometimes felonious, behavior. From the moment I met him, David became the object of my narcissistic obsession. Thank goodness my parents intervened and got me the help I needed."

"That must have been quite an experience, working through a serious psychological issue. You deserve a lot of respect for all the years of hard work." Philip's voice was filled with admiration.

"That's kind of you Lord Crosswick, but—"

"It's Philip, please."

"Of course, Philip. It's kind of you, but I was lucky. My parents had means and spared no expense getting me the best help possible. There are so many people who suffer from mental health issues but are left on their own." Becca's eyes misted. "One of the first things I did when I left Winthrop Hills, was to volunteer with a grassroots organization in Lexington: NAMI, the National Alliance on Mental Illness. I began fundraising for them and now sit on their national board. And I'm going to stop lecturing now!" Smiling a self-conscious smile, Becca blushed and looked down at her elegant boots.

"As they say, 'I knew you when'. And to say you have come a long way appears to be an understatement." David put his arm around Becca and gave her a squeeze. "If you can help solve this case, all will be forgiven!" Stepping back, David grinned and gave Becca a chummy punch on the arm. "How are your brothers?"

"They're terrific." Becca's smile oozed pride. "Conner is a psychiatrist in Boston. Considering my past, it's wonderful to have a shrink in the family." Becca's laugh filled the salon. "He's married to a concert pianist, Calliope Stanhope, and has two spectacular boys, Max and Henry. My brother James has been at the distillery since he graduated from business school. When Kentucky legalized same-sex marriage, he and Michael, the man he's loved since they were undergrads, had a big wedding at our farm. Best wedding I've ever been to. Sadly, Mother and Dad missed seeing James happy. They died in a plane crash nine years ago. I had been Harris Distilleries Vice President of Marketing for several years, so took over as CEO and James became CFO. We're a good team. It's wonderful to be in business with people you know, love and trust."

"I remember reading about the plane crash." David's face clouded. "I liked your parents very much. They were good to me that summer in Cambridge."

"It's been a long time. I'm just happy they saw me come out the other side of a very dark period in my life."

Striding into the grand salon, Duncan added his greetings. "Ms. Conway, welcome. I'm Duncan Warwick, the son," he said, shaking Becca's hand.

"The resemblance is striking. What lucky girls we are, Genevieve! We're surrounded by handsome men!"

"Aren't we? Not only are they hunky, but they're pretty nice most of the time. Come on, I'll show you to your room" Genevieve led the way through the grand salon toward the stairs. "You and David will have plenty of time to catch up over the next few days. Chief Superintendent Darlington wants to gather at two o'clock, so we'll have lunch at twelve thirty. Are you exhausted or did you sleep on the flight?"

"I'm fine. As much as I travel, I find I sleep as well on my plane as anywhere. You'll have to give me the grand tour of Wilmingrove Hall. I spent a lot of time with Jonathon at Margrave House, but I've never been here. It's magnificent. From the moment we turned down the driveway, I've been mesmerized."

"I'd love to, and we'll bring our head housekeeper, Mrs. MacIntosh, with us. She's the Hall's docent. You'll love her! She knows everything about everything in the house. And, who knows? We might even meet up with Charlotte!"

"Oh my God! Charlotte. I haven't thought of her in years. How is the old girl?"

"She seems to have come with us to Wilmingrove Hall. I smelled her just the other day."

The two women headed up the grand staircase side by side, chattering like old friends.

Watching the two women walk up the steps, a wave of exhilaration swept through her. It wasn't part of the plot, but what if they both tumbled down the stairs at the same time, bouncing, smashing, cracking. Then there could be two more beautiful ghosts wandering through Wilmingrove Hall.

THIRTY-TWO

B Y T H E T I M E everyone gathered in the library, the sun had disappeared behind banks of clouds that had rolled in during the early afternoon.

Becca sat next to the fire. She had changed into a starched white shirt topped by a camel cashmere sweater-jacket. Brown and camel tweed pants draped her long legs. Only someone born into wealth could have such natural authority and appear so comfortable in the old-money environment of Wilmingrove Hall. She sat calmly, hands folded in her lap.

On the other side of the fireplace, in direct contrast to his old nemesis, David's nerves danced close to the surface. His body was taut and the ankle resting on his knee bounced. After a moment, he uncrossed his legs, reversing his position, then finally put both feet on the floor and rested his hands on his knees.

Seated on the sofa in front of the hearth, Philip patted the cushion next to him as Genevieve entered the room. He inhaled the hint of the perfume she had worn for forty years. He could not smell the aroma without thinking of his wife. He placed his hand, palm up in the space between them. Genevieve reached out, intertwining their fingers without looking at him. Sneaking a sidelong glance, Philip could see a smile just for him pulling at the corners of her mouth.

Each man on the Met team was in his place. Chief Superintendent Darlington had exchanged his suit pants for more casual cuffed wool trousers. He no longer wore a tie and had pulled a heavy, collared sweater over his dress shirt, which was now open at the neck. Becca couldn't help wondering if all Scotland Yard coppers dressed so nattily. Then she looked at Chief Inspector MacTavish and Inspector Franklin and had her answer. No, they did not.

"Are we ready to begin?" Chief Superintendent Darlington looked around the room. In return, each person nodded. "MacTavish, Francis, are you ready?"

"Yes, sir," they said in unison.

"If I may, I'd like to give a brief recap of events starting when Sir David was shot six weeks ago. I think it would help focus our conversation today."

"I know I would appreciate it," said Philip. "So much has happened since then."

"Needless-to-say, as the late-comer, it would be very helpful to me." Becca's voice was low and steady.

Darlington nodded to Franklin. "Inspector."

In the silent room, a soft click could be heard as Franklin pressed the record button.

Chief Superintendent Darlington started with the shooting in September and droned on about the events until he got to the findings two days ago, excitement crept into his voice. "Since

Monday, forensics has been analyzing the shirt we found in the rubbish bin. They found a short black hair inside the collar."

"Well, that's exciting, isn't it?" David sat straighter in his chair.

"We hoped they could extract DNA from it," Darlington continued. "But the hair is synthetic, no doubt coming from a wig."

'Well, crap," Philip said.

"It's not all bad news. No doubt it means the person who prepared the mead was in a disguise. We believe that was the barmaid."

"But you can't find her," Duncan stated.

"True, we've had no luck so far. But Ms. Conway coming here and sharing her theory about the murderer could very well be the break we need. With that said, Ms. Conway, could you please start from the beginning? This is your official statement, so please don't leave anything out. Is there anything you need before we begin?"

"Thank you, Chief Superintendent Darlington. I'm quite comfortable, maybe a little nervous."

"There's no need to be nervous, Ms. Conway. We can take a break at any point. Just say the word."

A soft smile curled her lips and Becca began. "Two months after my graduation from Harvard, I came to England." Becca paused, glancing at David. "By then, David had been back here for two years and, I'm sure, hadn't given me a thought during that time. I, however, was still obsessed with him. I intended to stalk him until he fell madly in love with me." Becca nodded at the smirks and sly smiles around the room. "No, really," she pressed. "There was no doubt in my mind I could bend David to my will. Delusional? Yes." She stopped for a moment, chuckling. "I had won a Laney Museum of Fine Arts Fellowship."

She gestured to Philip and Genevieve. "You both know what a plum grant that is. My parents were thrilled. Little did they know that I had applied and been accepted under the name of Revy Harris."

Genevieve asked, "Why did you do that?"

Becca sat forward in her chair, her elbows on the arms. "Because I didn't want anyone to recognize my name."

Philip looked puzzled. "Why would they recognize your name?"

"Before she married my father, my mother's name was Katherine Robeson."

Gasps and questions filled the room.

"Katherine Robeson was your mother?" Duncan snorted a laugh. "This just keeps getting curiouser and curiouser."

"Doesn't it just," Becca confirmed.

"Who's Katherine Robeson?" Darlington asked.

"Katherine Robeson had once been engaged to the 12TH Earl and I didn't want anyone to find out she was my mother."

Questions began to fly.

"Was the 12TH Earl your father?" Philip couldn't ask fast enough.

"No. Jonathon was not my father."

"When did Katherine marry your dad?" Genevieve asked.

"About a year after Jonathon sent her back to the States, she met my father, who was a wonderful man. They dated for a couple of years before they got married.

"How did you find out your mother was engaged to the Earl?" Duncan wanted to know.

"I found a letter to Jonathon my mother wrote and never sent, telling him how devastated she was when he broke off their engagement.

"I don't understand, Ms. Conway. Why didn't you want the Earl to know your true identity?" Darlington looked puzzled.

"I was afraid if he realized I was Katherine's daughter, he would have me thrown out of the fellowship program. Then, much to my surprise, I was chosen to help catalogue Lord Crosswick's collection at Margrave House. It wasn't what I wanted to do," Becca shrugged, "but in the end, it turned out to be spectacular for me."

"So, you spent your time at Margrave House organizing the collection?" Chief Superintendent Darlington asked.

Becca inhaled and gave a soft laugh as she breathed out. "Yes, Chief. I did a little cataloguing, but I spent most of my time flirting with the Earl. With great success, I might add. Not long after I started working at Margrave House, he and I started having intimate dinners, and eventually we became lovers."

The statement was so matter of fact, it almost went unheard, then Genevieve gasped. "You were lovers with your mother's ex-fiancé?"

"I know," Becca rolled her eyes. "Hard to imagine a daughter would do that, right?" "Wait a minute!" Duncan shook his head.

"Wait just a minute. I thought Jonathon was, um, well you know, um, paralyzed."

"He was paralyzed, but he wasn't impotent. In fact, he was a very good lover." Becca took a long drink from her water glass. "Of course, like everything else about my story, it's complicated."

Pushing herself from her chair, Becca strode to the windows to admire the acres of green dotted with remnants of snow.

"During my years of therapy, I learned the motive behind my rebellious behavior was to hurt my parents—my kind, loving parents. I excelled at fulfilling that goal. I've always been a high achiever." She turned to the group and smiled a melancholy smile. She began to wander around the room. "When I realized I could have an affair with my mother's former fiancé, I couldn't believe my luck. I was drunk on the idea of how much pain I could cause her." She caught David's eye and held his gaze. "It even took my mind off you."

Pink crept up David's neck and into his cheeks until even the tips of his ears were blushing. "So, that's why you stopped stalking me. Better offer, better pedigree."

"Better return on investment." Becca wiggled the ruby on her finger.

Everyone laughed at the witty parry and thrust.

Philip had said little since Becca began telling her story. He cleared his throat before he spoke. "Did Jonathon ever realize you were Katherine's daughter?"

"You know, Philip, I didn't think so at the time. But in retrospect, it may have been one of the reasons he broke off our relationship." She picked up a tiny bronze statue of a hunting dog. She turned it over in her hand, running her fingers back and forth over the cold, silky surface of the belly. "A month before my fellowship was up, Jonathon told me I needed to go home as soon as it was finished. I was shocked. I was furious." She looked at David. "You remember how angry I could get."

David blanched.

Becca closed her fist around the bronze puppy until her knuckles whitened. "He said all the right things: that I was young and had my life ahead of me, that he was too old and feeble. I didn't want to hear any of it. I didn't want any of his self-sacrifice."

Draped in sadness, Becca drifted back to her chair and sank into the cushion. "I had fallen in love with him. Deeply. But there was no changing his mind. The last time I saw him, he gave me this ring." She looked down at her hand. "And he thanked me for all the joy I had given him." Tears trailed down her cheeks, dripping from her chin onto her sweater.

Genevieve walked to Becca, squeezed her shoulder, and offered unused tissues from her pocket.

"Thinking about Jonathon still brings me to tears." Looking down at the carpet, Becca blew her nose. "But that's not the worst part."

"What could be worse than unrequited love?" David asked.

Becca looked at him through wet lashes. Outside, the sun played hide-and-seek as the clouds broke apart and raced across the slate-gray sky. The library filled with a golden glow, then darkened into dusky gray before brightening again.

Becca took a sip of her cold coffee. Setting her cup back in its saucer, she looked around the room. "When I got home, I was out of control. I was angry. I was mean. I was hateful. I took out all of my fury on my parents."

"As you said, I've been on the other side of that anger and it's not a good place to be."

"You're right, David. I even frightened myself. For a month my mother and father tried to deal with me alone, but it was impossible. After consulting with the medical staff at Winthrop Hills, a psychiatric clinic, my parents decided to commit me. Two weeks after I was committed, I learned I was pregnant with my mother's ex-fiancé's baby. Welcome to *Days of Our Lives,* Rebecca Conway style."

No one in the room spoke. There were no words to be said. The stunned silence lasted until Darlington said, "Please go on, Ms. Conway."

Becca nodded. "My daughter was born six weeks after I left Winthrop Hills. My parents were extraordinary and by the time I moved home, I was beginning to understand my misplaced anger toward them. They doted on Olivia. Olivia Harris Conway. She was a beautiful little girl: blond curls and blue eyes ringed with violet. But even as a toddler something about her worried me. She was never warm and cuddly. She never wanted or needed my approval like most babies. Something about my beautiful child haunted me.

"I refused to tell my parents who the father was. Can you imagine how horrified my mother would have been? Even

I couldn't do that to her. My father implored, threatened, begged. My mother convinced him, after several weeks, to stop haranguing me. I think she was relieved they wouldn't have to deal with a father who might cause problems. Several times I wanted to call Jonathon and tell him about Olivia, but I always thought better of it. The only person I ever told was my brother, Conner."

Becca stood up and walked to David. With tears in her eyes, she took his hand in both of hers. "David, I'm so sorry. I believe what I'm about to tell you is what set everything in motion to bring us to where we are today. If I could, I would change everything."

Nearly growling, David said, "What in the world did you do?" He felt the old sense of dread creep into the pit of his stomach. Déjà vu swept over him in a wave of nausea.

Becca moved away from him to face the fire, her back to the room. She stood motionless until Darlington asked, "Ms. Conway, are you all right to continue or would you like to take a break?"

Becca turned around to face the room. Her eyes glistened and her cheeks were moist with tears. "I, um… I didn't expect this would be so emotional." She smiled and sniffed. Reaching into her pants pocket, she pulled out a tissue and dabbed at her eyes. "This is embarrassing," she said, offering a weak smile.

Genevieve moved to Becca with outstretched arms. Holding Becca by her shoulders she said, "You're telling a roomful of strangers an incredibly personal story. I think you're remarkably brave!"

"And I think a brandy would be helpful." Philip went to the sideboard, pulled the stopper from a decanter, poured generous servings into snifters, and passed them around. He sat down, handing a glass to Genevieve.

"Becca, would you please get on with it?" David snarled. "I'd like to know what you've done to put my life in danger."

"David!" Genevieve shot him a scathing look.

"It's all right, Genevieve," Becca said. "I deserve David's anger, and so much more." She took a fortifying drink. "I'm not proud of what I'm about to tell you. But then, I'm proud of very little I did in my youth. But I never imagined what damage my actions would cause.

"I had several photos of David from the summer in Cambridge and a couple at Harvard. Some were of him alone; some were of us together. I lived in those pictures and created an entire life for the two of us, in my head. Scary, isn't it?" Becca said, looking at David. "I never told Olivia you were her father in so many words, but I let her draw her own conclusions."

David slumped in his chair. As Becca spoke, he stared at her, shaking his head back and forth, seeing only the Becca who terrorized him for years.

"When she was little, it was easy. She just saw lots of pictures of a very handsome man and some pictures of that man with her mommy. As she got older, she began to ask about her daddy. I simply told her that he didn't live with us.

"When she was almost seven, Olivia began to show signs of some disturbing behavior. One day the housekeeper found a dead cat in her toy chest, dressed in some of Olivia's doll clothes. She had brought one of the stable cats into her room for a tea party. When the cat objected to being dressed up and scratched her hand, Olivia strangled it trying to make it more compliant. My parents and I immediately called in a child psychologist. The psychologist wasn't as concerned about the act of strangling the cat as she was about Olivia's lack of remorse at what she had done."

"That must have been terrifying." Genevieve couldn't imagine having to deal with such a thing.

"With my history, red flags were waving all over the place. Olivia began to see a therapist once a week. By that time, I was working at the distillery and rebuilding my life. I felt strong and healthy, but as time went on, I became concerned that my neuroses had transferred to Olivia. There's no question that narcissistic personality disorder can be genetic.

"By the time she was eight, she started obsessing about her father, whom she thought was David. Even if her classmate's parents were divorced, most of the kids had fathers in their lives. There were father-daughter dinners at school and father-daughter dances at cotillion. I should have told her from the beginning that her father had died, but by then it was too late. She constantly asked me questions about him: how did we meet, where did he live, why didn't he live with us, when would she meet him, did he love her? It was easier for me to build my answers around David than to tell her the truth. I didn't realize I was enabling her fixation on a man who didn't even know she existed."

Becca unclasped her hands in her lap and placed them on the arms of her chair. "We spent two years with psychiatrists, psychotherapists, behavioral psychologists… anyone we thought could bring our darling Olivia back from her place of darkness. No one could help. All I could imagine was Olivia spending her life in an institution. We were at our wits' end when we met Miriam and George Conrad. They came from England to buy a horse at a neighboring farm. During their visit, they came to tour Harris Distilleries. Because all the guides were busy, the front desk called me. It was serendipity. They were charming, funny, and full of life. We spent a wonderful afternoon together and we stayed in the tasting room until early evening. It turned out Miriam, Dr. Conrad, was the head of the Langston School, a boarding school for children with challenges in Burnstall."

"Burnstall, England?" David asked, surprised.

"Yes."

"But that's only about twenty miles from here," David said.

"Ironic, isn't it? I thought I had heard all there was to hear about new therapies and cutting-edge approaches but the more we talked, the more interested I became in their program. The school specialized in highly intelligent children with emotional and psychological problems. It was academically rigorous, which gave the students a focus beyond their mental issues and an opportunity for success. Every student was required to master a wide range of sports: riding, archery, shooting, cross-country running, swimming, skiing. When they were not studying or in therapy, their bodies were working hard."

David looked incredulous. "I've known about the Langston School for years. They have an amazing reputation for success. Several well-known writers graduated from Langston, and even a couple of MPs. I can't believe Olivia went there. I can't believe your daughter has been right down the road all this time."

"Quite a coincidence, isn't it?" Becca swirled the last of her brandy then tipped it to her lips. "When Miriam finished telling me about Langston, I was convinced it was the right place for Olivia. The next day my parents, Olivia, and I flew to England. The school had a two-year waiting list and extensive testing program before accepting a student, but a child Olivia's age and with Olivia's profile had just been asked to leave. Understanding our desperation, Miriam was kind enough to offer the place if testing proved it was the right school for her. It did. Within the week I left my nine-year-old daughter at a boarding school four thousand miles from home." Becca looked at David. "I know you English consider that normal, but I'm an American. We don't do that. Even though it was a relief, it was also agonizing.

"Since that day eleven years ago, Olivia has been home only six times, one of which was when her grandparents died. She distanced herself from me more and more each year. After the first four years, she chose to spend her holidays with friends or at school. She was an excellent student and excelled at every sport, but it's questionable how mentally stable she was. She would make good progress, then regress. Periodically there were incidents that indicated Olivia was more fragile than she appeared. But nothing was ever significant enough to cause the therapists serious concern. In retrospect, I don't believe her mental health was improving. I believe she was becoming masterful at hiding her psychoses; a useful skill with a treacherous outcome."

"In her last year at Langston she decided to take a gap year before going to Oxford. She had been an excellent student, and reports from all her teachers and therapists weren't glowing but were positive enough. Miriam's one serious concern was that in her last year, Olivia had become obsessive about the man she thought was her father. She had been spending a great deal of her therapy time talking about how she needed to connect with her father, discussing the importance of father figures, parental rejection, and the consequences of being raised by a single mother. In my opinion she should have been thinking about everything that her single mother had done for her." For the first time since Becca began her statement, her voice filled with anger. Though her composure was intact, fatigue was creeping into her eyes and her shoulders were beginning to droop.

"Becca, do you think we should take a break?" Signs of Becca's weariness had not escaped Genevieve's notice.

"No. I want to get through this. Bear with me, I'm getting to the end."

Genevieve slipped off her shoes and pulled her legs onto the couch, so she was sitting crossed legged. She wiggled her shoulders into the down-filled cushion behind her until she was comfortable.

Anxious to finish her statement, Becca pressed through her thickening exhaustion. "During her years at Langston, Olivia developed into an accomplished writer. She had an idea for a novel and wanted to spend her gap year working on it." Becca sat taller, summoning the last of her energy. "I was thrilled at the prospect of her doing something creative, delving into something she loved. Her plan was to live in London and work with a successful murder mystery author, S.J. Smythe. Smythe was her best friend's mother and agreed to mentor Olivia for the year, reading and critiquing her work.

I went to England as soon as she finished her exams to help her move from Langston to London. I hadn't seen her since the previous September and was thrilled at how healthy she seemed, both physically and mentally. We spent two weeks together, settling her into her cheery apartment in Holland Park." Becca smiled as she reminisced about helping Olivia set up house.

"We had Indian food delivered, drank wine, and sang to rock and rap music blasting from her new speakers. We laughed. We talked. We shared. We cried. For the first time, I felt the loving bond with Olivia I had longed for since my daughter was born. When it was time for me to leave, I didn't want to go, and it appeared Olivia wanted me to stay. But we agreed she needed to get on with her project and I needed to get back to work. We pledged to FaceTime and visit each other as often as possible. I have wondered every day since: if I had stayed, would things have turned out differently? Those two weeks were the most cherished two weeks of my life. I'll never know if they were precious to Olivia or if she was playing me the entire time." Becca looked around the room, smiling an exhausted smile.

"Call me cynical, but yes, I was suspicious of how genuine Olivia's feelings were. What stunned me, however, is Olivia took her gap year to write a terrifying piece of fiction that she is turning into reality." Becca reached into her tapestry tote at her feet, pulled out a book with violent red ink splashed across the dustcover, and put it on the coffee table.

Everyone leaned forward to see the volume. There was an audible gasp as people read the name of the book and saw the name of the writer. It was the same book Fenton Morrissey had found in the library weeks ago. *How I Killed My Daddy.* The author's name emblazoned across the bottom was Olivia H. Conway.

For well over an hour, she barely moved a muscle. Now, watching people drift from the library, she could breathe again. Euphoria flooded to the very tips of her fingers and toes. She heard nothing but the blood rushing in her ears.

Now everyone would marvel at how clever she was. Reaching into her pants pocket, she pulled out a small squirt bottle. She spritzed the air once, twice. Sniffing, she smiled.

Out of the corner of her eye, she noticed Harrington moving onto the stables screen. He looked around, walked to the office then walked back down the aisle. She could tell he was calling out.

She grabbed her jacket, doused the lights, and dashed out of the room, down the secret passageway and out onto the back path.

THIRTY-THREE

Anxious to review Becca's testimony and immerse himself in Olivia's book, Darlington suggested they call it a day and the Scotland Yard trio headed back to the village and Wilmingrove Inn.

Remaining in the library, Philip uncorked a bottle of Bordeaux and began to pour. Before he could pour the fifth glass, Becca stood, fatigue shadowing her eyes. Succumbing to jet lag and the stress of the day, she excused herself to take a nap before dinner.

Philip, David, Duncan, and Genevieve watched Becca retreat to her room, shoulders drooping, exhaustion slowing her pace. No one spoke until everyone was sure she was out of earshot.

"So, what do you make of all of this, David?" Philip massaged his temples. "Do you think Becca's story is real or invented?"

Genevieve jumped in. "Before you answer, I have a million questions. The first of which is the big one. Why would anyone planning a murder write a book telling the world 'I'm going to commit murder and here's how I'm going to do it?' That's crazy, isn't it?"

Looking bewildered, David set his glass on the table next to him. "The whole thing's crazy. I don't know what I was expecting, but it wasn't all of this." He flailed his hands to emphasize his confusion. "If there is an Olivia, she's a maniac! She must be clinically mad. And all her life she has believed I'm her father. I... I... I'm speechless." David shook his head, then shrugged. "I don't think Becca is making this up... do you?"

"If she is, it's a complicated lie." Philip said. He drained his wine glass. "I have no idea what to make of her story."

"Mom, I think your question's a good one." Duncan stretched his long legs in front of him. "Who details their plan to murder their father in a book she then publishes? I'm assuming it wasn't just a mockup. It looks real enough."

"Oh, I know!" Genevieve grabbed her phone from the coffee table and typed furiously.

"What are you doing?" Philip leaned forward to look at Genevieve's screen.

"I'm checking Amazon to see if they have *How I Killed My Daddy*. Give me a second." Genevieve punched search and realized she was holding her breath. "Voila! Here it is! It was just published in September." She scrolled down and clicked on customer reviews. "I don't believe it. *How I Killed My Daddy* has sixty-eight reviews and four and a half stars." She looked up from her phone. Philip and David were staring at her. "Am I getting off track?" she asked, sheepish.

"Maybe a little," Philip said.

"That's interesting, though. The murder plan is selling well. Not many authors can make that claim," David laughed.

"David, on a different subject, how do you feel about seeing

Becca after all this time?" Genevieve had been wondering what was going through David's mind since Becca arrived. Today's Rebecca Harris Conway was an elegant, accomplished, woman, seemingly kind, and remorseful about her misspent youth. Genevieve wondered if David could embrace the Becca who had flown four thousand miles to come to his aid, or did the specter of Becca's old self overwhelm who she was now?

"I must say, I'm on a bit of an emotional rollercoaster. When I first saw Becca, I was wary, but relieved by her warmth and how guileless she seemed. As she began her statement, old feelings of dread and fear crept into my psyche. Then, when she described how she encouraged Olivia to believe I was her father, all the distrust and suspicion I've felt since I met her came flooding back. I think everything she said is probably true. Between Becca believing her own child could be a murderer, and Olivia's book outlining all the events, I think it's the best explanation we have."

THIRTY-FOUR

I F *How I Killed My Daddy* proved to be the guidebook for this case, the mystery just got a great deal easier to solve. Becca's testimony, however, came first. Drinking pints from the bar and gobbling crisps from a bag, Chief Superintendent Darlington, Chief Inspector MacTavish, and Inspector Franklin huddled in a small meeting room in the Wilmingrove Inn, slogging through Becca's lengthy recorded statement.

They listened to Becca's steady, polished voice for several minutes, then clicked off the recorder. Darlington asked a question, MacTavish and Franklin offered an opinion, then the three discussed the point, and jotted down follow-up questions. It was a slow, methodical process, one each of them had executed hundreds of times over their careers.

"There was an element of fiction to Ms. Conway's story that's nagging at me." A small piece of crisp danced at the corner of the Chief's mouth as he spoke. "As genuine as she seems, could anyone spend years as a highly dysfunctional youth and evolve into such a productive adult?" he posed. He believed in the effectiveness of therapy. He had seen it in his own family, but he wasn't sure he believed in miracles.

"Do we need to bring our psych people in to interview her, sir?" McTavish said.

"I've encountered my share of psychopaths, schizophrenics, people living with all kinds of neuroses, and I've been duped more than once by a clever criminal. In our business, it doesn't take long to develop a healthy skepticism of humanity and a respect for the capacity of humans to lie, but," Darlington picked at a piece of skin on his thumb and chuckled, "in my gut I believed every word of Becca's testimony. I think we're okay for now," he said.

Everyone at Wilmingrove Hall seemed helpful, forthcoming, and truthful, but somewhere in all the polite willingness to help, someone was lying. It may be just a small untruth, or even an unwitting inaccuracy, but it could be the loose bit of string that would unravel the entire ball of yarn. With Olivia's novel, that thread might be easier to find.

"So," he said to himself, "you'd better get to it.

Bleary-eyed from late night reading, Chief Superintendent Darlington nursed his first cup of coffee. Nearly alone in the inn's cozy breakfast room, he looked out over a field of late autumn weeds, browned by the recent freeze. A seasoned cop of thirty-two years, he could say, without reservation, that he had never experienced anything like this case. Lying on the table was the novel that not only reviewed what had already happened but showed how the story would end. He should be confident about the swift resolution of this case, but instead, a sense of dread sat in the pit of his stomach.

"Good morning, sir."

Darlington looked up into the earnest face of Inspector James Franklin. A tiny piece of toilet paper stuck to his skin just above his shirt collar, blooming red from a razor cut. He tapped *How I Killed My Daddy* with his index finger. "What did you think of the book, sir?"

"I'm about three quarters of the way through. What about you, Franklin?"

"I finished it."

"Really?" Darlington was impressed. Sales had gotten quite a boost yesterday when everyone downloaded the book.

"I love reading and I'm fast." He flashed a proud smile. "Wasn't it amazing to read about what's already happened? The two crimes in her story didn't turn out like she wrote them. I bet she was surprised when she found out she actually hit Sir David rather than just shooting into the car like she said in the book." Franklin's pace sped up with each word. "And when she killed Sir Mark, wow! Do you think that frightened her or was she excited to see a twist on her own story? Maybe she decided she shouldn't carry out the rest of the book. You know, we haven't heard anything from her since Sir Mark's death… except when she delivered the tankard of mead, of course," he corrected himself. Pausing to take a breath, Franklin realized Darlington was staring at him. "Sorry, sir. As you can tell, I'm excited to be working with you on this investigation."

"No, no, Inspector. Please go on. Coffee?" Darlington caught the server's eye and mimed pouring coffee, then turned his attention back to his young protege. "Tell me more. What do you think will happen next?"

Thrilled his boss was asking his opinion, Franklin offered it. "Olivia is cunning, probably brilliant, and she seems to have mastered the art of disguise. She's a chameleon who can blend into the woodwork one moment and be blatantly obvious the next, whatever the situation calls for." Stopping to gulp his coffee, Franklin looked at Darlington for any sign of approval.

The Chief nodded his encouragement.

"I'd say the most dangerous thing about Olivia is she has no moral compass. She believes Sir David is her father and he abandoned her. Nothing will stop her from revenging this slight. Thanks to her book, we know how she plans to do that and when."

The Chief sat upright as if he'd touched a live wire. "We know when she'll kill Sir David?"

"Ah, right." The lightbulb switched on. "You haven't finished the book. In the last chapter, Olivia reveals that Bonfire Day is Doomsday."

"Jesus! That's in a couple of days!" As if on cue, Darlington's phone vibrated on the table. 'Rebecca Conway,' the screen announced.

Keeping his voice calm, he answered. "Good morning, Ms. Conway. You're up early. Jet lag?"

"Good morning, Chief Superintendent. No. I was awakened by a text from Olivia." Becca's voice was tight. "I thought you'd want to know immediately."

'What did she say?"

"The message said, 'How wonderful we're on the same side of the pond, my darling mother. It's been too long. Shall we get together? How about we see each other at the funeral?'"

"Well, that's quite a message. Did you respond?"

"I did not. Should I?"

"Don't do anything until we get there. I'll be at the Hall within the hour." He swiped his napkin across his mouth as he stood. "We should be able to pull a lot of information from the text. Ms. Conway, it may not seem like it, but this is excellent news."

"Oh, Chief!" Darlington could hear Becca stifle a sob. "We have to find Olivia before she can do any more harm. She's my daughter, but I have no illusions. She's a sick, dangerous young woman. The worst thing we could do is underestimate her."

Darlington signed his bill and strode back to his room as he continued his conversation. "Ms. Conway, give me ten minutes and we'll be on our way."

Thirty minutes later, the team gathered in the library, which had turned into investigation headquarters. As two digital forensic experts arrived, Rebecca walked in holding her phone. "Anyone looking for this?" She raised the mobile for all to see.

The forensic officers looked as if Becca were about to give them a bag of gold, eyes bright with anticipation.

As Becca handed the prize to Officer Simons, the data specialist, an incoming message sounded.

A chill shot through Becca. "Should I check the text?"

"Simons, take a look," the Chief ordered.

"Ms. Conway, what's your passcode?"

"204279."

Simons unlocked the phone and tapped the message icon. He scrolled to the most recent text, then handed the phone back to Darlington. As he silently read, furrows marched across Darlington's brow.

"Chief Superintendent, is it from Olivia?" Becca gasped, realizing she had been holding her breath.

Darlington paused. When he spoke, his voice was brittle. "It is."

"And?"

He looked at Becca, then back at her phone. "She says, 'Mommy, I'm disappointed you're with Daddy and didn't invite me. I bet the makeup sex was hot! Enjoy it while you can because he won't be around much longer. By the way, I love your red cashmere pants and sweater. Blood is my favorite color.'"

Becca gasped and looked down at the crimson trousers she was wearing. "What the hell?" she whispered.

Darlington laid a notepad on the table in front of Becca. He rose from his chair and said, "I'm going to get my briefcase. I left it in the car." He strode from the room.

Becca glanced down at the pad. Written in a hasty scrawl it said:

Follow me in five minutes.
I'll meet you in the Range Rover.

Becca noted the time on the library clock and mentally added five minutes. She stood and walked to an imposing giltwood mirror hung above a low, upholstered bench next to the library doors. She surveyed her reflection, looking at her vivid sweater and matching trousers, tears burning her eyes, fear pulsing through her.

Her daughter was here, in Wilmingrove Hall. Somehow Olivia had seen her this morning. Terrifying, simply terrifying. For years, Becca had feared Olivia might be capable of violence but had clung to the hope that her child was not that damaged. But now, knowing what Olivia had done to David and to Sir Mark, an innocent bystander, she could no longer ignore her daughter's criminal insanity. Olivia was watching the residents of the Hall like ants under a magnifying glass and planning how and when she would turn the next chapter of her novel into non-fiction.

Becca glanced at her watch. Knowing Olivia might be watching her at that very moment, she pulled her shoulders back, jutted out her chin and walked out of the library.

THIRTY-FIVE

"WHAT PAGE ARE you on?" Genevieve closed her Kindle, laying both hands on top. "Finished," she said.

Not included in the morning meetings with Darlington and his team, she and Philip knew nothing of how things had progressed since last night. Understanding they would not be needed at all today, they had buried themselves in the book.

"I'm on page two ninety-seven. You're a faster reader than I am. I'll be finished in an hour. From your expression, I'd say this novel doesn't have a happy ending." Philip chuckled.

"I'm overwhelmed by how the plot mirrors the last two months. Hurry up and finish." Though she was sitting close to the fire, and had a coverlet thrown over her lap, Genevieve shivered. What she had just read chilled her. Cradling her mug in both hands, she took a long drink. The Stroh rum in her tea, helped it slide down easily.

The Grand Salon clock bonged once. Genevieve rose, folded the lap robe, and placed it over the back of her chair. She walked to Philip, who was sitting on the opposite side of the fireplace buried in the story. She needed to be close to him right now.

She took his reader from his hands and set it on his side table. Putting her hands on each arm of his chair, she leaned toward him until her lips were only a breath from his. "I'm going to take a shower." She closed the tiny gap between them. "Would you like to join me?"

"You wash my back, I'll wash yours," he said, then gave her a noisy kiss.

"Good idea." She pulled Philip out of the chair. "I think we should finish this in the shower. I'd hate for Mrs. Macintosh to pop in on us with a lunch tray. She'd never recover!"

"You're probably right. On the other hand, she may have secrets that would shock us! You realize this interruption will delay me from finishing the book."

"A small price to pay, I'd say." As Genevieve turned to walk to the bathroom, Philip gave her a hearty smack on the bottom. She stopped, looked over her shoulder and said tempting him, "I dare you to do that again, I just dare you."

Philip shot out of his chair and the chase was on!

Hair piled into a damp knot on top of her head, cheeks flushed from her romp with Philip, Genevieve was refreshed, relaxed, and energized. Black jeans hugged her lean frame, her long legs stretching from under an oversized camel sweater. She trotted down the grand staircase, anxious to see what Mrs. Lomax was cooking in the kitchen.

"Nothing like shower sex to stir up your appetite," she said out loud.

"I wouldn't know," David said from the bottom of the stairs, mischief sparking in his eyes. "At least not recently."

"David!" Heat rushed into her cheeks. "I didn't see you there… obviously!" Laughter bubbled up from deep in her throat. "I'm expecting attorney-client privilege to apply here. We shall never speak of this again, right?"

David mimed locking his lips, then threw the imaginary key over his shoulder.

She linked her arm through David's, and he matched his stride to hers as they headed to the kitchen. "Any idea what's been going on this morning?" She assumed David would have the up-to-the-minute developments.

"I know nothing."

"Really?" Genevieve pulled back in surprise and narrowed her eyes.

"No. Really. I've heard nothing. I've been in my room reading the book just like you and Philip. Well, not exactly like you and Philip." David wiggled his eyebrows and grinned at Genevieve.

She responded with a sharp punch to his arm. "Behave yourself!" She failed at looking stern and laughed in spite of herself.

"I must say, it's fascinating to read about myself being terrorized, then barbecued. Olivia is a terrific writer, but I didn't particularly like the way I was killed. Too bad her editor didn't suggest something a bit less gruesome."

"David," Genevieve looked at her friend. "We're joking about Olivia and her crazy plan, but it's a deadly serious matter. You can't be as calm as you appear."

"The whole thing seems too much like a novel to be real. I

understand I was shot in the head and Sir Mark died from Olivia's handiwork…" David's voice trailed off. "Hmm. When I say it out loud, it does sound rather sinister, doesn't it?"

"It does, indeed."

As they approached the kitchen, the smell of freshly baked bread assaulted the two famished readers. Red-faced from pulling loaves from the oven, Mrs. Lomax beamed at Genevieve and David.

"Good afternoon, my lady, Sir David. As long as you're hungry, your timing is perfect."

"We're starving!" Genevieve and David said in unison.

"We're just setting luncheon for the Chief Superintendent, his team and Ms. Conway in the library. They're going to work while they eat. Where would you two like to dine? Or is it three? Will Lord Crosswick be joining you?"

"Let me check." Genevieve pulled her phone from her jeans pocket and tapped in a text.

Almost instantly, the phone pinged.

She glanced at the screen. "Yes, Elsie. Lord Crosswick will be joining us. Let's eat in the conservatory, in front of the fire. Will that work?"

"Of course, my lady."

"Thank you, Elsie. And could you ask Mrs. MacIntosh to come see me when she has a moment, please?"

As Genevieve and David walked through the kitchen, David tore a piece of fresh baguette from a loaf and popped it into his mouth. He groaned a note of pleasure, bringing a smile to Mrs. Lomax's face.

"Still warm from the oven," David said. "Oh Elsie, will you marry me?"

"Of course, Sir David. Just let me finish up here." Still smiling, Mrs. Lomax turned back to the job at hand.

Sitting in front of a bank of screens, Olivia's wide, violet eyes watched every movement of everyone in the Hall. Her flawless skin was marred only by a slight crinkle between her brows.

She watched Daddy and Genevieve walk away from the camera toward the kitchen. Her eyes darted to an adjoining screen as the twosome came through the swinging door and into view. She could almost smell the warm bread as she watched Mrs. Lomax pull baguettes from the oven. Saliva flowed into her mouth at the thought of the steaming, yeasty flavor. She took a bite out of a pear and, with the back of her hand, wiped a trickle of juice as it slid down her chin.

And there was Duncan, alone in the library, reading her book. Thank God he hadn't left with Julia and the kids. Ahh, Alex and Ella. She missed them. Though they weren't originally in the book, she had decided to add them to the real-life plot. And then they left…too bad. Maybe next time.

She began making small alterations in how she would execute the real-life *How I Killed My Daddy.* Her mother's arrival had thrown a wrench into the scheme. After all, her mother wasn't a character in her book. She could have included Becca in the murder scheme, but her creative integrity wouldn't allow it. She would have to work around this inconvenience. It might be fun to see how much pain the sight and smell of burning flesh would cause her mother. She smiled at the thought of Becca sobbing, realizing there were no limits to the horrors her clever daughter was capable of committing. This could be fun. All the cunning psychological tricks and physical skills she had honed over her brief life were serving her well.

She wanted them to be dazzled by how brilliant and skilled she was. She wanted them to be awed by her. Just days before the climax of her story, the volcano inside her was about to erupt. She leaned back in her chair, pulled at her blond, pixie hair with both hands, and screamed, "I'm special! Love me, damn you!"

THIRTY-SIX

G ENEVIEVE'S FULL-THROATED laughter wafted into the grand salon, making Becca smile as she walked through the vast entry hall.

"They're just finishing lunch." Mrs. MacIntosh sensed Becca was looking for Philip, Genevieve, and David, and directed the American beauty to the conservatory. "Should I have Lottie bring you coffee, Ms. Conway?"

"Thank you, Mrs. MacIntosh." Becca flashed an irresistible smile. "You are pretty wonderful."

At the outset Mrs. MacIntosh hadn't known the full story about the anguish Rebecca Conway had caused Sir David over many years, but she knew enough to dislike the woman. Now, Mrs. MacIntosh was surprised how she was warming to Becca, despite her initial reservations. The more she got to know the American, the more she liked her.

Becca opened the conservatory door and stepped into the cozy room. Giggling, Genevieve stopped long enough to drain her wine glass and hold it out for a refill. The three people seated around the table looked up in unison.

"To the illustrious American who's here to save my life." David raised his glass toward Becca.

Not to be left out, Philip and Genevieve hefted their glasses to join in. "Here, here," they chimed.

"Where have you been? What have you been doing, beautiful lady?" David's cheeks and the tip of his nose looked as if they had been kissed by crimson lips.

Taking in the tipsy scene, Becca's eyes widened. "Are you three drunk?"

"Drunk? No." Philip straightened in his chair. "A little mellow, maybe, but drunk, absolutely not."

"Join us?" Genevieve shoved a chair out from under the table with her foot and motioned for Becca to sit.

"It appears I have a lot of catching up to do." Becca took the goblet David offered her, swirled the ruby liquid, then took a drink. "You realize, while you three have been eating, drinking, and leading slothful lives, I've been working like a demon to figure out if my daughter is executing her novel as she wrote it or writing a new chapter as we speak?"

"You're right," David said. "While you're doing the difficult things, we three are drowning our fears."

There was a loud knock, and the door opened before anyone could say, "Come in." Chief Superintendent Darlington and Sean Harrington strode in, carrying Olivia's book and filling the room with tense energy.

"Is something wrong, Chief Superintendent?" Philip stood, his wine buzz vanishing.

"I wouldn't say 'wrong.' We have some new information that

could explain the mystery behind the Purdey rifle that was used to shoot Sir David. Mr. Harrington, please." Darlington pulled a chair up to the table, sat, and motioned for Harrington to do the same.

"Lord Crosswick," Harrington began. "Do you remember in September, just before Sir David was shot, a police officer came to Wilmingrove Hall to start the transfer of all the gun licenses from the former Earl to you?"

Completely sober now, Philip squinted his eyes, thinking. "Yes, yes, I do. It was the day we arrived at the Hall. It seems like years ago."

"Remember, Philip, I was in the middle of the tour of the house, and you called me to join you."

"Right." Harrington pointed to Genevieve and nodded. "As I remember, the police officer had all the appropriate identification and was very professional. She wanted to see where the shotguns are secured, where we keep the key to the gun safe and how many duplicate keys there are. She asked all the right questions about gun maintenance, who used the guns and how often they were used. All the questions the police routinely ask."

Genevieve recalled that day with a roll of her eyes. "She spent at least fifteen minutes lecturing on procedure and gun safety. She went on and on and on."

"The first time we interviewed Mr. Harrington," Darlington explained, "he told us about the visit. If it weren't for Olivia's book, we would never have circled back to him. But what he told us mirrors the chapter in Olivia's book."

Slack-jawed, Philip looked at Darlington. "I read the part about how she got the Purdey rifle. How did I not connect the dots?"

"In all fairness, darling, we had just arrived and were pretty overwhelmed with just being here. And that was quite a while ago."

"I agree with Lady Crosswick. But I do need you both to think back." Darlington pressed on. "How did she get a key to the gun safe? Mr. Harrington told me his recollection of how it could have happened. I need for you, Lord Crosswick, to search your memory for any opportunity she had to make an impression of the key. As I understand it, you went back to the house, Lady Crosswick. Is that correct?"

"Yes."

"Lord Crosswick, please tell me what you remember."

Philip rested his elbow on the table and cradled his chin in his hand. Looking at nothing, he tried to recall that day in the estate office. Light flickered in his eyes as he began to remember. "As I recall, I went with you, Sean, to help Andrew Frazier with one of the Harris hawks. Kafritz would have been alone in the office then. When we left, she was checking the inventory list against the guns in the safe and the key was on the desk. We were gone ten, maybe fifteen minutes, plenty of time for her to take an impression of the key. When we got back, she had finished the inventory. She stayed long enough for Sean to sign a couple of forms, then she left." Philip sat back and laid both hands on the table palms down.

"Do you remember what she looked like?" Darlington gave no hint of whether or not he already had a description.

"Oh! I can tell you exactly what she looked like." Genevieve jumped in. "Without a doubt, she was one of the homeliest women

I've ever seen. She had mousy brown hair, and she wore thick glasses that looked a bit like she had an artificial nose attached to them. Her police uniform was too big on her small frame."

Darlington smiled at Genevieve's vivid description. He pulled a photo from the pocket of his jacket and handed it to her. "I took this from the dust cover of Olivia's book."

"I'm anxious to see what you think, Lady Crosswick," Harrington said. "When the Chief showed me the picture of Olivia, I couldn't believe it was the same person."

Genevieve's eyes hardened. "Oh, yeah. Olivia could change her hair. She could make her nose bigger. She may even have altered her teeth somewhat, but that mouth. Kafritz had the same mouth."

"Exactly!" Harrington shouted. "I was gobsmacked what sexy lips she had, especially for such an, um, uh, unattractive woman." He looked at his shoes, hoping his words weren't too coarse.

Genevieve smiled at him then passed the photo to Philip.

He gazed at Olivia's mouth. "I think you're right, Sean. Becca, do you think this is possible?"

"Of course, it is." Becca's shoulders slumped. "My daughter's always been good at changing her appearance and she's very clever."

"She is that, Ms. Conway." Darlington had the rapt attention of the people around the table. Each leaned forward, elbows balanced on the table's edge.

"When I finished the book this morning, I wondered how much you can trust Olivia's novel to be her actual plan." Becca's mouth drew down at the corners. "Do you think she'll stay true to her plot, or do you think she'll deviate from it?" Becca asked. "What's your best guess?"

"Ms. Conway, your daughter is a shrewd adversary. She's talented and smart and, I fear, has skills that will make it challenging to disrupt her plan. According to our forensic psychologists Olivia will follow her plot as closely as possible. The shrinks said she feels her novel is flawless, so her ego won't allow her to alter it, unless there's a compelling reason. Our strategy is to follow the storyline and snare her before the climax."

Darlington pulled himself away from the door jamb where he had been leaning. He looked down at his well-buffed brogues, then at the group. "As I told you last week, we appreciate how you have all done your utmost to cooperate, which leads me to extend an invitation for this evening. Would you all please join me for dinner at the Lion and Lamb?"

"Oh, I love that pub!" Genevieve clapped her hands in delight. "That would be wonderful. You will be off duty, right?"

"We will, indeed. It's just a small thank you for your hospitality."

"Totally unnecessary, but we look forward to it. Thank you," Philip glanced at Genevieve. "I think there's more to this invitation than meets the eye," his arched eyebrow said.

"Shall we say half seven?' Darlington shrugged on his overcoat. "I'll take my leave now. I have some calls to make, but I'll see you all this evening."

At that, Philip, Genevieve, Duncan, David, and Becca raised their glasses and with a hearty "cheers," toasted to the night ahead.

THIRTY-SEVEN

CHIEF SUPERINTENDENT FRANCIS Darlington, Chief Inspector Morris MacTavish, and Inspector James Franklin walked through the door of the Lion and Lamb at 7:15 p.m., fifteen minutes before their guests would arrive.

"You old plonker!" A stout, ruddy-faced man greeted Darlington like an old friend, which indeed he was. Reid Moore, the publican, wore slouchy tweed pants and a cabled turtleneck sweater that had seen better days. He had spent thirty years with the Met before retiring to the Yorkshire Moors, where he had grown up. After a year's search for the ideal English village, he fell in love with Wilmingrove and bought the Lion and Lamb. Dating from 1789, it was a picture postcard pub, long cherished by the county and beyond. With a thatched roof and ivy-covered stone, the alehouse sat in the middle of an untidy English garden, which provided a haven for butterflies, bees, and hummingbirds all summer. But now, as the autumn wound down, tight pods of spent blossoms clung to browning marigold stems and the last roses of the summer faded almost as soon as their buds opened. As the weather cooled, ferns that filled the gaping mouth of the fireplace throughout the summer were replaced by the glow of fire in the grate. In the place of honor, just to the right side of the hearth, a round table was set for six, bearing a 'reserved' sign that was hard to miss.

"Reid, this is perfect. Thank you, mate." Darlington slapped his friend on the back. "Did you know Lord and Lady Crosswick like your little hole in the wall? They were pleased when I told them where we were having dinner."

Reid beamed. "They've been here four or five times. It isn't bad for business to have our county peers pop in now and then. The locals get excited about brushing elbows with the rich and famous."

Chief Superintendent Darlington pulled Reid into an alcove and spoke in a low voice. "It was brilliant of you to suggest we meet here, mate. It's possible we could snare her tonight." Since he arrived in Wilmingrove over a week ago, Darlington had dined most evenings at the Lion and Lamb, discussing the details of the case over bangers and mash and a good local stout. Using his years of experience, Moore had given his perspective on the investigation. Fresh eyes were always welcome.

By 7:30, the pub was full of drinkers and diners, many of whom had been loyal supporters of the Lion and Lamb for generations. When he purchased the landmark pub, Reid had given every wall a new coat of paint and polished every piece of wood and brass, giving the watering hole a sparkle without changing the essence of the classic tavern. The menu still provided standard pub grub, but his talented chef peppered the bill of fare with gourmet specialties, resulting in an influx of younger diners. The expanded wine list became an attraction as well.

Surveying the three connecting rooms, Darlington took an inventory of the patrons. Most tables were filled, with about eighty-five to ninety people packing the alehouse. The seven waitstaff were all attractive, young, and each wore a white shirt with the pub's logo on the left breast pocket, black jeans, and a knee-length black apron.

"They've all been working for me since I bought the pub, so Olivia can't pose as a waiter," Reid told Darlington. He had confirmed the kitchen staff as well, all five being long-term employees.

Darlington's sharp eyes moved from table to table, person to person. He saw withered and fresh-faced, smart, and dowdy. At most tables, people were enjoying themselves, full of laughter, smiles, and energy. Faces glowed from drink and the warmth of the rooms. People flirted and leaned into each other for intimate conversations. He saw two women, heads together, sharing gossip while their partners had a heated Premier League discussion about the merits of Leeds and New Castle. In a corner booth a family of five laughed at their toddler, face smeared with shepherd's pie.

The Chief Superintendent ducked, walking through a low door into a smaller dining room with six tables, each a four top. Two of the tables had been pushed together to accommodate a party of six. The room had three small windows along the wall to his left, that overlooked the carpark. At the far end was a small fireplace where embers waited for a few sticks of wood to spark them back to life. Darlington identified no one as suspicious.

He looked into the taproom, where about forty people, mostly men, gathered near the bar, some playing darts, others dealing cards. He noticed one young woman of Olivia's build, but her hair was long and raven. It could have been a wig, but her features were coarser than Olivia's. She was in a brutal battle at the pool table with a lad whose tattooed arms told the story of Lady Godiva and her infamous horseback ride.

"I don't think that's our girl," Darlington said to himself, turning back to the main dining room just as his guests walked in.

Two beautiful women and three handsome men coming through the door were enough to capture the attention of the diners within view. For a moment, there was a sharp drop in conversation as patrons swiveled their heads to observe the newcomers. Many people recognized the Earl and Countess of Crosswick, and the brief silence turned to an excited buzz.

Much to his surprise, Darlington found himself warmed at the sight of his five guests. He moved across the room, hand outstretched. "Welcome! Welcome. I'm pleased you could come tonight."

Reid came up behind him and slapped his back. "Lord and Lady Crosswick, the Lion and Lamb is so happy you're spending the evening with us, thanks to my old mate, Francis."

Darlington beamed as he explained his connection to Reid. "We've known each other since we were young, dashing sergeants together at the Met. I've been using Reid as a sounding board on this case, tapping his keen cop mind to help us think outside the box."

"I had no idea you two knew each other." Philip's expression was a mix of surprise and delight. He liked each man and was comforted knowing they were both looking out for David's welfare.

Darlington completed the introductions and Reid escorted the group to the fireside table.

"Reid, this is perfect." Genevieve admired the blazing fall centerpiece. "What stunning flowers. I can't imagine a more inviting setting."

The pub owner beamed. "Thank you, Lady Crosswick. I'm pleased everything is to your liking. My wife will be delighted you like the posies. She attends to all the details that make the Lion and Lamb a special place."

"Is she here? I could tell her myself."

"She took the night off. Her sister is visiting from Gretna Green. If they come in, I'll be sure to introduce them." Reid was the quintessential host, just the right amount of familiarity, charm, and warmth. "Unless you object, Francis has asked our chef to prepare a tasting menu for you. Is that all right with everyone?"

Agreement was unanimous.

Two servers approached the table and filled each Champagne glass with Veuve Clicquot.

"Oh my!" Genevieve's eyes sparkled. "My favorite!"

Becca held her glass aloft. "Mine, too," she said. "We have a

French friend whose family has been supplying grapes to Veuve Clicquot for six generations. When you ask him if he would ever drink Dom Perignon, he says, 'Perhaps I would drink Dom Perignon if all the Veuve Clicquot were gone and if all the water were tainted!'"

The table roared with laughter.

Darlington stood to offer a toast. "To an extraordinary case and its successful conclusion. But most of all to the House of Crosswick and all who dwell within."

With resounding "Cheers," everyone clinked glasses and drank.

With his back to the fire, Darlington scanned the room. He had a full view of the main dining room. Though people kept glancing at their table, the attention appeared to be curiosity rather than malice. He was about to sit when he noticed a woman he had not seen earlier. Seated alone near the door to the taproom, she was plump with graying brown hair pinned into a topknot. Her clothes, though dowdy, were clean and tidy. Next to her on the floor was an oversized tapestry bag. Rimless, rose-tinted glasses hid her eyes.

Darlington excused himself. "I'll be back in just a moment," he said. Before he reached the kitchen, Reid came through the swinging door carrying a tray of amuse bouche.

"I need to talk to you." Darlington snarled. "I spotted someone, and I need to see if you know her, if she's a regular."

Reid stopped a server heading into the kitchen. "Michael, take these to the Crosswicks' table." He handed off the tray and turned his attention to where Darlington nodded.

He squinted at the frumpy diner. "I don't recognize her," he said. "Let me see if she had a reservation or is a walk-in. We only had one or two tables unreserved for this evening."

He sauntered through the lounge, stopping at tables, chatting with patrons on his way to the hostess stand. Glancing over the reservation list, he saw table four, where the woman in question sat, had been reserved earlier that day. A definite red flag.

Reid walked to the table next to number four, where a couple was in the midst of a lively conversation. He asked them if they were enjoying themselves, the woman said something witty in response and the three laughed.

He turned and sauntered to table four. "Good evening."

Hunched over her meal, it took the woman several seconds to realize Reid was addressing her. When she glanced up, she looked startled, her eyes magnified by her thick glasses.

"I'm Reid Moore, the proprietor of the Lion and Lamb. I believe this is your first time dining with us, isn't it?" Reid smiled and leaned casually on the table.

"I—I—I'm having a brilliant time, thank you," she mumbled. She looked up at Reid, offering a shy smile. "It's my birthday, you see, so I thought I'd give myself a special treat. I've always wanted to come to the Lion and Lamb, but one doesn't like to dine alone."

Caught off-guard by the woman's lack of guile, Reid took her hand. "We're honored you would choose to spend your birthday with us. May I ask your name?"

Color bloomed in her cheeks. "Mary. Mary Sloan." She smiled. "I'm hoping my daughter can join me in time for pudding. She works late at the hospital but thought she could get away."

"I'll cross my fingers that she makes it. Thank you for honoring us this evening, Mary Sloan. I hope it's the first of many more occasions you share with us. If there is anything you need, please let our servers know. And I am always at your service." Reid squeezed her hand, nodded, and turned away from her table. As he headed back to the kitchen, he stopped a waiter. "Take a glass of Champagne to table four. It's complimentary." Reid wanted to make certain Mary Sloan felt special tonight.

"Well, she's not Olivia," he said to himself. He caught Darlington's eye as he walked by the Crosswick's table and subtly shook his head.

Darlington nodded in response but couldn't resist confirming Reid's conclusion for himself. As he sauntered toward Mary's table, she pulled her cell phone from her tote. He stood by the hostess stand and heard her say, "Oh, pet. I'm so disappointed. I was looking forward to you joining me. The restaurant is just lovely, and the proprietor has been so nice to me."

Darlington could see disappointment cloud her face and he dismissed her as a threat. He and Reid were a good team.

At the fireside table, the courses came and went, each perfect morsel more delicious than the last. Wine flowed and laughter came easily. Around the table, there was a sense of release after so many days of intense conversations and fear of the unknown. The group was loud and jolly and enjoying themselves. By eleven o'clock, they were alone in the dining room.

Ready to bring the revelers back to reality, Chief Super-intendent Darlington began to review the events of the last two days. He talked about Becca receiving the texts from Olivia and about the cameras planted throughout Wilmingrove Hall.

"We thought Olivia would come to the Lion and Lamb tonight in disguise, but it doesn't look like that happened," Reid interjected.

With each disclosure, the light-hearted mood of the evening faded a bit more and the reality of imminent danger came clawing back.

Her eyes glossed with tears, Genevieve brought her hands to her cheeks. "Chief, reading Olivia's book has made a grisly ending seem inevitable. You can't let anything happen to David."

Before he spoke, Francis Darlington, sat straighter in his chair, took a deep breath, then released it. It was difficult to read the look on his face. When he spoke, his voice was measured, steady, and firm.

"We cannot for one minute assume Olivia Conway's objective is anything but homicidal. She has twice proven her intentions, so we must believe she will not be satisfied until Sir David is dead. If she continues to execute her plot, then we can expect her to lure Sir David to a bonfire on Guy Fawkes Day, November 5TH and incinerate him. *Our* goal is to prevent her from accomplishing that."

Darlington's candor sobered the group.

Silence blanketed the table until a server approached. "Excuse me, Reid," the young man said. "A woman left these for you." He held out a beautifully wrapped package about the size of a book, and Mary Sloan's tapestry bag.

"Interesting." Reid looked at Darlington then down at the bag.

Always prepared, Darlington pulled a pair of plastic gloves from his jacket pocket and tossed them to Reid, who put them on and unlatched the satchel.

"Jesus," Reid said, peering into the bag.

"What is it?" the others asked in unison.

Reid pulled out a thick notecard. He read it then handed it to Darlington.

"What does it say?" Genevieve's eyes were wide with dread.

"It says, 'Thank you for the glass of Champagne. It was a lovely touch. O'"

Next, Reid held up a brown and gray top-knotted wig, then a frumpy flowered dress and last, a pair of tinted glasses. "Shit," he said under his breath. "Shit."

"Open the package, Reid," Darlington directed.

He ripped the crimson paper off, tossed it on the table, and held up a copy of *How I Killed My Daddy*. He opened the book to a notecard, which marked the first page of the last chapter. The notecard read:

It was such fun seeing you all tonight.
You looked like you were having such a good time.
The story is almost over
and you know how it ends…
in a blaze of glory!
Yours,
Olivia

Intoxicated by power, Olivia raced her Ducati down dark lanes through the Yorkshire countryside, banking around curves toward her secret command post in the walls of Wilmingrove Hall. Swaying with each bend in the road, she slalomed from side to side and relished the wind ruffling the short locks on her helmetless head. She laughed into the bank of air, exhilarated. She had them all fooled. They were confused and frightened with no idea what to do next. She was smarter than all of them and they were her stupid little pawns.

She geared down as she approached the back lane to the stable. The engine's throaty rumble sent a thrill up her spine. This had been a good night.

With the surge of adrenaline waning, a sudden wave of exhaustion swept over her. She rolled her Ducati through the narrow entry way to the abandoned storage shed. She pulled a tarp over the bike, piled three bales of hay around it, and closed the door behind her as she walked out. Overwhelmed with fatigue, she could barely drag herself up the stairs to her cozy room over the barn. Too tired to pull back her bed linens, she collapsed onto her bedspread. Within seconds, she was deep in a dreamless sleep.

THIRTY-EIGHT

WHILE CHIEF SUPERINTENDENT Darlington called his Met team from their beds and ordered them to gather at the Lion and Lamb, MacTavish, Franklin and three local constables escorted the three Warwicks, David and Becca to Wilmingrove Hall. To confirm Olivia was not lurking in the house, the police swept the Hall before allowing the residents to go in. To assure no one could enter or exit without their knowledge, officers were posted at each door.

Bustling about, preparing a hot toddy for herself, Mrs. MacIntosh looked up from the tea kettle as five frightened people walked into the comforting warmth of the kitchen.

"This is the perfect place to be right now." Genevieve pulled out a chair and plopped down with a heavy thud, propping her elbow on the table, her head in her hand.

"You all look dreadful," Mrs. MacIntosh said. "The evening was a bit botched, was it? Sit down, all of you. I believe a cup of tea is in order." Mrs. MacIntosh was in mother mode, chiding everyone to be seated. She delivered tea to the table along with a bottle of Dalmore Scotch. "For medicinal purposes," she said.

"We're absolutely gutted, Mrs. Mac," David said. "Olivia was at the restaurant the entire evening in a disguise. All the coppers were looking for her, thinking she might show, but none of us had a clue that the middle-aged frump at table number four was Olivia."

"My goodness. What a shock for all of you." Mrs. MacIntosh patted David on the back and handed him a cup of tea.

Becca stared into the room. "What kind of mother doesn't recognize her own daughter?" Tears filled her eyes, a lone drop plopping in her lap.

David covered her hand with his and squeezed. "I won't allow you to fault yourself for not knowing that a dowdy, forty-something matron was your beautiful twenty-year-old daughter. That's absurd!" He was gentle but firm.

"But—" Becca started.

"But nothing," Duncan interrupted. "David's right. Unless you sat with her and had a conversation, there's no way you could have known. And even then, you may not have realized it was Olivia. That girl is talented!"

"She should have been on the stage!" Genevieve agreed. "The productive thing to do right now is figure out ways to help Darlington find Olivia before she does any further harm. Focusing on that will make us all feel better."

Philip leaned forward in his chair. "The Crosswick family motto is 'Garde Le Roi.' Guard the king. In this case, David, you're the king and we're here to guard you. Of course, the real line of defense is the Met. They're good, David, really good."

THIRTY-NINE

CHIEF SUPERINTENDENT DARLINGTON sat with his back to the fireplace, a stoked blaze sparking back to life on the hearth. Around the table were six groggy forensic specialists, including two technology experts and Reid Moore.

Every muscle in Francis Darlington's body tensed. A toxic combination of frustration and anger throbbed in his temples. Olivia's wig, her dress, and spectacles lay lifeless as a corpse in the middle of the table that, less than an hour ago, was surrounded by high energy, laughing people. Next to the pile, the dustcover on her novel screamed, "How I Killed My Daddy!", taunting the group of seasoned detectives.

Glancing around the table, Darlington began. "Here's what we know. Olivia Harris Conway was on the premises tonight for at least two hours. During that time, she was disguised as a middle-aged matron treating herself to a birthday dinner. Always the consummate host, but sadly not a very clever chap, Reid gave her a glass of Champagne on the house!"

"Way to go, Reid!" The group hissed, booed, and banged on the table, razzing the former detective.

Darlington allowed himself a robust laugh, reveling in his mate's embarrassment, then he held up a hand. "Okay, okay, lads. Settle down. We've all read Olivia Conway's book. Assuming she follows her story, we know how she intends to proceed."

Darlington reached across the table and picked up the copy of *How I Killed My Daddy*. Next to it, Olivia's wig looked like a curled-up cat. "Franklin, you've thought a lot about this novel. Or should I say, autobiography. I think it would be useful if you read the last couple of pages to everyone. Do you mind?"

"Of course not, sir." Surprised by his Chief's suggestion, Franklin took the book from Darlington's outstretched hand. "You know, sir, this is going to be weird, because it's written in first person."

"That's fine, Franklin. You don't have to read in a lassie's voice." A wave of laughter circled the table.

Pulling his glasses from his rumpled shirt pocket, Franklin cleared his throat and began to read.

> *The night is perfection—black as the inside of a buried coffin. I'm waiting. I'm waiting for my Daddy. Every few minutes the sky explodes with fireworks, turning the night to day. I flatten myself into the shadows so I can't be seen. Aha, here he comes. He still has my note in his hand. It's hard to believe someone so clever could be stupid enough to fall for my little ruse, but curiosity is a powerful drive. 'Come meet me behind the bonfire.' I wrote. 'I'll make it worth your while.' Then I*

signed it with lipsticky lips. I thought maybe that was too much, but it worked. By now, I'm sure he wants to know who his temptress is.

"Hello, Daddy," I say. I'm impressed how much I sound like Mommy.

He's still walking toward me. He's just a few feet away now. I put the dart blower in my mouth. I inhale and taste the bitter fumes from the curare, then blow out with all my might… thwap! Right in the neck. Just as the sky cracks with a kaleidoscope of reds, greens, yellows, he sees my face. The shocked surprise in his eyes makes me laugh. He wafts to the ground like a pricked balloon.

Now for the fun. My very own grownup doll. My tapestry satchel holds everything I need. Here's the black cape, black hat, and wig. The creepy Guy Fawkes mask is the cherry on the sundae.

"Daddy, I need you to sit up so I can drape the cape around your shoulders. Oh, my. Hi. It didn't occur to me that you'd be looking at me. Of course, you're not dead…yet. Let's get your mask on so I don't have to see you watching me. Now the wig. The hat should be at a jaunty angle, don't you think? Let's put the elastic under your chin. Ooo. Sorry. I didn't mean to snap it like that, but you can't feel it anyway, can you? You look good."

I fold my tongue into my lower lip. My piercing whistle cuts through the noisy night and four local tipsy boys pop out of the shadows. It's amazing the talent a few quid and a nickel bag will buy you.

"Okay, boys. Let's get this mannequin on the bonfire. You, there. You with the Man City t-shirt and you with the tats, take his arms. And you two each take a leg. Let's go! I'll watch you from here."

The climax is so close now I can taste it. I can taste the metallic tang of blood. My heart is beating so fast, I gasp for air. I'm trying to count the thuds pulsing in my neck, but it's impossible.

As I watch the four lads carrying Daddy to the back of the bonfire, I don't know how they're staying upright. They're staggering, they're stumbling. But they are moving forward and are there at last. Now if they can just get him onto the pile.

Here we go.

One swing.

Two swings.

Three swings and up. Good for them!

And the timing is perfect. On the front side where all the people are standing, the mayor is touching his blazing torch to the pile, unaware Daddy is lying helpless on the opposite side.

The bonfire bursts with color and heat. The flames dance and surge higher and higher, devouring leaves and twigs and branches. It's creeping toward him.

I plop down on the ground, so dizzy from the thrill I think I may faint. I sniff the air for the telltale sign the raging beast is devouring Daddy. His sweet smell wafts to me on the night air. As the life leaves his body, I feel his spirit come to me, infuse me with all that he was.

I look one last time at the inferno, pick up my satchel and walk back into the black of the night.

Inspector Franklin closed the book and laid it on the table. No one spoke. His throat parched from reading aloud, Franklin took a long swallow of water. "Sir, if Ms. Conway adheres to her storyline, we have to find her before Bonfire Day. That's tomorrow."

FORTY

Genevieve and Becca trotted across the meadow on a matched pair of black Friesians, Onyx and Dutch, drops of frosty moisture spraying from their hooves, as they pranced through the pasture. After spending days cloistered in Wilmingrove Hall putting the pieces of a bizarre mystery together, it was a joy to breath crisp air and feel the chill of autumn.

The women whooped with laughter as they nudged their horses into a gallop. The release was exhilarating. They raced along a ridge overlooking the Hall, until they came to a stream that flowed into the dense forest at the eastern border of the estate. They reined their steeds to a halt. The magnificent horses tossed their heads, anxious to continue.

"That was the best thing I've done in days!" Genevieve gasped.

Becca had to catch her breath before she spoke. "My God! I haven't ridden like that for years! I've forgotten how spectacular it is to fly across the earth on a gorgeous animal like Onyx."

Genevieve pulled on her reins to turn Dutch around, then pressed her calves into his side to spur him forward. Over her shoulder, she yelled to Becca, "Last one to the river buys breakfast!" and she streaked off down the slope toward the riverbank.

FORTY-ONE

STILL DOZING, WAFTING in and out of fragments of dreams, Duncan heard his phone ping, announcing a text. He ignored it. A few seconds later it sounded again, urging him to look at the message.

Eyes still closed, moving as few muscles as possible, he groped the side table until he felt the coolness of his iPhone. He opened one eye and looked at the screen. He blinked, opened both eyes and read:

"Duncan, we're at the stable. Come ASAP. Darlington discovered information that will lead us to Olivia."

He read the text twice, then glanced at his watch. It was 7:30 a.m.

He stumbled out of bed and into the bathroom, where he splashed water on his face, brushed his teeth, and patted water on his bed-ruffled hair before pulling his clothes on. He wrapped a muffler twice around his neck and tucked the ends into his black wool duffle coat as he loped down the grand staircase.

He couldn't imagine what Darlington had discovered between midnight and seven o'clock this morning. But, given the serious character of Francis Darlington, Duncan assumed whatever had been uncovered was important. As he dashed onto the terrace, he passed Lottie coming in from the herb garden.

"Lottie," he said, keeping his pace. "If you see Lady Crosswick, would you please tell her I'm meeting Chief Superintendent and my dad at the stable?"

"Of course, sir. I'll tell her as soon as I see her." The fresh-faced kitchen helper was always eager to please.

He headed for the series of stairs leading down the hill to the stable and saw Genevieve and Becca on two black stallions, trotting across the field away from the barn. They had talked last night about going on an early ride. He smiled, watching them canter toward the ball of sun, inching above the horizon.

Deep in thought, Duncan walked into the stable, glad he'd stay at Wilmingrove Hall until everything was resolved. It took him several seconds to realize the only sounds in the barn were the normal rhythms of horses eating oats, swishing their tails, blowing raspberries and the occasional whinny. There was no sign of Darlington or Philip.

"Chief Superintendent Darlington," Duncan called out. At the end of the double row of stalls, a horse snorted.

"Dad," Duncan bellowed, hoping to hear a response.

Behind him, a sweet voice cooed, "Hey cuz. It's wonderful to see you."

Duncan whipped around at the saccharine sound, just as he heard the whistle of a dart pierce the air, followed by a sharp pain under his jaw. In an instant, his muscles began to relax. He gasped and took a tentative step forward, discovering he had little control over his body. He hovered for a moment, then crumpled to the wide-planked walnut floor. Though his body had abandoned him, his mind was even sharper than usual. He forced himself to focus on Olivia's angelic face and knew his terror must be evident in his eyes.

Olivia dropped to her knees beside Duncan's limp body. She leaned down on all fours until her cheek was on the floor and she was nose to nose with Duncan. She said nothing, just stared into Duncan's panic-filled eyes until, at last, she whispered, "I bet you're so surprised." She lingered for what seemed like forever, a demented smile curling her blood-red lips. "I have an exciting morning planned for us."

Duncan's mind raced to Olivia's book, trying to remember why he was paralyzed and why he—and not David—was here with Olivia.

As if reading his mind, Olivia said, "Curare, Duncan. You're paralyzed by curare. I don't know how long it will last. I tried to give you a dose that would just paralyze you until I can get you on my little bonfire. You're going to make a beautiful blaze!'

Olivia sat up, clapping her hands with glee. "I bet you thought David was going to be the Burning Man!" She cackled, eyes wide and blazing. "Let me tell you a little story. For such a long time I thought David was my father. I ached for him to love Mommy and me, he didn't even know I was alive until I got his attention. I know that now. My book was published before I knew about you and your very perfect family. Your perfect parents and perfect Julia and perfect little Alex and Ella. You all make me sick." She shook her head as if to refocus. "After my Uncle Conner read

How I Killed My Daddy, he sent me a long letter explaining that David wasn't my father. He said he was the only one in the world, besides my mother, who knew Jonathon Laney, the 12ᵀᴴ Earl of Crosswick, had sired me, as they say in your circles. Conner's a psychiatrist. I think he was afraid I was going to execute my book and he was right, of course. But when he told me the truth, well," she shrugged her shoulders, "I had to change my plot a bit. It didn't take long for me to realize you're the one. You're the one who has to go. There can only be one special one in the Crosswick line and I'm it. Besides, I'm the real heir." She clinched her teeth and growled. "Wilmingrove and all of this belongs to me, not to you."

The more she spoke, the more frightened Duncan became, her madness filling the stable like a suffocating vapor. Breathing as deeply as he could, he tried to calm himself. Keeping his wits might be his only chance to survive.

"Well, our moms will be back soon, and we don't want to run into them. And, since I'm not sure if I've given you too much or too little curare or if it's just the right amount, I'd better get busy." Olivia hopped to her feet. She jogged down the aisle toward the far end of the stable and was gone.

"What the hell?" Duncan's mind raced. "Surely somebody will come before she moves me or I die, whichever comes first." Duncan listened for any sound but heard nothing.

At last, he felt, more than heard, a faint rhythm on the wood floor. The rumble of tires? Maybe it was Darlington or one of his men. He closed his eyes and focused on the intensifying rhythm of whatever was coming. The low whomp, whomp, whomp morphed into a soft hum, then amplified into the gentle whine Duncan recognized as an electric motor. The sound bore down on him until it came to an abrupt stop. Then, slowly, it jerked toward him until he sensed a nudge in his upper back and thighs.

"Damn! I don't quite have the hang of this yet." Olivia sounded annoyed. She walked around and squatted in front of him. Grabbing his jacket in her right hand, his jeans in her left, she pulled him toward her until he was balancing on his left side. "That should do it," she said, giving Duncan a pat on the cheek. The engine started again. There was another nudge, and again, Olivia bent over him, but this time she rolled him away from her, so he was on his back.

Olivia could see the confusion in Duncan's eyes when he realized what she was doing. "Can you believe it, Duncan?"

Her open-mouthed grin filled Duncan with horror.

"You're going for a ride on a forklift. La, la, la, la, la, la." She sang a little ditty while she figured out how to raise the forks. "Just give me a minute and we'll be on our way. I love this little forklift. It's perfect for doing things in the stable, but it isn't as easy to drive as I thought it would be. Not to worry, practice makes perfect. I know it's not for outdoor use, but I think it will be just fine to get you down to the river. Next stop, your blaze of glory!"

Olivia started the forklift, put it into gear and rolled slowly toward the stable door. Duncan lay on his back like a ragdoll, limp legs hanging over one prong, the other tine supporting his back. He lolled back and forth with the rhythm of the lift, his head hanging back between his arms, elongating his neck, and exposing his throat.

Once out of the barn, Olivia turned left, away from the Hall. She accelerated onto the gravel path, which sloped to the river's edge. For the last few days, the Wilmingrove Hall grounds staff had been gathering forest debris, which they would float down the river and add to the town's ever-growing pile. Little had they known they were creating a funeral pyre right here at the Hall.

She was unhappy about having to change the timing of her storyline. She loathed having the blaze during daylight but, knowing Darlington was closing in on her, she didn't feel she had a choice. The fire wouldn't be as glorious during the day as it would be at night, but it was the best she could do under the circumstances. Sometimes you had to make concessions, just like she had to change her victim.

As they bumped along, Olivia belted out the words to the primal rhythm of Talking Heads' "Burning Down the House". She pumped her shoulders, her left hand pounding out the beat on the steering wheel.

FORTY-TWO

THE SKY STILL blushed with a hint of pink when Philip set out on an early morning walk to survey the Wilmingrove Hall grounds. In his green Barbour jacket and wellies, he looked like an ad from *Horse and Hound*. With him were King George and Prince Albert, the matching pair of Labrador Retrievers Harrington had trained to perfection.

The dogs raced ahead of Philip, barking, and chasing each other. Circling back, they would streak by their master before shooting out again across the field. The more Philip wandered the estate, the more he could feel it in his blood. He was getting to know the hills, the valleys, the fields, the streams, and had befriended a two-hundred-year-old tree on the property. His love for his family's land grew each time he ventured out. Standing on a knoll surveying his estate, he saw Becca and Genevieve on horseback, walking through a meadow. He pulled his phone from his pocket and was just about to take a photo of the two riders just as it rang.

Julia's picture filled the screen and he answered.

"Thank God, Philip! I've been trying to get ahold of Duncan and he's not answering."

Hearing the alarm in Julia's voice, Philip was on high alert. "What's the matter? What's happened?"

"Listen, Philip. This is important."

"I'm listening, Julia."

"Last night when I walked into the playroom, the kids were playacting they had a room full of computers and they were watching everyone in Wilmingrove Hall. They had set up boxes, pretending they were monitors and they were describing what was happening on each screen. When I asked them where they got the idea, Ella said it was like the room inside the walls in Wilmingrove Hall." Her panic reached across the ocean. "Philip, there is a statue in the music room that opens a panel in the wall. The ballerina."

Philip whistled the dogs to him and raced toward the Hall. "The surveillance equipment is somewhere in the walls?"

"I believe Olivia set up a room of monitors and has been watching our every move from inside the house."

"Julia, I've got to call Darlington. I'll call you as soon as I have anything to tell you."

"And have Duncan call me as soon as you see him."

Lungs on fire, Philip burst through the Hall's kitchen door. Mrs. Lomax stopped midway through pulling a tray of cinnamon buns from the oven, her eyes popping at the Earl's frantic entrance.

"Is Darlington here?" Philip barked, his face crimson.

"I don't know if he's arrived yet." Mrs. Lomax wiped her hands on her apron. "If he's not here, he's on his way. What's wrong? Something's wrong."

Ignoring her questions, Philip ordered, "I need to see him as soon as he gets here." He pushed through the swinging kitchen door and smashed into Sean Harrington. "Come with me, Sean," Philip commanded.

As the two men bolted to the music room, Philip briefed Harrington on his new information. Philip walked straight to the ballerina, pulled backward on the statue and the panel slid open.

"Did you know we had secret passages in the Hall?"

From Harrington's look of surprise, Philip guessed the answer.

"I did not, my lord." A bark of laughter escaped Harrington's throat. "This is absolutely brilliant!"

"I don't think we should go in until Darlington gets here." Philip was trying his best not to storm headlong into what might be disaster. "Let's wait for him in the grand salon."

"I just got off the phone with him. He'll be here any minute. His men have been doing a drone search through the night and he has some results."

"I need to call Genevieve and tell her and Becca to get back here. Assuming Olivia is on the estate grounds, I want everyone here in the Hall. I guess David is still asleep. And I don't know where the hell Duncan is." They left the study and headed through the hallway, where the library clock struck eight. The hour was still early and so much had already happened. A pit in Philip's stomach warned him that it was only the beginning.

FORTY-THREE

THE WIND WHISTLED around Genevieve's riding helmet, her body an extension of the thundering black stallion beneath her. She could feel Becca pressing forward on her left and smiled at the competitive surge spurring her on. The howling wind and the pounding hooves filled her ears.

"You haven't won yet," Becca laughed into the wind. Thirty yards to the bank of the river. Thirty yards for Onyx to champion her to victory. Eager for just a bit more speed, she softened her hands on the reins and increased the pressure of her calves and heels around the horse's girth. She inched closer to Genevieve and Dutch, now only half a length ahead.

"Come on, you magnificent boy!" Becca urged her steed forward, her body flowing with the movement of her horse.

With twenty yards left, the Friesians and their riders were in a dead heat, racing at a breakneck pace. At ten yards they each reined in their mounts to a canter then slowed to a trot until they stopped near the river's edge, breathless and exhilarated.

Genevieve unstrapped her helmet and pulled it off. Shaking her head, her hair fell from the band holding her ponytail. She ran her free hand through her mane, allowing the breeze to lift the ends.

"I've never ridden that fast!" Genevieve's eyes flashed from the thrill of competition.

Becca couldn't stop grinning. She leaned down and patted Onyx on the neck. "What a gorgeous ride you are, my man." She smiled at Genevieve. "Have you ever had so much fun? Thank God neither one of us has to buy breakfast! What a perfect finish to a spectacular race, my friend!"

"Speaking of breakfast, what time is it? I'm starving!"

Becca looked at her watch. "It's 8:10. I bet Mrs. Lomax has something wonderful just coming out of the oven. I can just taste her cinnamon buns! I'd suggest we race back to the Hall, but I'll be lucky to make it at a slow walk."

Genevieve pushed her hair behind her ears and pulled her helmet back on. "I'm with you, Becca. I can't imagine how sore I'm going to be tomorrow.

"I bet I won't be able to walk by this afternoon," Becca laughed.

"Small price to pay, though. Wouldn't you say?"

Turning their horses away from the river, they started ambling toward the Hall. It had just come into view in the distance when Becca pulled abruptly on her reins. She squinted across the field toward a path leading out of the woods. "What the hell is that?"

"That's the pile Harrington's men cleared out of the forest. They're taking it down to the village today for the Guy Fawkes bonfire tonight."

"No, not that!" Becca was becoming more and more agitated.

"There! There!" She pointed beyond the huge pile of branches and twigs. Something moved toward them.

"What the hell, indeed!" Genevieve focused on the small image bumping along the ground. "It looks like a forklift carrying a big bundle."

They watched for a few seconds as the figure approached and they could see her better. The blinding sun glanced off the driver's short white-blond hair.

"Jesus!" Becca growled. "Jesus, Genevieve. That's Olivia and I bet you any amount of money, that's David on that forklift!"

FORTY-FOUR

PACING THE GRAND salon waiting for Chief Superintendent Darlington to arrive, Philip finally heard the crunch of tires on the gravel drive. The slam of two car doors was followed seconds later by the creak of Wilmingrove Hall's massive front door. Looking short on sleep and long on stress, Chief Superintendent Darlington burst into the cavernous room, accompanied by Michael Flynn, the head of the tech squad. Darlington's usually manicured appearance was disheveled, his short hair sticking up at the crown of his head and his clothes rumpled.

Dispensing with all pleasantries, Darlington opened his mouth, but before he could speak, Philip motioned them to follow him to the music room. On their way, he told them what Alex and Ella had found in the wall.

Using his phone as a flashlight, Darlington led the anxious band down the hall to the closed door.

When the door opened, he gave a soft, "Whoa" and flashed his light around the room.

Philip flipped a wall switch, and the room came to life.

"Jesus." Darlington looked around, his mind racing. "Flynn, get your team in here and get to work." His voice was terse and urgent. He motioned for the other two men to head back out the door.

When they crossed back into the warm glow of the music room, Darlington said, "Lord Crosswick, we have drone images of a bonfire pile by the river. Could Olivia have built a pyre without anyone noticing?"

Stepping out from behind Philip, Harrington said, "The pile by the river is from the forest. For the last week, my men have been clearing rubbish from the woods. It never occurred to me that Olivia might use it for her Guy Fawkes bonfire. Holy shite! Do you think that might be her plan?"

"It deviates from her plotline, but she has to adjust details as she goes, doesn't she?" Darlington's brow furrowed as he rubbed his temples with his thumbs "When our forensic psychologists told us Olivia would follow her plan, they didn't take into consideration how many circumstances have change since she wrote her book.

"We need to get David down here." Until now, Philip had been silent, but now he was anxious to account for his friends and family. "Chief Superintendent, I want Becca and Genevieve back here. The Hall may not be as safe as we thought, but at least I want us all together until this is over. They're out riding. I called Genevieve about ten minutes ago, but she didn't answer. I think David's upstairs and I want Duncan here as well."

As the group returned to the grand salon, David sauntered

down the stairs. "Good morning, all," he said, looking remarkably rested for a man in the crosshairs.

"We were just going to roust you out, David. A lot is happening." Philip squeezed David's shoulder. "We want to keep our eyes on you today."

"Excuse me, Lord Crosswick."

"Wallace. Just the man I wanted to see. Could you please let Duncan know he needs to join us?"

"That's what I was coming to tell you. Lottie saw him about half an hour ago. He wanted Lady Crosswick to know he was meeting you and the Chief Superintendent at the stable."

Darlington's face was blank.

"Did you meet up with him, sir?" Wallace asked.

"What the bloody blazes are you talking about? I haven't seen or talked to Duncan since everyone left the restaurant last night. Where would he get the idea I was meeting him this morning at the stable?" Darlington pulled his phone from his pocket, punched one number, and waited seconds before someone answered. "Immediate Priority. All available units to Wilmingrove Hall." His voice was commanding and hard as steel. He mashed another button. "Flynn, get drones to the stable and riverbank straight away! I want eyes on both locations. Lord Crosswick, keep calling your wife. When you get her, tell her and Ms. Conway to come back to the Hall immediately."

He spun around and was out the door, leaving Philip, David and Sean Harrington looking at each other with no idea what to do.

FORTY-FIVE

Without a word to Genevieve, Becca kicked Onyx to a trot and headed toward Olivia.

"Becca!" Genevieve hissed. "Becca, wait!" She moved forward to Becca's side and grabbed her arm. "Stop! We need a plan before we go charging at Olivia."

Becca reined Onyx to halt and looked at Genevieve, eyes briming with anger and tears. "You're right, of course, Genevieve. I'm just so angry I could wring Olivia's neck with my bare hands. I knew this was coming, but a part of me held out hope that she would stop before it went too far. What an idiot I am to keep believing my child is salvageable, to believe she has a soul."

Glancing beyond the wood pile towards Olivia's steady approach, Genevieve reached out, took Becca's gloved hand, and squeezed. "We need to figure out right now how to prevent a troubled young woman from killing our dear friend. I don't think she's seen us yet. Between the sun in her eyes and the woodpile, I think we can stay out of her line of vision until we're close to her. Is there any possibility of reasoning with her?"

Becca barked a single laugh and shook her head. "No!" She snarled.

Genevieve's phone rang from deep in her riding jacket. Pulling her iPhone from her inside pocket, she saw Philip's face on her screen. She punched "accept" and his urgent voice shot through the phone. "G, where are you? You need to get back to the Hall. Don't go to the stable. Get back here!" His rapid-fire instructions took her by surprise.

Looking up, Genevieve saw Becca and Onyx walking on the riverbank's soft edge, trying to stay hidden behind the bonfire heap. She was heading straight toward Olivia.

Turning her attention back to Philip, Genevieve covered the phone with her hand to muffle her voice. "Philip," she whispered. "We're at the river near the big pile of branches."

"Oh shit!" Genevieve could hear Philip's rapid breathing.

"Olivia is heading there on a forklift with David hanging on the prongs. She's done something to David to make him—" She cut herself off. "Of course, the curare."

"Genevieve." A coldness took over Philip's voice. "It's not David."

She narrowed her eyes, laser-focused on the figure bouncing on the forks. "Not David? But in the book—"

"Forget the book."

"But the book outlines what she's planning to do, Philip. It says—"

"It's Duncan."

"Duncan?" she asked, confused. "Why in the hell would Duncan be on he forklift?" She squinted to focus on the body swaying from the forklift, then panic filled her voice. "Oh my God, Philip. You're right! It's Duncan." Tears closed her throat. "What if he suffocated from the curare? Oh Jesus. What if he's dead?" She was barely breathing.

"Genevieve, listen to me." Philip's voice was like a slap. "Darlington and a shitload of cops are on their way to the river. Just stay away from Olivia. They'll be there any minute. Did you hear me?" Raising his voice, Philip yelled at Genevieve to confirm she would stay put.

"I heard you, but I have to get to Duncan! I have to. Oh, Philip, I can't believe this is happening."

"I'm on my way with Harrington and you should see the police any minute. Stay put!"

"Just get here, Philip. Please, just get here." Genevieve ended the call, shoving the phone back into her pocket.

As Becca and her horse moved closer to Olivia, she gasped. She yanked on Onyx's reins, halting him, stunned at what she saw. Duncan, not David, hung from the forks. She turned in her saddle. Did Genevieve know it was her son who was about to become a human torch? Seeing her friend's fear-stricken face, there was no question, she knew.

Olivia was no more than twenty yards away, singing at the top of her lungs and bumping along with Duncan dangling from the forks. Excited about placing Duncan on the wood pile, Olivia had raised the mast to its full extension.

Trying to keep her rage in check, Genevieve breathed slowly and deeply. Nudging Dutch forward, she timed her inhale and exhale with her horse's stride, slowly bringing her anger under control. Moving closer to Olivia with every step, Genevieve assessed what items could serve as weapons. She had her crop and a two-thousand-pound horse.

She reined Dutch to a stop. An idea flashed to mind. It might work. She needed to think for a moment before charging ahead. Genevieve closed her eyes, visualizing her plan. This just might work. This just might startle Olivia into making a mistake.

She leaned forward, patting Dutch on the neck. "Okay, you magnificent beast. My darling boy is relying on us to save his life. We can do this." Her voice was soft, coaxing. She felt the ridged firmness of her crop and she was ready.

Genevieve sat erect, sinking her bottom into her saddle. She took a deep breath and exhaled. Reins in one hand, her crop in the other, she struck Dutch on his hindquarters and drove her heels into his sides. He burst forward like shot from a cannon, skirting the wood pile, flying past Becca, and heading straight for Olivia.

Stunned at the sight of the jet-black horse and rider roaring toward her, Olivia yanked the forklift to the left, driving onto the riverbank.

Genevieve reined Dutch to a sliding halt and jumped out of her saddle to a standing crouch, coiled, ready to strike.

The forklift's small tires stuck in the riverbank's muddy grass, stopping the vehicle's forward motion with the left side just inches from the edge. Olivia sat stone still, moving only her eyes to glance down at the cold water rushing below. Looking up ten feet above her, she could see Duncan starting to move his head and heard his raspy voice as the curare's effects began to wane.

Duncan felt a fork at the joint of his thighs and knees, his muscles coming back to life. "Jesus, Olivia! What have you done?" Like a trapeze artist gripping a high bar, he squeezed the tine as hard as he could with his weakened muscles.

The forklift listed to the left, its weight too much for the soggy bank. In slow motion, it eased onto its side, the mast stretching out into the air above the river, almost horizontal to the embankment.

Olivia froze in the driver's seat.

Hanging out over the icy water, Duncan struggled to pull his dangling arms from above his head, trying to reach the fork pressing against his back. If he could grasp that tine, he could hold on until someone could rescue him.

"Olivia, don't move!" Genevieve screamed. "Stay where you are! If you move, the forklift will go over the edge!"

The buzz of drones and screaming sirens pierced the air. Six police cars, a specially equipped Road Policing Unit, and an ambulance, all with lights blazing, raced toward them from across the field. Overhead a police helicopter shared the sky with the drones, keeping watch over the scene.

With the onslaught of arriving emergency vehicles, Becca and Onyx streaked across the field to join in the mayhem. Becca threw herself off the steed and was running to Genevieve before Onyx came to a full stop.

Coming from the Hall, the fastest way to the river was on foot. Philip, David, and Harrington bolted across the terrace then flew down the stairs, taking two at a time. They raced between the parterre and croquet lawn, past the falconry field, and whipped by the quince trees to the river's edge where all three bent over, gasping for air after their sprint.

Genevieve scanned the crowd of police, looking for Chief Superintendent Darlington. She found him in the middle of a sea of dark blue, barking orders and pointing toward the forklift where Olivia and Duncan teetered.

"Get that forklift stabilized!" Darlington shouted. "Get a harness around Warwick and get your hands on Conway! I want that woman in handcuffs!"

Before anyone could stop her, Olivia pushed herself out of the driver's seat, balanced on the edge of the forklift's frame, then dove into the river. The forklift shuddered, tilting a bit more toward the water.

Duncan's voice could now be heard above the din of all the activity. "Help!" he rasped. "Help me!"

Lying flat on her belly, Genevieve scooched to the edge of the bank until her torso hung out over the water. She extended her hand as far as she could, trying to touch Duncan. Not quite able to reach him, she sucked in a breath. Then, exhaling, she stretched a bit further and grabbed a fistful of his pant leg.

"The police are here, Duncan. It's going to be all right. I promise you," she sobbed. "Everything's going to be all right. Just stay still. Don't move. We'll get you back on the embankment. I promise. You're going to be okay."

Blinking to clear her tears, she felt weight pressing her into the ground. Glancing back, she saw Philip sitting on her butt so she wouldn't fall over the embankment.

She couldn't believe the absurdity of this situation. Duncan was hanging from a forklift, tipped on its side, while she stretched across the ground, torso hanging out into thin air, holding onto their son's pantleg, while her husband sat on her butt to keep her from tumbling over the bank into the water. It would be hilarious if only it weren't so terrifying. Genevieve tightened her grip even more. She vowed to cling to Duncan's pants until he was in the grasp of the police.

The Met team moved a vehicle fitted with a winch into position. They hooked cables to the Mini, one to the frame, another to the mast, stabilizing the forklift. Well-developed muscles straining his black uniform shirt, a SWAT officer crawled out onto the mast to wrap a harness around Duncan. The rescue team pulled the forklift to an upright position and three officers held the limp man as they lowered the fork. When it was four feet off the ground, paramedics grabbed him off the lift and strapped him onto a gurney.

"It's curare," Duncan rasped to the EMT's. "She used a dart to inject me with curare." His voice was stronger with every word.

Within seconds Duncan was in the ambulance. The SWAT officer pounded twice on the closed doors and the hospital wagon took off, bouncing across the field, siren blaring.

In the river, the current and her strong stroke carried Olivia swiftly. Ten feet above her, a police helicopter hovered, its blades whipping the water into white caps. Downstream, a small, inflatable motorboat churned against the current, closing in on her. She bobbed in the waves like a buoy, coughing and sputtering as water rushed into her mouth. The boat slid beside her while two officers hung over the side. One grabbed the collar of her jacket, the other grasped her under her arm.

"We're pulling you out!" one cop shouted above the din as they plucked her from the churning river. They sat her on the bench seat, zip tied her wrists and wrapped a mylar blanket around her shoulders. Rivulets from her drenched hair streamed down her face. She glared at everyone on the riverbank high above her. They were watching her. She saw her mother sobbing and she sneered.

She jumped to her feet and the officer yanked her back down. She shook her fisted hands at everyone on the bank. "It's not over!" she screamed. "Tell Duncan it's not over!"

But it was. The drama of the last two months was over.

FORTY-SIX

BECCA LOOKED AT her reflection in the walnut cheval mirror. Her eyes were ringed with dark circles, confirming her lack of sleep and the tears she had shed since the climax at the river's edge six days before. Dressed in simple navy wool pants, jacket, and a white silk shirt, she was ready to see her daughter for the first time since the police fished her out of the river.

So much had happened since that terrifying morning. After Olivia's apprehension, Becca's first phone call was to Henry Fitch, who had come immediately to represent Olivia. Having an old friend on their side was a great comfort. At Henry's suggestion, her second call was to the director of the Langston School, where Olivia had thrived for so many years. Thanks to Henry and the school, Olivia was remanded to a private psychiatric hospital: Blain Lodge, near York.

After four days of court appearances, helping police tie up loose ends, and fending off the tabloid press, Becca was a cauldron of emotion: anger, frustration, sadness, self-pity, guilt. She was determined to accomplish two things during today's visit with her daughter. First, she would tell Olivia about her father, Jonathon Laney, the 12TH Earl of Crosswick. She wanted Olivia to know how much the couple had loved each other. Second, she would apologize. She would tell Olivia how guilty she felt and how sorry she was for all the years she nurtured Olivia's fantasy that David was her father. After years of her own therapy, Becca knew she had contributed to Olivia's struggles, but this would be the first time she would share just how responsible she felt. It would be a painful meeting.

Becca heard a soft knock on her door. "Come in."

The door opened just enough for Genevieve to stick her head in. "Just checking to see if you need anything. Are you okay?"

Becca offered a joyless smile. "I'm fine, as well as one could expect. But thank you, Genevieve. Everyone's support means a great deal to me."

At that, Genevieve walked across the room and enveloped Becca in her arms. They lingered until Genevieve gave a squeeze and then held Becca at arm's length. "Well, my friend, you look ready to go into battle."

"Let's hope it's only a small skirmish." Becca's laugh was brittle. "Do you know if David is downstairs?"

"He is. He's waiting for you in the car. You're sure you don't want Philip and me to go, too?"

"Absolutely not." Becca gave Genevieve a kiss on the cheek. "David will be there after my visit. He's more than enough support."

During the forty-minute drive to Blain Lodge, BBC Radio York droned on and on, filling the Range Rover with news of local holiday fetes, international news of skirmishes and protest marches and the Prime Minister's latest embarrassing behavior.

Becca didn't hear any of it. Gazing out the window, she stared at the endless fields. Not long ago, they were golden with wheat. Now, resown, they waited for their snowy winter blanket to protect them from the icy months ahead. The cycle of life, Becca thought. Come spring, these fields will be green with new life and hope. She smiled at her musings. It was her first real smile in a week, and it felt good. Deep in her own thoughts, she was unaware the car had stopped until she felt David's hand squeeze hers.

"Becca, we're here."

Nothing registered.

"We're here," David repeated. "Do you want me to walk you to the door?"

Several seconds passed before Becca's eyes sparked. "Wow! I was lightyears away!" She smiled again. "No. No. I don't want you to come in. I'll be fine. I'll be fine." She took a cleansing breath, held it, then exhaled. "I guess it's now or never!"

David walked around to Becca's door and opened it. She grasped his hand and let him help her from the Range Rover.

He held her shoulders, looked into her eyes, and said, "You're one of the bravest people I know. What you did for us, coming here and exposing Olivia, is something few people would have done."

David pulled her into his arm, holding her there longer than he had intended. Before releasing her, he kissed her lightly on the lips. Much to his surprise, she pulled his face to hers, parted her lips and planted them firmly on his. "To be continued," she said.

Becca walked away to face her troubled daughter, head high, back erect. David couldn't take his eyes off her until she disappeared into the building.

FORTY-SEVEN

HAVING NO IDEA how Becca would feel after her time with Olivia, Genevieve wanted everything to be perfect when she returned. This evening she wanted to wrap Becca in a blanket of love. She stood back to admire her efforts.

"Pretty, very pretty," she said to herself.

Set in front of the music room fireplace, with a fire waiting to be lit, the round table was just the right size for an intimate dinner for five. A square damask tablecloth, heavy tassels hanging at each corner topped a floor-length blue, green, and gold plaid cover. Royal Doulton Carlyle china was the perfect dinnerware for the fall with its blue and gold rim and center rosettes. A cluster of Waterford crystal sparkled at each place with the reflection from lamps dotted around the room. Votives and a nest of blue and violet hydrangeas finished the tableau.

In the kitchen, Mrs. Lomax was doing her part to make the evening comforting and special. When they talked menu, there was no question. It would be Beef Wellington, Joel Robuchon's mashed potatoes and Mrs. Lomax's own nutty Brussels sprouts.

Glancing out of the towering widows, Genevieve noticed a

few flakes of snow wafting from low clouds. She heard the crunch of tires on gravel and saw the black Range Rover make its way around the circle, stopping at the front door. She glanced at her watch. 5:30.

Genevieve heard voices before she got to the salon. David and Becca were chatting with Wallace in the cavernous room. She heard laughter. She heard banter. Genevieve frowned, searching for a word to describe how Becca sounded. She listened a bit longer before it occurred to her. Happy! Becca sounded happy! Throughout the afternoon Genevieve had thought about her friend. She thought about all the emotions Becca might be feeling, but not once did 'happy' occur to her.

"You're back!" Genevieve crossed the great hall with outstretched arms. "David, you brought our girl back in one piece. Well done!" She wrapped her arms around Becca. "So, how did it go?" Genevieve pulled back, looking at Becca's face for any clue.

"It was an extraordinary afternoon. Not at all what I expected." The relief in Becca's eyes was genuine. "I'll tell you all about it at dinner. Right now, I want to shower and change. What time do I need to be down?"

"Are we having a party or a wake?" Genevieve asked.

Becca looked at David. "I'd say we're having a party." She looked back at Genevieve, grinning.

"Then the party starts when you arrive," Genevieve said. "Philip and Sean Harrington are in York finishing a few things with Chief Superintendent Darlington. Philip just called to say they're about to leave so there's no rush. And I ordered Duncan to rest so he'll be ready to enjoy the evening. According to Mrs. Lomax, dinner will be served at 7:30, but the Champagne is on ice just waiting to pop."

"Alrighty then. I won't be long. I don't want to miss anything, and I have a lot to share." Becca pressed her lips to David's cheek. "Thank you, David, for your support today. You were wonderful." She swept up the staircase and was gone.

Genevieve looked at David, with amused surprise.

David shrugged his shoulders, a sheepish grin on his face.

"Has something happened between you two?"

"I don't know. Maybe." David started up the stairs, stopped and turned around. "Can we talk about this later?"

"Oh, you can count on it," Genevieve confirmed.

Bubbles teased the top of Genevieve's Champagne flute. "Philip, stop!" Genevieve begged him as he coaxed just a bit more Veuve Clicquot into her glass. He filled his glass then set the bottle back in its silver cooler.

"To happy endings." Philip and Genevieve clinked glasses.

Philip smiled at his wife and took a drink. "Can you believe all that's happened in two short months? The inheritance alone would have been enough to change our lives, but the madness of Olivia trying to kill Duncan… I mean, who experiences such wild events, except in the movies?"

"It's hard to imagine. And speaking of all that's happened," Genevieve lowered her voice and leaned toward Philip, "I think something's going on between Becca and David."

"What do you mean by 'some—'" Philip stopped, seeing

Becca, David, and Duncan in the doorway. Philip raised his glass then took another drink. "Come in. As you can see, we didn't wait."

Genevieve held flutes while Philip poured. The trio took the glasses, and the toasting began.

"Julia's devastated she's not here," Duncan said. "She almost cried on the phone. It's good I'm going home tomorrow."

"Then our first toast is to Julia." Philip raised his glass and the chorus of "To Julia" rang out.

At precisely 7:30, Wallace announced dinner would be served. The diners were very happy indeed, and the Champagne bottle was empty, he noted.

Genevieve rose from the love seat where she and Philip had been sitting opposite Becca and David for the last half hour. "Come on, everyone. Mrs. Lomax is very serious about her meals being eaten hot. We don't want to suffer her wrath, do we?"

"I should say not." David held out his hand, helping Becca to her feet. "She's been very good to me while I've been at the Hall. Lord knows I've overstayed my welcome!"

David slipped his arm around Becca's waist, escorting her to the table.

"Tell me, David," Genevieve said. "Where else would you rather have been? Where else could you have been the center of attention for the last two months?"

David held Becca's chair, scooching her closer to the table "This kind of attention, I could have done without," he said.

When everyone was seated, Wallace led a parade of servers into the music room. Each placed a silver-domed plate in front of a diner. On the silent count of three, they removed the domes to reveal Mrs. Lomax's exquisite meal, which was greeted with "ooh"s, "aah"s and applause.

Wallace poured a splash of Chateau Beaulieu Bordeaux, the Crosswick's own vintage, into Philip's glass. Philip swirled it, admiring its legs, then stuck his nose into the goblet's tapered mouth to inhale the rich aroma. He slurped a taste into his mouth, closed his eyes, then swallowed. "Wallace," he said, "we make a hell of a wine!"

"We do indeed, my lord." Wallace poured the rest of the glasses. When he was finished, he bowed at the waist. "Lord and Lady Crosswick, Lord Crosswick, Sir David, Ms. Conway, may I say, it is with the greatest happiness the staff and I serve you this evening. We could not be more pleased that Ms. Olivia's novel had a happier ending than planned. My lord," Wallace nodded at Duncan. "We are all delighted you did not die." Wallace's sober voice betrayed nothing, but the curl of his lips brought his audience to laughter.

"I, too, am pleased I'm not dead," Duncan deadpanned.

"Lord, Lady Crosswick, just ring when you need me." Wallace caught Duncan's eye and winked as he left the room.

"There aren't many like Wallace," Becca said. "He's in a class all his own. How long has he been at the Hall?"

"He was born here, in the stable," Genevieve said, poker-faced.

"You don't suppose he'd like to come to the U.S. to work, do you?" asked Becca.

"Pull something like that at your peril." Philip pointed his dinner knife at Becca.

"Just testing the waters! I can't imagine Wallace putting up with us insufferable Americans, although he's put up with the Warwick family pretty well!"

"Okay. Okay. Changing the subject." Genevieve gestured toward Becca with her wine glass. "Tell us about seeing Olivia today. Judging from your high spirits, things must have gone well."

Looking around the table, Becca smiled, her eyes brimming with happy tears. "In such a short time I've grown to trust this special group as much as I've ever trusted anyone. Though my own daughter has terrified you for the last two months, you welcomed me into your lives, embracing me from the moment I arrived on your doorstep." She paused, looking down at her napkin twisted in her fingers.

David offered his hand.

She took it and went on. "Dr. Morgan, the lead psychiatrist on Olivia's case, is on the cutting edge of treating mental illness. Over the next month, they'll do a thorough assessment of Olivia's mental state and create a treatment plan. That's all very normal and as I expected. What excites me is Dr. Morgan's success using several of his new therapies. Olivia's only been at Blair Lodge for four days, but already Dr. Morgan seems to have a good read on her. He's not taken in by her guile. He is, however, impressed and interested in her ability to manipulate and influence people. He seems excited to have her as a patient. There's no question she's brilliant and can charm her way out of most trouble. But not this time. I think she's met her match with Dr. Morgan. I can't believe I feel such happiness, such—well—such hope. Over the years there were more than a few times I thought we were on the right track with Olivia, but never have I truly believed Olivia might someday be able to lead a happy, productive life. I may be a fool, but I…" Becca's voice trailed off into silence. For several seconds, the only sound in the room was the crackling fire and the pretty pink marble mantle clock's tic toc.

Still holding Becca's hand, David pulled it to his lips and kissed her knuckles. "I will never understand how such a brilliant mind, who carried out her plotline so well, made such a dog's breakfast out of the climax. Thank goodness she did. Right, Duncan?"

Leaning back in his chair, Duncan's serenity belied the anxiety gnawing at him. Only his fingers tapping on the table's edge gave him away. "When Olivia squatted down beside me and said that she was the special one in the Crosswick line and the true heir so she had to eliminate me, the hate in her eyes is something I will never forget."

Becca started to speak, but her voice failed. She cleared her throat and tried again. "From the time she was born, my parents and I told Olivia how special she was. She was the prettiest, the smartest, the best at everything. Of course, we were overcompensating for her not having a father. What a mistake!"

"But understandable," Genevieve sympathized.

Becca leaned forward, elbows on the table. "Duncan, Dr. Morgan said that watching your loving family over the course of several weeks fueled a jealousy that overwhelmed her. When Conner wrote to her to tell her that Jonathon, not David, was her father, she transferred her rage from David to you. She felt you were trying to take her special place. You had everything she longed for, and she felt by destroying you, she would have your life."

Duncan stopped drumming his fingers. The corners of his mouth lifted, and he said, "If Olivia had executed the end of her story as well as she did the rest of her tale, I'd be toast! I'd be just a bar of charcoal you could use on the grill to cook some ribeye steaks. I trust you'd serve a nice Petrus with that, Dad. I know it's not our vintage, but at least it's a Bordeaux."

Duncan's comic observation pierced the heavy cloud that had gathered, and the room exploded with laughter at his dark humor. They laughed until their eyes streamed with tears. They laughed until their faces hurt. They laughed weeks of tension away.

Surprised and pleased by the jovial mood when he entered the music room, Wallace offered a reserved smile. "My lady, may we serve dessert?"

Still breathless from laughing, Genevieve nodded. "Thank you, Wallace." She dabbed at her eyes, hoping she didn't look like a racoon. "We've been having the most marvelous laugh about everything that's happened over the last two months."

"That must sound deranged," David said.

"Not at all, Sir David. Indeed, laughter is the best release in the world. Let me pour more Champagne. Champagne always helps the laughter bubble up." Pleased with himself at his bon mot, Wallace refilled the flutes as servers placed puffy chocolate souffles in front of each diner.

"Wallace, would you ask everyone in the kitchen to come in, please? And if Mrs. MacIntosh and Harrington are available, please ask them to join us as well." said Genevieve. "We need to give them an ovation for all they've done, not just this evening, but since we arrived. And we'll need glasses for everyone and more Champagne. We always seem to need more Champagne, don't we, Wallace?"

He smiled. "What is life without Champagne, my lady? Everyone will be delighted to come in."

A few minutes later, Wallace returned, carrying a tray of glasses, followed by Mrs. Lomax, Lottie, Claire, and two girls who would have been called scullery maids a century ago. A moment later Mrs. Lomax and Harrington joined the growing crowd.

Brimming with emotion from an evening spent in his ancestral home, Wilmingrove Hall, Philip stood in front of the elegant marble fireplace, fire dancing on the hearth. He was unsure how the Hall managed to be both grand and embracing, but it was. Each day, the connection to the generations of Laneys who preceded him grew stronger. The longer he sat at the helm of this vast empire built by clever, courageous men and women, the more responsibility he felt to secure the continued success of the family going forward. He could envision one day handing the reins of the Laney dynasty to Duncan and Julia, who would continue nurturing the family legacy until ultimately Alex and Ella would take their place as Crosswick heirs. At the thought, his eyes stung with tears.

Philip walked around behind Genevieve and rested his hand on her shoulder. He waited while Mrs. MacIntosh and Wallace organized Champagne for everyone.

Taking a deep breath to get his emotions under control, Philip began. "Just a few months ago, we were all strangers. Genevieve, er, Lady Crosswick and I arrived here out of our depth. We are not unsophisticated people, but as Lord and Lady Crosswick, we stepped into roles that very few people in the world experience. Those who do, are usually born into this wealth and responsibility rather than thrust into it as we were. Honestly, it was terrifying." He looked around at the faces he had grown to know and admire. "After years of managing the estate very well on your own, you could have resented us coming to Wilmingrove Hall, but you didn't. All of you welcomed us with extraordinary grace, for which we thank you. The presence of a new lord and lady would have been unsettling enough but add to that the upheaval of Olivia Conway's attempts on Sir David's and Duncan's lives, and the last few weeks have been quite, um…" Philip searched for just the right word. "Exciting, haven't they?" Giggles rippled through the room.

"Genevieve and I—" this time he did not correct himself, "can't express how much we have grown to love Wilmingrove Hall, and each of you." He nodded to Duncan, David and Becca. "Like the three people sitting here, you are our family. And, like family, we will always be here to support you, protect you and share all of our happiness with you."

Philip raised his glass. "To Wilmingrove Hall and all of you who nurture her. We will cherish you forever."

EPILOGUE

"**B**UMPA, I'M NEXT, I'm next!" Ready to perform the song she had prepared for the *Christmas Eve Musicale*, Ella danced with excitement. Cocky and self-assured, she stood in front of the guests assembled in the music room, anxious to begin. Genevieve sat at the piano waiting for Ella's nod, while her brother was at the ready with his harmonica.

Ella curtsied, holding the skirt of her red velvet dress in each hand. "Ladies and gentlemen, tonight I'm going to perform my Bumpa's favorite Christmas song, Santa Baby." She looked back at her grandmother and nodded.

Genevieve played the introduction and Ella began to perform.

For years, the Warwick Christmas Eve tradition had been an evening filled with performances by everyone, followed by a sumptuous dinner. The meal's climax was the discovery of *the almond* buried in someone's dessert, which won them a prize. And then, accompanied by sleighbells and booming "ho, ho, ho's," Santa's arrival was almost more excitement than one could bear.

It was an elegant, black-tie evening. Even the children dressed in their best party clothes. Philip and Genevieve made sure this year would be no different. They committed to incorporating their Christmas Eve ritual into Wilmingrove Hall's traditions, offering their own addition to the Laney heritage.

David travelled from London the day before and Becca had flown in a few days earlier to spend time with Olivia. Duncan, Julia, Alex, and Ella had been at the Hall since Thanksgiving and planned to stay until the new year.

Like a scene from a Currier and Ives lithograph, snow floated down just outside the windows, fires crackled on hearths, and as was the tradition of the Hall, Champagne flowed.

David stood to deliver a poem he had written for the occasion. Becca played the guitar and sang "Silent Night" in German. Duncan and Genevieve sang a fractured version of "A Partridge in a Pear Tree" which included the entire group's participation. For the grand finale, Philip and Julia joined their talents lip syncing "All I Want for Christmas is You," which brought down the house.

Just as the applause died and as if on cue, Wallace entered the room and announced, "My lords and ladies, dinner is served."

Accompanied by Alex on his harmonica, Wallace led the parade out of the music room, and across the grand salon to the dining room. With great flourish, he opened the double doors to reveal the room dressed in all its Christmas glory. The soaring tree was decked with a thousand lights and hundreds of antique English ornaments representing generations of Laneys. The magnificent table twinkled and beguiled with sterling and candles and crystal and flowers. No one could imagine anything more holiday perfect.

When everyone was seated, Genevieve stood. Glass in hand, she smiled at each glowing face looking back at her. "Every Christmas is special and every year we say, 'This holiday was the best ever.' This year I believe it's true. As our wise Julia says, 'We have so much we'll never get over, but so much we've gotten through.' With that in mind and knowing how much each of you means to Philip and me, I propose the toast our family has offered on Christmas Eve for many, many years."

She raised her glass and said:

"On this happy Christmas tide,
Gathered round our table here
Are those we love and hold so dear.
To you, we wish good Christmas cheer.

"We love you all and will see you at Chateau Beaulieu after the new year. Please come whenever and as often as you can. We'll drink our lovely Bordeaux and see what mischief we can get into in France. Joyeux Noel!"

Above the clink of toasting glasses and the din of happy voices, the faint sound of jingling bells could be heard. Santa was on his way… and the aroma of Charlotte's Rose Otto wafted through the Hall.

ART, WINE, *and* CRIME

Tana L.H. Boerger

ONE

THE PLANE PLUMMETED toward earth with a searing whine and thunderous shudder of the fuselage. These could be their last moments before slamming into the ground and exploding into a million bits. Tears stung her eyes, but Genevieve was calm, dead calm.

"Lord and Lady Crosswick, brace for impact," Captain Bruni barked over the intercom.

With their heads between their knees, Genevieve and Philip locked on each other's gaze. If these were their last moments, they would cherish each other until they perished in a ball of flames.

She stretched toward him, brushing his lips with hers. Philip's hand cradled the back of her head, pulling her to him and firming what was probably their last embrace. Each could feel the other's taut muscles and prayed their combined strength might ease the plane to earth.

And then, the jet engines roared back to life, their thrust pressing Philip and Genevieve back into their seats. The front of the plane nosed up. Outside the window, the horizon leveled.

"What the hell?" Philip gasped under his breath.

The hum of lowering landing gear filled the cabin with a glorious moan.

"Lord and Lady Crosswick." They could hear Captain Bruni's smile and relief through the speaker. "It appears our engines had a change of heart and have decided to take us into Paris rather than smashing us into a farmer's field. We shall be on the ground shortly."

Overcome with relief, Philip and Genevieve's whoops and whistles bounced off the walls of the Bombardier jet. Still gripping Genevieve's hand, Philip brought it to his lips and kissed each knuckle.

She croaked a laugh, tears streaming down her adrenaline-flushed cheeks. "That's quite an entrance into Paris," she said, glancing down at her trembling hands.

"After what we've been through since September, all I wanted was a few calm months in France." Philip shook his head. "This does not bode well."

Lights flashed, sirens screamed, and three ambulances clustered in front of the General Aviation Terminal at Paris-Le Bourget Airport, waiting for the Warwicks' jet to ease to a stop. Unsure what to do next, Genevieve and Philip didn't move, didn't release their seatbelts, barely breathed.

After what seemed like an eternity, the cockpit door opened. Filling the doorway with his tall, broad-shouldered frame, Captain Francesco Bruni paused before he entered the owners' cabin.

"Well done, Captain Bruni." Philip mopped his brow with a crumpled linen napkin left from lunch. "What the hell just happened?" He motioned for the captain to sit in the seat across from him.

Bruni hesitated, then sat. In his lilting Italian accent, he began. "Lord, Lady Crosswick," he said, hands clasped between his splayed legs, his handsome face pale from strain, "until the mechanics investigate, it's difficult to say what caused the flameout, but I wouldn't—"

"Flameout?" Philip interrupted.

"This term is often used for any failure in a turbine engine, but its technical meaning is a power loss not associated with mechanical failure. In this case, though the engines stopped, we were able to restart them."

"For which we are grateful." Genevieve reached out and touched the captain's sleeve, her eyes still sparkling with tears of relief.

"If it wasn't mechanical, what could have happened?" Now that the unthinkable was behind them, Philip wanted answers.

Captain Bruni cleared his throat, his gaze riveted on Philip. "Lord Crosswick, the problem could have been caused by a number of things: birds flying into the engine, a compressor stall, or…" Bruni glanced down at his interlaced fingers, looked at Genevieve, then back at Philip. "Or perhaps water in the fuel. If we find that is the problem, there will be serious consequences for whoever is responsible."

"I don't understand. How does water get into the fuel?"

"Under normal circumstances, it does not. I don't want to speculate, but we're scrupulous about testing before we refuel, so I would say if that turns out to be our problem, we need to find the person responsible."

Philip ran his hands over his face. "Are you saying if the

engines stalled because of water in the fuel, someone intended to make that happen?"

"As I stated, I don't wish to speculate. I shall work with the authorities to uncover the problem and, I assure you, we'll discover what happened. Please, leave it in my hands. You will have a report as soon as possible. And now, Lord, Lady Crosswick, your car is waiting to take you home. I would suggest you do your best to enjoy the rest of your day."

Through the window, Genevieve saw a silver Rolls Royce Ghost at the ready. She unsnapped her seatbelt and gave Philip a nudge with her shoulder. "Philip, if there's nothing we can do here, we should go."

"I guess we'll leave you to it, Captain Bruni. And again, thank you." Philip extended his hand, a rare gesture for an earl to a member of his staff. Without hesitation, Bruni gripped Philip's hand.

With the door open, cold January air rushed into the cabin, chilling Genevieve's cheeks as she walked forward. She stood at the doorway, felt Philip next to her and laced her fingers through his. "Here we go again," she said.

He felt his phone vibrate. It was out of his pocket and at his ear before the second ring.

"Tell me," he demanded.

Silence filled the line.

"Tell me." This time he whispered through clenched teeth.

"Sir," the caller's voice cracked. The caller cleared his throat and started again, his cockney accent thick. "Sir, I did it, but the pilot was able to restart the engines."

He yanked the phone from his ear and smashed it against the wall.

Henri, their driver, maneuvered the Rolls through midday Paris traffic with the skill of a Formula One driver. Exiting from A1 onto Boulevard Périphérique, Philip and Genevieve could see Sacré-Cœur in the distance, regal atop Montmartre like a queen on her throne.

As the ring road made a graceful sweep around Montmartre, Genevieve smiled. Releasing her seatbelt, she cuddled close to Philip and prickles of excitement began replacing the terror of the morning. "Remember our ride through Paris on the quad last year?"

"Do I?" Philip gave Genevieve a sidelong glance that said, are you kidding me? "That was one of the greatest travel adventures we've ever had."

Genevieve recalled mounting an ATV at 5:00 a.m., Philip driving, Genevieve's arms wrapped around him from behind. She tested the GoPro on top of her helmet, and then for the next two hours, they roared through Paris, their guide leading the way, the wide, empty boulevards all their own. Just before sunrise, at the foot of Sacré-Cœur's extravagant stairs, they drank mimosas, ate croissants still warm from the baker's oven, and toasted the sun as it rose over the Basilica's glowing dome. It was an experience to remember.

Now, as Montmartre faded into the distance and the warm glow of the memory vanished, the reality of their brush with disaster came flooding back. "How are you feeling after our near-death experience this morning?" Genevieve asked as much to explore her own thoughts as to take Philip's emotional temperature.

"I'm grateful we didn't die." His wan smile confirmed he was still shaken.

"You're not alone. But I have to say I'm shocked at how serene I was when I thought we were going to crash. The thing that went through my mind was I'm here with Philip and the kids are well taken care of." Genevieve squeezed Philip's hand. "I was okay."

He leaned into Genevieve and kissed her forehead. "While you were totally Zen as we plummeted toward death, my mind was racing trying to figure out if someone was trying to kill us. That's how suspicious I am of everything and everyone, after what we've just been through in England."

Genevieve nodded her agreement. "What a rollercoaster our lives have been since our phone rang that Sunday morning." She closed her eyes, a whirlwind whipping through her mind: an inherited title, a huge fortune, and a maelstrom of murder and mayhem. She shook the thoughts away, grateful for the calm they had been living for the last three months in Wilmingrove Hall, their historic family seat near York.

As if he could read her thoughts, Philip sighed and leaned back in his seat. "I'm looking forward to exploring our Paris apartment," he said, and Genevieve smiled at the thought of their French inheritance, still as yet unvisited due to the upheaval in England.

When the car stopped in front of a wrought iron gate, they were not disappointed. Henri rolled down his window, smiled into a camera, and punched in a code on the digital pad. A pretty chime sounded, the gates lumbered open, and the car eased onto the stone driveway of their grand château in the middle of Paris.

"Of course," Philip said with a hint of awe. "What else would we expect?"

Genevieve craned her neck to peer up at the elegant Belle Époque building.

Though she had seen photographs of their Paris property, she was still impressed. "We own the entire building, is that correct, Henri?" Genevieve squinted, trying to see the small windows on the top floor.

"Oui, countess. Welcome to Maison de Laney, your home." Henri stopped in front of the arched doorway, swept out of the driver's seat, and opened Genevieve's door in one smooth motion. Philip waited for Henri to come to his side of the car. It had taken some time to become accustomed to having so much done for him, but at last, he was beginning to enjoy the perks of his position.

The chauffeur swung Philip's car door wide. "Merci, Henri," he said, nodding his appreciation.

As Genevieve and Philip walked up the stone path to the

entrance, the double glass and wrought iron doors parted. There to greet them stood Parisian perfection. Almost as tall as Philip and every bit as lean as Genevieve, Madame Morier, their chef de ménage, commanded the gateway to 22 Avenue Foch. At forty-five, she was all French demeanor and style. Her chiseled features were as elegant as a Degas statue.

"Whoa," Philip whispered to Genevieve without moving his lips. "Stylish or what?" He nodded at her French uniform of casual but sophisticated, thoughtful but thrown on.

"And *the scarf*," agreed Genevieve, her gaze drifting to the long, elegant neck where grey and black silk was tangled to perfection. Arrogance wafted from Madame Morier like an expensive fragrance.

Usually the most elegant woman in the room, Genevieve felt as dowdy as a washerwoman. For a moment, she longed for the warmth of stout, sensible Mrs. MacIntosh, their housekeeper at Wilmingrove Hall.

"Lord and Lady Crosswick. Bonjour et bienvenue." Madame Morier's thick chestnut hair swished at her chin with beveled precision, and her eyebrows arched into severe, straight bangs as she waited for a response from her new employers.

Genevieve decided there was nothing to do but rise to the occasion and replied to Madame Morier in her best French, saying that it was a pleasure to be here: "Quel plaisir d'être ici."

"S'il vous plaît, entrez." Madame Morier motioned for them to come in, making the Warwicks feel privileged to enter their own home. She switched to flawless English with ease: "I understand you had a difficult landing."

"Oh, no, madame." Charm poured into Philip's smile. "It wasn't difficult to land. It was just difficult to land without all of us dying."

Genevieve snorted a laugh, and Philip grinned at his wife. Nonplussed, the housekeeper could do nothing but shake her head and study her two employers with a judgmental stare.

Genevieve giggled a bit more, then said, "Madame Morier, I assure you we haven't lost our minds. We're just relieved that today we cheated death."

"Allons-y." Still baffled by Philip and Genevieve's casual regard for their dire experience, Madame Morier mumbled something under her breath and led them through the grand marble hall. "Why don't we go into the salon?" she tossed over her shoulder. "Perhaps a Scotch is in order."

Genevieve felt like an errant child as she and Philip followed their housekeeper. She caught Philip's eye and made a snooty face. In return, Philip flashed a stern look and shook his head.

Halfway along the fifty-foot foyer, they slowed to a stop. Philip's head pivoted back and forth. Genevieve circled in place, disbelieving. The realization hit them both: they were walking through a gallery of masterpieces, all of which belonged to them. Two O'Keeffes, a Kline, a stunning collage by Motherwell, a small Monet tucked into a recess, and a charming Andy Warhol screenprint of Mickey Mouse filled the corridor with creative energy. Philip and Genevieve looked at each other, then back at their collection, their eyes lingering over each canvas.

Madame Morier entered the grand salon and turned to speak to Lord and Lady Crosswick, but they were nowhere to be seen. When she walked back into the foyer, the two stood rapt, enthralled by the collection.

"My lord, my lady, you must stay with me," she snapped.

Intimidated by her tone, Philip and Genevieve obeyed and followed her into a room that glowed from the winter sun. Three sets of French doors lined the far wall. An enormous Frankenthaler canvas in blues, whites, and splashes of pink and rose dominated one end of the salon, while a massive fireplace had pride of place at the opposite end.

"Madame!" Genevieve strode the length of the room to the vibrant canvas. "I can't believe we have a Helen Frankenthaler. How long has this canvas been hanging here?"

A slight smile pulled at the corners of Madame Morier's mouth, as if surprised that the American recognized a great painting when she saw it. "It has been here as long as I have, countess, and I have been the head of Maison de Laney for more than fifteen years. You enjoy contemporary art?"

"Lord Crosswick and I value all periods and genres, but we both have a passion for modern art."

"I have an advanced degree in Art History and did my master's thesis on how the CIA used Jackson Pollock and other contemporary artists in the cold war." Philip seldom talked about his academic accomplishments, but, much to his surprise, he felt the need to impress Madame Morier.

"Hmm." Madame Morier hummed a mere flicker of acknowledgement. "Vraiment?" she said, splashing Scotch into three faceted glasses and handing one to Philip. "Then you will appreciate the paintings throughout the house. The head of your foundation, Lillie Langdon, keeps a close eye on your collection."

"That does not surprise me." Philip accepted the glass with a nod, amused that the house manager was joining them for a drink. "We spent time with Lillie when we were in London. She has a real passion for the foundation's work and for the museums. What about you, Madame Morier? Are you an art lover?"

She gave an arrogant flick of her head. "Of course, my lord. I love all beautiful things. After all, I am French."

"Naturellement, art, beauty, and the French go hand in hand," Genevieve said. As she walked back to the other end of the room, she admired the carved moldings nestled high up where plaster ceilings met silk-covered walls. Her steps were cushioned by a thick carpet of vivid color, which, overwhelmed by the Frankenthaler painting, she had not noticed until now. "Madam Morier, this carpet looks like a piece designed by Pierre-Josse Perrot, but that's not possible, is it?"

"I am surprised, my lady. Few outside the arts and antiquities world would recognize his work. And, sadly, this is not one of his originals. When the 12TH Earl repurchased Maison de Laney, returning it to the House of Crosswick, he commissioned the carpet a la Savonnerie. Though it is not 17th century, it is still beautiful and quite valuable."

"It's stunning." Genevieve accepted the tumbler Madame Morier held out to her, and the three clinked glasses.

"To beauty," Madame Morier said. "If you would like a tour of Maison de Laney, we shall do that now before you dine."

Though Genevieve would have enjoyed a quick shower, she was anxious to learn about their Parisian château. "I'd love that," she said, with a sweet smile she hoped would woo madame.

"If you'd like to be seated," she motioned to her audience of two to sit, "we can start here, in the grand salon. I'm sure you know nothing of Baron Haussmann, the Préfet of Seine, the man tasked with executing the reconstruction of Paris."

Not appreciating Madame Morier's condescending tone, Genevieve plucked up an arrogance of her own. "Of course, we know about Haussmann," she said.

Not bothering to suppress a smirk, Madame Morier said, "Vraiment? Perhaps I should not have assumed you were unfamiliar with his work, but I believe few Americans know about his extraordinary contribution to Paris."

Annoyed by madame's insinuation, Genevieve said, "The Opéra Garnier, the Opera House, is one of our favorite buildings in the world and it's very close to Boulevard Haussmann."

"Are you referring to the Palais Garnier?" Madam Morier raised one eyebrow.

Feeling foolish in her feeble attempt to impress Madame Morier, Genevieve waved her hand and mumbled, "Um, never mind."

Until now, Philip had been entertained watching the parry and thrust between Madame Morier and Genevieve, but he had questions. "Am I correct that, when the 9TH Earl of Crosswick inherited this property from his wife Charlotte Chaubert's family, the first thing he did was name the house Maison de Laney for his family?"

"Oui, my lord. Well done." She honored Philip with her first smile since they arrived.

"The 9ᵀᴴ Earl is one of my favorite distant cousins in my newly discovered family tree. His first name was also Philip." He flashed his most charming smile back at Madame Morier, and a flicker of approval crossed her face.

Genevieve watched the evolving interaction between Philip and madame, feeling more like a third wheel with each exchange.

Madame Morier set her glass down on the table next to her and crossed her legs. "The 9ᵀᴴ Earl spent ten years in Paris during Baron Haussmann's thrilling renovation of this decaying city. Though the earl was a titled Englishman with a substantial allowance, he loved the gritty side of Paris, befriending painters and spending his time in the ateliers of artists who were about to revolutionize the artistic world—and he began collecting."

"She's missed her calling," Genevieve thought begrudgingly. "She's a natural docent."

The room darkened as clouds raced across the sun, then brightened again as they streaked off to cast shadows elsewhere.

Madame Morier's energy began to build. "Lord Crosswick was awed by the artists' willingness to risk everything to follow their passion. Dedicated to acquiring works from friends and only works he loved, he began buying small pieces, reflecting daily life in Paris—a gathering in a bar, a bridge bathed in late-afternoon light, a flower past its prime. He was wild for the works of the Impressionists. He couldn't resist the beauty of the spontaneous brush strokes and ever-changing light covering these canvases, and soon, the pace of his acquisitions sped up dramatically."

Mesmerized by the captivating raconteur, Philip leaned forward, not wanting to miss a word. "Would you say my cousin was a patron of these Impressionists?"

"I would say oui," Her broad grin reached her eyes. "By the time he left Paris in 1870 to return to England, he shipped forty-two crates from Paris to Wilmingrove Hall, each containing six or eight paintings. He had, indeed, become a collector and, as a result, a patron in the true sense of the word."

"What about Charlotte? When did she and Philip meet?" Genevieve loved to hear stories about Charlotte Chaubert. The more she learned about the Countess of Crosswick, the more she liked her.

"Ah, Charlotte." Madame's smiles came easily now as she spoke of the Laney family. "They met two years before he went back to England. As the story goes, he was smitten, and she was not. He pursued her. She thought he was a soulless Englishman trying to buy affection from the artists he befriended. But, as she grew to know him, she succumbed to his charm, his elegance, and his passionate heart."

Genevieve watched the color rise in Madame Morier's cheeks and saw a flicker of affection in her eyes. "I do believe madame has a crush on Philip's long-dead cousin," Genevieve thought.

The house manager took a deep breath before continuing. "Lord Crosswick's most cherished acquisition was the beautiful, talented artist with whom he had fallen in love, Charlotte Camille Chaubert. Charlotte was a twenty-four-year-old free spirit with a fine pedigree. Philip's parents approved of her immediately and were relieved that their thirty-three-year-old only son was settling down at last. Philip and Charlotte were married at St Paul's Cathedral on September 7, 1871, with Charlotte's family in attendance. Though the townhouse in Kensington was their primary residence, they loved spending time in Paris and entertaining their creative friends here at Maison de Laney."

She drained the last of her Scotch, put the glass on the coffee table, and said, "Come with me."

Philip and Genevieve followed Madame Morier into the foyer, down the hall, and into a cozy room.

"This is your study, my lord." She walked to a painting over the fireplace. "And this is your cousin Philip and his beloved Charlotte."

The three of them gazed at an Impressionist work in soft blues and greens. A couple sat on a garden bench, surrounded by a soft halo of sunshine. The man leaned forward, captivated by the beautiful young woman. With her chin tilted down, the mademoiselle looked up at him through her lashes, a soft smile at the corners of her mouth. Almost closing the distance between them, their hands rested on the bench, just a whisper from touching. It was an exquisite homage to love.

"This was their engagement portrait," Madame Morier said, her hands folded in front of her and her head cocked to the side.

Philip leaned close to the lower right-hand corner of the painting. "B. M.; Is that Berthe Morisot?" His mouth hung open. He couldn't tear his gaze from the signature.

"It is," Madame confirmed. "Venez avec moi." Again, she directed them to follow her, and, like two obedient students, they did. They walked through the dining room to the two sets of doors at the far end.

"See the blue bench?" She pointed into the garden.

"That's the bench in the painting!" Genevieve cried. Overwhelmed at the idea that the portrait of the two lovers had been painted in this garden, her eyes stung. "I feel as if I'm in a dream." She looked at madame, her eyes glistening. "Madame Morier, though Philip and I are adjusting pretty well to our new roles as the Earl and Countess of Crosswick and all that it means, it's still staggering to realize we are responsible for so much heritage and so many treasures."

Madame Morier stared at her employer for a moment. Genevieve thought she was about to say something kind, but instead, she stiffened, said, "Allons-y," and forged on.

Two hours later, Genevieve sat in a picture-perfect petite salon. Challenged by their housekeeper's sublime French style, she had worried too much over what to wear for dinner and had changed clothes several times before coming down. At last, she decided on grey wool pants, a matching cashmere sweater and grey suede ballet flats. Understated but chic, she thought. When she was drying her hair, Genevieve smiled at the fact that she and Madame Morier had similar haircuts. At least, Genevieve thought, the cosmopolitan head of their household couldn't fault her hair!

Earlier, she had enjoyed the engaging, knowledgeable Madame Morier and had begun to think this woman was going to be a welcome ally as she and Philip navigated the complicated world of French society. And then, warm madame had vanished, and the cool, arrogant house manager who had greeted them upon their arrival reappeared. It was perplexing, to say the least.

She pulled her thoughts from Madame Morier to the straight line of perfect bubbles rising from the stem of her Champagne glass, breaking the surface and tickling her nose as she sipped. She had tried to wait for Philip, but after fifteen minutes, she could no longer resist the pretty pink call of the Widow Clicquot. As she savored the soft finish on her tongue, she stared into the fire crackling on the hearth. Scenes of the day floated through her mind, and she played the happy conclusion over and over. She closed her eyes and blew a little puff of air from her cheeks. She and Philip seemed to live a charmed life. From the time they met, Philip, about to finish his master's degree in art history, and she in her second year of law school, they had been lucky, indeed. And now, forty years later, with one adored son and his marvelous wife, two wild grandchildren, an unimaginable inheritance and death cheated, Genevieve felt she was living a life straight out of a novel.

"Okay, G." Striding into the room, Philip startled her from her thoughts. Admiring his classic, handsome features, she couldn't help but smile. She never tired of the crinkles at the corners of his bright green eyes, of his lean, muscular frame, or his thick graying hair she still thought of as blond. Soon to be sixty-five, Philip could fill a room with his easy charm, and she still adored him.

"Sorry, I didn't wait." She grinned and handed him his glass. "You've been on the phone?"

"I have. I was talking to Captain Bruni." Two furrows etched Philip's brow.

"From your frown, I'd say whatever he told you was not good."

Philip sat next to Genevieve on a camel-and-black-striped loveseat. He clinked her glass before taking a long swig from the flute. "Bruni said the BEA, Bureau of Enquiry and Analysis, the group responsible for investigating incidents in French airspace, has a preliminary report. One of their inspectors is coming in the morning to speak to us."

Genevieve put her glass on the coffee table in front of them. "He didn't tell you what their findings were?"

"He did not. He said Inspector Boucher, the BEA agent, will brief us when he comes."

"What do you think that means?" Genevieve twisted her wedding ring round and round on her finger and searched Philip's eyes for answers.

Philip picked up Genevieve's hand from her lap. "I have no idea," he said. We'll find out tomorrow." He turned her hand over and ran his thumb back and forth over her palm. "You know, since we inherited this fortune, we've been talking about how we can use the wealth to make an impact on as many lives as possible."

Genevieve nodded.

"I'd say our little brush with mortality today was the universe telling us to stop fiddling around and decide how we're going to do that."

A smile bloomed on Genevieve's lips. "Trust you to think of a way to turn today's fright into a motivating experience." She laced her fingers through Philip's. "Have you come up with the grand plan?"

Philip was animated as he spoke. "Not yet, but I was thinking. Since we have museums and an art foundation, we need to use those as the basis. Why can't we break out of the cloistered walls of the museums and reach kids whose lives might be changed or even saved by the power of art?"

Usually the one bubbling over with schemes, Genevieve loved when Philip took an idea and ran with it. "I think when we meet with Lillie, that should be at the top of our agenda," she said, then leaned forward and planted a kiss on the tip of his nose. "If we can stay alive until then."

TWO

GENEVIEVE GUIDED THE tip of her belt through the gold lion's head buckle. As she slipped her feet into cordovan ankle boots and tugged up the zippers, she heard a firm knock on her bedroom door.

"Come in," she said, massaging her forehead. She and Philip had talked long into the night, then finished their eventful day with some post-trauma lovemaking, leaving her groggy this morning from lack of sleep.

The door opened a few feet and there stood Madame Morier, looking expensive. She was dressed in black from her turtleneck sweater to her body-hugging jeans to the tips of her Chanel ballerinas. The only relief was a vivid yellow and red scarf wrapped nonchalantly around her neck. Genevieve caught the glitter of huge gold studs in Madame Morier's ears, almost covered by her shiny bob. "I wonder what we're paying her," she mused and mustered a shallow smile. "Madame Morier, good morning."

"Countess, Monsieur Boucher from the BEA is here." She walked several steps into the luxurious bedroom and placed a business card on a round table next to a mass of coral roses. "The earl is with him and asked me to summon you. And so, I have."

Genevieve's left eyebrow shot up. "Summon?" She tried her best to look down her nose at Madame Morier but, as Genevieve was several inches shorter than the housekeeper, it didn't quite work.

Standing even taller, Madame Morier said, "Perhaps 'request' is a better word." She turned and, just before she pulled the door closed, said, "They are in the grand salon, countess."

"Merde!" Genevieve loved swearing in French. "This woman's going to be a problem," she thought. "I wonder what the French is for 'pain in the butt'."

Genevieve trotted down the curved staircase at a fast clip, one hand on the wrought iron banister, her camel skirt swishing around her ankles with each step.

As she neared the bottom of the staircase, she could hear two men talking. Philip's voice she knew. The other, a rich and elegant accent, conjured an image of a well-built, sensuous man with a Gauloise hanging from the corner of his mouth, eyes narrowed against the wafting smoke. Her step quickened across the foyer to the grand salon. Standing in the doorway, she blinked. She searched the room from one end to the other and saw no one but her husband. Philip was seated on the biscuit-colored sofa. Across the coffee table from him were two massive, overstuffed chairs facing away from her.

"Philip, are you alone?" Confused, Genevieve's eyes swept the room again, but there was no sign of another man.

The sexy voice from nowhere said, "Non, countess. Je suis ici!

I am here!" Like a jack-in-the-box, a short, stout man popped out of one of the chairs, huge cushions hiding him from Genevieve. The petit Frenchman scurried around the chair and over to where Genevieve still stood in the doorway. He bowed from the waist. "Enchantée, countess, simply enchanted. I am Charles Boucher, Investigator with the BEA." He grabbed her hand and brought it to his lips. "Bienvenue à Paris. I promise we shall do better to make you feel at home than we did welcoming you into the country. Quelle entrée, oui?"

He still cradled Genevieve's hand. She could feel the sweat building between them and slid her hand from his gentle grasp. Looking over the top of his head, which was, at most, three inches over five feet, she saw Philip struggling to keep his laughter at bay. She scanned Boucher's round face and smiled at him. "I'm sorry we're meeting under such circumstances, Monsieur Boucher. Thank you for coming so promptly." Genevieve turned to Philip. "Is Captain Bruni joining us?"

Boucher answered for Philip. "Non, countess. I wanted to interview you and the earl without him present."

"Really?" Genevieve's eyes widened. She looked at Philip, then back at Boucher.

Boucher shoved his lower lip into a pout. "Baahh, oui. This is normal. We like to have each party involved in such an event give us their impressions." Boucher gave a sweep of his arm, ushering Genevieve into her own living room. "Please, sit down."

Genevieve ambled to Philip, skirting the coffee table until she stood in front of him. Before sitting, she held out her hand.

"Good morning, darling boy." Remembering their early-morning dalliance, Genevieve offered a sultry smile.

Philip took her hand and held her smokey gaze before pulling her down beside him.

The intimate exchange did not go unnoticed by Monsieur Boucher, who tucked it into his mental file. The investigator sat, scooching back into the deep chair. "Allons. Shall we begin?" He dug in one sagging pocket of his jacket and pulled out his leather-covered notepad, scuffed from use. In the other, he discovered the nub of a pencil, the erasure well-gnawed. He licked the pencil lead and was ready to go. "D'accord. So, tell me. Who would very much like you dead?" His voice was so cheerful, both the Warwicks thought they had misheard the question.

"Pardon, Monsieur. Did you just ask who would like us dead?"

"Oui, my lord. There is nothing but to be direct." His eyes sparkled and his face shone with enthusiasm. Then he slapped his forehead as if remembering something. "Ah, but of course, no one has told you." He reached into his battered briefcase and pulled out a few sheets of paper and handed them to Philip. "Significant water was found in your gas tank. Someone put the water there intending to cause the plane to crash."

A little choking noise rose from Genevieve's throat. "What do you mean?" Her head swiveled to Philip then back at Boucher. "Are you saying it was intentional? Maybe the gas cap was loose, and water seeped in from condensation, or…?" She threw out explanations that seemed plausible, anything other than someone wanting them dead.

Boucher's eyes filled with concern. "I understand this is upsetting, my lady, but I assure you, our people are excellent analysts and have ruled out all but this possibility. They are checking security cameras to see if they can identify the auteur."

"Auteur?" Genevieve cocked her head.

"Uh, the perpetrator," Boucher clarified.

Philip held up his hand to stop the inspector. " You're saying there could be cameras that will tell us who did this?"

"Oui. Security cameras will no doubt show us who put water in the tank, but that person will not be the real criminal." Boucher shrugged. "He—or she—is the hired hand." Without missing a beat, he said, "As I asked before, who would very much like you dead? Perhaps someone would receive great wealth if you and Lady Crosswick perished in a plane crash. Is that possible?"

Philip leaned forward, elbows on his knees, the muscles in his neck taut. His eyebrows almost touched as his forehead furrowed. "Our son and his family are the beneficiaries of the Crosswick estate, and I assure you they are not suspects."

"Mais, non, certainement. But I understand you had some difficulty the last few months in Angleterre; is that not correct?"

Sensing Philip's anger building, Genevieve put a cautionary hand on her husband's arm as he said, "Monsieur Boucher, that entire business in England was resolved and the person responsible is no longer a threat. There is no possibility the two situations could be linked. You're sure the water in the fuel tank was done on purpose? Are you telling us it couldn't be a simple mistake?"

The investigator shrugged his shoulders. "There is always a

possibility the refueler in Leeds made an error." He tented his hands. "But it is unlikely."

Genevieve examined her manicured nails and pushed the cuticles back with her thumb. "The incident in Yorkshire had nothing to do with our wealth. At this point, I can't imagine who would want to kill us, or why."

His pencil poised over a blank page in his small notebook, Monsieur Boucher asked, "What were the events at Wilmingrove Hall about?"

Philip eased back against the sofa cushion. "Monsieur, my guess is you already know what happened at the Hall. You strike me as a man who doesn't ask a question he hasn't already answered."

Boucher's grin squished his chubby cheeks up to his eyes. "My lord, you are très perspicace."

"Oh yes," Genevieve chimed in. "Philip is nothing if not perceptive. But I doubt if our combined intuition will discern who wants us dead."

Boucher scooted forward in his chair, so his feet touched the floor. He wrote some notes in his scruffy notebook, then squinted at Philip and Genevieve. "My lord, my lady, why are you here?"

Confused, Philip and Genevieve looked at each other then back at the investigator. "What do you mean, why are we here?" Philip asked, his head cocked to one side.

"I mean what caused you to leave the safety of Wilmingrove Hall and come to Paris?"

"That's an interesting interpretation of what we did." Philip's anger simmered just below the surface.

Genevieve glanced at his profile. His jaw tensed and his eyes narrowed.

"With the resolution of what happened at the Hall, it never occurred to me Paris would be a dangerous proposition. What about you, G?"

"I wouldn't have thought so."

"I'm assuming you know about my recent inheritance."

Boucher nodded, "Uh, oui."

"I'm sure you also know we've been at the Crosswick family seat in Yorkshire since September. We've come to France, first to spend time at this property." Philip offered a sweeping gesture around the salon. "While we're here in Paris, we'll get to know our art museum, the Laney Musée des Beaux-Arts. We'll be working with Lillie Langdon, the executive director of the Laney Museum of Fine Arts Foundation that supports our two museums. We'll determine if we need to make any changes in order to ensure the integrity of the collection and the foundation's work. In fact, we're meeting with her this afternoon at the musée. From here we'll go to our vineyard in Saint-Émilion. Though everything appears to be well-run on paper, it's easier to make those determinations in person."

Boucher scribbled in his notebook as Philip spoke. When the investigator said nothing, Philip continued.

"Though we've read all the files on the vineyard staff, we haven't met any of them. Most of the permanent employees have been with the vineyard for years. In fact, the managing director has been at Château Beaulieu for almost forty years. Is any of this helpful?"

Boucher tapped his stubby pencil on the half-full page, then chewed his eraser. The only sound in the room came from a painted clock hanging between the French doors to the garden. The tick-tock of the swinging pendulum gave way to chimes announcing eleven o'clock.

Genevieve slipped off her shoe and drew her leg up under her on the sofa. She looked at Philip, who was watching Boucher.

Boucher jotted a note. "Hmm… almost forty years," he said under his breath. At last, he flipped his notebook closed. "D'accord." He stood, clicked his heels, and bobbed his head. "Merci beaucoup. I believe I have what I need for the moment."

"You do?" Surprised by his abrupt announcement, Genevieve stood and struggled to get her foot back into her shoe. "I don't understand. What just happened? Do you think you know who put water in our fuel?"

Boucher's head bounced up and down like a bobblehead doll. "I may have une idée that perhaps will grow into something significant."

Still seated, Philip snorted, then asked, "Would you care to share your thoughts with us, Monsieur Boucher?"

Putting his notebook back in his left pocket and his gnawed pencil in his right, the investigator said, "When I am a bit more certain of my theory, I shall be delighted to share it with you. I trust I may return as questions arise?"

"Of course. We'll help any way we can." Still confused, Genevieve extended her hand. "Thank you, Monsieur Boucher."

"C'est mon plaisir, countess."

Philip was unwilling to let the investigator go without him

offering at least a hint of what he was thinking. "Monsieur, s'il vous plaît. Do you have a specific idea who put water in the fuel, or do you just have a general hunch?"

"Hunch. I like this word. Let us say I have a hunch that, if it proves correct, will lead us to a specific person. I will tell you one thing. I believe this mystery is tied to the art or perhaps to your vineyard."

Hugging herself, Genevieve rubbed her hands up and down her arms. "Hmm. I, um… Monsieur Boucher. Are you suggesting someone wants to steal our art or our wine, so they decided to kill us to make it easier?"

"My lady, perhaps it is a bit more complicated. Maybe steal art, maybe take your vineyard, maybe protect their jobs." Boucher shrugged. "I think each one is possible—a good start."

"Wow," Philip said as he stood, towering over the investigator. "That sounds, as you French say, un peu fou; a little crazy."

Bucher flashed an impish grin. "I assure you, my lord, I am completely mad. But in this case, I am right. Now, if I may, I shall leave you. But I shall be in touch." He headed for the door, then turned around. "In the meantime, please be cautious. I would like to solve the mystery before it becomes a fatal crime." He nodded, scuttled down the gallery and out of the front door, leaving Philip and Genevieve gaping at each other.

THREE

PHILIP AND GENEVIEVE waited for Lillie Langdon in a small conference room overlooking one of the museum galleries. When the door opened, she blew in like a breath of fresh air. Ballerina slim, she floated rather than walked. Her blond curls were piled high on her head, held with a single sterling silver clip, stray tendrils bouncing around her sculpted face.

"Lillie, how wonderful to see you again." Genevieve rose from a leather and chrome chair, a dramatic contrast to the elaborate nineteenth-century surroundings. She extended her hand, her eyes crinkling with an affectionate smile. From the moment they met four months ago in England, she had fallen in love with Lillie.

"Lord and Lady Crosswick!" Lillie grabbed Genevieve's hand in both of hers. "I can't begin to tell you how happy I am you're here. Since we talked at your fabulous party at Wilmingrove Hall, I couldn't wait to get you to the Laney Musée des Beaux-Arts." Lillie squeezed Genevieve's hand. "And Lord Crosswick." Lillie turned her radiance to Philip. "I've been so excited about showing off the LMBA and sharing all our plans, I couldn't sleep last night."

"Genevieve and I want to hear everything." Philip gave Lillie la bise, the traditional two-cheek French greeting. "But I insist you call us Philip and Genevieve."

As they took their seats around a small, round table, Genevieve jumped in. "Lillie, we have two things on our agenda. First, we want to hear all about your ideas for the future of the foundation. We've heard the most marvelous things about what you've already done. I'm wondering how you'll top your past successes." Genevieve scooted her chair closer and leaned forward, her elbows on the table. "We've heard about the exhibition two years ago where you combined paintings and sculptures of Degas' dancers with the London Contemporary Dance Theatre and the Experimental Strings Ensemble."

"We read the reviews in *The Times*." Philip smiled. "Brilliant, Lillie. Just brilliant."

"And what about the opening gala for 'The Circus Through the Eyes of an Artist', when you brought in performers from Cirque du Soleil to entertain the guests? Didn't the gala sell out the first day?" Genevieve heard herself gushing but didn't care.

"As I recall, the event netted over two million pounds for the foundation." Philip was impressed. "Do you think we can be that successful here in Paris?"

"I do." Her cheeks glowing from the praise, Lillie put up her hands. "But please, please," she said. "This is too much. I want to leave room to dazzle you. If you're overawed by my past accomplishments, it will be difficult to impress you in the future!" Her smile was irresistible.

"Not to worry, Lillie." Charmed by this sprite, Philip couldn't help but gush a bit himself. "As you know, art is one of our great loves. Inheriting responsibility for the Laney Museum of Fine Arts in London, Laney Musée des Beaux-Arts de Paris, and the foundation is thrilling for us. I hope it doesn't scare you when I tell you we want to become hands-on with the foundation and help any way we can."

"Which brings us to our second agenda item. Philip, tell Lillie what we want to accomplish."

"I can't wait to hear." Lillie straightened in her chair as Philip explained they didn't know what the project should be, but they knew they wanted to reach and enrich as many lives as possible. And they wanted to get started immediately. "We're thinking about something connecting art and children—art changing children's lives or something like that."

"That's smashing news," Lillie beamed. "And a challenge. I love a challenge. We do have a remarkable program called the Children's Art Forum already in place but let me gather my thoughts and I'll give you some ideas of projects as soon as I think of something brilliant."

Lillie looked up and saw someone struggling through the glass door with a tray. "Aha." She dashed across the room and pulled open the door for a young man bringing refreshments. "Lord and Lady Crosswick, this is Émile de Laudre, one of our interns. Émile is in his last year of the art history program at the Sorbonne." Lillie motioned to a carved chest sitting along one wall of the conference room. "Émile, you can put the tray over there."

Close to six feet tall and rail thin, Émile could have just walked off a Paris runway. His luxurious mane was parted in the middle and waved to his chin. In contrast to his dark good looks, his heavy-lidded eyes were pale blue. A waist-cinching olive-green jacket topped narrow black trousers tucked into polished black ankle boots. His demeanor was not subtle. Everything about him shouted wealth, privilege, and ennui.

"Bonjour," Émile threw in Philip and Genevieve's direction. He plunked the tray on the sideboard with a clatter that rattled the cups and French press. With a dramatic sigh, he looked at Lillie and said in French, "You asked for coffee; here it is," and he sashayed out.

"Oh my." Genevieve was unsure what else to say.

Philip's brows arched. "Um, Lillie. That, um… that young man is a Musée des Beaux Arts intern?"

"He is, Philip." Lillie blew out a puff of air. "I assure you there is a good explanation." She let silence fill the room.

Genevieve leaned forward, her elbows on the table and her eyes on Lillie while Philip tipped his chair onto the back legs, folding his hands in his lap. He waited several beats before he said, "Well, are you going to share this explanation with us, or do you want us to guess?"

"I thought I'd let the suspense build just a bit before sharing why this arrogant little tosser is filling a coveted spot at the museum when there are so many more deserving students. You see, his father is the Baron de Sézanne, one of the foundation's biggest donors."

"Enough said." Philip put his chair back on the floor, dropped his head back and studied the ceiling before turning his attention back to Lillie. "As I recall, the baron's name has been at the top of our donor's list for the last few years. Didn't he become one of our patrons with a huge initial gift?"

Lillie cocked her head. "If you call twenty-five million euros a huge gift, then I would have to say yes. As part of his patronage, he committed to an additional five million euros a year for ten years. This year marks the halfway point in his commitment. And he rather likes that Émile is an intern at the museum."

Her elbows still on the table and her hands pressed together, Genevieve tapped her fingertips on one another while she thought. "So, at this point, the baron has supported us to the tune of fifty million euros with another twenty-five on the horizon. Is that what you calculated, Philip?"

"Yup," Philip said, smiling at his wife. "And after hearing Émile's sterling credentials, I'd say he's our favorite intern, wouldn't you, G?"

Genevieve nodded. "I love everything about him, especially his winning attitude. Excellent job finding such an outstanding young man, Lillie."

"I live but to serve," she said, rolling her violet eyes.

With the question of the errant intern asked and answered, the three moved to the topic of future plans. Lillie's vision for the museums and the foundation was aggressive and creative. Some of her ideas were provocative. All were fresh and exciting. Throughout the meeting, Genevieve sat on the edge of her seat. Lillie answered every question with a quick response, demonstrating her deep knowledge of the foundation and describing future plans with enthusiasm.

After two hours of rapid-fire conversation, Philip asked, "Lillie, how can we use our properties to benefit the foundation? Could we create an event in conjunction with an exhibition, a gourmet and art weekend, maybe 'Palette and Palate' for the art gourmet at our Saint-Émilion vineyard? I'm sure we could raise a few euros with an event there, don't you think?"

"Lord Crosswick, that's the spirit! I'd love to do an event at Château Beaulieu. That would be smashing! And, since you've opened the door, I'm going to walk right through it." Lillie vibrated with enthusiasm. "We have a new show of Abstract Expressionists at the musée opening in three weeks. Would you consider hosting a cocktail party the evening before? You can't imagine how thrilled our patrons would be to meet you and be in your beautiful home."

"That's a fantastic idea. Let's do it. Philip and I need to meet the people who support our museum, and that sounds like a perfect opportunity to get to know a lot of them at once."

Lillie clapped her hands and smiled at her two bosses. "Thank you, Philip and Genevieve, for your enthusiasm, your support, and most of all the commitment to your personal involvement. We're going to have the most marvelous alliance, we three."

The glass door opened, and a studious-looking young man popped his head in. "Pardon, Lillie. "

"Ah, Bernard! I was just about to text you to join us. Come in, come in." Lillie bounced out of her chair and threw the door wide. "Lord and Lady Crosswick, may I introduce Bernard Reines, director of the Laney Musée des Beaux Arts."

Bernard smacked his forehead with his palm. "Merde, j'ai

complètement oublié," he swore, rolling his eyes. "Excusez-moi, I completely forgot." As he nodded an apology, his chestnut hair flopped over his brow. "Enchanté, my lord, my lady," he said, his chocolate eyes, sparkling at them through his horn-rimmed glasses. He raked his hand through his thick bangs, sweeping them back in place. "We have been anticipating your visit. Have you had a tour yet of your musée?"

"Not yet, Bernard." Lillie grinned. "I thought we could do that together. I was hoping you'd be back from your meeting in time, and so you are. But, you need me?"

"Oui, juste pour un instant, s'il te plaît. Rohh la la." Bernard growled and threw up his hands. "Nous avons un problème de livraison."

"A delivery problem? Is it serious?" Philip piped up.

Not expecting Philip to understand French, Bernard grinned. "It is just a little bit serious," he said. "Last month, La Cité du Vin in Bordeaux bought two paintings we had in storage. They were supposed to be picked up this morning and delivered before the end of the day, but our trucking service still hasn't collected them." He turned back to Lillie." Would you mind double checking the transfer documents? Émile did them and," Bernard rolled his eyes, "I need for you to make sure they are properly executed.

Lillie stood. "If you'll excuse me, I'll go down to the loading dock with Bernard."

"Of course, Lillie, go. Please don't mind us. Genevieve and I can wander on our own until it's convenient for you two to join us."

"Good plan," Lillie said as she headed for the door. "Never fear; we'll find you wherever you are. This first gallery is a perfect place to start. I'll text you as soon as we've sorted this out." She flashed a dazzling smile at Philip and Genevieve and dashed out the door with Bernard hot on her heels.

When Lillie and Bernard had disappeared, Genevieve turned to Philip. "Bernard seemed pleased when he realized you speak French."

"He did, didn't he? I'm sure my excellent command of French would shock most people."

"I'm glad you have such a healthy self-image." Genevieve patted him on his bottom, and they began to wander through their museum. "Well, well. Look at this, G." Philip grinned at the dynamic canvas of Lee Krasner, one of his favorite abstract expressionists and the wife of Jackson Pollock, another artist he revered. "In your wildest imagination, did you ever think we would own such great works of art?"

"It's not terrible to be outrageously wealthy, is it, my darling?" Genevieve slid her hand through the crook of Philip's arm, and they moved to the next canvas, a colorful painting full of movement and drama by Mary Abbott.

For an hour, Philip and Genevieve strolled from canvas to canvas moving from the Abstract Expressionists gallery to a salon filled with strange, avant-garde works by French artists.

Arms crossed and squinting, Genevieve stared at a white porcelain commode with a red and purple striped seat. The installation was tucked into the corner of the room. She turned to find Philip across the gallery, studying a thick rope hanging from the ceiling, with about six feet puddled on the floor.

"Am I to assume the significance of this toilet is that the artist feels the world is shit?" Genevieve said, adopting an intellectual tone. "Or, perhaps, it's just a convenient place to go to the bathroom, albeit not very private."

Unable to tear himself from the hemp cable in front of him, Philip said, "I'm fairly sure this installation is entitled 'When You Learn How Much You Paid For Me, You'll Hang Yourself.'"

At that, Genevieve exploded, her laughter bouncing off the soaring ceilings and marble columns.

"I've missed a great joke!" Lillie said, gliding into the room. "Tell me, what's so hilarious?"

Shaking his head, Philip smiled. "We're laughing at these two installations. I thought we had moved beyond this sort of thing in the late eighties, early nineties, but these are recent works. I can't wait to learn about our acquisition process."

"Please, Lillie, don't tell us you're on the acquisition committee," Genevieve begged.

Lillie wiped her hand across her forehead in mock relief. "Whew!" she said. "I am not, but it's something I want to discuss with you. I hope you've enjoyed wandering on your own. I'm so sorry our delivery issue took so much time and Bernard won't be able to join us."

"That's a shame," Philip said. "I was looking forward to getting to know him. I read his resume and wanted to ask him about his time at the China Academy of Art in Hangzhou. I'm hoping he's considering expanding our collection in contemporary Chinese art. I suppose I can get together with him later."

"We'll make certain that you do. You won't believe this, but the family who owns the château near you, Château Pitique, is the family with whom Bernard lived when he studied in China. They bought it three or four years ago. How's that for a small world?"

Philip's eyes rounded. "That's extraordinary. Do they live at the château?"

Lillie's curls bounced as she shook her head. "The parents live in China. They're huge in import-export. Their son, Hank—his name is Han Shou, but he goes by Hank—lives in Saint-Émilion at the château. He and Bernard are close, and Hank is a museum donor. Bernard makes sure of that."

"We'll take it any way we can get it," Philip said.

"I think his father bought the vineyard so Hank would have something to do." Lillie leaned in. "He's pretty much mucked up everything he's tried since he graduated. His father hopes he can make a success of the vineyard." She raised her brows. "The wine business is difficult enough if you have generations of winemaking behind you. I can't imagine how he's going to succeed with no experience, but so far, according to Bernard, he's doing a decent job exporting to China."

Philip scratched the back of his neck. "Jeeze, I can't imagine running a vineyard without any background in the industry. I can tell you, Genevieve and I are nervous about jumping into the world of fine wine and we have a spectacular team in place. It's one thing to be proficient at drinking great vintages—we're good at that—but it's a different challenge to ensure the continuity of winemaking at the level Château Beaulieu has maintained for over two hundred years. The idea that we could be the first generation to allow the quality to diminish is terrifying."

"Philip, Lillie has many other things to worry about besides us driving Château Beaulieu into the," she smiled, "terroir. Getting back to the subject, is everything all right with the delivery issue?" Genevieve asked. "Anything we need to worry about?"

"It's all taken care of. Shall we?" She led them into the center of the museum, a circular three-story hall, glorious to the eye with ornate plaster moldings, light pouring in from soaring windows.

Philip strained to look up at the domed ceiling. "As I recall, Philip Laney, the 9TH Earl, bought the building just after Haussmann built it."

Seeming delighted that the Warwicks were so well informed, Lillie's eyes sparkled at Philip and Genevieve. "You have done your homework. I'm impressed."

"And the collection we've seen is exceptional, with a few questionable choices," Genevieve chuckled.

"We're impressed with the quality of the works," Philip added. "The Laneys have done a wonderful job over 150 years and four generations, haven't they?"

"Indeed they have, and we want to continue that impressive record. The three of us are going to do exciting things." Lillie threw her coat over her shoulders. "Now, it's time for Champagne and gateau. How does that sound?"

From behind a column on the second floor, he watched the three leave the building, laughing, and talking as they went. He swiped tiny beads of perspiration from his upper lip with the back of his hand, then raked his fingers through his wavy hair. Now that everything was in place, the game could begin. And if the earl wouldn't play, there would be a high price to pay. Either way, this was going to be fun.

FOUR

TWO WEEKS LATER, as RSVPs poured in for the Abstract Expressionist pre-opening gala at the Earl and Countess of Crosswick's home, Philip stood in the doorway of the study. He brought treats to the two women organizing the invitation responses, most of which were "oui": he carried a tray with coffee, cups, and a plate of hot pink, blue, mint green, and yellow macarons. Winter sun slanted through the French doors, filling the charming room with warmth, belying the chilly temperature outside. On opposite sides of an antique writing desk, Genevieve's straight chestnut hair huddled just inches from Lillie's mass of blonde curls. Philip smiled, watching the two chatter, make notes, laugh, erase one name, and add two more.

Philip crossed the room with his tray of goodies. "Ta da!" he said. "Your cookie daddy has arrived."

Rubbing her hands together, Lillie eyed the macarons and licked her lips. "Philip, you're a master at understanding what a woman craves."

"Only sometimes," Genevieve said, slicing open another envelope with her sterling paperknife.

As she reached for a cookie, Philip skirted her and held out the tray to Lillie. He looked at Genevieve with a sly grin. "Not so fast, my little ingrate. She who appreciates the giver gets the treats first."

"Men are so easy." Genevieve snatched a cookie from Philip's tray and popped the entire thing in her mouth. "Praise their egos and you own them for life."

"No wonder you and Philip have been married so long. You play him like a Stradivarius," Lillie said, two macarons safe in her possession.

"If you two aren't careful, I'll take my treats and go home."

"You are home." Genevieve licked crumbs from her lips.

"Ah, yes. So I am." Philip pulled up a chair and joined the two cheeky women. "I just got off the phone with David."

A smile glowed in Genevieve's eyes as she held up a cream-colored envelope. "We just got his RSVP and he's coming. I'm so pleased. Do you know when he'll be here? What did he say when you talked to him? We haven't heard from Becca yet. Does he know if she's coming?" One question tumbled over another.

"Whoa, there." Philip surrendered, holding both hands up in self-defense. "You're the one whose nose is buried in the responses. I should be hammering you with questions."

Enjoying the banter between the two, Lillie swiveled back and forth between Philip and Genevieve, like someone watching a tennis match.

Genevieve whipped her focus to Lillie. "You remember David, don't you, Lillie? You met him at our party at Wilmingrove Hall."

"Of course I do. He's your solicitor, isn't he? And very dishy, as I recall." As soon as the words were out of her mouth, Lillie grimaced. "Perhaps I shouldn't have said that." She scrunched her shoulders toward her ears and offered a sheepish grin.

"You're right. David is absolutely a hunk." Genevieve sat back in her desk chair. "But beware, Lillie, my girl. I'm pretty sure he and Rebecca Conway are an item." She gave Lillie a sympathetic look. "I don't think you've met Becca. You'll love her. I hope she's coming to the opening."

Her elbow on the desk, Lillie leaned forward, cradling her chin in her hand. "That's not the Rebecca Conway with the lifestyle channel, *The Most Interesting Woman in the Room,* is it?"

"One in the same." Philip took a bite out of a hot pink macaron. "And I have to say, she often is."

"Is what?" Genevieve and Lillie asked in unison.

"The most interesting woman in the room," he clarified.

"Aah." Both women nodded.

"You do, of course, mean when the two of us," Genevieve pointed to Lillie, then to herself, "aren't in the room."

"Mais oui." Philip threw up his hands. "That goes without saying. But, if I may, I'd like to turn the conversation from the two most interesting women in *this* room back to David. Lillie, will G and I have anything to show him on our world-changing project when he comes for the gala?"

"Voila! So glad you asked." Lillie reached into her tote on the floor beside her and pulled out a slim, spiral-bound booklet. She handed it to Philip. "I think you'll like the proposal."

As he leafed through the pages, Genevieve saw the cover. "La Cité du Vin. Interesting. Are we changing the world one glass of wine at a time?"

"Not a bad idea," Lillie said, "but there's a little more to it than that."

"While Philip's reading, give me the executive summary."

"The idea came to me the moment you mentioned creating something to change lives." Lillie grinned as she spoke. "The foundation, LMBA, and La Cité du Vin have been partners since 2016, when la Cité opened. We loan them artwork on a rotating basis, and, as you know, we recently sold them two paintings. In turn, they provide support for various programs at the museum."

Philip laid the proposal in his lap and listened to Lillie's overview.

"The gist of your new partnership is to create a work-study program we'll call "The Art of the Vine.""

"I like the name," Genevieve said, anxious to hear more.

"The year-long program would accept students interested in learning about French viticulture. Their fees would be completely covered, but their obligation would be that, on completion of the program, they commit to work a minimum of two years at a vineyard in Bordeaux. As you know, there's a dire labor shortage in the wine industry in France. This would help both the wine growers and the students. There are a lot of kids who can't afford school fees, so they never learn a skill and eventually end up on the dole."

"It sounds like a good program, but it doesn't get my blood racing, Lillie." Philip picked up the prospectus. "Are all the details in here?"

"Yes, they are. I understand, Philip. It's not curing cancer, but I think it's exactly what you're looking for." Lillie still smiled, but her eyes no longer sparkled. "I promise, this program has the power to change the course of a young person's life. Spend some time with it and let me know what you think." She dug back in her bag, pulled out another copy, and handed it to Genevieve. "Ask me questions as they come up."

"Excusez-moi." Three heads turned to find Madame Morier standing in the doorway, holding a tray of envelopes. "Plus des réponses." She walked across the room and placed the tray on the desk.

"Just what we need." Genevieve rolled her eyes. "Merci, madame."

"How many are there so far?" Madame Morier asked. As she was responsible for the house looking its best and for the event running smoothly, she was anxious to assess how much trouble the cocktail party would cause her.

"Lillie?" Genevieve deferred to the foundation's director.

Lillie pointed to the stack in front of her. "Before this new batch, we have 122 'oui' and four 'non'. There's no question, people want to meet the Earl and Countess of Crosswick. What do you think, Madame Morier?"

Annoyance radiated from the statuesque woman. "Bernard told me when we spoke yesterday that everyone in Paris wants to come to this event." She arched a single brow, shrugged, and pouted, "Uuh bof."

Surprised that Madam Morier and Bernard had spoken, Genevieve asked, "Do you talk often to Bernard?"

"We have a little gossip from time to time." Before leaving the room, she handed Philip a large cream-colored envelope. "This was hand-delivered for you, my lord."

"Merci, madame." Philip dropped the mail into his lap.

"And, Lady Crosswick, Madame Beaufoy is here to see you," Madame said as an afterthought.

Genevieve looked blank. "Madame Beaufoy? Do I know her?" She frowned at Madame Morier, hoping the house manager would give her a clue who her visitor was.

Instead, Lillie spoke up. "I don't think you've met her yet."

Genevieve narrowed her eyes at Lillie, trying to decide if the fact they hadn't met was good or bad.

"She and her husband are big supporters of the foundation."

Genevieve brightened. "Wonderful."

"Hmm. We'll see what you think after you've met her. And another thing; she is the Presidente of the Board of Cité du Vin." Lillie pointed to the study door. "Go on. Go charm our donor and potential partner. And remember, she has no idea what we are about to propose."

"She is in the salon," Madame Morier said as she walked out.

Genevieve followed her through the door then headed to the grand room.

"Madame Beaufoy, bonjour." Genevieve crossed the room to greet a woman who was fighting against time and losing the battle. Her eyes looked permanently surprised, her cheeks overfilled, and her lips too Brigitte Bardot for her advancing age.

Elise Beaufoy avoided Genevieve's outstretched hand and went straight for la bise. "Please call me Elise, Ah, ma chérie," she gushed. "I am so happy to meet you. Thank you for seeing me. I should have called, but I was just around the corner at my dressmaker and thought I would take a chance that you had a moment for me to say hello and welcome."

She spread her arms and turned a full circle. "This room," she said. "This manoir. C'est parfait. And the art. Mon Dieu!" She walked to the coffee table and picked up a box wrapped in heavy royal purple paper. Fresh gardenias tucked under its thick grosgrain ribbon, wafted scent through the room. "Happy crémaillère!"

"Elise, that's kind of you, but unnecessary." Genevieve was touched. "Crémaillère. Is that what we call a housewarming gift?"

Elise nodded, then leaned into Genevieve like a conspirator. "I could have waited until your gala, but it is important you know how much I want to be on the foundation board. I thought perhaps a very special bottle of Dom Perignon would help you decide I'm the best person to fill the next vacancy." She winked at Genevieve.

"Oh," was all Genevieve could say. "Um…" She searched for a few gracious words. "As you can imagine, I'm just getting my bearings with the foundation and—"

"Let's talk more later this week," Elise interrupted, then kissed Genevieve on both cheeks again. "I shall call you to make a plan, and we shall have a lovely lunch in a couple of days." She gathered her purse and her coat, which she had slung over the back of a chair, and was through the doorway, down the foyer, and out the front door before Genevieve realized she was gone.

When she returned to the study, Genevieve dropped into her chair, bewildered. She plunked the gift box on the desk, and all she could say was, "That was a lot."

Lillie's laugh started with a giggle and grew into a full-blown guffaw. "She's a handful, isn't she? Did she press you for a seat on the board?"

"You knew she was going to do that, and you sent me out there anyway?" Genevieve wadded a piece of paper and threw it across the desk at Lillie.

Grinning as he watched the back and forth, Philip picked up the ivory packet Madame Morier had brought in earlier and looked at the front. His name was written in calligraphy. "Hand me the letter opener, G." He held out his hand and Genevieve slapped the silver knife into his palm. He caught the corner of the flap with the tip, sliced the envelope open, and pulled out two pieces of cardboard. As he held them up by one corner, four photos slid from between them and drifted to the floor, one facing up and three facing down. The color glossy facing Philip was of the Jackson Pollock that filled the wall on the landing at the top of their staircase.

Genevieve stood up and stretched across the desk. "What in the world are those?"

Philip gathered the four photos from the floor. "They seem to be pictures of our Pollock." A handwritten note was clipped to the cardboard. Philip cleared his throat and read aloud.

Lord Crosswick,

We regret the inconvenience we are about to cause you. The Jackson Pollock hanging in your home is not an original, but rather an excellent forgery. If you alert the gendarmes, you shall never see the original painting again.

We would accept a small donation of €5,000,000 for the return of your painting. If we do not receive the money, we would be sorry to destroy such a magnificent work , but one must do what one must do.

We shall be in touch within twenty-four hours to provide the terms of exchange.

With best regards,

M. Gieleur

He dropped the photo as if it had singed his fingers. "G, call Monsieur Boucher. We're either the targets of a bad joke or the victims of a robbery. Let's not touch any of this." He pointed to the envelope, cardboard, and glossies.

Lillie clutched each arm of her chair, her knuckles turning whte. For a moment she sat frozen, then shot out of her chair. "Bloody hell!" she shrieked, tearing out of the study, her blond curls dancing.

Genevieve's hand flew to her mouth as she watched Lillie streak from the room. She dug her fingers into her temples, trying to massage away the fierce throbbing already starting, then she pulled Boucher's business card from a small onyx box on her desk. She tapped a number into her cell and waited for a connection. After two rings a voice croaked, "Oui?", followed by a sneeze and a sniff.

"Monsieur Boucher?" Genevieve said.

"Oui," he said again.

"C'est Genevieve Warwick, La Countess de Crosswick. Hallo.

Monsieur Boucher, we have another problem. It could be a joke, or it could be a spectacular robbery."

Genevieve told the BEA investigator what had just happened.

"Oui…Oui," she said. "Of course, we will. Bon. À bientôt." She ended the call and laid her cell phone on the desk. "He'll be here within the hour. He's alerting the Paris police detectives as well. If it doesn't have anything to do with our fuel tank issue, it's not in his purview. Oh, and he said not to touch anything." She nodded at Philip, acknowledging his earlier advice.

Just as Genevieve asked, "Where did Lillie go?" she burst back into the room swearing like a sailor.

"That bloody bastard! The painting hanging on the landing is a goddamn giclee!" She spat out the word, fire in her eyes. "That's why he signed the note M. Gicleur. Giclee comes from the French word gicleur," she snarled.

"A giclee is made on an inkjet printer, isn't it?" Philip asked. His eyes closed as he pinched the bridge of his nose, trying to relieve the pressure building there.

Lillie rubbed her glazed eyes, thinking. "But once they had the print, swapping it had to be next to impossible. How did they take a five-by-eight-foot painting off the wall, replace it, and get the painting out of the house without being detected?" she said. "I bet Madame Morier keeps firm reins on who comes in and out of this house. It shouldn't be difficult to figure out who had the opportunity to swap the canvases."

"She keeps a close rein on us," Philip nodded, "so I wouldn't be surprised if she has a log of everyone's comings and goings."

Genevieve tapped her chin with a pen. "And, of course, we

have security cameras. I don't know for sure, but I would imagine there's one focused on the stairs and landing." She stood up. "I have to agree with you, Lillie, this seems like an easy theft to solve. I want to see this giclee we've been walking by every day for who-knows-how-long."

Lillie grabbed Genevieve's hand and said, "I've got to get to the museum." Her voice was frantic. She turned and dashed for the door, then stopped. "Go look at the painting. I bet you won't be able to tell it's a fake until you run your hand over the canvas. And have the police call me if they need me. I'll be back as soon as I check on things at le Musée." Then she was gone.

Philip shoved himself out of his chair and put his arm around Genevieve. He could feel the tension in his wife's shoulders. "What was that all about?"

"I'm assuming Lillie wants to make certain nothing similar has happened at the museum."

Philip and Genevieve stood in the foyer at the bottom of the staircase, gazing up to the landing at the rectangular canvas hanging there. Philip pulled Genevieve into his side and kissed the top of her head. As if on cue, they each put a foot on the first tread and began ascending the stairs, unable to take their eyes off the forged Pollock. They trudged closer and closer, trying to detect the artifice with each step.

At the top of the stairs, Philip said, "I can't tell a thing, can you?"

Genevieve shook her head, then tiptoed forward. When she was within a foot of the painting, she pulled her glasses from her trouser pocket, put them on, and leaned in until her nose was just inches from the riot of sweeping, swirling strings of paint.

She squinted, walking back and forth in front of the long canvas. She stopped and turned to Philip. "What am I supposed to see? It looks good to me."

"Lillie said to close your eyes. Run your hand over the surface of the painting and tell me what you feel."

Genevieve's eyes squeezed tight as she concentrated on what she felt, her hand skimming over the canvas. "I'm stunned." She opened her eyes to look again at the drips. "There's no texture. One of the wonderful things about a Pollock is the texture of the drip layer."

Standing at the edge of the landing, Philip had been watching Genevieve's experiment. "You mean to tell me the canvas is flat?" He shook his head, disbelieving.

Genevieve turned from the wall. "Come feel for yourself."

Rather than close his eyes, Philip watched his hand brush over the painted surface before him. Even feeling the flatness of the canvas, it was hard for him to believe the texture didn't exist when his eyes insisted that it did.

"I had no idea a giclee could be so convincing."

Philip jumped at the "dring" of the doorbell. When he turned to look down the length of the grand foyer, Madame Morier was already opening the front door. From their perch on the landing, Philip and Genevieve could hear a rapid exchange in French before Madame Morier stepped aside and allowed three men to enter. Just inside the door, all three men pulled white booties over their shoes.

"Restez ici," Madame Morier demanded, with a gesture even a puppy would understand meant "stay right here!"

The house manager stormed toward the landing, her expensive pumps clacking on the marble floor. "My lord! The police…" but before she could finish her sentence, the bell sounded again. Without missing a step, she turned and charged back to the front door. She threw it open and there stood Monsieur Boucher, blowing his nose into a white handkerchief. He took two huge sniffs, winding up for an enormous sneeze.

Madame Morier stepped back to avoid his spray. "Mais bien sûr." Her words dripped with sarcasm. "Inspector, but of course, you're here as well. And you have un rhume," she said, disgusted by his cold. "Vous restez ici, aussi."

Embarrassed by his Rudolph-red nose, Boucher blinked his watery eyes. "Mais oui, madame." Not wanting to incur her wrath, Boucher stood frozen to his spot. He bobbed his head at the three men from the Paris police, who were also standing firm. They nodded back.

Boucher started to speak to them, then thought better of it. He'd wait for Madame Morier to tell them what to do next.

By the time Madame Morier reached the other end of the foyer, Philip and Genevieve had descended the stairs and were bracing for her fury. Madame Morier's posture was even more rigid than usual. Before she spoke, she took a shallow breath and looked at her employers with narrowed eyes. "My lord, que se passe-t-il? What's happening? With the Paris police here, this is not about the jet fuel."

Philip mustered his courage. "Madame, you are correct. This may not be related to the airplane incident. The envelope you gave me a few minutes ago was filled with pictures of the Pollock painting." He pointed back up to the landing. "There was a note from someone who says he has the original and replaced it with a forgery."

"Mais, non." Her voice was barely audible. "Ce n'est pas possible."

Philip leaned toward the stunned woman until their faces were just inches from each other. "It's not only possible," he said, "but it happened. The painting you're looking at is a giclee."

"Non, non, non." The blood drained from Madame Morier's face. "Ce n'est pas possible," she repeated. "How could this happen? There is always someone here."

"Madame," Genevieve moved closer to the distraught woman. "If that's true, it should be easy to find out who did this."

She took Madame Morier by the elbow. "Let's go sit down for a moment," she said, guiding her into Philip's study. They sat on the loveseat, their knees almost touching.

"Madame Morier." Genevieve started to put her hand on the house manager's knee but thought better of it and put her hand back in her lap. The comforting overture would not be welcome, she decided. "Madame," she started again, "this is not your fault."

"Of course, it is not my fault," Madame Morier snapped. "But it is my responsibility to keep Maison de Laney secure."

"Fair enough," Genevieve agreed.

"I need to consider when the criminals had time to commit this crime."

Much to Genevieve's surprise, she felt a pang of pity for the distressed house manager. "Madame, I know you said the house is never vacant, but if you think hard, maybe you can remember a time recently when no one was in the house for a few hours?"

Madame Morier stared at the engagement portrait, above the fireplace, of the 9TH Earl and Charlotte, as if she were looking for the answer in the thick brushstrokes.

For a long time, the two sat in silence—Madam Morier as still as a statue, legs together, crossed at the ankles, Genevieve with her legs crossed, foot bouncing.

"Les fumigateurs," Madam Morier mumbled at last. "Bien sûr. C'est les fumigateurs."

"Are you saying fumigators?"

"Oui. Fumigators came just before you and the earl arrived last week. The renovations on the house next door have disturbed some of les rats. We found evidence they had come into the manoir, so the fumigateurs came just before you arrived. No one could stay in the house for twenty-four hours, so the house was unattended for that long. That must be when they exchanged the painting. Mon Dieu!" Madame Morier ran her hands through her hair. Her bangs stuck out as if she had a cowlick. It was the first time since they arrived that Genevieve had seen her in any state except perfection.

Genevieve decided a hand on Madame Morier's shoulder wouldn't kill either of them. When she touched her, she felt madame flinch, but didn't care. A kind gesture was never wrong.

"Come on, Madame Morier." Genevieve stood. "We need to tell someone about your fumigator theory."

As they emerged from Philip's study, the four inspectors were making their way down the hall and Philip was coming down the stairs.

The alpha male from the Paris police spoke first. "My lord." He clicked his heels and gave Philip a brisk nod. "I am Capitaine Fabré. I head the task force for art theft and forgery." His erect posture relaxed as he turned to Genevieve, snared her in a heavy-lidded gaze, and said, "Countess, it is a pleasure to meet the magnificent Lady Crosswick at last. My wife showed me your profile in the holiday issue of *Vogue France*. Magnifique! She will be thrilled to know I met you, though not under the best of circumstances."

Much to Genevieve's surprise, Fabré took her hand from where it rested at her throat and brought it to his lips. Surprised by the gesture, she pressed her mouth into a tight smile. His velvety brown eyes caressed her lovely face, and then he winked. Genevieve coughed, trying to stifle a laugh. She cleared her throat, sniffed, and looked at Fabré with as much innocence as she could muster. "Excuse me, please, Capitaine Fabré," Genevieve said. "Perhaps I'm catching Inspector Boucher's cold." She cleared her throat again and turned to Fabré's sidekicks. "Now, who are these two gentlemen?"

Fabré's eyes lingered on Genevieve for a moment, then he turned to his underlings and introduced them. "My lord, countess, may I present Lieutenants Delique and Laurent."

Nodding at the BEA investigator, Philip said, "Gentlemen, I assume you met Inspector Boucher. Lillie Langdon, our Foundation Director who confirmed the Pollock is a giclee, went to the museum to make certain everything is all right there. She'll return as soon as she can. The ransom note is still in the study.

As Inspector Boucher instructed, we left everything untouched after I opened the envelope."

Not quite sure who should take charge, the police stood together in an awkward cluster. The cop quartet was a mismatched set: Boucher with his Danny DeVito looks and sexy Charles Aznavour voice; Fabré, swoon-worthy but smarmy; and the two lieutenants: a tall, thin man in his early twenties with remnants of acne near his thin-lipped mouth, and a middle-aged man so bland it would be difficult to pick him out of a lineup.

"Would you like to see the photographs and the note?" asked Philip, anxious for the investigation to get going.

Genevieve held up a hand. "Before you go to the study, I have a question. Are there any forensic people coming?" She wondered why the house wasn't already swarming with a team peering through magnifying glasses, combing through hours of security video and dusting anything that could be dusted for fingerprints. "No doubt this crime is a couple of weeks old. How in the world can you gather any evidence?"

Fabré regarded Boucher. Boucher nodded his deference and Fabré took over. "First, let me say, Inspector Boucher and I are quite certain what happened with your Jackson Pollock is not associated with what Inspector Boucher is investigating for the BEA. If that is confirmed, my team and I will take over all aspects of the investigation of this crime. The forensic squad is on its way and will be here soon. As for the delay in discovering the robbery, that should not be a problem. There are many things that will make it quite easy to track the perpetrators. Number one is, if this is a giclee, there are few printers in this country who can print on such a large scale. It will not be difficult to find who created the forgery."

The doorbell sounded again, and Madame Morier opened the door for the third time in less than ten minutes, this time ushering in a crew of six men and women, each carrying a bulging satchel. Fabré strode the length of the foyer to the front door and spoke to the group, gesturing at the forged Pollock still hanging on the landing. Even while he was issuing orders, the team dug in their bags, pulled out white hooded jumpsuits and booties, and suited up. Within minutes, the sleuths had dispersed, with their forensic tools, ready to gather any clues remaining from days ago.

"Inspector Boucher, Capitaine Fabré." Genevieve tilted her head as she spoke. "Shall we go into the study?" She smiled at the two policemen, turned, and led them toward the door. "Philip, could you please ask Madame Morier to bring coffee?" Genevieve caught the flash of terror in his eyes. "You'll be fine." Genevieve patted him on his back, happy he was the one imposing on the housekeeper.

Motioning for one of the forensic experts to follow them, Fabré, Boucher, and Genevieve made their way to the study. Still lying on the floor were the photos, envelope, and letter. Fabré pulled latex gloves from his suit pocket, tugging them on with a flourish and a snap. He squatted, his elbows on his knees. He stared for several seconds, then gestured toward the strewn paper and pictures and spoke to his crime scene technician in rapid French. The specialist began to photograph the room, starting with the evidence on the floor.

"Shall we leave our forensic team to do what they do best?"

Fabré ushered the others toward the door. "Is there someplace we can talk?" Fabré asked.

"Of course." Genevieve led the way to the petit salon.

The forensic team was in full action. Some members dusted for fingerprints. Others bagged bits of thread they discovered near the painting. For two hours, they examined every inch around the painting but didn't touch the canvas itself. Before they removed the painting from the wall, they wanted to make certain they had captured every fiber, print, morsel, and microscopic clue left behind.

When all their painstaking work had been photographed and videoed, they were ready. An officer gripped the thick stretchers at either end of the gallery-wrapped, eight-foot-long canvas. In the middle, a third investigator squatted to stabilize the structure by holding on to the bottom. On the count of "un, deux, trois," they lifted the painting off its cleats. Easing it onto the floor, the two men at the end angled the large piece away from the wall to inspect the back.

"Qu'est-ce que c'est? What's this?" One analyst thumbed the edge of the giclee that had been wrapped around the top rim of the stretchers and stapled on the back. Just below the straight edge of the forged painting, a frayed canvas showed itself, teasing the investigators like the flash of a lacy slip beneath a maiden's frock. The technician tugged gingerly on the loose piece of giclee, trying to release it from a staple.

"Don't pull on that," his colleague warned. "I think we had better get the capitaine."

"We need to see what's under the fake." The technician

persisted, pulling a small screwdriver from his pocket and wedging it under the staple.

Rising from his haunches, the senior specialist settled the question. "Put that back in your pocket," he ordered. "I'm calling the capitaine."

Far away, in another part of the house, they could hear a phone ring twice.

"Fabré."

"Capitaine, please come to the landing. I am not certain what we have here, but I believe we may have another canvas under the giclee."

They heard Capitaine Fabré's footsteps hammering toward them. He burst into the foyer, bounded up the stairs two at a time, then took two deep breaths before he said, "Tell me. What have you found?"

Still holding each end of the painting, the forensic investigators again angled it away from the wall.

"Capitaine, if you look here," the head of the team tugged the border of the forged painting so Fabré could better see what was under it, "it appears the giclee has been stretched over another canvas, a canvas with a frayed edge. A much older canvas." Though he tried to keep his voice even, his excitement was hard to hide.

Fabré stared, confused. "Qu'est-ce que je regarde? What am I seeing?" he murmured to himself. Taking the edge, Fabré pulled hard enough to dislodge one staple, then another. The three analysts gasped. Fabré glared at his subordinates, daring them to challenge him. He wrenched the canvas away from three more staples. With six inches of the underpainting exposed, Fabré's hand fell to his side. He stepped back, keeping his eyes on his work. "Get the rest of the staples off," he said. "Let's see what we have here."

The investigators laid the canvas face down on the thick oriental carpet running the length of the landing and went to work. While Capitaine Fabré loomed over them watching their every move, they slipped their small screwdrivers under the staples, wedged them up, and plucked them out with tweezers. Within minutes of starting their work, the giclee had been released from the stretchers and the edge of the aged under-canvas was visible.

Fabré stood, hands on hips, a scowl creasing his brow. "Lift it back up and lean it against the wall," he said, holding his breath as the men raised the picture until it was upright. Not believing what he saw, Fabré squeezed his eyes shut, rubbed his hand over his face, and opened his eyes again. "Mon Dieu," he whispered. Puckering his lips, he let out a long, low whistle. "Boys." He looked at the three police standing with him. "I think we've just recovered our original Jackson Pollock."

FIVE

THE FOUR POLICE officers stared at a wall of squiggles, drips, swirls, rhythm and energy. This time there was no question. The texture was not just texture to the eye, but texture to the touch as well.

Philip puffed out a short breath that vibrated his lips. "Tell me again what happened."

A gentle smile played on Fabré's full lips. "When this officer took the painting off the wall," he nodded at the young man in a white jumpsuit, "he noticed an old, frayed canvas peeking below the edge of the giclee. When they finished unstapling the forgery, the original Pollock was there, underneath. It's been here the entire time. Very clever, but not very productive for the thieves." Fabré scoffed. "This was not a well-thought-out crime, certainment not the work of professionals."

Genevieve's mind raced. "Whoever did this must have known the original would be discovered before the ransom was paid. This seems more like a prank than a crime. It seems like something kids would do for fun or a dare."

Inspector Boucher sneezed into the crook of his arm. "Whatever the motive, it doesn't appear it has anything to do with my investigation." He pulled a red handkerchief from his jacket pocket, blew his nose, then shoved the soiled rag back into his pants. "If no one objects, I shall take my leave."

"By all means." Philip looked down at the stumpy figure, offering a sympathetic grin. "Inspector, you should be at home in bed with a hot toddy."

"Mais non, my lord," Boucher wheezed. "Ma mère swore by semolina." He wiped a knuckle under his damp nose. "First semolina, then a hot toddy." He returned Philip's grin, then winked a rheumy eye at him.

The inspector extended his hand to Fabré. "Capitaine, if I can be of any future service, please call me." He gave Fabré his business card then turned to Genevieve. "Countess, I shall be working avec diligence to discover who tampered with your avion, your airplane. Bien sûr, it will take longer to find the perpetrator of that mischief than the buffoon who committed this joke." He swept his arm around the landing, stopping at the painting. "This mystery should be solved by tomorrow. Any detective worth his salt will make short work of it."

Though he didn't disagree with the inspector, Fabré bristled at Boucher's dismissal of how complicated his job would be. Fixing the stubby, disheveled inspector with dagger eyes, he said through clenched teeth, "Inspector, please feel free to scurry home to your sickbed. I'm sure we'll manage very well without you."

Swooping in to avert further unpleasantries between the rival police officers, Genevieve took Boucher's arm. "I'll walk you out, Inspector," she said, pressing him toward the staircase.

Flattered by the countess's personal attention, Boucher didn't resist and gloated at Fabré, as he waddled—and Genevieve floated—down the stairs. They stood at the front door talking for several minutes before Genevieve extended her hand. Boucher cradled it in both of his, then bowed at the waist. Genevieve opened the door, and the BEA Inspector was gone.

Where just an hour ago there had been three forensic specialists assessing the Pollock and a few officers milling around, the house was now pulsing with people. On the landing officers rolled the giclee into a long cylinder. The original painting was hanging back on the wall. Fingerprint experts dusted everything that wasn't moving. Downstairs, detectives had taken over the study and were interviewing the entire staff one by one, and Madame Morier hovered and scolded and spat out orders to the police, over whom she had no authority.

At the base of his skull, Philip felt a pinch of tension he knew would soon bloom into a throbbing headache. A lesser man would have slipped off to a quiet corner of the house and pretended none of this was happening; instead, he closed his eyes and inhaled. As he exhaled, the trilling of someone's cell phone brought his attention back to the organized chaos whirling around him.

Fabré answered his phone with a terse, "Fabré." He held the phone so tight, the veins popped out on the back of his hand. "Oui. Déjà? Qu'avez-vous découvert? Vraiment? Bon. Appelez-moi dès que vous y êtes."

Philip's breath quickened as he listened to Fabré's side of the conversation.

As soon as the capitaine was off the phone, he turned to Philip.

"We have found the printer of the giclee. Two of my officers are on their way to speak to him."

"Already? That's amazing." Philip slapped Fabré on the back, much to the policeman's surprise. "Well done, Capitaine!"

"It was, wasn't it?" Well pleased with Philip's praise, Fabré worked to keep his smug smile in check. "They will call as soon as they have spoken with the owner of the shop. In the meantime, I must check on the progress of the interviews."

As Philip and Fabré descended the stairs together, Genevieve stepped into the foyer from the grand salon. She looked at the hive of activity on the landing and heard herself sigh. Then, her eyes lit on Philip standing with Fabré. Though Fabré was film-star handsome and at least twenty-five years Philip's junior, Genevieve would choose Philip's classic good looks and easy elegance every time.

"Is there any news?" she asked the pair as they approached.

Philip opened his mouth, but Fabré jumped in before he had a chance to speak: "My officers are on their way to the shop responsible for printing the giclee."

"My, that was fast," she said, echoing Philip. "It's going to be interesting to see what the printer can tell us." Genevieve slipped her arm through Philip's and the three strolled into the grand salon. She looked at Fabré, then her husband. "I don't imagine whoever did this would use their own name or pay with their own credit card, do you?"

Fabré walked to the sideboard where the kitchen staff had laid out coffee service. "May I?" Not waiting for permission, he filled a cup. He perused a tray of sweets, put a sablé Breton on his saucer and sat in a chair facing the garden. "What a charming view, even in the middle of winter."

Genevieve watched as Fabré took a bite of his cookie. A quiet "mmmm" vibrated at the back of his throat as the buttery confection melted in his mouth. His gaze panned from one end of the elegant room to the other, his eyes lingering on a four-foot-tall figure. "Is that a Giacometti bronze?" He put his cup and saucer on the table and pulled a small notebook from his inside jacket pocket. He uncapped his expensive Mont Blanc fountain pen, made a note, and said, "You live very well, don't you, my lord? Very well indeed."

Philip stopped in the midst of pouring Genevieve a cup of coffee and turned to look at the detective. "What an arrogant son of a bitch," he thought. He glanced at Genevieve, but she was focused on Fabré. Philip finished pouring her coffee and walked to where she was sitting on the sofa opposite the detective. He set the cup and saucer on the table in front of her and sat down close to his wife.

Philip fixed Fabré with an icy stare. "We have always worked hard and been smart about our money. As a result, we've lived well, but never so well as we are living now, since I inherited the estate from my cousin, the 12TH Earl of Crosswick," Philip said, his voice frosty. "Is there something you're implying, Capitaine? If there is, you're barking up the wrong tree."

Unphased by Philip's remark, Fabré continued, "My lord, I'm not implying anything, I am stating the obvious. You live very well. Very well, indeed. I imagine it costs a great deal to maintain all your properties and keep your private jet and helicopter flying." Fabré lifted one leg, intending to put his foot on the coffee table, thought better of it and crossed his ankle on his knee. "I was just wondering what the insured value of the Pollock is." His foot began to bounce on his knee.

"What are you suggesting?" Genevieve leaned forward on the sofa, her green eyes narrowing. She felt Philip's hand squeezing her bicep, pulling her back until she eased against the sofa pillows.

Philip watched as Fabré dropped his Mont Blanc between the upholstered chair arm and the seat cushion. As he dug the fountain pen from the crevasse, Philip could see a blue ink stain blooming on the expensive silk fabric. Fabré eased the edge of his suit jacket from under his right hip, and draped it over the blotch, saying nothing.

"I am sure you understand. We must look at every possibility." He resumed his explanation as if he hadn't just defiled a chair that no doubt cost more than a month of his wages. "Insurance fraud is always considered in cases such as this. You would be surprised how often it is the culprit. A hundred million euros would buy a lot of jet fuel."

Philip shot Genevieve a look that warned her to say nothing, then waited a moment before speaking. He relaxed deeper into the sofa and crossed his long legs. He draped an arm behind Genevieve's shoulders along the top of the couch. Before speaking, he cleared his throat.

"Capitaine," he began, his tone razor sharp. "I appreciate your need to turn over every stone, but it seems to me you are following this line of interrogation for your own amusement, or because you're curious about us and our lifestyle. Either way, I don't blame you, but I can't imagine you believe I'm behind this amateur crime." Philip was not a man to flaunt his talents or use his connections, but at the moment he was relishing this little drama in which he played the all-powerful lord of the manor and Fabré was at his mercy. "You can believe two things: first, if I had done this, it would have been flawlessly executed. I do nothing half-assed and I'm very clever."

Amused by what she was hearing, Genevieve turned her head to look at Philip.

"Second, with well over a billion pounds in our accounts, the chance is infinitesimal that I would put our fortune and our lives in jeopardy, period. So, shall we move on to something more productive or do I need to reach out to the Minister of the Interior? He'll be here at our cocktail party Saturday night before the opening at our museum, so I can speak to him then."

Realizing he had overstepped the mark and put himself in jeopardy, Fabré shot to his feet. "My lord, my lady," he said, his voice quivering. "I apologize for any implication that you attempted to deceive la compagnie d'assurance. Of course, the idea is preposterous! I shall take my leave and return to you as soon as I have plus d'information."

Philip remained lounging on the sofa. "By all means, let us know when you have additional information." Philip dismissed Fabré with an arch of his eyebrow. "I assume you can find your way out."

Chastened, the police officer turned and almost ran from the grand salon.

SIX

THERE WAS NO reason to believe he was not the architect of this ridiculous attempt at extortion.

Lillie's lacquer-red Porsche raced out of Avenue Foch. She darted in and out of the maze of traffic around the Arc de Triomphe, worked her way to the far-right lane, then streaked up the Champs Élysées. Sixteen minutes later she arrived at the LMBA, and slid into her reserved parking place behind the imposing building. She threw the car door open and pushed herself from her bucket seat in one explosive motion. Swiping her pass card over the electronic pad, she yanked open the employee door and raced up the back stairs until she hit the landing three flights up.

"Bugger," she swore, trying the door handle and finding it locked. Glancing at her mobile screen, she saw there was no service in the stairwell. Back down the three flights she flew, taking two steps at a time until she burst out of the building.

Without breaking her stride, Lillie loped to the front and tugged on the heavy entrance door, which, pushed from the other side by two exiting museum visitors, opened easily. She nodded at the aging, well-dressed couple and held the door for them. They stood in the doorway and blinked at the afternoon sun before sauntering onto the sidewalk.

Tapping her manicured nails on the edge of the door, anxious to dash inside, Lillie let the pair clear the entrance before she dashed into the building and bolted to the sweeping staircase. She put one foot on the first step, then stopped. Her chest rose and fell with each gasp of breath and her rapid pulse boomed in her ears. With a mighty inhale, she forged up the marble stairs, tripped once, recovered, and raced on.

One more flight and she burst into his office. "Bernard! What the hell have you…" She stopped mid-sentence, seeing Émile de Laudre, their intern, sitting across from the museum director.

Bernard's head jerked up from the brochure he was holding.

"Émile, get out," Lillie barked.

Eyes wide, the intern shot from his chair and ran from the room.

Bernard sat in shocked silence, his mouth hanging open. He watched as Lillie stormed across the room, slammed both hands down on his desk and loomed over him.

Her voice was low and dangerously calm. "Tell me. Tell me right now."

Bernard held Lillie's glare. "I have no idea what you're talking about. Qu'est-ce qui te prend?"

"I'll tell you what's gotten into me." Lillie's eyes were slits. "Someone did what you wrote in your novel. Someone—and I assume it was you—attempted to extort five million euros from the Earl and Countess of Crosswick by stretching a giclee over the original painting. They executed the plan to perfection, except that I discovered the giclee and the earl called the police. Tell me it wasn't you! Tell me, Bernard!"

A thunderous silence hung in the room for several seconds until Bernard leaned forward and the squeak of his chair split the air. "Mon Dieu," he said under his breath. "Impossible! There are three people who have read my manuscript: you, my brother, and Alain. You know Alain, my friend from uni." Lines etched his forehead. "Lillie, you couldn't possibly think I did this." His eyes clouded as he looked into Lillie's stormy face.

She looked away and took several deep breaths. When she turned back to him, her eyes had softened. "It's such a clever crime, such an original idea. You have to admit it's a bit too coincidental for there not to be some connection." Lillie sat down, settling into the chair facing Bernard on the other side of the desk.

He nodded. "It's hard to argue that point. But you know how I guard my writing until I send it to my publisher. In fact, this is the first time I've ever let Alain read anything before it's been published."

"Why did you let him read your book this time?"

"Remember he came to stay with me for a few days last month?"

Lillie nodded.

"He was not a happy man. His wife found out he was having an affair and threw him out, so he came knocking on my door. I let him read my manuscript to cheer him up. There's nothing better than a good novel about an art heist to raise a person's spirits." He chuckled and started to relax.

"My darling Bernard," Lillie pressed, "is there any chance Alain could have taken a page from your book, quite literally, and attempted to extort money from the earl and countess?"

"Absolument pas!" Bernard assured her. "Absolutely not," he said again, but with less conviction. "Non, non, non."

He stared at his fisted hands and shook his head. "He wouldn't." He looked up at Lillie. "I don't think he would. I've known him for twenty years."

Lillie moved around the desk to stand in front of Bernard. She squeezed his shoulder. "We should call Lord Crosswick and tell him about your book and who had access to the story."

"Bien sûr." His shoulders slumped and his head hung so low that his chin rested on his chest. "Je suis désolé," he mumbled. "I can't believe he would do such a thing, but I know he was terrified of losing everything in a divorce. Perhaps he saw it as a way out of financial ruin. It was an easy crime in my novel." Bernard looked up at Lillie.

With a reassuring smile, Lillie cupped his chin. "Let's call Lord Crosswick."

Philip answered at the first ring. "Lillie, where are you?"

"I'm at the museum. I have an idea who may have tried to extort money for the Pollock." Lillie told him about Alain and why she thought he would be worth questioning.

When she finished, silence filled the line for several seconds until Philip said at last, "Lillie, you can tell Bernard his friend is not the culprit. The police found the shop that printed the giclee and the idiot who had it done, used his own credit card. They're on their way to the museum."

SEVEN

Tiny beads of perspiration sparkled on his forehead, but the Baron de Sézanne's cool, arrogant voice gave no hint that he was trying, yet again, to snatch his son from the jaws of ruin.

The baron had pulled Émile out of trouble on many occasions throughout Émile's twenty-two years, but the stakes had never been this high. Breaking and entering, art theft, fraud, and intention to extort: each was a serious crime, but the four together could put Émile in prison for years. Having a child behind bars would blacken the family name and his wife wouldn't stand for it.

He looked around the Warwicks' sophisticated salon and knew he was dealing with a man of substance. "Do you have children, my lord?"

Philip nodded. "One son."

The baron looked down at his folded hands, then back at Philip. "I'm sure your son has caused you plenty of anxious moments."

"Not many." The corners of Philip's mouth pulled up and he chuckled under his breath. "My son's greatest transgression was when he and a friend drove his father's Porsche without permission. They got away with it and Duncan told us the story just last year, twenty-five years later." Philip shook his head. "Hardly Émile's situation, is it?"

The baron ran his hand over his face then shifted in his chair, uncrossing his legs. He leaned forward. "You see, my friend, my son—"

"Let's be clear, Baron. I am not your friend." Philip's voice was cool, and he could feel the slow burn of anger begin. All his life he had believed the best about people, but with his newly inherited title and wealth, he was discovering that people often didn't deserve that trust. Because of the pressure of his new responsibilities, his temper was closer to the surface than ever before. Much to his dismay, he was beginning to wonder if their inheritance was becoming more of a curse than a blessing.

"Of course, of course." For the first time, the Baron de Sézanne was flustered. He fumbled with the tip of his tie, picked imaginary lint off his sleeve, then looked out the window.

Philip crossed his arms and waited for the baron to go on.

"My lord, I am appealing to you as a father. Émile has always been a challenge to his mother and me. He was a beautiful little boy, and clever." The baron smiled at the thought of his son as a child. "He was a little cherub and he could always make me laugh, so it was easy to spoil him. And now, the spoiled child has become a spoiled man. It is my fault, and his mother's. If Émile is prosecuted for this," he paused, searching for the right word, "this serious prank, it will ruin his life and his mother will not survive the humiliation."

Philip rose and walked to the French doors overlooking the manicured garden. He stood for several minutes, staring at nothing. The room was quiet, each man deep in his own thoughts. After a few minutes, they heard the front door open and the clack of high heels approaching.

"Here come reinforcements," Philip said under his breath, just before Genevieve burst into the room.

Her cheeks pink from the cold and hair tousled by the winter gusts, she filled the salon with energy. "Bonjour, mon amour!" she said and blew a kiss to Philip before noticing the baron. "Ah, pardon. I'm so sorry. I didn't know you had company. I didn't mean to interrupt."

The baron sprang to his feet and smiled, encouraged by Genevieve's lively spirit.

Philip stood and accepted the kiss Genevieve planted on his cheek. "Darling, this is the Baron de Sézanne, Émile's father."

"Oh!" Genevieve made no attempt to hide her surprise.

"He's here to talk about his son and appeal to our better angels."

Genevieve walked to the baron, who shifted from one foot to the other. "Baron de Sézanne, I'm Genevieve Warwick."

The baron accepted her extended hand, shook it once, and gave her a curt nod. "Please, my lady. Call me Émile, just like my son. It is an honor to meet you."

"When you say the baron is here to appeal to our better angels, what do you mean, Philip?"

"He was just getting to that. Baron, proceed."

"Lord and Lady Crosswick." He stopped, cleared his

throat, and went on. "I assure you, my son will be grateful for any consideration you may give him and will execute any consequence you feel is just. S'il vous plaît, my lord. S'il vous plaît." Émile stretched forward in his chair, his hands folded and pleading. For a moment Philip thought he was going to drop to his knees, but he didn't.

"Baron, if you were in our shoes, what would you do?" Philip relaxed, interested to hear Émile's solution.

Feeling he had just been offered a sliver of hope, the baron sat back and unclenched his hands. "My lord, I've given this a lot of thought since the call from the gendarmerie. I believe my son would benefit from hard work and simple living. Perhaps he could work at Château Beaulieu, in the fields, and live with the workers."

To the baron's surprise, a scoff stuck in Philip's throat. "That's rich." A disbelieving smile crimped the corners of his green eyes. "Let me see if I have this right. Your son tries to rob us of a multi-million-dollar painting, and you want us to save his ass by employing him and offering him accommodation at our vineyard? Have I left anything out?"

Émile shook his head. "Oh, la la. When you say it like that, I am embarrassed to be asking such a thing." He turned to Genevieve. "Countess. Vous avez un fils." Émile's pleading eyes begged Genevieve to hear him out. "You have a son. Lord Crosswick told me he is spectaculaire! Intelligent, aiment, un fils merveilleux."

Philip looked at Genevieve, his shoulders next to his ears, his palms turned up. "I didn't say any of those things."

"But I'm sure they're all true," The baron said, his eyes wide, imploring. "Your son has two wise, loving parents who challenged him to be the best person he could be." Genevieve rolled her eyes. "My wife and I gave our son more money than he could spend, bailed him out of endless, uh, how do you say, um, scrapes, and never made him accountable for his actions." Émile plopped back into his chair, his elbows on his knees and his head in his hands.

Philip and Genevieve looked at each other, clueless about what to do next. Genevieve thought she heard the baron whimper but wasn't sure. She gave Philip a nod in the direction of the sofa, and they sat.

"Baron," Genevieve said, her voice soothing. "I can imagine how frightened you must be."

When the baron looked up, his eyes brimmed with tears and his hands trembled. "Countess, I will do anything to save mon enfant. I think he could learn a great deal from hard work and deprivation. It would be an opportunity for him to make something of himself rather than spend his life as a self-indulgent morveux—how do you say," he looked at the ceiling then back at Genevieve, "brat."

"Philip, what do you think?"

"I think it's too much to ask us to be responsible for changing the life of this twenty-two-year-old criminal."

Émile pulled a linen handkerchief from his pocket, wiped his eyes, blew his nose, and tried his best to stifle a sob.

Sensing Genevieve was about to go to the distraught father, Philip put his hand on hers. He shook his head and gave her a warning look. He knew his wife well and was sure she yearned to comfort the tortured man, but he was not going to make it easy for the baron. Genevieve's eyes pleaded. Philip shook his head again. Genevieve stiffened at his side, pulled her hand away and set her lips in a tight line.

"Émile." Philip crossed his legs and sighed.

"Oui?" Dark rings encircled the baron's eyes. His hair sprang out in random spikes where he had stroked his head in distress. He looked up with such hope that Philip couldn't help but smile.

"Émile," Philip started again. "If Genevieve and I were to agree to your proposal, your son would have to come to us himself. He must convince us that he wants to do this, that he wants to change his life. We need to believe that he will work hard and do everything our vigneron asks of him. He'll work long hours, have little time for himself and will live with the workers. It will be an enormous change in his lifestyle."

Genevieve turned toward Philip, tucked her legs under her and smiled at her husband. He rarely disappointed her. She looked at the baron. "What do you think, Émile? Do you think your son can do this?" She reached for Philip's hand and squeezed it. "Thanks to Lord Crosswick, Émile has two options. Whichever one he chooses, his life will change forever."

EIGHT

Genevieve leaned against the molding of the wide doorway to the grand salon, her arms folded. She watched as the young, elegant Émile wandered from painting to painting, his fingers laced behind his back, drifting around the room until he saw Genevieve.

"Ah, countess, bonjour." He swanned over to Genevieve, his right hand outstretched. With his other, he tucked a lock of hair behind his ear.

She was slow to shake his hand, but at last gripped his palm in hers, giving it a firm squeeze. "Émile, sit down," she said, motioning to a chair that faced the French doors. "Would you like coffee?"

"Oui. Café noire." He draped the overstuffed chair with his lanky body.

"I'm sure you meant to say café noire, s'il vous plaît," Genevieve chided.

"Hein?" Émile shrugged and took the cup and saucer, but Genevieve didn't let go.

"Do you have anything else to say, young man?" She had often used this tone with Duncan when he was growing up, to remind her son of his manners.

Émile's brow furrowed and he stared at the coffee, then it dawned on him. He threw a lopsided smile at Genevieve and said, "Merci."

"De rien." Genevieve relinquished the cup. She poured coffee for herself and returned to the sofa. She stared at Émile for several seconds and, before she sat down, she said, "Let me give you a little piece of advice, Émile. Lord Crosswick is on a phone call. When he comes in to speak to you, it would be in your best interest to convince him that you're grateful he's giving you an alternative to prison." She took a drink of her coffee. "I suggest you tell him not only will you do everything you are asked to do at Château Beaulieu, but you will strive to become a credit to your family and to everyone who helps you at the winery." Genevieve pointed her finger at Émile and continued, "I would also suggest that you assure him you will not betray his trust and you will never be able to repay his kindness. Can you do that?" She could feel the heat in her cheeks. "Émile, I'm rooting for you, but you don't make it easy."

Émile's eyes were wide, his mouth hung open, and he looked like a little boy. He blinked, then blinked again.

"Émile, I asked you a question." Genevieve was still pointing her finger at him, waiting for a reply.

"Merde, why did you speak to me that way?" His lower lip quivered, and Genevieve thought he was going to cry.

"Émile!" She dropped onto the sofa. "My goodness!" She shook her head in disbelief. "You are such a spoiled little baby, aren't you?"

He sat forward in his chair. He looked at his sleeve, picked an imaginary piece of lint from the tweed just as his father had done, then said, "That is not a very kind thing to say. Why are you being so mean to me?"

"Émile, you realize you tried to steal a priceless painting from us, don't you? You broke into our home, sent a letter demanding five million euros and cost the Parisian taxpayers a great deal of money. Don't you think you deserve a firm scolding, at the very least?" Genevieve felt her patience dwindling.

"But it was just a joke," he whined. "While I was copying Bernard's manuscript for him, I read about covering the canvas with a giclee and thought it was clever. I thought it would be fun to see if I could do it." He smoothed a wrinkle on his trousers. "If it hadn't been for Lillie, I think I would have gotten away with it." He looked at Genevieve, shrugged his shoulders and pouted his lips. "Je ne sais pas. It's really Lillie's fault."

At that, Genevieve leaned toward him. Her eyes turned flinty. Her voice hushed, but steel-edged, she said, "I don't think this is going to work. The only way you're going to understand who you are now, and who you need to become, is to spend some time in prison. You're not just a brat, you're a delinquent. You've been handed everything anyone could ever want in life, and you think you're owed even more, yet you've given nothing in return." Genevieve was on her feet and began to pace back and forth in front of Émile, who relaxed into his chair. "If you were my son," she said, her temper beginning to boil, "I'd send you to the most destitute country in the world to build hospitals and schools for children who have nothing, who yearn to be given a scrap, any kind of help. I'd make sure you slept on the dirt floor of a mud hut and ate bugs for your meals. I wouldn't expect your victims to send you to a beautiful vineyard surrounded by luxury, hoping you'd become a better person." She stopped in front of him and put her hands on her hips. "If that's what you expect us to do, you're delusional, Émile."

She glared at him and waited for a response. "Well?" she said.

He sat in silence, staring at the floor and twiddling his thumbs in his lap.

"You have nothing to say?"

When she saw Philip standing in the doorway, they locked eyes and she shook her head. Looking back at the young man, she said. "I was rooting for you, Émile. I thought you were a young man worth saving, but after our one-sided chat, I can't imagine there is anything inside of you to salvage. My friend, you're on your own." She gave him a final look of contempt and stalked out of the room.

"He's all yours," she said as she stormed past Philip, his eyes wide and his lips curled in amusement. He was looking forward to playing good cop to Genevieve's bad.

He ambled to the sideboard, poured a coffee, and turned to Émile. "Well, I don't know what you said or did, but it seems you have rather pissed off the countess."

Émile rolled his eyes. "Women," he huffed. "All I did was tell her that my little prank would have been successful if it hadn't been for Lillie, and, of course, you called the gendarmes even though I told you not to in my note." He sighed. "It would have been such a funny joke, but I don't believe the countess saw the humor in it."

Philip let out a long, low whistle. "Imagine that." He stared at the young man before him and tried to peel away the layers of bravado. The boy couldn't be as unconcerned about his situation as he appeared unless he was confident the Warwicks were going to bail him out.

Philip sat down, drank his coffee, and tried to bore into Émile's soul. From what he saw when they met at the museum, the kid's hubris was as thick as his hair. Philip had never witnessed such arrogance.

Émile pushed the sleeves of his khaki-green jacket up his forearms and fixed his eyes on the ornate ceiling. His ankle rested on his knee and his foot bounced, the only indication he might be anxious.

"All right, my friend," Philip said at last. "I think we've spent more than enough time on this." He put his cup on the coffee table and sat back, his arms spread on the sofa back. "I'm inclined to let you spend time as a guest of the Paris police."

"Pardon?" Émile shot forward in his chair. "Vous ne pouvez pas être sérieux!" The blood drained from his face.

"Oh, but I am. I'm deadly serious." Philip sat still as a stone and glowered at Émile. "You've given me—given us," he corrected himself, "no reason to help you. You have no respect for us, for your family, for anyone, as far as I can tell. Am I wrong?" he said, giving the kid an opportunity to help himself.

"Mais, mais…" Émile stuttered, panicked, realizing for the first time that he might be heading to jail. "S'il vous plaît, Lord Crosswick. Please give me a chance to plead my case. I cannot go to prison." His eyes were wide, moistened with tears. "Imagine what they would do to me!"

"Yes, Émile." Philip leaned forward, elbows on his knees and his hands tented. He smiled and said, "Just imagine what they would do to a beautiful boy like you in a place like that." He shook his head. "Tsk, tsk, tsk, not a happy thought." He stood. "Well, if we have nothing else to talk about, I should call the police and tell them how our conversation went. They may want to send a car and take you directly to the magistrate." Philip had no idea what he was talking about, but by now was having fun terrifying this little plonker. At least the brat was showing some signs of fear, some inkling that he might be in real trouble.

Émile's forehead glistened with a layer of sweat. He clutched his hands, walked around the coffee table and leaned within inches of Philip. "My lord, s'il vous plaît," his voice cracked. "S'il vous plaît. You have frightened me."

Delighted at Émile's confession, Philip nodded for the boy to continue. "Go on."

"I don't know what you want me to say. I don't know what you want to hear. I don't know where to begin. It doesn't seem to me that I did anything so bad. I never intended to take your money. My family is very wealthy. I did not mean to frighten anyone. When I read Bernard's idea, I just thought it would be a clever prank. It never occurred to me it would be considered a crime."

Philip poked Émile in the chest as he spoke. "And that's why I think you need a much harsher experience than you would have at Château Beaulieu, working in the fields and living in a very nice cottage. You don't understand how serious this is.

To his surprise, Émile grabbed Philip's hands and clutched them in his. "Please, please, my lord." Tears oozed over the rims of his eyes. He whimpered as he said, "I promise I will go to the vineyard and work hard. I swear you will be proud of me."

"Why in the world should I believe you, Émile?"

"You should believe me because I am telling you the truth." He dropped to his knees, sobbing now and still clutching Philip's hands as if they were his last lifeline, which, indeed, they were.

Reaching down, Philip pulled the lad up by his elbows and handed him a napkin from under his coffee cup. He didn't know if this sobbing kid was being genuine or genuinely playing him.

Émile stopped to wipe his nose, "There's a very good psychiatrist on YouTube." His brow furrowed, and his lips puckered. "Hmm. Maybe she's not a real psychiatrist," he waved his hand. "Anyway, she said, I have never had to take responsibility for anything naughty I've ever done. According to her, my parents were afraid I wouldn't love them if they disciplined me. You're the first person who has ever threatened me with consequences for my actions and I'm terrified."

"That's quite a self-analysis. Who knew you could be analyzed on YouTube?"

Émile dried his eyes with Philip's hankie and hiccupped. "I thought she was really good." He smiled at Philip. "She was very pretty."

Philip threw back his head and laughed. He slapped the spoiled, young Frenchman on the back. "Okay, Émile. We'll give this a try, but if you screw up even once, you'll be in the Bastille so fast, you won't have time to say *Les Misérables*. Is that clear?"

"Mon Dieu! Mon Dieu!" Émile threw his arms around Philip, wrapping him in a grateful hug. Philip staggered back onto the sofa with Émile falling on top of him just as Genevieve walked into the salon.

"My goodness," she said, looking at the two of them lying on the couch in a tight embrace. "It appears as if you've come to some kind of an agreement!"

NINE

WINTER RAIN PELTED the château windows and lights flickered throughout the house as the sound of thunder rumbled through Maison de Laney. Tucked into a cozy room just off the kitchen, Philip, Genevieve, and Château Beaulieu's Managing Director Daniel LaGrande enjoyed a hearty winter lunch of white sausage with truffled pasta.

"I know a grape who spends all his time in the sun. It's his raisin d'etre," said Philip, lifting his glass in Daniel's direction.

Daniel groaned at Philip's joke.

"I promise, Daniel, my business acumen is better than my jokes."

"Mon Dieu. I hope so." LaGrande's throaty chuckle filled the pretty salon. He had arrived a day before the Laney Museum party to spend time with the château's new owners. It hadn't taken long before Philip and Genevieve were Daniel's captives. His warmth, his passion for the grape, and his lust for the world of wine made him irresistible.

Anxious to know more about his personal life, Genevieve asked, "Daniel, do you have a family? We haven't heard if there is a Madame LaGrande at the château." She hoped she wasn't being too forward.

"Alas, no. I have no wife or children. I am married to the vineyard and the grapes are my babies."

Genevieve smiled at his poetic description of his life.

He turned the conversation back to Château Beaulieu. "Though we are one of the smaller vineyards, we were one of the original First Great Classification Growths when the designations were established in 1955 and we continue to deserve our fine reputation." Daniel swirled his glass of cabernet sauvignon before bringing it to his lips. "The Château Beaulieu name conjures images of life's most special occasions: an important birthday, a milestone anniversaire. We are too expensive to drink every day, but, then, we are not a vin de table. Our pricing reflects quality, and we sell everything we produce."

"So," Genevieve said, "if we wanted to grow the business, we would need to bring in cheaper grapes from another vineyard and add a mass-market wine to our offering or raise our prices. Is that right?" Noticing Daniel stiffen, she raised both hands. "Don't panic. I'm not suggesting we do either of those things. I'm just asking an academic question."

He relaxed back into his chair.

"That must sound very American to you," Philip said. "We know Château Beaulieu was founded before the US was born. I promise you we respect the history of the vineyard and what has been accomplished over the centuries. We're in awe of how you and your team have kept the château on an ever-upward course, and we have no intention of interfering with success."

Philip lifted a linen napkin from three small baguettes, still warm from the oven. He offered the Quimper breadbasket to Daniel, who plucked a piece from the ceramic platter and ripped a bit from the end of his loaf. With his elbows on the table, he popped the yeasty morsel into his mouth. A few crumbs fell on the sky-blue scarf around his neck.

The rain had stopped, and clouds were breaking into whimsical shapes before blowing off to the east. The sun slanted into the small dining room, splashing Daniel's shock of white hair with a golden light. "Are you familiar with Clos Peyra?" he asked.

Philip and Genevieve looked at each other. "No," they said in unison, both shaking their heads.

"What is Clos Peyra?" Philip asked.

Daniel sat back and took a drink, savoring the wine before answering. "It's the vineyard next door to Château Beaulieu. It is maybe four hundred years older than we are. They say their history dates back to the eleventh century." He shrugged. "It may. It may not, but it is an old vineyard."

"Why is it called a clos rather than a château?" Genevieve was curious.

Daniel smiled. "Ah, une bonne question. A clos is a walled vineyard. It was used to protect the grapes from theft. Some clos were monasteries, and some vineyards still use the term even though they are no longer walled."

"You said Clos Peyra is our next-door neighbor?"

"Oui. After hundreds of years of ownership by the same French family, a Chinese family bought the vineyard ten years ago. Since then, they have tried to buy Château Beaulieu several times, twice while your cousin was still alive, and most recently just after he died."

"Really?" Philip's eyebrows arched. "That's very interesting. Lillie Langdon, the director of our foundation, told us the château across the road from us is owned by a Chinese family, too. Is that possible?"

Daniel's ice-blue eyes saddened. "It is. And that winery, Château Pitique is, well…" Daniel couldn't find words for what he wanted to say, so he left the sentence unfinished and went on to explain. "In the last decade, the Chinese began an intense love affair with French wine, particularly those of Bordeaux. Twenty percent of our wines are now exported to China. Those with means came to Bordeaux, began buying our vineyards and shipping home eighty percent of the wine they produced. By 2010, Chinese individuals and businesses owned more than a hundred seventy-five vineyards. It sounds like a lot, but with almost six thousand vineyards in Bordeaux, it's only about three percent of our wineries." He paused, filled his fork with the last bite of pasta, and popped it into his mouth.

Genevieve sat back. "I had no idea there had been a Chinese invasion in Bordeaux. Are they still buying?"

Daniel swallowed his food, wiped his mouth then draped his linen napkin back in his lap. He drained the last of his cabernet sauvignon, then said, "The pace has slowed to a trickle, in great part due to China's tighter control on overseas investments. Also, they have made it more difficult to get a visa to France. Those who made the investment early were lucky." He turned up his palms. "And then, there are some who are wishing to expand, like the Wangs wanting to buy Château Beaulieu."

"Do you know who handled the request on our behalf?"

"I don't, but I suppose it was someone at Holmes Fitch Smythson Morrow, the trustees who managed all the properties until you were found."

"Do you know David Weatherington?"

Daniel grinned and nodded his head. "He is fantastique, is he not? He has been to the château several times in the last few years. He is supérieur to work with. I do know it was not David who spoke to the agent from Clos Peyra." He knitted his brow and hummed for a moment. "Perhaps it was someone named Michael Holmes?"

"Sir Mark Holmes?" Genevieve said.

"Peut être."

"That makes sense. He was the principal trustee."

"Obviously, each overture was rejected," Philip said.

"Mais oui. There was never a question. The earl would never sell. He loved the château."

"Daniel, do you know why they want to buy Château Beaulieu?" Genevieve said.

"Ah, oui. It is a matter of growth and quality. It is impossible to grow a vineyard if it is run at maximum efficiency and you sell all your bottles at the highest price possible. It is very different than most luxury products. If Louis Vuitton wants to expand, they can buy more leather, make more bags, sell more product." He pouted his lips. "We cannot make more grapes, hein?" Daniel took Genevieve's hand. "And always remember, Genevieve, we do not grow grapes. We grow soil. If we grow the right soil, everything else will be fine. For Clos Peyra, acquiring Château Beaulieu gives them two things they need."

"What are those?" Genevieve asked.

"Terroir et Prestige."

TEN

The Earl and Countess of Crosswick
request the honor of your presence
at their home,

MAISON DE LANEY,
22 AVENUE FOCH,
75116 PARIS

SATURDAY, 28 JANUARY 2023
AT 5:30 P.M.

to celebrate the opening of
Le Musée des Beaux-Arts exhibition,
"The Women of Abstract Expressionism"

PARIS IN FULL designer regalia was a sight to behold. Through the Warwicks' front door, one dazzling couple after another made their entrance. A statuesque woman draped in a silver sheath with plunging neckline paused to pose for the *Vogue France* photographer and anyone else who might be looking. She accepted a faceted flute of Champagne from a tuxedoed server, greeted Philip and Genevieve, then disappeared into the growing throng of France's elite.

Jazz wafted from the landing at the top of the stairs where a quartet played in front of the Pollock. The music wove its way throughout Maison de Laney, sophisticated and cool.

Watching Philip and Genevieve greet their guests, no one would have ever known they were newcomers to the world of aristocracy. Philip was the picture of elegance in his Givenchy tuxedo. Not wanting to offend the French supporters of the musée and foundation, he had agreed with Genevieve that he should wear a French designer. He had, however, drawn the line when the House of Givenchy's personal shopper suggested an avant garde, star-patterned tuxedo that Philip thought would look perfect on a circus ringmaster.

Echoing the Helen Frankenthaler painting hanging in the grand salon, Genevieve carried out the theme of the evening, "The Women of Abstract Expressionism". Her long-sleeved gown, belted at the waist, was a showstopper with yellow, periwinkle blue and red splashes of color spilling across a billowing floor-length skirt. Diamonds flashing at her ears, a Crosswick heirloom diamond on her right ring finger, and her wedding band were just enough sparkle. She and Philip greeted each guest with the perfect mix of hauteur that the French love and elegant informality, making each person feel special to be in attendance.

Lillie Langdon had created the initial list, which Genevieve supplemented with a few friends and several English philanthropists she and Philip hoped would become donors. Few had declined the prized invitation.

Just as Philip and Genevieve finished greeting the Mayor of Paris, Genevieve looked back at the entrance and squealed. Through the doorway breezed a dazzling blonde, looking like an F. Scott Fitzgerald heroine. She held the arm of a dashing man, his warm good looks a perfect foil for her cool elegance.

"Becca! David!" Genevieve grabbed a fist-full of skirt in each hand, hiking it to mid-calf, and sprinted to the couple. She threw herself into Becca, squeezing hard. The pale beauty returned her lusty hug.

Genevieve released her friend into Philip's embrace and moved into David's outstretched arms. "You can't imagine how thrilled we are that you're here."

"I knew we'd be welcome, but I had no idea you'd be this overjoyed to see us." David Weatherington held Genevieve at arm's length, giving her a critical look. "What's going on that Becca and I don't know about?"

Philip pumped David's hand and slapped him on the back. "There's plenty of time to bring you up to date, but right now come in and meet some of Paris's posh people. Your job tonight is to schmooze them and convince everyone to donate lavishly to the foundation and the musée."

Genevieve looked around for someone to take Becca's coat,

but there was no one to be seen so she laid it on a bench. She slid her hand through the crook of Becca's arm and the two chatted their way into the music and laughter of the party. "After the masses have gone, we'll tell you all about what's been happening in the last few weeks."

There was mischief in Becca's eyes when she said, "David and I have something to tell you, too."

"What is it? From your smile, I bet it's something wonderful." Genevieve badgered Becca as she plucked two flutes off the tray of a passing server. "Tell me, tell me."

"I'll tell you after the party; after we hear all your news."

"You go ahead and start enjoying yourself." She put her hand on Becca's arm. "I've got to go tell Madame Morier no one's manning the door. Brace yourself for a small explosion when she hears the staff is falling down on the job."

She strode toward the kitchen, pushed through the swinging door, and squinted. The bright white lights were a stark contrast to the soft warm glow of lamps and the candlelight flickering throughout the party salons. Looking around the bustling room, Genevieve saw no trace of the woman in charge of Maison de Laney.

A chef was fussing with an hors d'oeuvre of potato slices, crème fraiche and caviar. Genevieve was about to ask him where Madame Morier might be, when the woman in question emerged from the dark kitchen office, smoothing her hair, and buttoning the front of her black silk blouse.

The moment she saw Genevieve, her eyes popped wide, and scarlet flooded her cheeks. "My lady," she said, rushing to

Genevieve. "Please excuse me." She plucked at her skirt to make certain it was in place. "I was just, um," she ran her tongue over her lips then wiped the edges of her mouth with her finger, "um, checking the wine. What may I do for you?"

Over madame's shoulder, Genevieve caught a glimpse of a man slipping from the shadow of the office and out the back door.

Genevieve was so surprised she couldn't speak for several seconds. At last, she said, "I, I… uh, came to tell you that no one is at the front door to greet people or take coats."

Thunder flashed across Madame Morier's face. "My lady. I shall remedy that at once." She spun on her heels and marched toward an unsuspecting underling. There was nothing for Genevieve to do but go back to the party.

Slipping his arm around Becca's waist and gripping David's shoulder, Philip ushered his two close friends into the midst of diving necklines, haute couture tuxedos, and flashing jewels.

At the far end of the room, Lillie Langdon stood in front of the glowing fireplace chatting with a group of men twice her age, all of whom were hanging on her every word. She dazzled, draped in midnight blue velvet, neckline high in the front and sweeping low in the back. Her long arms and elegant hands fluttered through the air emphasizing a point, teasing her admirers, touching a shoulder or patting a back as her laugh filled the air. Philip could feel her energy even from across the room.

"Brace yourself," he said. "We're going to make our way over to Lillie." The three of them wove through the salon, stopped every few feet by someone who wanted to meet Philip or tell him what a smashing party it was.

A breathtaking young twenty-something brunette grabbed his shoulders, kissed him on one cheek then the other, then planted her ruby lips on his mouth.

"Je suis Bernadette Lavigne, Émile's girlfriend. Thank you, my lord, for saving my darling boy from prison. He is so grateful, as am I." She held Philip's gaze and pressed her body against his. "I would do anything to repay you," she said. "Anything."

Her plea was melodramatic and filled with clumsy sensuality, and Philip couldn't help but smile. He took her hands from around his neck and let them fall to her side. "Lady Crosswick and I are glad we could help. I hope you enjoy the evening." As he moved back into the crowd he felt her eyes following him.

"What was that all about?" Becca snickered. "That young lady looked as if she wanted to take a bite out of you." She laughed. "Not that I blame her." She gave Philip a loud smack on the cheek. "You could get into quite a bit of trouble around here, couldn't you?"

"You have no idea, my friend." Philip rolled his eyes at Becca, then pressed forward until they got to Lillie.

"So, what's happening in this little corner of the world?" Philip leaned in and kissed Lillie on each cheek.

"Philip! Sir David!" Pleasure lit Lillie's face. She put a hand on Becca's arm. "Ms. Conway, I'm delighted to meet you and so pleased you were able to come. Genevieve hoped both of you would make it, and voila! Here you are."

She turned to the four men who were waiting to be introduced to Philip and his entourage and made the presentations. Then with a flourish, Lillie said, "Lord Crosswick, I'm happy to tell you that this evening, these four gentlemen have told me they have formed an alliance. Each of them will match the other's donation to the foundation's education fund starting this year, with a spectacular contribution of one million euros each."

"Indeed?" Philip said, eyes twinkling. He raised his Champagne glass and nodded. "Lady Crosswick and I will not forget your generosity. Thank you, gentlemen."

"What a smashing way to kick off Lord and Lady Crosswick heading up the musée and foundation," David chimed in. "Bully for you, chaps," he added, in his poshest English accent.

"Lillie, I'm sure you already have plans to make a big splash of this news, don't you?" Philip smiled at the four new donors.

"Oh, yes. We were just talking about grand ways to make the announcement. Monsieur Beaufoy has several clever ideas." She nodded at the president-directeur general of Credit Alliance. "We'll have a big reveal at the donors' party next month." Lillie beamed at her four conquests. "How does that sound, gentlemen?"

Though these men were top players in the world of finance, they were no match for Lillie's charm. Each was putty in her hands.

Philip leaned to whisper in her ear. "Well done, Lillie. It's obvious they never knew what hit them. You're pretty good at this."

Lillie felt a rush of pleasure at Philip's compliment and moved on to her next conquest.

Philip turned and, without taking a step, found himself in another small group comprised of David, Daniel LaGrande, and Émile de Laudre.

"Look who we have here." David slapped Philip on the back.

"David, you and Daniel are old friends, right? And it looks like you've met Émile. Daniel, have you two had a chance to talk?"

Daniel put his arm around Émile's shoulder and gave it a firm squeeze. "We have indeed, and I'm quite certain we understand each other perfectly. Don't you agree, Émile?"

Émile stood straight as a soldier. "Oui, Monsieur. Absolument." He gave Daniel a sharp nod and Philip a nervous smile.

Yesterday, within the first few minutes of the meeting, Philip and Genevieve were smitten by their charming managing director. They were lucky to have LaGrande heading Château Beaulieu and didn't want Émile upsetting the status quo. From all appearances, Daniel had the newest member of his staff well in hand.

Philip stopped a passing server, said something, then let him go about his business. "As you know, Daniel, after we spoke yesterday, I was anxious for you two to meet." Philip put his hand on Émile's shoulder. It was important for you to approve of this grand experiment before thrusting this bad boy on you and the vineyard."

"It's going to be my pleasure to torture this jeune coquin."

Everyone laughed but the young rascal Émile.

The server was back. "You requested whiskey shots, my lord?"

"I did, indeed. Perfect timing." Philip took small, faceted glasses from the server's tray and gave one to each person in their circle. "I think we need a toast. Here's to Émile's miraculous and hopefully speedy reformation, with special gratitude to everyone who is about to help him on his way."

"Santé," the group cheered, before tossing back their shots.

Hearing the shout, Genevieve searched the room for the uproar. Everywhere she looked, she saw beautiful people. There was no denying, the French were attractive. She grabbed a Champagne flute off the tray of a passing waiter and began to snake her way toward Philip.

"Geneviève! Geneviève, darling!" Genevieve stiffened hearing the French pronunciation of her name. She recognized the nasal accent of Elise Beaufoy. Though Elise was high on the Parisian social pecking order, it was clear that she wanted to add Lady Crosswick's title to her close circle. Genevieve wasn't having it.

She planted a smile on her lips and turned to greet the social climber.

"Ah, ma cherie. Quelle belle soirée." With her hair pulled back into a tight bun at the nape of her long neck, it was impossible to miss the stunning chandelier diamond earrings dangling from Elise's lobes. Genevieve felt them flap against her cheeks as Elise came in for la bise. "You have all the best people here, don't you? Have you heard? My husband is donating one million euro to the foundation."

"No, I hadn't heard, but that's wonderful." Genevieve was sure surprise shone in her eyes. "How marvelous! When did he decide to do that?"

"He decided last week when I told him what wonderful work the education fund is doing. I went to the Children's Art Forum you recommended and was very impressed avec les enfant."

"Elise." Delighted Elise would spread the word about their children's program, Genevieve offered a genuine smile. "I'm so pleased you attended the event. And I'm not surprised you were excited by what you saw. What the foundation team has accomplished on a shoestring is quite remarkable." She clinked the rim of her glass to Elise's flute. "Your contribution will give the program a real boost."

"C'est notre plaisir. Now, perhaps you will find a place for me on the foundation board." Her eyes had turned from warm to glacial and her over-plumped lips drew into a tight, frosty smile.

"There's no free lunch," Genevieve thought. "Well, Elise, I'll be happy to have that discussion with the board members." She had a sick feeling in the pit of her stomach. "Now if you'll excuse me, I need to circulate." She was already edging backward, trying to escape into the crowd.

Craning her neck, she again searched the room for Philip, who was nowhere to be seen. She drained her Champagne glass just as arms encircled her waist and hot breath teased her ear. "What's up, Lady Crosswick?"

She twirled in Philip's arms and planted a kiss on his lips. "Well, well, well. If it isn't my favorite husband." She kissed him again then leaned back in his arms. "I'll tell you what's up. Did you know Michel Beaufoy donated a million euros to the foundation's education fund?" She felt smug with her insider information.

"I did know that." Philip grinned. "He and three of his buddies each tossed in a million euros a year for the foreseeable future."

"How did you find out?"

"When I took Becca and David to see Lillie, she was with Beaufoy and his boys, and they shared the news." He loosened his arms from around Genevieve's waist. "According to Lillie, they just decided to do this last week."

Genevieve straightened his bowtie. "I know all about that." She went on to tell Philip about her conversation with Elise Beaufoy, ending with, "I can't believe we're going to have to work with her as the Presidente of the Cité du Vin Board and now she's trying to extort a position on our foundation board."

"Is there a seat open?"

"There is."

"Would it be so bad to have her on the board?"

"It would." Genevieve was emphatic.

"Really?" Philip looked surprised. "Why?"

Genevieve stuck three fingers in Philip's face. "She's a social climber, she's overbearing and I couldn't get the votes to put her on the board even if I wanted to, which I do not." She lowered a finger as she recited each reason. "Since just after we arrived in France, she's been trying to insinuate her way into my life and I don't want her there

Philip threw up both hands in defense. "Okay, okay. This is your territory, G. Yours and Lillie's. But you two might have to find a way to offer her a seat at the table."

"I guarantee Lillie will echo my sentiments when she hears what Elise is demanding. You should have seen how she turned from warm and saccharine sweet to frosty and frightening in the blink of an eye. It was clear she was daring me to cross her."

Genevieve felt a push in the back. When she turned, she was nose to nose with Bernard.

"I am so sorry, Lady Crosswick. I did not mean to shove you."

"That's quite all right, Bernard. There are a lot of people in this room, aren't there?"

"It is a beautiful party," he said, smiled, then turned back to his group of friends.

For a moment, Genevieve had forgotten they were surrounded by ears that shouldn't be hearing their conversation. She leaned into Philip and whispered, "Do you think anyone heard what we just said?"

"I hope not, but there's not much we can do about it now." He took her hand and led her into the foyer. "Where've you been? The last time I saw you, you were headed to the kitchen to find someone to greet guests and take coats."

Genevieve took a deep breath then blew it out. "You're not going to believe this." She proceeded to tell Philip about what she had witnessed in the kitchen.

Philip's laugh boomed through the hall. "Wow, who knew? I thought she was too frosty to…" he wiggled his eyebrows, "you know."

"God, Philip. Don't be such a twelve-year-old." Genevieve gave him a light shove on the shoulder.

"Did you recognize the guy?"

"No, thank goodness. I don't want to know who it is."

Philip's laugh ebbed to a chuckle.

"When she saw me I thought she was going to faint, she was so embarrassed. She couldn't get away from me fast enough." Genevieve bit her lower lip. "I guess I'm not so surprised that she has a lover, but I am surprised that they were in the kitchen doing whatever they were doing during the party. That seems out of character, doesn't it? I know she's used to having the run of the house, but do you think by having a tryst in the middle of our party she's flipping us the bird? I wonder if she's thinking about resigning as our chef de menage."

Philip smirked. "How would you feel about that if she did?"

"I don't know." She looked at the ceiling and thought for a moment. "She's terrifying, opinionated, inflexible, and has a rather nasty streak, but she knows everything about this property. She knows the history of the house. She runs it to perfection. And, as we know, having looked at the books, she's almost miserly with the household budget and won't spend anything that's not absolutely necessary." She shook her head before saying, "You're going to be surprised to hear me say I think she's exactly what we need at this property."

Taking her face in his hands, Philip stared into Genevieve's eyes before brushing a kiss on the tip of her nose. "Actually, G, I'm not the least bit surprised. One of the many things you do well is recognize quality and Madame Morier is quality from the top of her well-coiffed head to the tip of her Louboutin-shod tootsies."

"Whoa, you know Christian Louboutin shoes?" Genevieve's eyebrows shot up.

"Embarrassing, isn't it? I must have overheard you talking about them to someone." Philip spun her around and swatted her on her bottom. "We need to get back to our guests, cute girl."

Genevieve looked at her watch. "Seven thirty. People should start leaving soon, don't you think?"

Philip shook his head. "I don't think so. Not while there's still plenty to drink and a morsel left to eat."

Genevieve groaned, and as she and Philip moved back into the fray, they heard angry voices bellowing from the salon, followed by glass breaking. The crowd silenced, then resumed almost immediately.

"What the hell?" Philip craned his neck in the direction of the ruckus but could see nothing but people eating, drinking, and enjoying themselves.

"What in the world was that?" Genevieve tugged Philip's arm, pulling him into the crowd. "I think it came from over by the fireplace. I hope no one's hurt."

They snaked their way to the far end of the room. When they edged out of the crowd, they found Daniel and Bernard hissing at each other, hushed, angry words flying back and forth in rapid French. Hank Shou, Bernard's long-time friend from China, watched the heated exchange, fear in his eyes and beads of sweat glistening on his upper lip. At their feet, one server picked shards of glass off the plush rug while another sopped up Champagne from the precious Savonnerie replica carpet.

Philip saw Daniel's hand clench into a fist and grasped his wrist before he could draw back and punch Bernard. Philip's face froze in a smile meant for the few guests near enough to see the confrontation. Most of the partygoers were so consumed by their own conversations and merrymaking that they hadn't noticed the brouhaha.

"What the hell?" Philip hissed, drawing the two into a tight circle. "What's going on here?" He looked from Daniel, red faced and wild eyed, to Bernard, who had already composed himself.

"Lord Crosswick, please accept my deepest apologies

for our outburst. Daniel and I simply had un malentendu, a misunderstanding, and allowed it to get a bit out of hand." He put his arm around Daniel, who stiffened at his touch. "I assure you it was nothing. N'est-pas vrai, Daniel?"

Daniel pushed out of Bernard's grasp. "Lord Crosswick." He stood in front of Philip, head bowed. "There is nothing I can say."

Watching the events unfold, Genevieve had no idea what had just happened between the two men, but her heart wrenched when Daniel raised his head and she saw the tortured look on his face. She grabbed his hand. He patted hers, squeezed her shoulder and walked into the crowd. She searched the guests for Bernard, but he was nowhere to be seen, nor was Hank.

"Well, that was a strange scene," Philip muttered into her ear. "I don't think those two like each other very much."

"To say the least. I thought Daniel was going to punch Bernard. Thank goodness you stepped in to save the day." She stretched on tiptoe to kiss Philip on the cheek.

Just as Philip started to reply, Lillie appeared with an elegant, aging couple, donors who were anxious to meet Lord and Lady Crosswick. Philip and Genevieve plastered their benefactor smiles on their faces and went back to work.

ELEVEN

THE CLOCK IN the foyer chimed eleven o'clock. The last party guests had just been ushered out the door and five exhausted people were draped across the overstuffed sofas and chairs of the grand salon. An army of catering staff rolled through the room like a Zamboni, leaving everything pristine in their wake, glasses, napkins, and plates gone as if they had never littered the salon. Surfaces were polished and the floor had been vacuumed without disturbing the weary bunch.

"Who's hungry?" Philip dragged his feet off the coffee table, put them on the floor and pushed himself to a more upright position.

Perking up at the idea of food, Becca said, "I bet none of us had much to eat during the party, which was smashing, by the way. Let's go to the kitchen before the caterers take away all the food."

"Great idea," David agreed, getting a second wind at the prospect of eating.

They dragged themselves through the house and into the kitchen, still bustling with end-of-party activity.

Madame Morier stood in the center of the room watching

every person, particularly those returning wine bottles to storage. She trusted no one and thought everyone suspect. When she saw the group push through the swinging door, she moved to intercept them.

"What are you all doing in here? What do you need?" she snapped, her tone sharp enough to cause the group to take a step back.

David nudged Philip forward. He scowled back at his friend, then looked at madame with pleading eyes. "We've come begging for food. None of us ate during the party, too busy trying to pry money out of everyone's pockets. And that's made us very hungry. Is there anything left?"

She flashed an uncharacteristic smile, much to the relief of the beggars. "Mais oui. I'll have Chloé fix plates for you. She'll bring them to the study. You will be comfortable there, and out of the way," she added. "Allez, allez." She shooed them from the kitchen with a flick of her hand.

As directed, they ambled back across the foyer and through the double doors into the cozy study. Philip put a flame to the fire already set on the hearth and they settled in, each person flopping into a comfy chair.

"Crikey! She's no Mrs. MacIntosh," David said, referring to the motherly Scottish head housekeeper at Wilmingrove Hall.

"You have no idea how often Genevieve and I have lamented that in the last few weeks. At first, she scared the hell out of us. Now we're just grateful when she's civil."

David slapped Philip on the back. "I never thought it would suck to be you, old man, but in this case…"

Lillie leaned forward in her chair. "The last couple of weeks while I've been working with her on this event, I've gotten to know her and I quite like her," she said.

"Do you?" Genevieve scoffed. "What's your secret?"

"I think my secret is, I don't have any power over her. I don't hold her fate in my hands. She doesn't fear me."

Genevieve and Philip barked a laugh in unison. "You're not suggesting she's afraid of us?" Philip said.

"I don't think she's afraid of you, but maybe she fears what you could do to her. You know what I mean?"

"Maybe I do." Genevieve furrowed her brow, thinking. "You mean she's been running Maison de Laney for the last fifteen years without interference, and now we're here, and she's concerned we might want her gone. Is that what you're saying?"

"It is." Lillie crisscrossed her legs on the cushion of her chair. She pulled the full skirt of her gown over her knees, so she looked as if she were sitting on a blue cloud.

"You know, that had never occurred to me," Philip said as he sat down in a chair next to the fireplace. "You might have something there, Lillie."

"I guess the best thing would be for us to tell her we appreciate how well she runs the Maison, don't you think, Philip?"

"We'll do it tomorrow. Why don't we add a raise and an additional week of holiday to prove our point?"

David grimaced. "I think you'd better check to see what you're paying her and how much holiday time she gets now."

"Spoken more like our accountant than our attorney, David."

Philip laughed then put his finger to his lips. "Shh," he said, as the sound of a trolley could be heard in the foyer.

Over a feast of leftover hors d'oeuvres and Champagne, Lillie reported what a success the night had been. Several people had committed to making sizable donations to the Foundation. Toasts were made and applause filled the room. Philip and Genevieve updated David and Becca on the past week's events, starting with their near-disastrous arrival in Paris, moving to the story of Émile's botched attempt to extort five million euros from them, and ending with the ultimate resolution of Émile going to Château Beaulieu to work as a laborer. Lillie interjected, telling David and Becca how Émile had gotten his idea from a book written by Bernard Reines, the LMBA's director.

"You're kidding me!" David choked, laughing. "That's unbelievable! You two caught up in another book-inspired crime. Wow."

Genevieve threw up her hands. "I know, David. We Warwicks are becoming a bit of a cliché, aren't we?" She turned to Becca. "Before we talk about anything else, how is Olivia?" Becca's daughter, who had caused havoc at Wilmingrove Hall last fall, was a patient at a private mental hospital near the Warwick's family seat. It could be years before she was released, if ever.

"We saw her just last week," Becca's eyes misted. "She's doing well, making excellent progress."

"I'm so pleased. Maybe there will be a happy ending to this story."

Becca's cool smile didn't reach her eyes. David squeezed her hand and warmth flowed back into her lovely face.

"On another subject, as you two know, Philip and I want to do something meaningful with the wealth that fell into our laps. We're working with Lillie on a project in Bordeaux that will impact both young people and wine growers. So, beware: we're going to be picking your creative minds."

"That sounds exciting. Can you tell us more?" Becca said.

"By all means." Genevieve directed everyone's attention to Lillie, who described the project with enthusiasm.

"So, there you have it," Philip said. "All it takes is lots of organization, creativity and euros."

"You know, Philip, you can count on us to spend your money!" David gave his friend a sly smile.

"We know we can," Genevieve said. "But enough about us. Becca, you said you and David had something to tell us." She rubbed her hands and curled her lips into a Cheshire cat smile. "I think I know what it is."

"There's no way you can know," David said.

Beaming, Becca looked at David. "I bet she does."

"I am very much an outsider in this group and I'm quite sure I know what your news is," Lillie chimed in.

Philip looked blank. "What are you all talking about?"

"Wait, wait, wait. Before you say anything, just in case I'm right." Genevieve grabbed the bottle of Veuve Clicquot and went around the room refilling glasses. She returned the bottle to the chiller and sat back in her chair. "Okay. Tell us. What's your news?"

David stood up, walked to Becca, and pulled her to stand. "Last week, Becca and I went to Gleneagles for a few days before coming here." He took Becca's hand and grinned at her. "While we were there, I asked her to marry me."

"I knew it, I knew it!" Genevieve shrieked. She shot from her chair and engulfed Becca in a hug. Then she moved to David. "You! You!" She kissed him on both cheeks. "You're smarter than you look, aren't you? I knew at Christmas something serious was going on."

Becca pulled a ring from her skirt pocket and slipped it on her finger.

"Stunning," Lillie said, examining the large square-cut diamond. On her other hand, Becca wore the Laney family heirloom given to her years ago by Philip's cousin, Jonathon.

David beamed. Philip shook his hand, then pulled him into a bearhug. "Good job, man. I can't wait to hear how you're going to manage living on two continents. Ha!"

"We're still working that out. It's all rather new," David said.

Genevieve squealed when she saw the ring. "That's a stunner," she said, her excitement bubbling over. "Now, Philip, will you please make a toast?"

"It would be my pleasure." Philip raised his glass. "To two of our favorite people. It's been a bumpy journey that's brought you to this very special place. Thank you for letting us be a part of the road you've traveled and thank you for letting us continue to walk down the path with you. We know it will be an exciting journey. Here's to your happiness." Glasses clinked, kisses were exchanged all around, and the promise of a bright future filled the room.

TWELVE

"I LOVE THIS." GENEVIEVE looked out of the window at the fields racing by. "I've always wanted to take the TGV. Look, Philip." She pointed to the electronic board on the wall at the end of the aisle. The digital readout announced 297 kilometers per hour. "That's almost 185 miles an hour, isn't it?"

"It is. Not as fast as a Formula One race car, but pretty fast."

"And a heck of a lot safer." Genevieve put her hand on top of Philip's, lying on the armrest. "Yet another adventure," she said, turning back to the window.

Philip's phone vibrated on his tray table. Though he didn't recognize the number, he hit accept anyway. "Oui," he said. "Daniel, bonjour." A smile curled his lips. Let me put you on speaker so Genevieve can hear."

"Bonjour, Lady Crosswick." Daniel's sober voice crackled through the weak connection. "I am just calling to see if you are still coming to Château Beaulieu."

"Of course, Daniel. We're on our way. Did you think our plans had changed?"

There was silence on the line. "Daniel, did we lose you? Can you hear me?" Philip asked.

"Non, non. I am here. I just want to tell you how wonderful it was to spend time with you in Paris. I loved meeting you." Again there was silence.

"We so enjoyed meeting you, Daniel. We're looking forward to working with you." Genevieve smiled at Philip.

"Is there anything else?" Philip looked at his screen that was announcing a call from Duncan. "I have a call from our son that I should take. I can call you back."

"No, Lord Crosswick. That is not necessary. I shall just say goodbye. Goodbye, Lady Crosswick, goodbye."

"We'll see you soon, Daniel," Genevieve said, but he said nothing in return. "We're looking forward to having dinner with you this evening. Bye."

Philip hit 'accept' and put the phone to his ear. "Hi, buddy. We've been calling you." He was silent for a moment before he said, "Huh. Okay, Okay. Let me put you on speaker."

"Hi, darling. What's going on?"

"Hi, Mom. I was just telling Dad that Ella has bronchitis, so Julia is going to stay here with the kids. I'm taking a commercial flight tonight. When Ella's well the three of them can come on the Bombardier if you don't mind the plane being here for a week or so. What do you think of that?"

Genevieve looked at Philip. "Your dad and I think you shouldn't come until we find out for certain what happened to the plane."

Philip leaned closer to the phone and kept his voice quiet. "We have no idea yet what's going on and until we do, nobody should use the plane."

Duncan hesitated. "That makes sense. I'm sure Julia will agree the smartest thing is to wait until Ella recovers and we know there isn't any danger flying the plane. But I'll be there tomorrow," he said firmly.

"All right, if you're not worried about coming. We're anxious to see you. We're disappointed Julia and the kids won't be with you, but we don't want them here until it's safe."

"Where are you two?"

"We're on the bullet train to Bordeaux."

Excitement buzzed in Duncan's voice. "How fast are you going?"

Philip looked back up at the monitor. "We're slogging along at 299 kilometers an hour. Wish they'd get this old crate moving." The three of them laughed.

"Text us your arrival time and we'll pick you up. It's going to be exciting to explore the vineyard together." Genevieve couldn't stop smiling at the prospect of her son coming to Château Beaulieu. "Bye, sweetheart. Give Julia and the kids a kiss and tell Ella to get better fast."

"Bye, buddy." Philip hung up and chuckled under his breath.

"What?" She gave him a playful shove on his shoulder. "Why are you laughing at me?"

"I'm not laughing at you." His gaze lingered on his annoyed wife. "I'm just enjoying your enthusiasm over Duncan coming. You're such fun to watch."

She shook her head and patted Philip's hand. "I know I'm cheap entertainment."

"I wouldn't say cheap." He gave her a full-throated laugh.

"In keeping with my spendthrift reputation, I think I'll go get something to drink." She reached into her handbag and pulled out her wallet. "What do you want?" She kissed his cheek.

"If they have an iced tea with lots of ice, that would be perfect."

"That's unlikely. Second choice?"

"A beer and a bottle of water, but not mixed, please."

"I'll see what I can do." She slid between Philip's knees and the seat in front of him, felt him pinch her bottom, and knew she would have been disappointed if he hadn't.

The line was long at the café-bar, but the service was efficient and within a few minutes Genevieve was headed back to the first-class car with drinks and plenty of things to nibble. Humming and smiling, she moved down the aisle, swaying with the movement of the train.

As she approached their seats, ice hit the pit of her stomach. Philip stared at a piece of stationery, his jaw clenched, lips drawn tight, and color flooding his cheeks. After loving this man for forty years, Genevieve knew when something was wrong. Three more steps and she was in front of her husband. "What is it? What's the matter, Philip?"

"Sit down," he said through clenched teeth.

Genevieve edged back into her seat, holding on to her goodies as best she could. "Philip, what the hell is going on? What is that?"

He took the drinks and she put the chips and peanuts on her tray. He handed her a sheet of paper.

"I opened my briefcase to get the report on this year's wine sales and this was on top." He waved a thick, cream-colored envelope. Philip's name was scrawled across the front in black ink. In the same strong handwriting, someone had written:

The water in your gas tank
was only the beginning.
Your lives are in danger at the vineyard.
People will die.
Stay away.

THIRTEEN

T HE BLOOD DRAINED from her face. Genevieve couldn't breathe. She had stood next to death at Wilmingrove Hall and she didn't want to do it again. She tried to reread the note, but the words swam on the page. She blinked. She blinked again and drops of water plopped onto the stationery. She looked at Philip. His face was stone, his eyes steel.

"This is a little late," he spat. He took the note from Genevieve, put it flat on the tray and snapped a photo with his phone. With his thumb, he scrolled through his contacts until Boucher's name appeared.

"I just opened my briefcase. This was sitting on top of my papers. Call me," he wrote, then sent the text. Before he could lay his phone back on the tray, it rang.

"Boucher, I…" Philip was immediately interrupted.

"Où êtes-vous? Are you on your way to Bordeaux? Mon Dieu, you are not flying in the Bombardier, are you?" Boucher's rapid-fire questions shot through the phone.

"No, we're on the TGV. The jet is in Washington, D.C. Captain Bruni flew there two days ago to bring our kids to Bordeaux tomorrow." Philip brought the BEA detective up to date with the family's change of plans. "And now, according to the note, Genevieve and I are headed into the eye of the storm." Beads of sweat lined Philip's upper lip.

"This is good that your children are not coming. Lord Crosswick, I am certain the note was written to frighten you. You survived an aeronautical event, what could possibly happen at a vineyard, you drink some bad wine?" Philip could hear Boucher chuckle at the other end of the phone. "Pardon. I made a petit blague, a little joke."

Philip put his head in his hand, not at all amused.

The inspector went on. "Put the envelope and note back in votre briefcase. Try not to touch them. Use a tissue, anything to keep your hands off the paper and the case."

"What should we do with it?"

"I shall send an officier to meet the train. When you arrive in Bordeaux, remain in your seats. The officier will board the train and come to you."

Philip massaged his left temple. "So, you need my briefcase as well as the note?"

"Absolument." Boucher was emphatic. "Disturb nothing. Now, if you will excuse me, I shall call our bureau in Bordeaux."

"Of course, Inspector. Merci."

Philip stared past Genevieve at the fields streaking by. For a long time, he didn't speak and, though she knew him better than anyone in the world, she couldn't read his expression. She put her hand on his cheek and studied his blank face before saying, "I can't tell what you're thinking. What's going on in this head?"

Philip twisted in his seat to look at Genevieve. He laced his fingers through hers but said nothing.

"Philip," Genevieve said, trying to control her annoyance.

"You're not going to like what I'm about to say." His expression gave away nothing and a seed of fear began to blossom in the pit of her stomach.

"I've had enough."

Confused, Genevieve waited for him to explain, but no explanation came. "What do you mean?"

Her vacant expression told Philip she didn't understand what he was saying. Though he didn't mean to, he raised his voice. "I'm telling you I don't want the money anymore. Since we received this inheritance, we've been plagued by one dangerous event after another. We had a wonderful, perfect life before all of this. We were prosperous, happy, and safe. This isn't worth it. I don't want the title and I want to give the money back."

Struggling to believe what she was hearing, Genevieve searched his eyes for any indication he was making a joke. There was none. "You're serious."

Philip attempted a smile but failed. "I told you that you wouldn't like what I had to say."

"That's the only thing you have right in this conversation." Her head swimming, Genevieve pulled her hand from Philip's, sat back in her seat, and stared out the window until they pulled into the Gare de Bordeaux-Saint-Jean.

Passengers struggled into coats, gathered newspapers and magazines, and made their way down the aisle to the exit.

Still reeling from Philip's announcement, Genevieve turned from the window to look at her husband. "Obviously, we need to talk more about the inheritance, but for now, shouldn't we keep this between the two of us?"

"Of course, we should." Philip reached for her hand and squeezed it. "I just wanted you to know what I've been thinking."

Genevieve rolled her eyes and said, "*Now* he wants to share his feelings. This is going to be quite a back and forth. And for the record, I think now that you've embraced your link to the past and the future, you're crazy to even consider giving back the inheritance." She tilted her head then went on. "Changing the subject dramatically, I wonder how long we'll have to wait for Boucher's people."

"I'd say not long. Look." Philip nodded toward a lean woman of about forty, wearing a limp trench coat, her short, brown hair fringed around her square face. She pushed toward them against the wave of departing travelers. "You think she might be the officer?"

"Hmm. Maybe." Genevieve chuckled under her breath.

"Bonjour. Lord and Lady Crosswick?" she said when she arrived at their seats.

"We are." Philip stood up and moved into the aisle, now clear of passengers. "And you are with the BEA?"

"Oui. I am Officiere Palmarie. You have the briefcase?"

Philip reached up to the narrow luggage shelf above his seat. Careful to only handle his valise where he had wrapped his

Burberry scarf around it, he handed it to the officer. "I'd like the scarf back and do you have a receipt for the briefcase?"

Palmarie looked surprised at the request. She shrugged her shoulders. "Rohh la la," she grunted. "Call the Paris bureau if you wish." She took the case and was gone before Philip could respond.

"Well, that was strange," Genevieve said as she slid across Philip's seat to the aisle. "I thought the officer would want to talk to you and find out the details of what happened." She tugged on her coat then plucked her purse from the hook.

"Maybe they'll call later to set up an interview. Don't forget your gloves." He pointed to where the fingers of her black kid gloves peeked out from between the seats.

As Genevieve reached back across the seats for her gloves, she looked through the window and saw Palmarie flanked by two burly men, all hustling toward the exit. "Look at that," she said to Philip. "She has a security escort. I'm glad to see they're taking this so seriously."

He leaned over her shoulder just in time to see the three agents retreat through the door to the street.

"Lord and Lady Crosswick."

Philip and Genevieve turned in unison to see a tall man with short salt-and-pepper hair standing in the aisle.

"Yes," Philip said.

"I am Detective Boulaine from the Bordeaux bureau of the BEA." He offered an official-looking badge, then put it back in the pocket of his topcoat.

"You're from the BEA?" Genevieve asked.

"Oui. Were you not expecting me? Inspector Boucher said he told you I would meet you on the train, did he not?"

"Shit," Philip said under his breath.

"Monsieur? Qu'est-ce que c'est?" Boulaine cocked his head. "What is the matter? Do you have the briefcase for me?"

"No." Philip and Genevieve looked at each other in disbelief. "I'm afraid we gave the case to someone else, perhaps the people who are trying to kill us."

FOURTEEN

FTER TWO HOURS of intense conversation with officials at the BEA and Inspector Boucher on Zoom from Paris, Philip and Genevieve were now speeding through the countryside on their way to Château Beaulieu on the outskirts of Saint-Émilion, a picturesque medieval town whose fame far exceeded its size. Exhausted by the day's events, the pair had retreated into their own thoughts during the forty-five-minute ride to their château.

Henri navigated their Citroen C6 limousine through undulating fields lined with rows of bare winter vines. Though they were dormant above ground, below they were busy drawing energy from the soil into the roots in preparation for spring, when the plants would explode with new shoots.

Just as Genevieve was about to ask Henri how much farther it was to the château, the car turned left between two stone walls inset with large, bronze plaques that announced, "Château Beaulieu." They proceeded slowly down a lane flanked on both sides by linden trees, which touched each other's outstretched branches overhead. Now leafless, they stood at attention, greeting everyone who drove beneath their glory.

"Venus's very own trees," Genevieve said to herself.

"What was that?" Philip said.

She turned her head from the window to look at him. "I just said how wonderful it is to have the allée lined with linden trees. They're dedicated to Venus, you know, the goddess of love and fidelity."

"Interesting."

"Just wait until the spring. The smell is wonderful." She smiled at Philip. "I love linden trees. They're a very old species. You'll see. They have a mysterious, spiritual aura."

"If you say so." Philip took Genevieve's hand and squeezed it. "I'm so lucky to be married to someone so full of useless information."

"You're such a wise ass." She shook her head and smiled at Philip. "Trust me, there's more where that came from." She looked back at the road just as they came to the end of the lane and made a slight right onto a circular drive. "Philip, look!"

Before them stood a classic château, its limestone glowing in the winter sun. On either side of the four-panel burgundy door, arched French doors graced the length of the elegant façade, while white shutters stood at attention like soldiers guarding each window.

"What do you think, Lady Crosswick?" Henri asked as he pulled to a stop at the front door. "Is it what you expected?"

Genevieve admired the ornamental olive trees, planted in aging stone pots, dotting the front terrace. "It's perfection, Henri. Absolute perfection."

"But, given the House of Crosswick's taste for excellence,

I'm not the least bit surprised." Philip opened the car door. He stepped out and, mesmerized by the grandeur of their château, tried to channel the spirit of his ancestor, Philip George Winston Laney, 9TH Earl of Crosswick, the force behind the family's two acquisitions in France. He closed his eyes, waiting for his distant cousin's spirit to course through his veins. It did not. He opened his eyes and looked again at the château, feeling nothing but admiration for the stunning property.

"What are you doing?" Genevieve took his hand.

"I'm just trying to feel the 9TH Earl's presence."

"Are you?" She snorted and peered at Philip through dark glasses. She leaned into his side and whispered, "And you want to give all of this up?"

Ignoring her, he said, "Maybe you should try to get in touch with Charlotte. I bet she spent a lot of time here."

Genevieve snatched her sunglasses from her face and squinted at the top floor of the house. "Of course she did!" She gasped. "I hadn't thought about Charlotte's ghost since Madam Morier showed us the wedding portrait." She clapped her hands. "Won't it be wonderful if she's here? You can bet, I'll be sniffing for roses."

"I'm sure you will be." Philip blew into his fisted hands. "Let's go in. It's cold out here."

Henri pushed open the heavy front door and stood aside.

Genevieve held her breath as she crossed the threshold. This was the fifth property of Philip's inheritance they had visited in the last six months. Each residence was breathtaking, beyond anything the couple could have imagined owning, and each residence had been full of history and adventure. Genevieve hoped Château Beaulieu would treat them well and allow them to live the simple, beautiful life associated with a vineyard in Bordeaux.

"In this fantasy château, what could possibly go wrong?" she said under her breath and walked into the bright foyer.

"What did you say?" Philip asked as he leaned over her shoulder and took in the warm beauty of the entry hall.

"Oh, nothing," she said. "Isn't this perfect?" She turned where she stood, admiring the glowing limestone floors, boiserie paneling scrubbed to a dusty green patina, and light, graceful furnishings.

"Bonjour, bonjour!" Through a doorway under the sweeping stairs, a woman strode into the foyer. She was about forty, wearing a navy-blue apron and wiping her hands on a white linen towel. "Lord and Lady Crosswick, bienvenue. I am Delphine Dumont, house manager for Château Beaulieu." She glanced at her palms, grabbed a fist full of skirt in each hand, and bounced an awkward curtsy. She looked at the driver. "Henri, take the bags to Lord and Lady Crosswick's room. Do you know which one it is?"

"Mais oui." Henri was already on his way up the stairs, a bag in each hand.

Turning her attention back to Philip and Genevieve, she said, "You were quite delayed, weren't you?"

Unprepared for the question, Philip stuttered. "Uh, well, uh, yes. Yes, we were."

Genevieve jumped in. "Madame Dumont—"

"Please, call me Delphine."

"Of course, Delphine. We decided to spend a bit of time in

Bordeaux before coming to the château. We went to Le Quatrieme Mur, the restaurant in the Opera House, drank some crémant and people watched. We had a wonderful time. I hope we didn't upset anyone's plans."

"Non, non, non. C'est bon." She shook her head and the banana clip wrangling her thick hair wobbled back and forth. "Come with me. I shall show you to your room." She dashed up the stairs, with Philip and Genevieve trying their best to keep up. "I am certain you want to rest," she said, looking back at them as she hit the top step. "Dinner will be served at seven thirty, unless you would prefer a different time? And Daniel is joining you, n'est ce pas?"

"Yes, he'll dine with us. But I want to see him before dinner. We have greetings from Madame Morier to deliver to him."

Delphine whipped around on the stairs to face Philip and Genevieve. "Oh la la!" She threw her hands up. "That woman has such a beguin on Daniel!"

Philip and Genevieve stopped just short of smashing into Delphine.

"A beguin?" Philip's mouth twisted as he said the word.

"I think you say crush. She fancies him. You know…" She pooched her lips together and made kissing sounds.

Genevieve's mouth dropped open. When she realized it was agape, she shut it with a loud snap of her teeth. "You think Madame Morier likes," she wiggled her eyebrows up and down, "you know, really likes Daniel LaGrande?"

"Absolument. They used to go back and forth from here to Paris, then back here again. But that was years ago. For quite a while now they have been just friends, but perhaps, how do you say…?" She pouted her lips and drew her brows together, then her face brightened. "Ah oui!" She raised her finger in the air and said, "Friends with benefits." She turned back around and ran the rest of the way up the stairs while Genevieve clamped her hand over her mouth to stifle a laugh.

"Daniel is in the wine office. I shall get you settled, then I must get back to the kitchen."

"If you can just show us where our room is, we'll take it from there," Philip said.

As soon as Delphine left, Genevieve collapsed onto the bed, laughing. "Can you imagine, Philip? Mean Madame Morier has a crush on darling Daniel? But that makes no sense. I'm pretty sure I witnessed her with another man the night of the party."

"I have to admit, I didn't see that coming. But who says she has to be a one-man woman?"

"Good point."

"I didn't know what to say when Delphine questioned us about being late. Since we aren't supposed to tell anyone about the note and the woman stealing my briefcase." Philip pulled his shirt out of the waistband of his jeans and began unbuttoning it. "You, however, were brilliant." He leaned over and kissed her on the nose. "Listen, cute girl, I'm going to stay here while you go see Daniel. I want to shower and unpack. I'll see him at dinner."

"Okie dokie." She returned his kiss, but hers was full on the mouth.

Genevieve skipped down the stairs, excited to see their new friend again, and perhaps learn more about his relationship with their Paris house manager. Thinking about the two of them together, she couldn't help smiling. As she crossed the back terrace, she stopped. The sun hung low in the sky, just above the hundreds of perfect rows of vines and she felt the sting of tears as she stared at the stunning panorama. Maybe Philip couldn't feel the 9TH Earl's presence yet, but Genevieve was sure Charlotte's spirit wafted beside her.

She shivered at the cold and continued to the small building, which had a sign that said "Bureau de Vin." Pulling open the door, she breathed in the warm air and found herself in a small lobby. Classical music wafted from an open door and soft light spilled out into the hall.

"Daniel," she called. "Daniel?" she called again as she walked to what she assumed was his office.

The room was classic, just like the man. Rugged brick floors complemented hand-buffed oak-paneled walls. On the corner of Daniel's massive desk, a vintage cut-glass bowl was filled with corks and an open bottle of Château Beaulieu cabernet sauvignon sat on a copper tray.

Genevieve cleared her throat. There was no answer. Daniel's tall-backed leather chair was turned toward the window so he couldn't be seen. Perhaps he's on the phone, she thought. She walked around his desk. He didn't look at her. She walked toward him until they were just feet apart. His elbow rested on the arm of the chair, but his fingers were splayed; they had not long ago held a glass of wine. The glass lay in his lap, ruby red wine spilled across his grey wool pants.

Genevieve didn't understand what she was seeing… until she

looked into Daniel's intense blue eyes that had sparkled with life the last time she saw him. Now, all their exuberance and vitality was gone. And so was Daniel.

Daniel LaGrande was dead, and the note on the train was coming true.

FIFTEEN

T HOUGH IT SELDOM snowed in Bordeaux, a few flakes wafted past the window in the study. Genevieve sat staring into the fire, a paisley pashmina snug around her shoulders. The pot of tea Delphine had left steaming on the table next to her an hour ago was untouched and cold. The sorrow of Daniel LaGrande's heart attack yesterday sat in her chest like a stone.

"This is irrational," she told herself. "We only knew him briefly and he was not a young man." She rose, took a poker from the fireplace and stirred the fire before adding another log.

"G, we're back. I brought you a present." She jumped at Philip's voice and turned to see two handsome Warwick men walk through the door.

"Hi, Mom." Duncan's broad smile washed over Genevieve like the sun coming from behind a cloud.

Her eyes brimming with tears, Genevieve rose on tiptoes and threw her arms around her son. His firm hug quelled her sadness and replaced it with strength and a calming energy.

"It seems I got here just in time." Duncan held his mother at arm's length to look at her. "I leave you for a month and everything falls apart! The jet, the painting, our managing director! What the hell, guys?" Duncan's grin crept into his eyes, and he wiped away a tear clinging to his mother's jaw, then he sobered. "I have to say, I'm pretty concerned about what's going on here."

Genevieve gave him a kiss and another squeeze before releasing him. "I can't say it's been smooth sailing since we got here. But before we get into the discussion of the perils of France, are you exhausted? Are you hungry? What do you want to drink?" Now in full mom-mode, Genevieve bombarded him with comfort questions.

"It's taken care of, G. We saw Delphine on the way in. She's bringing a tray." Philip slid his arm around her and stuck out his cheek. "Do you have a spare kiss for me?" He accepted the peck and ambled to an overstuffed chair opposite Genevieve, then motioned for Duncan to sit on the sofa facing the fire.

"Duncan, tell your mom what you and Julia talked about before you left."

Duncan unwound the burgundy scarf from around his neck and sat down. "Jeeze, Dad. You want to get right down to it, don't you?"

"Why not? This is going to make your mother very happy."

Genevieve looked back and forth between them, feeling a tickle of anticipation. "All right, you two. What is it? Do you want me to start guessing?"

Duncan studied the muffler and flipped the fringe with his fingers before looking at Genevieve. He took a deep breath and let it out.

Exasperated, Genevieve threw up both hands. "Duncan! Out with it."

"Okay, okay." He lay the scarf on the sofa beside him and rested his hands in his lap. "As you know, Julia and I have been talking about how we could help with the estate and all its moving parts. When you called yesterday morning with the news about LaGrande's death, it seemed pretty obvious what we should do."

Genevieve leaned forward in her chair, watching Duncan fold and unfold his hands. "And what do you and Julia think that is?"

For several seconds, the room was silent except for the crackling fire. Before Duncan could speak, Delphine came through the door carrying a large brass tray filled with tempting treats.

Duncan jumped up, took the heavy tray from Delphine, and put it on a small, ornate sideboard. She pulled a bottle of white Bordeaux from an apron pocket and handed it to Duncan with a wink and a quick smile.

Duncan tore a small baguette lengthwise, smeared the bottom with butter, piled it with thinly sliced ham and Gruyere, popped the top on and took a bite. "Hmmm." His eyes rolled as he inhaled the smell of the fresh bread and chewed. He picked up the bottle. "Shall I?" he asked, his voice muffled through the jambon beurre.

"By all means." Genevieve watched her son slice the foil, screw the worm into the cork and pull it out with a quiet thunk. He poured a glass and handed it to Genevieve.

"Thank you," she said. "Now, maybe you could tell me what your big revelation is."

Duncan handed a glass to his father then poured one for himself. "It's not a big revelation, Mom. It's an idea we think has merit."

"Go on."

He sat back down on the sofa and put his plate on the coffee table in front of him. "I realize you two have been blindsided by Daniel's heart attack." He looked at Philip, then Genevieve. "I'm assuming it was a heart attack."

Philip nodded. "That's what the doctor put on the death certificate."

"I'm sure you haven't had time to figure out who will take over the managing director position. True?"

Genevieve leaned forward and nodded, waiting for Duncan to continue.

"So here's the proposal. Julia and I think we should move here." Duncan watched his mother, looking for a reaction.

Genevieve pursed her lips. "And?" She waited.

"And I should take over as managing director and learn the wine business… post-haste."

Now on the edge of her seat, Genevieve squinted. "And Julia's on board with this?"

"She thought of it first. She thinks it would be good for Alex and Ella to live in France, be exposed to another culture, learn a second language." He paused and squinted at his mother before saying, "What are you thinking? I can't tell what you're thinking."

"Hmm," Genevieve said. "What about her practice? She wouldn't be able to practice medicine here, would she?"

"That's the best part. For several years, a colleague of Julia's at Georgetown Hospital has been after her to be a visiting professor or take a research fellowship at the University of Bordeaux. His father is on the executive board, which, I assume is like our board of trustees. He says they're always looking for skilled physicians, particularly from the US." Duncan's eyes flashed with pride as he talked about his smart, skilled wife. "Visiting professors and researchers from the States are prestigious for the university."

"Would she want to do research rather than be with patients?" Genevieve tried to temper her excitement at the prospect of her family being together at Château Beaulieu.

"She's ready for another challenge. Learning French and teaching the crème de la crème of medical students fills that bill. We've been talking about it off and on since you learned about your inheritance, Dad." Duncan nodded at Philip. "At first it was just a 'wouldn't it be fun' kind of conversation. But after the extraordinary Christmas at Wilmingrove Hall, we got serious."

He walked to the fireplace, gazed into the blaze, then turned to face his parents. "Just last week we decided we'd talk to you about it when we were here." He ran his hand through his cropped hair. "I had no idea how I could best help you here at the château, then Daniel died. It seems almost like a sign."

Genevieve blinked and tears plopped into her lap.

"Mom, are you crying?"

She went to her towering son, slipped her arms around him, and squeezed. "You know I believe there's always a glimmer of sun, no matter how dark the situation. Losing Daniel is devastating. But having you, Julia, and the kids here would be an incredible gift." She leaned back and smiled.

Then her mind began to work. "This is just perfect," she began. "All your hospitality experience is perfect for running the business side of the château." She began to pick up steam.

"We need a huge announcement. Then a big party introducing you and…"

Philip interrupted. "G, don't you think we should get Daniel's death, the cremation, his celebration of life, all the administrative things taken care of first?"

"Of course, of course." She leaned back in her chair, looking sheepish. "This is just so unexpected and I'm… well, I'm just overwhelmed." Tears streamed down her cheeks, and she made no attempt to stop them. "I'm just so happy," she said, grinning. "Have you talked to Alex and Ella?"

Duncan shook his head. "We didn't want to say anything until we talked to you two. Whenever they get here, we'll have a big jolly family dinner and tell them how their lives are about to change, drastically."

Her husband and son could see the wheels spinning in Genevieve's head and smiled at each other, knowing that the matriarch of the family was about to kick into high gear. They were aware she was already plotting and planning and knew that soon Château Beaulieu would be a bubbling caldron of activity, energy, and boundless creativity. The next few months would be challenging, but exciting, and the Warwicks were up to it all.

But first, Daniel LaGrande's work and memory had to be honored. In two days much of Bordeaux would come to the château, not just to pay tribute to an extraordinary man, but to see if the next generation of owners could carry the Château Beaulieu mantel. It was the Warwicks' task to show the gathering that they were ready to step up and take the helm.

SIXTEEN

NGRY CLOUDS HUNG over the rows of naked vines. There were two hours until Daniel's celebration of life, where people would say goodbye to the man whose name had been synonymous with Château Beaulieu for decades. The stage was set.

In jeans and a baggy sweater, Genevieve strode from room to room with Delphine at her side, making notes of things that were not perfect. When they arrived at the tasting room, the fragrance of lilies and roses was overwhelming. Sent from all over the country, sumptuous bouquets lined the limestone walls of the tasting room, two deep in some places.

Genevieve wrinkled her nose. "Delphine, should we take some of these arrangements out of here?"

Delphine sniffed. "They are a bit strong, non? Perhaps we should put a few of the larger ones in Daniel's office. No one will go in there."

"I think that's a good idea. This is just too much. Why don't you ask Émile to move them?"

"Mais oui, my lady."

"Do you think we have enough chairs?" Genevieve turned in

a circle, trying to assess if they were prepared. "We have no way of knowing how many people will be here, do we?"

Delphine shook her head. "No, but there will be hundreds. The overflow will have to stand in the vat room."

They peered into the vast adjoining space where oak barrels lay side by side, aging their precious liquid to perfection. The two women shrugged their shoulders in unison.

"They may even have to flow onto the terrace," Delphine said.

"That would be perfect if it weren't February. I suppose if everyone has several glasses of wine, they'll be fine."

"A very good point. And what do you think of this? Do you like it here?" Delphine pointed to a heavy column carved with grapes and vines, which stood in front of the wall of French doors that overlooked the broad terrace and the vineyard beyond. On the pillar was a large photograph of Daniel smiling into the camera, his eyes crinkled at the corners and his lips curled into a relaxed grin.

Genevieve ran her hand over the picture of the man she had known for such a short time but liked so much. She returned his smile. Behind Daniel's photo was a massive bouquet of yellow roses tinged with orange, his favorite. They were the roses planted at the head of every row of vines; the rose that stood guard over his beloved grapes and served as an early warning system to announce any pest or disease that intended to harm the vines.

"Everything is perfect, Delphine. Just perfect." She squeezed the housekeeper's hand, then glanced at her watch and was surprised that an hour had flown by. "I'd better get going. I've got to shower and change. Is there anything else we need to check?"

'Non, madame. Tout est prêt. Daniel would be proud."

Genevieve felt a lump forming in her throat and forced herself to swallow it. "I'll be back in a minute."

With her head down and her mind a million miles away, she raced out the door straight into a wool-covered wall of muscle.

"Crap! Oh my goodness, I'm so sorry." When she jerked her head up, she was nose to nose with a stunning man, his perfect features just inches away.

She took a step back, realized her palms were still resting on his well-formed chest, and said again, "I'm so sorry."

Assuming he was a guest, she extended her hand. "Welcome. I'm Genevieve Warwick."

His brows shot up. "Ah, Lady Crosswick. C'est mon plaisir. Je suis Paul LaGrande. Daniel was my uncle."

Confused, she pulled her hand from his. "Your name is Paul?"

He nodded. "Oui."

"Paul, you've caught me by surprise. It was our understanding that Daniel had no relatives."

Understanding flashed in his eyes. "Ah, of course, you wouldn't know about me." He put his hand on her arm. "My father and Daniel were brothers. They hadn't spoken in many years. They had a… umm, I think you say falling down?"

Genevieve smiled. "A falling out?"

"Ah, oui. A falling out." Paul shrugged. "It is a long story, and it was a very long time ago."

"Perhaps you can tell us about it later. We're having a dinner tonight for everyone who was close to Daniel. I hope you'll join us." Knowing she was running out of time, she looked at her watch again. "Right now, I'm going to have to excuse myself."

She gestured toward the tasting room. "Please go on in and make yourself at home," she said, and shot out the door.

As she loped across the courtyard, Philip and Duncan walked out of the château. She stopped just long enough to tell them about Paul.

"Daniel's nephew?" Philip said. "How odd."

"You didn't know about this guy?" Duncan tilted his head.

"No, we didn't. The time we spent with Daniel was brief, but I got the impression he had no family, didn't you, G?"

"I did. But right now, I have to shower and change. You two go make him feel welcome."

"We'll take care of him. You just hurry. Duncan and I don't want to be left with all these elegant French people. You know how shy we are." He slapped his son on the back.

"Yeah, Dad. We're a couple of shrinking violets," Duncan chuckled as they walked toward the tasting room.

Duncan heard a grand march playing faintly and rolled his eyes.

"Dad, your phone's ringing. *Les Marseilles*? Really?"

Philip dug in his pants pocket. "I think it's perfect, don't you?" he said, defending the French national anthem as his ringtone.

"Jeeze, Dad, just answer your phone."

When Philip saw his screen, his brows shot up. "Inspector Boucher, bonjour. Ça va?"

Listening to Boucher on the other end of the line, Philip looked at Duncan and nodded. "Yes, he arrived yesterday." He smiled at his son. "Yes. Yes, we were." His smile dissolved as he listened to the inspector.

Duncan motioned that he would go into the gathering, but Philip shook his head.

"Of course… of course." He held up his index finger indicating he wouldn't be long. "Just ring us with your schedule and we'll send a car to pick you up at the station." A brief silence, then, "We look forward to your arrival. It sounds as if you have a lot to tell us… Indeed, au revoir."

"So, what was that all about? Boucher. Isn't he the officer who's investigating the issue with the jet fuel?"

"He is. He's coming the day after tomorrow. He has a lot to tell us, and he thinks it's best if he comes here rather than discussing the new information over the phone."

Duncan put his hand on his dad's back. "This is getting interesting, wouldn't you say?"

Philip looked up several inches into his son's blue eyes. "Duncan, ol' buddy, I can honestly say, since this inheritance dropped into our family's lap, life has been one adventure after another."

When Philip and Duncan walked into the tasting room, there were already people milling around, each clutching a glass of Château Beaulieu's finest red. Almost immediately, a line had formed near Philip and was growing. People wanted to meet Lord and Lady Crosswick, but instead were greeted by Lord Crosswick the older and Lord Crosswick the younger. Genevieve had not yet returned.

The line moved at a snail's pace. French and English ebbed and flowed and sometimes merged. Laughter came easily to most people as they shared charming memories of Daniel. Young, old, those who worked with him or for him, business associates, friends. Everyone was richer for having known him and everyone was sad to have lost him.

A classic, aged beauty stood next in line. "Je suis Madelaine Duveau," she said, her voice somber and her accent refined. Her fine, white hair was pulled into a chignon and her black wool crepe dress was perfectly tailored to her petit frame. She held Philip's hand in both of hers. "Daniel and I were close friends for forty years. We told each other everything. He telephoned me when he returned from your merveilleuse soirée à Paris." She dabbed at the corners of her mouth with a lace handkerchief then tucked it into her sleeve. "I could tell Daniel was very excited about working with you and your wife here at Château Beaulieu."

Philip couldn't look away from her piercing blue eyes, the deep crow's feet only making them more compelling.

She motioned for him to come closer. Philip leaned over until he was eye to eye with the petite woman. She brought her lips close to his ear and whispered, "Daniel told me something I must share with you, but not here. Come to 5 Avenue de Verdun tomorrow at four o'clock." She tucked a folded piece of paper into his hand. "I do not believe Daniel's death was from natural causes. I believe it was tricherie."

"Tricherie?" Philip had no idea what the word meant.

"Foul play," she said and moved into the crowd.

SEVENTEEN

NOWING SHE WAS late, Genevieve ran across the courtyard between the château and the tasting room, her low-heeled boots tapping on the smooth stones. As she dashed through the door, she remembered a beautiful medal she had seen lying on Daniel's desk. How perfect it would be draped across his photograph, that was standing on the column. Making a detour, she trotted down the hall to Daniel's office. Even this far away, she could smell the flower arrangements Émile had put there. When she was just outside the door, she heard rustling, then a drawer open and close. She stopped. She listened. Nothing. She held her breath, closed her eyes to listen more intently. And then, the crash of broken glass sent Genevieve's heart into her throat and before she realized it, she was through the door.

"Paul!" She looked down where Paul LaGrande squatted, picking up shards of glass that sparkled on the floor. A photograph of Daniel holding a prize-winning bottle of wine was still in its frame, but the glass was shattered.

He looked up, wide-eyed, open-mouthed. "Lady Crosswick, mon Dieu! Je suis d— d— désolé," he stammered.

"What are you doing in here?"

Paul's hands covered his face, and he said nothing.

"Paul, what's going on?"

With a grunt, he stood, pulled a tissue from his trouser pocket and blew his nose. "I must sit down," he said, and walked to a leather armchair in front of Daniel's desk. He plopped into the chair with a great sigh, and his head dropped forward.

Anxious to get to Daniel's memorial, Genevieve felt her annoyance rising. "Paul, I don't have time for this. I should have been in the tasting room half an hour ago. What's this all about? What are you doing here? Do I need to call the police?"

With that threat, his head shot up. "Non! Mais, non, madame," he wailed.

She crossed the room and loomed over the weeping man. "Stop it," she commanded through gritted teeth. "Tell me this instant. What are you doing in here? And what's that?" She pointed to the corner of a blue file folder he was trying to hide inside his jacket.

She stepped even closer. "I want to know why you're stealing a file folder, and I want to know what's in it. And, for god's sake, stop sniveling!"

He inhaled with three gasping breaths and sniffed, wiping his sleeve across his nose. Genevieve grimaced to see his nose had left a slug-trail up his arm.

Genevieve pulled up a chair, so she was almost knee to knee with him. "Well?"

Paul held up both palms in defense. "Bien sûr, of course. I know this looks suspect, uh, how you say, suspicious?"

"To say the least."

He gazed at his Italian loafers. "Daniel was a kind man."

"Yes, he was."

Paul blew his nose again with the crumpled tissue. "Even though he and my father hadn't spoken since they were in their twenties, he always sent me birthday cards and a small cadeau de Noel, you know, Christmas present. He was a good uncle. When I was at université, I would visit him here at the château and once I met him in Paris, where I met Clarisse." He tore his gaze from his shoes. His eyes met Genevieve's and the corners of his mouth lifted.

"Clarisse?" Genevieve said.

"Madame Morier."

"Ha! It never occurred to me that Madame Morier had a first name."

"Doesn't everyone?"

"Of course. I've just always thought of 'Madame' as her first name." Genevieve caught a glimpse of the time on a brass clock hanging on the wall, ticking the seconds away. Philip was going to be irritated with her absence from the celebration, which was about to start.

"Please, Paul, get to the point so I can decide whether or not to call the police." She tapped her wrist. "I have to get to Daniel's celebration of life."

"Please, Lady Crosswick, go. This is nothing. I was just looking for some business papers relating to an arrangement I had with my uncle."

"Don't take me for a fool, Paul. If, as you said, this is nothing, you've picked a very bad time to do it. With everything that's happened to us over the past month, Lord Crosswick and I are more suspicious every day of anything even slightly out of the ordinary, and you breaking into Daniel's study certainly qualifies." She made a show of looking at her watch once more. "Out with it, now."

He slid the folder from inside his jacket. "Here. Just take this and we shall be done with it." He thrust it into her hands then stood and walked toward the door. "Daniel is dead. There is nothing he can do to make difficulties for me now."

"What do you mean, 'we shall be done with it'?" Genevieve was so confused, she felt lightheaded. "We are not finished with this." She glanced at her watch one last time. "Jeeze," she said. "I have *got* to get to the tasting room. You, Philip and I will talk about this tomorrow."

She followed him, then remembering the medal, grabbed it from Daniel's desk. "In the meantime, stay out of Daniel's office. Is that clear?"

Paul didn't miss the razor edge in her voice. "Oui, countess. Je comprendre."

With a sweep of her hand, Genevieve indicated he should precede her out the door. She pulled it closed and walked behind Paul to make certain he made it to the tasting room without any more detours.

EIGHTEEN

After an hour of meeting and greeting, Philip took his place at the podium and surveyed the guests who filled every nook and cranny of the tasting and vat rooms. He was relieved to see Genevieve enter the room, Paul LaGrande at her side. Still carrying the folder Paul had given her, she brought the medal to the podium, draped it over the corner of Daniel's photograph, kissed Philip on the cheek and took her chair between Duncan and Paul.

As people noticed Philip standing at the front of the hall, conversations began to quiet. He switched on the handheld microphone and tapped the wire mesh head.

"Bienvenue. Welcome." He waited for the last voices to still, then began again. "Je suis Philip Warwick et," he swept his arm toward Genevieve in the front row, "c'est ma femme, Genevieve." He gave the crowd a sheepish grin. "Et maintenant, je vais passer à l'anglais." Polite laughter rippled through the crowd as Philip warned them he was switching to English. "We join you today to honor a man Genevieve and I met only recently, but who became an instant friend."

He told the rapt audience about the day the three of them spent together in Paris. He talked about the plans they had discussed for a radiant future and how he and his family would protect all that Château Beaulieu was now and would become in the future. "For almost forty years, Château Beaulieu enjoyed the energy, the excellence, the creativity and the joy of Daniel LaGrande."

Though Philip's words were eloquent, Genevieve couldn't focus on his tribute. What had just happened in Daniel's office? The scene was on a loop in her head, playing over and over. Fingering the edge of the folder, she wondered what she would find when she read it. She forced her attention back to Philip's final words.

"Genevieve and I experienced his extraordinary spirit for just one day, but we consider ourselves lucky, indeed." Philip's eyes swept the room. "Please raise your glass to un homme magnifique. To Daniel LaGrande."

Everyone stood, held their glasses high and said in unison, "À Daniel."

He handed the microphone to Edouard Comte, the next person to speak, and sat next to Genevieve, who grabbed his hand and squeezed it hard.

The twenty-seven-year-old vigneron gripped the podium, blinking hard, trying not to cry. Hired by Daniel just three years before, Edouard's sweet face was ruddy from long days among the vines. At first his voice was low and halting, but as he looked out at so many people he knew, his confidence grew. Soon he was sharing charming memories of his boss that brought many to tears.

Genevieve's foot bounced at the end of her crossed leg. The longer Edouard spoke, the more agitated she became. Longing for x-ray vision, she looked at the closed folder in her lap. What if it contained information that was so shocking, it had caused Daniel's heart attack? How much longer could she wait to see what the folder contained? She dragged her mind back to the tasting room. Edouard was still speaking. Would he never stop?

Edouard paused to survey the crowd and gather his final thoughts. "I am young and, some might say, arrogant. My responsibility at Château Beaulieu, as Daniel taught me, is to grow great dirt. If you grow outstanding soil, fine grapes and excellent wine will follow." His face clouded with emotion. "Before Daniel impressed that philosophy on me, I thought a great vintage was all about my skill as a vigneron, about how clever I am. Ah, the hubris of youth." He looked down at the podium and a sad smile played on his lips.

He paused and swallowed. The sadness passed. "Daniel was not a young man. He was a bit too cautious for my aggressive spirit, but I will always be grateful for that very special lesson, and I shall dedicate my life to growing extraordinary dirt as a steward of Château Beaulieu."

Throughout the room, guests sniffled, dabbed at their eyes, and wiped tears from their cheeks.

Edouard stepped from behind the podium and looked toward the heavens. He raised his glass and said, "Daniel, you will live in the soil of Château Beaulieu forever. À la vie!"

Together the people in the room repeated "À la vie," and drank.

With the tributes finished, everyone drifted toward the hors d'oeuvres table. Before he could move away, Genevieve slipped her arm through Paul's and pasted a dazzling smile on her face.

"Philip," Genevieve said through her artificial grin, "Paul and I have quite a story to tell you. Don't we, Paul?"

His face blank, Philip looked at the pair, connected by looped arms. "Am I supposed to know what you're talking about?"

"You are not, but tomorrow morning all will be revealed. Right, Paul?" She poked Paul in the chest with her finger. "We'll see you in the orangerie at nine thirty. Now go do your uncle proud. Have a glass of his favorite red."

Genevieve leaned into Philip. "I'll fill you in when this day finally ends." She gave him a kiss and walked toward the guests, looking for a safe place to stash the folder before delving back into the crowd.

Still confused, he watched her as she stopped at a massive sideboard. She opened the blue file she'd been carrying since her encounter with Paul and studied a sheet of paper. She closed the folder, slipped it between two thick books that sat on the chest and disappeared into the masses.

Three hours after Daniel LaGrande's celebration of life began, the hors d'oeuvre table was empty, the wine nearly gone, and the throng was at last thinning.

By the time the last guest was out the door, Genevieve was exhausted. But there was one more event before the day could end. In a little over an hour, a dinner in the château dining room would entertain Daniel's closest local friends, and out-of-town guests, many of whom had come from Paris.

Tonight the small group of Daniel's friends would feel his spirit in the food, the flowers, the wine, and the music. The dining room was a stunner and she smiled at the magic she and Delphine had created. It was the perfect backdrop to the quartet that would play his favorites during dinner, honoring his love of jazz. Genevieve was sure the evening would sparkle from start to finish and Daniel would enjoy it, wherever he was.

NINETEEN

H AND IN HAND, Philip and Genevieve descended the château's staircase. Looking like a fashion magazine photo, they were a perfectly matched pair. Philip was dashing in black trousers, a gray and black striped sweater, and a gray scarf looped once around his neck. With understated elegance, Genevieve dazzled in a black windowpane checked skirt that swished at her ankles and a black cashmere sweater, the generous cowlneck draping to the back, showing the curve of her neck.

Strains of Miles Davis's "So What" wafted from the dining room. Midway through the foyer, Philip stopped, pulled Genevieve into his arms, and swayed to the music. When their eyes met, his grin was full of mischief. In perfect time with the sultry jazz, he took four beats in place, twirled her away from him, her skirt lifting with the spin, then pulled her back into a dip. Her head dropped back, and he leaned forward to kiss her throat before folding her into his arms.

Much to their surprise, applause filled the foyer. Arriving guests who had wandered in just in time to witness Philip and Genevieve's spontaneous floorshow, clapped and whistled in appreciation.

Still holding her hand, Philip flung Genevieve to his right. She paused, bowed, swept her arm toward her partner and the hall erupted. "Bravo! Magnifique!" The guests engulfed their hosts, hugging, kissing cheeks and chattering their way into the dining room where glasses of crémant, Bordeaux's delicious version of Champagne, awaited.

Without any decoration, the dining room was a classic Bordeaux beauty. Centuries-old paneling lined the walls of the enormous room. A long table made of a single piece of white oak had pride of place in the center of the room, lustrous from years of oiling and rubbing. A coffered ceiling tamed the massive chamber, making it cozy and inviting, rather than cavernous. This evening, it had been turned into a magical vineyard wonderland, with vines, branches and curly willows lining the walls from floor to ceiling, hundreds of tiny white lights woven throughout, sparkling like stars.

For an hour, guests mingled, drank, nibbled exquisite morsels and introduced themselves to those they didn't know. By the time people were seated, everyone seemed like old friends.

Midway down the long table, Philip and Genevieve sat opposite each other. As soon as the servers poured each diner a glass of Château Beaulieu's grand cru, Philip stood and tapped his glass with a spoon, the pretty tinkle quieting everyone.

"Good evening to you all," he said, his smile lingering on each person around the table. "Genevieve and I love having Daniel's closest friends gather here for the final sendoff of a man who will leave an emptiness in all of our lives. For the second time today, I have the privilege of honoring Daniel LaGrande, Château Beaulieu's North Star for almost four decades.

"I'm told that when he first arrived at the vineyard, Daniel was a young, brash vigneron, full of new ideas and ready to implement them at Château Beaulieu. One of his first challenges was our soil. There was dire concern our vineyard's excellent dirt was compacting, and if we wanted to maintain the quality of our wine, we needed to improve our methods of cultivation. Daniel didn't miss a beat. After consulting with some of the most forward-thinking minds in the industry, he gave them a nod and looked to the past when horses worked the fields." Laughter rippled through the room.

Around the table, those who had spent their lives nurturing their vines, nodded.

"Many have followed Daniel's example of bringing horses back to the vineyard. We at Château Beaulieu are lucky. That decision, like so many others Daniel made over the years, assured that ours is a château that will continue to produce fine wines well into the next century. Daniel was an extraordinary friend to the vines and a beloved friend to all who were privileged to know him. Please stand and raise your glass."

Chairs scraped on the stone floor as everyone stood.

"Merci, Daniel pour tout. We shall always be grateful for your dynamic thinking, your wisdom, and your love of Château Beaulieu. To Daniel."

"To Daniel," the crowd said in unison, and drained their glasses of the wine he loved.

"Everyone please sit down, enjoy the meal, and enjoy yourselves. It's the best way we can honor our dear friend." He pointed to the musicians. "Maestro," he said, and the music resumed.

Before he sat down, Philip surveyed the sumptuous scene, the men and women laughing and talking around the table. When he got to Genevieve, he smiled to himself, watching her in animated conversation with the mayor of Saint-Émilion. As his gaze lingered on his wife, he felt the uncomfortable sense of someone's eyes on him, and continued his sweep around the table until he came upon Edouard Comte, staring at him. He shivered with a chilling thought. What if one of the guests celebrating Daniel's life were responsible for the note warning them to stay away from the vineyard. He shook his head to clear the absurd thought and sat.

The meal was everything Daniel loved. The five-course menu began with foie gras, followed by Aquitaine caviar, oysters, pavé de boeuf de Bazas, and a finale of canelés and dunes blanches, and a perfect wine paired with each course.

The guests assembled in the dining room were an interesting mix of young, old, urban, rural, sophisticates, and the unsophisticated. The one thing they all had in common was they were old friends of Daniel LaGrande, and they loved him.

Across the table, Madame Morier and Paul LaGrande sat with their foreheads nearly touching. Genevieve couldn't help but watch the two of them. "Curious," she thought. She remembered putting the madame's place card between the chairman of their biggest exporter and the president of the Bordeaux Institute, but seated in that place was a well-dressed, youngish woman Genevieve hadn't met. Her head whipped back and forth between the two men as she chattered non-stop.

When Genevieve glanced back at Madame Morier, Paul's

lips were at Clarisse's ear. He whispered something that made Clarisse raise her eyebrows and curl her lips into a coquettish smile. His arm was draped on the back of the chair, and he ran his thumb back and forth on her shoulder. Genevieve couldn't take her eyes off them. "I wonder what in the world is—"

"Lady Crosswick." Sitting on her right, Kim Wang jolted Genevieve from her musings. "This is a beautiful gathering. My wife and I appreciate you including us." His English sounded more Oxford than Hong Kong.

Genevieve smiled "We're so pleased to have you, Mr. Wang."

He took Genevieve's hand, held her gaze with his chocolate eyes. "I insist you call me Kim. And may I call you Genevieve?" His full lips curved upward.

She nodded. "Of course."

Genevieve was surprised at how young and good looking he was. When Daniel told Philip and her about Kim Wang owning Clos Peyra, the vineyard next door to Château Beaulieu, she had expected a middle-aged, solemn man. He was neither of those. She guessed he was in his mid-thirties at most. His fine features were chiseled just enough to make him handsome, not pretty, and his thick hair was stylish and spikey to match his whimsical personality.

Genevieve looked across the table at Kim's stunning wife, Jing, who sat next to Philip, smiling and laughing. Quite possibly the Warwicks were going to enjoy having the Wangs as château neighbors.

TWENTY

Philip's hand rested on Genevieve's hip as they waved the last of their guests goodbye.

Walking back into the foyer, Genevieve yawned, stretched her arms overhead and said, "Merde, I'm exhausted."

"Too exhausted for a nightcap with… 'the kids'?" Philip made air quotes.

"Yes, but I'd never tell." She tickled him in the ribs. "Come on ol' man. We have to keep up."

When she pulled him into the salon, a cheer went up from Duncan, David, Becca, and Lillie. The fire was crackling and the drinks were poured.

David jumped up from his cozy seat by the fire and handed Genevieve a glass of Veuve Clicquot. "Sit here." He ushered her to the chair where he had been sitting. "As wonderful as crémant is, I know you've been dying for a glass of The Widow all evening, haven't you?" He sat down close to Becca on the sofa, picked up her hand and smiled as he looked at her engagement ring.

"Get a room, you two," Genevieve teased. She brought the slender faceted glass to her mouth, closed her eyes, and took a long sip. "Yum," she said and smacked her lips. "Now that's more like it." She took another drink, then thought a moment. Her brow furrowed. "You don't think anybody could tell while I was drinking crémant I was longing for Veuve, do you?"

The group booed and laughed at her.

Duncan threw a wadded napkin at his mother. "I'm pretty sure most people were thinking about Daniel, Mom."

"Good point." Genevieve took another sip.

Duncan rolled his beer glass back and forth in his hands before savoring a swallow of Cool Jazz, a local craft beer. Holding up the glass, he assessed the color. "I'm surprised how delicious this is."

"May I have a sip?" Genevieve held out her hand.

"Sure, Mom, but you're not going to like it. It's too hoppy."

She whipped her hand back and wrinkled her nose. "Thanks for the warning." She held up her glass of Champagne. "I'll stick with this."

"Okay. Okay!" Lillie vibrated with excitement. "Enough about drinks! I have gossip! Well, not gossip, because I can confirm it's true."

Becca leaned forward on the sofa, eyes glistening. "What took you so long to tell us?" She licked her lips waiting to hear the scuttlebutt.

Lillie tossed back the rest of her drink. "Are you ready for this?" she asked and set her glass on the table beside her.

"Lillie!" Becca wailed. "Tell us."

She lowered her voice so everyone had to lean in to hear her.

"Well," Lillie began in a dramatic whisper, "during dinner between the entree and salad, I went to the loo and you'll never guess what I saw." She leaned back and paused for effect.

All eyes were wide with anticipation and glued to Lillie. Her lips drew into a smile.

"Well?" Genevieve pressed.

"Believe me, this is worth waiting for." She sat forward again. "When I came out of the toilette and walked back toward the foyer, I heard a sort of moaning as if someone were hurt." Lillie shook her head. "But when I crept around the corner to see if someone needed help, they did not." She stopped, enjoying the confusion on all five faces.

"I don't understand," Philip said.

Genevieve shrugged her shoulders, palms up. "I'm with Philip. I don't know what you're telling us, Lillie."

David took over. "I think what Lillie's saying is that there were two people... uh, where were they, Lillie?"

"In the little alcove under the main staircase."

"So, right there, under the staircase, Lillie saw two people in flagrante delicto." David rested his case.

"Wow," Genevieve said. "Trust the lawyer to use Latin! That's pretty dishy."

"So two people were shagging under the stairs? Were they staff or dinner guests?" Becca said.

"Ooooh, they were dinner guests, all right," Lillie said, relishing keeping her audience in suspense.

"Well?" Becca and Genevieve said in unison.

"Don't you want to guess?" Lillie teased.

Philip walked to the fire, gave it a poke, then tossed a fat log onto the glowing embers. A shower of sparks flew up the chimney and the wood burst into flames. With the poker still in his hand, he turned on Lillie. "If you value your life, you'll tell us who was under the stairs," he teased.

She raised her hands in defense, and a laugh rolled from her throat. "All right, all right. I'll tell you. It was Madame Morier and Paul LaGrande." She plopped back against the cushion, a self-satisfied grin on her lips.

"After what I saw at dinner this evening, I'm not at all surprised. Those two were very, very chummy. As the French would say, rohh la la." She shook her hand in French fashion. "And, Philip, remember I told you during our party in Paris I saw Madame Morier come out of her office, rather disheveled, with a man sneaking out behind her?"

"Of course, I do."

"I bet that was Paul LaGrande. What do you think?" She raised a questioning eyebrow.

"I suppose it could be. You didn't see his face, did you?"

"No, but given what Lillie saw, it seems logical."

"You saw madame in another compromising situation in Paris?" Becca said. "She gets around, doesn't she?"

"I don't care about how sexual she is," Genevieve said. "I'm just blown away that Paul and Clarisse are having an affair."

"Who's Clarisse?" the question rang out.

"Ha!" Genevieve laughed. "Who knew Madame Morier had a first name?"

"Clarisse, huh?" David said. "If you had asked me what her first name was, I would have said Cruella."

Snickers rippled through the room.

"Back to business, please," Genevieve said. "I'm assuming Paul is Madame Morier's Parisian mystery lover." Genevieve watched her hands fold and unfold in her lap. "But, in addition to being a boy toy," she lifted her gaze, "he's a snoop, if not a thief. I caught him nosing around Daniel's office just before the celebration of life."

"What are you talking about?" Philip set his goblet on the table beside him. "When you said you two had a story to tell me, I had no idea you meant he was trying to rob us!"

Genevieve raised her hand to Philip. "Calm down and I'll tell you about it," she said, and told the group about finding Paul in Daniel's office. "The infamous file," she said, holding up the blue folder. "When I opened this, there was a single sheet." She waved the page.

"And what does it say?" Duncan asked.

Genevieve held the paper so everyone could see.

"That's it?" David said. "Just this hand-written IOU for a hundred thousand euros?"

"Did he explain what this is all about?" Becca asked.

Genevieve shook her head. "He just shoved the folder at me, hoping that would be the end of it. I had to get to Daniel's memorial, so I didn't see the IOU until after the celebration of life." She turned to Philip. "I told him we'd discuss it with him tomorrow. We'll meet him at nine thirty in the orangerie and get to the bottom of this."

Genevieve rolled her shoulders. "I've got to go to bed. Philip, are you coming?" She stood, holding out her hand.

"There's one other thing," Philip pulled a crumpled piece

of paper from his pants pocket. "An old friend of Daniel's, Madelaine Duveau, wants me to come to her home tomorrow at four o'clock. She cornered me at the memorial. She said Daniel told her something just before he died, that she needs to share with me."

"Is that all she said?" Genevieve's body sagged from exhaustion. "You don't have any idea what she wants to tell you?"

"That wasn't quite all. She also said she thinks Daniel didn't die of natural causes. She thinks it was foul play. I'll find out more tomorrow at four o'clock."

TWENTY-ONE

Philip extended his leg, feeling for Genevieve, but instead of her warm body, he was greeted with the chill of unoccupied sheets. He opened one eye and saw the imprint in Genevieve's pillow where she had been not long ago. He listened and heard nothing. The only thing to tickle his senses was the faint aroma of baking bread, no doubt wafting from the kitchen.

As he pondered getting up, his phone pinged, announcing a text:

Were meeting with Pall at 9:30. Get your burt out of bef.

Chuckling, Philip wondered if Genevieve would ever learn to proofread her texts before sending them.

He threw off the covers, grabbed his heavy terrycloth robe and headed to the shower to start what he was sure would be an interesting day.

"Delphine, would you please ask Émile to bring the flower arrangements from Daniel's office here to the orangerie?"

"Mais oui, madame. I'll text him."

"Let's make sure they're all still pretty, then take them to the hospital where patients can enjoy them. What do you think about that?"

Delphine tapped a message to Émile on her phone and hit the send arrow. "That's a very good idea, my lady. Even though these flowers are for a sad occasion, they will brighten many spirits at l'hôpital."

Genevieve had been up since seven thirty and operating at full speed. She and Delphine were a good team. The housekeeper executed Genevieve's ideas almost before she came up with them. "Did you ask…"

Delphine answered Genevieve's question before she could finish asking it. "Breakfast has been laid out in the orangerie. Lizette and Chloé have outdone themselves. You will be pleased when you see the petit dejeuner they have prepared."

Genevieve was in awe of Lizette. Since they arrived less than a week ago, she had been devouring the cook's croissants and baguettes nonstop. Just this morning she had sworn off pastries, but her resolve dissolved when she walked into the orangerie. She couldn't resist a warm pain au chocolat with her rich, black coffee.

She was alone in the orangerie, a pretty building connected to the château by a stone and glass corridor. Even as late as the last century, it had served as a greenhouse, preserving delicate flora incapable of wintering outside. Today, orange and lemon trees lived in ornate pots around the room. They thrived, bathed by the sun streaming through a wall of French doors. During balmy weather, the doors were thrown wide to the broad terrace and vineyard beyond.

Sitting at a small table, Genevieve stared out at the naked grapevines while she sipped her coffee. She smiled as her mind replayed yesterday's send off, pleased with everything they had done for Daniel. But now, she was ready to move on. There was no shortage of things to be done. The sooner she understood the basics of how the château was run, the sooner she could move on to more complicated issues.

"My lady, plus de café?" Chloé pulled Genevieve from her thoughts.

"Ah, Chloé, oui s'il vous plaît. Merci."

Lizette's kitchen helper was petite, tidy and an Audrey Hepburn clone, and Genevieve had liked her from the moment they met, just days ago. She refilled Genevieve's cup and dusted a few crumbs from the yellow linen tablecloth. "Is there anything else I might do for you?"

Genevieve flashed a smile. "I think I'm fine, thank you."

She turned back to her notebook and ticked off several chores she had already completed, then began to add more to the bottom of the list.

"Madame." Paul LaGrande's voice cut through her concentration.

"Paul!" Genevieve said, startled. "Are you early?" She looked at her watch.

"No, my lady. I believe I am punctual."

Paul's fresh-from-the-shower fragrance wafted to Genevieve. His dark hair was still damp, and he was dressed in wool camel pants and a navy hooded sweater, a classic French look. "It's not hard to see how Clarisse is smitten," Genevieve thought. Her eyes lingered on Paul's elegant features, until over his shoulder she saw Philip walking across the room toward them.

Distracted, Philip nodded. "Bonjour, Paul."

"Bonjour, my lord. I am appreciative that you and Lady Crosswick will speak with me today and allow me to explain what happened yesterday."

"You need to give me a moment, Paul," Philip said with a quick nod. "G, could I borrow you?" He offered his hand and pulled her out of her chair. When they were in the corridor, he showed her his phone. "Read this," he said.

"Who is this?" She didn't recognize the name on the "From" line, which said, "DREETS."

Philip took a deep breath and said, "It stands for the regional directorates for the economy, employment, labor and solidarity."

As Genevieve opened her mouth to ask what all that meant, he held up his hand.

"It's the French regulatory agency that investigates cases of fraud, you know like counterfeit wine. It looks like someone named Jules Lambert is paying us a visit this Friday."

Scowling, Genevieve asked, "Why? Are we counterfeiting wine? Should we be worried?"

"I have no idea." Philip shook his head. "Duncan and I will sit down with Edouard and find out what this is all about. Find out why they might be coming." He sighed. "But right now, we need to deal with Paul."

Resigned to a lengthy session with Paul LaGrande, they went back to the orangerie. Philip sat across from Paul and noticed little beads of perspiration glistening on his forehead. "All right, Paul, where do we start?" he said and leaned back in his chair, settling in for a long haul.

"Let me begin by saying I meant no disrespect to my uncle, to you or to Lady Crosswick." Paul fiddled with the string of his hoodie like a nervous twelve-year-old. "Three years ago I got into a sticky financial situation. I discovered my partner in an import-export business was a man avec sans scrupules; unscrupulous I believe you say. He borrowed money from some very bad people to cover a…" He thought for a moment. "A shortfall in our company, then he ran away." Paul ran his hand over his face, then went on. "My father and I have an impossible relationship. I could not ask him for help. So, I asked my uncle to lend me the money."

"And that's what the IOU is?" Philip said.

"Exactly."

Genevieve began to understand. "So when you learned Daniel died, it was the perfect opportunity to retrieve the IOU. Is that about it?"

"Oui." His shoulders slumped and he hung his head.

Genevieve rolled her eyes and Philip stood.

"It seems to me this was between you and your uncle," Philip said. "I don't see any reason to be further involved, do you, G?"

"No, I don't," Genevieve said, anxious to bring this to a close and move on to more important things.

Genevieve handed Paul the file folder containing the IOU and the three agreed the matter was concluded.

They walked Paul to the front door, shook hands, then watched him get into his red Jaguar. The throaty engine hummed to life and as Paul backed out, Philip saw Clarisse Morier sitting in the passenger seat. It appeared they were quite the item.

TWENTY-TWO

Pleased to have the issue of Paul LaGrande behind them, Genevieve poured a second cup of coffee into a toile-patterned china mug and wondered where Émile was with the flowers. Annoyed that he hadn't done the job, she stabbed at her phone, texting Delphine.

Did you ask Émile to bring the bouquets to the orangerie?

Within seconds, her phone rang. "Oui, madame, I told him to do it an hour ago. Did he not do as I asked?"

"He did not."

Delphine could feel Genevieve's exasperation through the phone. "I am helping in the kitchen, but I shall go find him."

"Never mind, Delphine. I'll take care of it." She shoved her phone into the pocket of her grey flannel pants and, disappointed in Émile, charged out the French doors toward the vineyard office. As she stepped onto the terrace, an icy drizzle pricked her cheeks. She snuggled the collar of her grey sweater up to her ears and quickened her pace, more irritated by Émile with every step. They had given him an opportunity to save himself from prison, and all he had to do was what was asked of him. Moving a few vases of flowers was not a difficult task.

Opening the door to the building, Genevieve was hit with a welcome blast of warm air. She leaned over, shook her head like a puppy and a fine mist sprayed from her hair. She swept her hands over her hair, straightened her shoulders, and marched down the hall ready to give Émile a verbal spanking. She bolted through the office door expecting to see him lounging on the leather sofa, absorbed in his phone. But, except for the pungent aroma from the fifteen or twenty vases of flowers in the exact same spot they were yesterday, Genevieve saw nothing.

She felt an ache in her jaw and realized she was clenching her teeth. She released her bite, rolled her head to ease the tension and her neck crackled.

She heard a groan and stepped further into the room. She heard it again but, turning in a slow circle, saw nothing. She cocked her head and listened. This time the groan rolled into a low moan. She took another step forward and saw a foot sticking from behind the desk. As the memory of discovering Daniel's dead body just days ago splashed through mind, the blood drained from her head. Two long strides and she was there.

Émile lay on his stomach, his face smooshed against his outstretched arm, vomit oozing from his slack mouth onto the floor. On the desk was an empty bottle of Château Beaulieu's Bordeaux blend and a glass with a splash left in the bottom.

"Drunk," Genevieve spat out. "You little shit. You're drunk."

His moan was guttural.

Genevieve squatted next to him and pulled his eyelid up so she could see his pupil. She wasn't sure what she was looking for, so she released his lid. She slapped his cheek. "Émile." She slapped him again, harder this time. "Émile, are you drunk?"

A squeeze on her knee startled her. She clasped Émile's clammy hand and leaned over so her lips were close to his ear. "Émile, are you sick?" The longer she watched him, the more she thought he was ailing rather than intoxicated.

He whimpered and mumbled something. She leaned in to hear what he was saying, but the words were garbled and confused.

Genevieve pulled her phone from her pocket and pressed Philip's number. She counted the rings, tapping her fingernails on the brick floor.

At last, he answered.

"Philip, where are you?"

"I'm with Duncan in the study. Where are you?"

"I'm in Daniel's office and Émile is lying on the floor in a puddle of vomit. At first I thought he was drunk, but I've changed my diagnosis." Concern creased her brow. "I think he's sick; really sick. We should call an ambulance." Still holding Émile's hand, she plopped from her haunches to her butt, so she was sitting on the floor. "I don't know if it's an emergency, but he seems to be in pretty bad shape. He's clutching his stomach so maybe it's appendicitis. Whatever it is, we need help."

"Leave it with me. I'll ask Delphine to call an ambulance. Duncan and I will be right there."

There was little she could do but cradle Émile's hand in hers. She had nothing with which to clean his face or the floor around him, so he continued to drool into his vomit.

Within minutes, she heard footsteps racing toward her in the hall. She tried to stand, but Émile's grip on her hand was strong.

"Genevieve?"

"Mom, where are you?"

From where they stood in the middle of the room, Philip and Duncan couldn't see behind the desk.

Still clutching Émile's hand, Genevieve leaned on her elbow and stretched as far as she could to peek around the bureau. "We're here." She was surprised to hear her voice croak.

Philip and Duncan were stunned when they saw the pair, Genevieve sitting with her knees up to her chin and Émile sprawled on the floor, pink-tinged vomit everywhere.

"Mom, is he alive?" Duncan said, concerned by Émile's deathlike pallor.

"He is," she confirmed. "He's gripping my hand and moaning, both good signs under the circumstances."

They heard the door open down the hall and voices approaching.

"My lord. Ce qui s'est passé? Est-ce qu' Émile va bien? Les ambulanciers sont là. Que puis-je faire d'autre?" Delphine asked in rapid-fire succession.

Duncan slipped his arm around Delphine's shoulder and gave it a comforting squeeze. "Delphine, you've done a terrific job getting the paramedics here so fast. We're not sure what happened to Émile, but the medics will figure that out. The faster we get him to the hospital, the better."

Working efficiently, the medical team lifted Émile onto a gurney. One EMT listened to his heart, then took his blood pressure, which was dangerously low. Another collected a sample of the vomit from his blue-tinged lips and popped it into a vial. She cleared his airway, wiped his mouth, and eased the elastic over his head to hold an oxygen mask in place. The third medic bagged the empty wine bottle, poured the wine from the glass into a sterile jar, and put the glass into a separate bag. Within five minutes they were wheeling the sick young man across the terrace, through the house and lifting him into the ambulance.

Keeping pace with the EMT as he rushed to the driver's seat, Philip asked, "Do you know what's wrong with him? Will he be all right?"

The medic heaved himself up and behind the wheel. "It appears he has been poisoned. From his extremely low blood pressure, his abdominal pain and his ataxia, we believe we are dealing with methanol poisoning."

"What's ataxia?" Philip yelled as the medic pulled his door closed.

"His coordination is impaired. If we are correct about the methanol, he will be fine after we give him the antidote. As long as we don't waste time." He gunned the engine and gravel sprayed from under the wide tires. When they came to the D122, the siren began to scream, the ambulance squealed onto the main road, and was gone.

TWENTY-THREE

ELL, THAT WAS a hell of a deal." Shivering in the icy wind, Duncan blew into his fists. "I'd suggest we go in. It's cold out here." The wind was building, and clouds scurried across the sky. "Dad, what did you say to the EMT?"

Philip's hand rested on Genevieve's shoulder as they walked toward the house. "They said they believe Émile was poisoned."

"What?" Genevieve stopped in the middle of the driveway. "What do you mean he was poisoned? Why would they think that? Who would want to poison a kid who's just working in the vineyards and doing chores around the house?"

Philip slipped his hand into hers and pulled her toward the house.

"He hasn't been here long enough to make enemies, has he?" Genevieve frowned, bewildered. "Could it have been an accident?" A hopeful note hung in her voice.

"I'm sure it could have been. We'll just wait to see what the doctors say. I'll call in an hour or so and find out how he's doing. I suppose I should phone his father, but I'd like to wait until we have some positive news about his condition. Did Becca and David go into Saint-Émilion?"

"They did."

Philip pulled her limp body into a hug. "You look like you need a nap."

"I do. I'd like to go back to bed, pull the duvet over my head, and stay there until Émile is hale, hardy, and back at the château being his annoying self."

Tilting her chin up, Philip kissed her forehead. "I think this is all too much," he said. Not wanting Duncan to hear, he leaned down and whispered in her ear, "It would be a lot easier if we gave the money away."

Genevieve pushed out of his arms. "I'm not having this conversation out here in the cold."

"What conversation aren't you having?" Duncan asked.

"Never mind," Genevieve said. "Your dad is just being ridiculous." She looked up at the grey Bordeaux sky, searching for a sign that things were going to get better. Just then, a sliver of sun sliced between two black clouds. Taking it as a sign, she said, "I'll make you a promise. Things will be much better tomorrow."

"I'll hold you to that," Philip said, opening the front door for her.

For a moment, they stood together as if they were guests in Château Beaulieu, a house filled with the history of generations and the heritage of the great wine the family had nurtured. They admired the foyer in front of them: the graceful stairs to the first floor; the well-buffed limestone tiles; the view at the end of the hall through the French doors, onto the terrace and out to the vineyard. For a moment they stood in awe of the lineage that, until recently, they had not known was theirs.

"You know Julia loves Wilmingrove Hall," Duncan said, breaking the silence. "We still talk about the exciting time we had over Christmas. But I think she's going to be thrilled to live here. And Alex and Ella." Duncan glowed as he spoke of his family. "They're going to be crazy about every nook and cranny of Château Beaulieu."

Genevieve's eyes stung. She blinked and a lone tear trickled down her cheek. It hung on her chin for a moment then plopped to the floor.

Duncan put his arm around his mother and pulled her to his side. "You're pretty happy about this, aren't you, Mom?"

Their eyes met. Their smiles were identical, mother and son.

"It's a dream. What could be better than having my family all under one roof, working, playing, growing together?" She slipped her arm around Duncan's waist, holding him tight.

"It's going to be a wild ride." Philip chuckled then kissed the top of Genevieve's head. "Alex and Ella are going to keep us on our toes."

His phone vibrated. He looked at the screen and, not recognizing the number, tapped reject. Almost immediately, it rang again. "Given all that's happened this morning, I guess I should answer this," he said, and walked across the hall to his study.

As the creaking hinges of the front door echoed through the foyer, Duncan and Genevieve turned as Becca and David shivered into the hall, pushed by an icy wind, their scarves snapping at their faces.

"You're back." Genevieve strode across the foyer and gave them each a kiss on the cheek.

They peeled off their gloves, struggled out of their coats, unwound their mufflers and piled everything on an upholstered bench.

"Crickey, it got cold." David rubbed his hands then tucked them into his armpits.

Tucking her arm through Becca's, Genevieve ushered her shivering friend into the salon and to the fireplace where logs simmered, waiting to be brought back to life.

"I can't wait to hear how you liked Saint-Émilion." Genevieve tossed wood on the fire and it sparked to flames, then she walked to the corner of the room to an ornate pull and gave it a single tug, calling for coffee. "Did you enjoy your poke around our charming village?"

Stretching his legs in front of him, David leaned back in an overstuffed chair and crossed his ankles. "We did. We went to Chai Pascal, the café Philip recommended. It was wonderful, but we had the strangest experience with the wine."

"Let me tell," Becca interrupted, her cheeks flushed from the cold. "We ordered a bottle of the Château Beaulieu grand cru and had to send it back."

"How strange. Had it turned?" asked Duncan.

David shook his head. "No. It just wasn't good. It tasted like a cheap corner shop wine. They gave us a new bottle, which was superb. It was just odd how the first bottle was a completely different, certainly inferior, wine."

Philip walked in just at the end of the story. Looking at his sagging shoulders and weary eyes, there was no question he was about to tell them something serious.

"What's the matter?" Genevieve asked, instantly on high alert. "Did you hear something from the hospital? Is it Émile?"

"What about Émile?" David asked. Having been gone all morning, he and Becca knew nothing about what had happened.

"In a minute, David." Genevieve narrowed her eyes at Philip. "Something's wrong. What is it?"

Philip eased himself into a chair and leaned his head back against the cushion. "The call I got as you two walked through the door," he nodded toward David and Becca, "was from the hospital."

They could hear a cart rattling down the hall, and in a moment, Chloé wheeled through the salon doorway with trolley piled with pastries, coffee cups and an urn. "Excusez moi, madame. Would you like me to serve?"

"No thank you, Chloé, we'll be fine." Genevieve picked up a small linen napkin and a cup and saucer. The pretty gamine bobbed a curtsy and was gone.

Philip pushed himself to stand and trudged to the cart. He poured a cup of coffee and, spying a bottle of Irish whiskey on the cart's lower shelf, added a generous shot to his steaming java.

"Will you please finish telling us about the call from the hospital?" Genevieve's tone was sharper than she intended.

Returning to his chair, he set his cup on a small side table and plopped down. Every move seemed to be an effort. "So, I have the proverbial good news and bad news." He crossed his legs and sank deeper into the cushions. "The good news is Émile is going to be fine. The bad news is he was definitely poisoned."

As he scanned his friends and family, he looked from one blank face to another and another. His words had not registered.

"Dad, I don't understand. How was he poisoned? Did he eat something that was contaminated?"

"Wait a minute." Genevieve's voice was almost inaudible. "Wait a damn minute, Philip. I saw the EMS guys bag the wine bottle and glass. Those were still in Daniel's study from the day he died. That's where Émile got the wine, isn't it?" She could hear her heart pounding in her ears.

"And if Émile was poisoned from that bottle of wine, does that mean…?" Duncan couldn't finish the sentence.

"Yeah," Philip said. "That's what it means, Duncan." He drained his coffee cup. "Daniel didn't die of a heart attack. He was poisoned."

"But why wouldn't the police have discovered that?" David said. "Why would a bottle of poisoned wine be sitting there days after a man died in that room?"

"Very simple," Philip said. "Because Daniel was seventy-four and had a few minor heart issues, the police automatically ruled his passing a death by natural causes."

Genevieve jumped in. "Because everyone was busy organizing his celebration of life, no one has been in there to clean, so the bottle was still there."

"I'm assuming he was cremated," Becca said.

"He was, so at this point, there's no way to confirm if he was poisoned or not." Genevieve was on her feet and pacing. "Philip, did the hospital tell you what the poison was?"

"The chemical analysis says it's methanol, a very clever poison to use in wine. It's odorless and tasteless so it's difficult to detect, until someone goes blind or dies, of course."

"Yeah, that's kind of a dead giveaway," Duncan said. "Pun intended."

Becca had been silent, thinking. "I'm assuming the police will get involved now."

Philip nodded. "I expect to hear from them anytime. We've been in France less than a month and already we've dealt with dozens of cops. Now we're about to add another gendarme to our list of acquaintances." He cradled his head in his hands for a moment. He took a deep breath, then another "No one can say that our lives are dull, can they?"

"A little less excitement might not be a bad thing," Genevieve said.

As the sound of *Les Marseilles* announced a call on Philip's phone, everyone jumped and nervous laughter rippled through the room.

"This is probably the police now." He stood up and headed for his study as he accepted the call. "Hello. Oui. Oui, this is Lord Crosswick."

"My lord. This is Frederick Picard, Chef de la Police in Saint-Émilion. I am calling about Madelaine Duveau. She has written your name on her calendar for four o'clock today. Were you coming to see her, Lord Crosswick?"

"Yes, I was. Is there a problem?"

"Do you know Madame Duveau well?"

Philip sat in his desk chair. "Not at all. I met her yesterday."

"If I may ask, why are you coming to see her?"

He swiveled his chair back and forth, trying to imagine what Picard looked like, but the policeman's monotone voice conjured nothing. "She told me to come to her home today because she has information about our deceased general manager, Daniel LaGrande." He stopped moving and leaned on his desk. "Look, chef, you need to tell me what's going on here."

Without changing his tone, Picard said, "I'm sorry to inform you, Lord Crosswick, your appointment has been canceled. Madame Duveau died earlier today."

Silence filled the line for several seconds. "Lord Crosswick, did you hear me?" Picard finally asked.

"I did, chef. How did she die?"

"She was sitting in a sunny window overlooking the garden, drinking a glass of wine and reading a book."

Philip heard a smile in Picard's voice, his first emotion during their conversation. "Not a bad way to go at eighty-six," he said.

Philip imagined the elegant octogenarian enjoying a glass of wine and a favorite book as she sailed out of this world into the next. Then, the words "drinking a glass of wine" screamed in his head. "You said she was drinking wine?"

"Oui."

"What kind of wine?" Philip held his breath.

"Un moment," Picard said and yelled to someone, waited, then came back to Philip. "My lord, it was a bottle of your Château Beaulieu blend. Why do you ask?"

Philip ran his hands over his face as if he were trying to wipe an image away, then he repeated the words. "She was drinking a glass of wine… and then she was dead. You need to check the bottle for poison. Chef Picard, I don't know what the hell's going on here in Saint-Émilion, but whatever it is, it's not good."

TWENTY-FOUR

David poked the embers of the spent logs, tossed a chunk of wood on the pile and within seconds the fire was crackling, hungry flames lapping at the wood.

When Philip returned to the salon, he was as pale as snow and his brow wrinkled in a ferocious frown.

"My god, Philip," Genevieve said, looking at her husband. "Every time you take a call, you return looking like death warmed over. Who was on the phone?"

"Just as I thought, it was the police. But they didn't call about Daniel or Émile. It's Madelaine Duveau. The woman I was going to see this afternoon." His eyes clouded. "She died earlier today. Her daughter stopped by to bring her a gateau and found her. The police saw my name and number on her calendar on today's date and called me to let me know."

"How old was she?" Duncan asked.

"She was eighty-six. But, the big news is she was drinking a bottle of Château Beaulieu wine." He paused to let his words sink in.

On the sofa, Becca covered her lap with a soft wool throw

she had pulled from the basket next to her. "I don't understand," she said.

"I asked them to check the bottle to confirm there wasn't anything suspicious about it."

"What did they say?" David asked.

"At first they weren't interested, but their attitude changed pretty fast when I told them about Daniel, Émile and the poisoned wine in our vineyard office. Given Madelaine's note and the timing of her death, I won't be at all surprised if she was poisoned."

TWENTY-FIVE

RAP AT HIS study door caused Philip to look up from the stack of papers he and Duncan were reviewing.

"Ah, Edouard, come in." Philip shoved his glasses from the bridge of his nose to the top of his head.

"Bonjour, my lord. You asked to see me?"

"Oui, asseyez-vous." He motioned for Edouard to sit. "Duncan and I have several things to discuss with you."

Philip moved from behind his desk to a chair next to Edouard, who had flopped down on a loveseat.

Completing the cozy group, Duncan sat on the other side of their vigneron.

Philip looked down at his jeans and brushed away a crumb left from his lunch. "It's been a busy time since we arrived." He looked back at Edouard. He was in no hurry to fill the silence in the room.

Edouard cleared his throat and stared at the floor. He tapped his signet ring on the wood of his arm chair until he realized how annoying the sound was, and stopped.

At last Philip said, "I got a message yesterday that a representative from DREETS will be visiting us Friday. My understanding is that they are the agency that investigates fraud in the wine industry. Is that true?"

Surprise flashed across Edouard's young face. "Oui. That is the agency that looks into such matters. Why would they make a visit here?"

"That's what we're asking you, Edouard," Duncan said, his voice sharper than he had intended.

"Has there ever been an issue of counterfeiting wine at Château Beaulieu, that you know of?" Philip didn't hide his wariness.

Edouard stiffened in his chair. "No," he spat. "Absolument pas."

"All right." Philip reached out and put his hand on Edouard's knee. "We'll wait and see what they want. But we want you to meet with us when he comes."

Edouard laced and unlaced his fingers in his lap. "Friday morning, I must be at the Saint-Émilion growers' breakfast. But I can be back by eleven o'clock."

"That will be fine." Philip softened his tone and changed the subject. "Edouard, how are you doing? We know Daniel's death has been very hard on you and we want to do what we can to make the next few weeks as easy as possible for you; for everyone here at the vineyard." He paused, waiting for Edouard to say something.

The young man relaxed back into the cushions and said, "I don't think there's anything to be done. Nothing will ever be the same without Daniel. That may be a bad thing." He paused, looked down at his fidgeting fingers and quieted them. "Or it may be a good thing. We'll just have to wait and see, won't we?"

Duncan looked at his dad then back at Edouard. "Did you just say Daniel's death might be a good thing?" Furrows appeared between his eyebrows.

"What I mean is, Daniel had been here for a very long time. Perhaps it is the right time for new energy. We say un peu de sang neuf, some new blood." He tilted his head back and assessed Duncan with a critical eye. "My lord, you are not young, but you are not old."

"Thank you, I guess." Duncan shrugged.

"It is my understanding that though you have not worked in the wine industry, you are a businessman. Oui?"

"True." Duncan nodded and went on. "I'm going to rely on you to teach me about wine and this industry, Edouard."

Edouard shook his head. "No, no, no. I would suggest you manage the numbers, the cash flow, the paying of the bills, ordering of the supplies—all of that business." He fluttered his hands in the air. "And I shall manage the vineyard, the quality of the wine, everything that is the reputation of Château Beaulieu."

Stunned into silence, Duncan turned to catch his father's reaction. He wasn't surprised to see the color rising in Philip's face and his lips in a tight line.

"Edouard, I don't understand." Philip kept his voice even. "You realize we Laneys own Château Beaulieu, don't you?"

"You may own the vineyard, but you do not own the heart and soul of Château Beaulieu. That will take generations. Until then, your family will have to rely on me to be the—I believe you say—steward of the land, and all that comes from it." He rose and headed toward the door. Before making his dramatic exit, he turned and said, "Now if you will excuse me, I must attend to *our* land."

Minutes ticked by. Philip and Duncan didn't speak. Each sat, replaying what they had just heard, wondering if they had misunderstood this twenty-seven-year-old's arrogant words.

Duncan was the one to break the silence. "Wow, Dad. I didn't understand. I thought Daniel was Edouard's mentor, his close friend," he said. "And he couldn't possibly think he's not going to have to answer to anybody."

"He's going to have to answer to you, Duncan. Good luck with that." Philip scoffed, walked behind his desk and sat down. He rifled through a few papers and pulled out a sheet. "I found this when I came in here after lunch." He handed the stationery to Duncan.

"What is it?" Duncan scanned it and handed it back to his dad. "Very funny. It's in French."

"Oh, is it?" Philip smirked. "Is that a problem?" he teased. "It's from our bottle purveyor. It says the order for the extra bottles for our shipments to China will be delayed by two weeks. This leads me to ask: what do they mean by extra bottles?"

"I guess it could either mean that we're sending more bottles to China than we normally do, or we don't usually send wine to China and this year we are? Why didn't you ask Edouard about it?"

"Not that I suspect Edouard of anything, but I decided to show it to the DREET agent and see if they think it has anything to do with counterfeiting."

"Too bad Daniel's not here to guide us. No doubt he could answer a lot of questions." Duncan rose and started gathering the papers he'd been reading. "You know, Dad, we should be working in his office. That's where all the records are going to be." Duncan stuck a binder under his arm and grabbed the stack of file folders with both hands. "If there's anything incriminating in the office, the sooner we find it, the better."

Philip glanced at his watch. "I'll meet you there in thirty minutes. I want to bring your mother up to speed."

"Works for me," Duncan said and headed to the vineyard office as Philip went in search of Genevieve.

TWENTY-SIX

I N THE PETIT salon, which had become her favorite retreat, Genevieve nestled in a faded paisley chair, and Becca sat cross-legged on a down-stuffed sofa. The fire threw warmth into the room and a pretty glow onto the frescoed walls. Just across the hall from the kitchen, the cozy room caught all the aromas, from baking bread to the smell of quiche bubbling in the oven.

Brainstorming about the Cité du Vin project, the two women talked non-stop, posing one idea after another until they had a roadmap of how to make The Art of the Vine exciting and successful. They'd start with a launch at Château Beaulieu and build from there.

Genevieve's phone vibrated its way across the table. She grabbed it before it could dance over the edge and saw Lillie's face on the screen. "You're back in Paris safe and sound I trust?"

"I am" Lillie's spirited lilt shot energy over the line. "Do you have a minute? I have news."

"Of course, and Becca's here with me. We've been throwing ideas for the Cité du Vin program against the wall to see what will stick. You should be here."

"I'm glad you said that. I'll be back sooner than expected. I just got off the phone with Elise Beaufoy, the Chairman of the Cité du Vin Foundation board. I can't begin to tell you how thrilled she was that you and Philip want to create a work-study program with them. Usually people who donate bags of money want to throw it at something glamourous, something flashy. The foundation has been wanting to do something like this for years." She paused to take a breath.

"That's excellent. I'm putting you on speaker so Becca can hear." Genevieve flashed a smile and filled Becca in.

"That brings me to my next piece of news. You're sitting down, right?"

"We are."

"They have a quarterly board meeting in just over a week. It was supposed to be in Reims with each Champagne house trying to top each other to impress Cité du Vin, but the hotel where the board was going to stay burned to the ground two days ago. If you can believe it, there's a California growers conference in Reims at the same time, and all the hotels are booked. So, guess what. They're having their board meeting in Saint-Émilion. It starts with a cocktail party on Thursday night and an all-day meeting on Friday, followed by a dinner. They've already booked a hotel in Saint-Émilion that can accommodate them, but they want you, Philip, and Duncan to join them for the cocktail party, meeting, and dinner. They want to highlight The Art of the Vine. Elise knows you're incredibly busy, having just arrived at Château Beaulieu, but the next board meeting is in Italy, and they don't want to have to wait six more months after that to get the program rolling. Would you three be able to attend?"

"Hmm," Genevieve's mind churned. "That's next Thursday?"

"Yes."

"How many people are we talking about?"

"There are fifteen on the board and some ancillary staff, so maybe twenty or so. And of course, Bernard and I will be there. What are you thinking?"

"Only twenty or twenty-five? That's nothing, Lillie. We'll host the cocktail party, meeting, and dinner here. We'll make the Champagne houses look like amateurs. We'll blow their socks off. Right, Delphine?" She grinned at Delphine, who had been standing in the doorway, listening. Delphine smiled at the energy in the room, then, remembering why she was there, said, "Lady Crosswick, you have a visitor. Monsieur Wang est ici."

"Kim Wang?" Genevieve's eyebrows arched. "What in the world…" she caught herself and lowered her voice. "Did he say what he wants, Delphine?"

"Non, my lady, but he did come with a beautiful bouquet."

"Well, in that case, show him in."

She said into the phone, "Lillie, we have to go. Text me the specifics and let's talk later today."

"You're brilliant, Genevieve. You, too, Becca. Bye."

"Well, that's exciting. I can't wait to tell Philip."

Genevieve pulled a tube of lipstick from her pocket and applied it without looking in a mirror. She smoothed her hair and was ready for Kim. "Becca, did you meet Kim Wang at Daniel's celebration of life? He sat next to me."

Becca shook her head. "I don't think so. Who is he?"

"His family owns Clos Peyra, the vineyard next door. He's

seriously handsome," she said, lowering her voice to a whisper as he walked into the room.

What an understatement, Becca thought as she looked at Kim Wang's elegant, classic features.

Genevieve stood and extended her hand. "Kim, what a wonderful surprise."

Avoiding her hand, he pulled her into la bise, careful not to crush the bouquet he was carrying.

She heard Becca's hum of approval and shot her a look that said, "Stop it."

"For you, Genevieve." He handed her a stunning assortment of hydrangeas, lilies, roses and stock, a riot of purples, deep blues, and oranges, that smelled of spring.

"How lovely." She buried her nose in the blossoms. "You would have been welcome without such a beautiful offering, but if you're going to come bearing gifts, please, come often." She flashed a dazzling smile. "Delphine, would you mind putting these in water?"

"Certainement, my lady."

"Kim, I don't believe you met our dear friend, Becca Conway, when you were here yesterday."

Becca's stomach fluttered as Kim turned his velvet brown eyes on her.

He held her captive in his gaze for several seconds before he took her hand and brought it to his lips. "I would not forget such an encounter, I assure you," he said.

At a loss for words, Genevieve stood by watching until Delphine came to the rescue. "Monsieur Wang, voulez-vous boire quelque chose?" she asked, her voice formal and cool.

He dragged his eyes from Becca to the housekeeper. "Le Champagne serait parfait," he said in flawless French. He nodded to the bottle of Veuve Clicquot.

Within moments, Delphine returned with a glass, filled it, and extended it to Wang. "Monsieur."

Hearing an icy note in Delphine's voice, Genevieve made a mental note to ask her about it later.

"Will there be anything else, my lady?"

"Not for the moment, Delphine. Thank you." She gave the housekeeper an affectionate nod.

"Please, Kim, sit." She motioned to a chair near the fire. "To us." She raised her glass and the three drank.

"If I may," Kim began, looking at Genevieve, who smiled for him to continue. "My wife Jing and I would like you to join us for dinner Friday evening." He looked at Becca. "And we would love for you and your fiancé to join us, Mademoiselle Conway. We can make it quite a party."

Becca flopped back against the cushion. "How disappointing. David and I have to go to London Friday morning. May we have a raincheck?"

"Raincheck?" Kim's cocked his head.

"I mean, I hope you'll invite us again."

"Of course. It will be our pleasure. When you return, you and Sir David must come to the Clos."

"Too bad for you, Becca, but, Kim, we'd love to come. I look forward to getting to know our next-door neighbors."

"Excellent," he said. He drained his flute and stood. He smiled at Becca. "You will be missed."

Genevieve rose to see him out, chatting until they arrived at the front door. Kim wrapped his scarf twice around his neck and draped his coat over his shoulders. He turned to Genevieve, took her hands in his and asked, "How are you doing?" his voice filled with concern.

"Why do you ask?" Genevieve said, surprised.

He studied her for several seconds until he knew she was growing uncomfortable. "I'm just a concerned neighbor," he said at last, and released her hands. "Aren't you worried about Daniel's death?" His gaze was riveting. "Look after yourself. I wouldn't want anything to happen to you." Then, without warning, he flashed a broad smile. "Jusqu'a vendredi," he said.

"Yes, we look forward to seeing you on Friday," she said, glad he was leaving.

TWENTY-SEVEN

FRIGID WIND WHISTLED through gnarly vines, warning tender buds not to make an appearance yet. Looking out at the wintery scene, Genevieve sipped her steaming coffee and scrolled through her calendar. She made two more entries, then looked up to see Philip stroll through the door, looking very continental in snug jeans, a black turtleneck and a scarf knotted through a loop around his neck. The sight of him still made her stomach flutter. A good sign, she thought.

"Good morning, darling." He kissed her. He kissed her again. "Mmmm. Coffee." He licked his lips, took her mug and gulped the steaming java. She watched with admiration as he took another swig.

"How can you do that? It's almost boiling." She grimaced, imagining his scalded mouth.

"It's not that hot," he dismissed, and ran his fingertips over her cheekbone. "You know, you're a real beauty," he said, lured by her green eyes. With his fingers under her chin, he tilted her face up, leaned over and covered her mouth with his. He lingered there until his body told him to stop or find someplace more private to continue. He could feel her smiling and pulled his lips from hers just enough to say, "You think this is funny? It's going to be hilarious if Delphine walks in here and sees what state I'm in."

His lips still on hers, her giggle turned into a throaty laugh.

"What's the big joke? What did I miss?" David asked, making his entrance and heading to the sideboard, where fresh pastries were waiting to be eaten. He piled a croissant and a pain au chocolat on a plate, then turned back to Genevieve, who was still giggling. "So? What's so funny?"

"It was nothing, David." She waved him off. "Philip just told me a joke and it made me laugh." She gave him a sly smile and pulled a tissue from her pocket to blow her nose.

"You're joining us for our conversation with Inspector Boucher, aren't you, David?"

"That's my plan." He put his plate and mug on the table, pulled out a pine armchair and sat. He took an enormous bite of a warm croissant and flakes sprayed the front of his hunter-green sweater.

Genevieve smiled at the crumbs littering his chest. "Good, isn't it?"

"Mmmm." He chewed, then swallowed. "Scrumptious. Worth the mess," he said as he picked pastry from his pullover and popped it into his mouth.

Philip refilled his cup from the French press. "I've got to go. Duncan's been in the vineyard office for an hour. We're trying to get through the files before the agent from DREETS comes tomorrow. Boucher will take up most of our afternoon today, so we're running out of time."

"What are you looking for?" David asked. "Is there any way I can help?"

"We're not sure what we're looking for, but whatever it is, six eyes are better than four. Come on."

"And they're off," Genevieve said to herself. As she watched them hustle out the door and stride across the terrace toward the vineyard office, she heard a growling in her stomach and realized she needed to eat. As if reading her thoughts, Delphine appeared with a new pot of coffee and a narrow tray of mini baguettes. "What are the chances I could have an omelet with mushrooms, olives and cheese?" she asked Delphine, knowing the chances were excellent.

"Lizette will have it done dans un moment. Fruit aussi? And what may I get you, Mademoiselle Conway?" she said as Becca walked in.

"Just coffee, please, Delphine." Becca sucked in her stomach. "I have to watch out for you and Lizette. You're treacherous with your fresh pastries and fabulous meals. She puffed out her cheeks.

"Madame, it would take many croissants before you have to worry about your waistline." Pleased with the praise, the house manager scooped up a tray of dirty plates and headed toward the kitchen. As Genevieve watched her leave, she marveled at how she and Philip had so quickly adjusted to having a small army of people care for their every need. It hadn't taken long to go from being self-sufficient to having most of their needs catered to.

"Becca." Genevieve took a sip of coffee and put down her cup before continuing. "You grew up in a very wealthy household. Did you always have a lot of staff to take care of you and your family?"

Before answering, Becca thought for several seconds. She draped her linen napkin in her lap and leaned her elbows on the table. "We did. When I think about it, I'm sure it was part of why I was such a mess for a long time."

Genevieve leaned forward, surprised.

"For years I was indulged and pampered. When I look at Émile, I see a lot of myself. Speaking of Émile, when will he get out of the hospital?"

"Funny you should ask. Henri went to pick him up about an hour ago. They should be back any time."

"I didn't hear what Émile's father said when Philip called to tell him his son had been poisoned. Was he furious?"

The shake of her head was almost imperceptible. Then, Genevieve said, "I was surprised by his comments, but Émile has been a problem for his parents for a long time."

Becca sat back in her chair. "What in the world did he say?"

"He said he shouldn't have been drinking while he was supposed to be working."

"Wow! That's heartless!" Becca snorted a laugh. "Compared to Baron de Sézanne, my parents were Mother Theresa and Gandhi. When Philip called him, was Émile out of danger?"

"He was. I don't think Philip dwelled on the fact that Émile could have died. My guess is he minimized that little piece of information. No need to worry the baron unnecessarily." She rolled her eyes.

"Wise thinking on Philip's part."

As if on cue, Émile ambled through the door carrying Genevieve's omelet and an array of fresh melon and raspberries.

"Well, speak of the devil. Émile, ça va?" Genevieve asked.

He smirked at her. "I am not as well as I would be if I had not been poisoned."

She couldn't help but smile. "I guess that's the last time you drink from a random bottle of wine," she deadpanned.

He set the plate in front of her. "You are correct." Having something more to say, he lingered, shifting from one foot to the other, then back again.

"Thank you, Émile." The dark circles around his eyes accentuated his ghostly pallor and he was even thinner than before he was poisoned. "We're happy you're out of the hospital and on your way to your old self. Lizette needs to ply you with lots of pastries so you can put on a few pounds." Still, he remained until Genevieve said, "Is there something else?"

"Yes, Lady Crosswick, there is." He studied the floor for several seconds. When he looked up, his eyes were moist. "Lady Crosswick, I want to thank you." His voice cracked. "The doctor said if you had not found me when you did, I could have died."

Genevieve's chair scraped on the floor as she stood. She clutched Émile's shoulders, then pulled him into a hug. His rigid body neither resisted nor surrendered. They stood in an awkward embrace, Émile's arms at his sides, until Genevieve decided she should let him go. As she released him, she felt his muscles relax.

He stepped back and gave her a stiff pat on the shoulder. He looked at her, then at Becca. "If there is nothing I can do for either of you, I should see if Delphine needs me."

But before he could escape, Becca moved in to give him a peck on the cheek. "Welcome home, Émile. We're glad you're back."

Crimson crept up his neck to the tops of his ears. "Merci," he mumbled, then turned and fled, passing Delphine as she walked back into the orangerie.

"What did you two do to that poor boy?" Delphine asked as she cleared plates and refilled coffee cups.

"We were just showing him we care," Becca said. "I think it might have been a bit too much for him." Her lips parted in a broad grin.

Genevieve rolled her spoon between her fingers. "He seems so vulnerable. I'd almost say sweet." She looked at Becca and Delphine for confirmation.

Becca nodded. "Sweet is the perfect word. Quite a change from the would-be art thief who tried to steal your Pollock."

"He's going to be fine," Delphine said with confidence. "The house staff is working him hard, but he's not complaining, and the vineyard workers are making him earn his place. That is as it should be." Her eyes softened. "And, I am happy to say, he is making friends."

Through the windows, they watched Émile lope across the terrace toward the vineyard, then turn as a young worker, about his age, called to him and waved. A lopsided smile plastered on his face, Émile waved back, and they walked together into the vines. With the sun brilliant in the winter-blue sky, the two were soon lost in its blaze. Watching them, Genevieve felt a glow of pride that she and Philip were helping this lad change the course of his life.

"My lady, may I get you anything else?" Genevieve's attention was pulled back into the orangerie.

"Delphine, could you please sit down for a minute?"

The house manager's brows arched. She hesitated for a heartbeat then said, "Mais oui," and sat on the edge of a paisley-covered dining chair.

"Yesterday, when Monsieur Wang was here, I got the impression you don't like him very much. Or perhaps I'm wrong." She studied Delphine's expression, but it gave away nothing. Waiting for a reply, she rose and picked up the carafe.

"Coffee?"

"Oui, s'il vous plaît." As Genevieve poured, Delphine folded her hands on the table. "You are perceptive, my lady. Or, perhaps I am too transparent." She draped her napkin over her knees. "I am not, as you Americans say, a fan of Monsieur Wang."

"And why is that?" Becca eased into the conversation.

"Alors, I can only say it is a feeling I have gotten over the years." Her eyes were glued to the napkin she was now twisting in her lap.

"There's nothing specific, no event, no one thing he has done to make you suspicious of him?" Genevieve looked at Becca, then back at Delphine. "Nothing?" she pressed.

Breathing a deep sigh, Delphine dropped the wrinkled serviette and locked Genevieve in her gaze. "If you must know, there are two reasons I believe Kim Wang is not the homme charmant he would like everyone to believe he is."

"Do tell." Becca leaned forward anticipating some great gossip.

"The first incident was when the Wangs had just moved into Clos Peyra. Monsieur Wang's father owns the conglomerate that bought the vineyard from the original French owners."

"I assume you were not happy about that."

"No one in Saint-Émilion was." Delphine sipped her coffee, wrinkled her nose at the cold brew, and shoved the cup away. "According to the potins, uh, the gossip, Kim was sent to make the clos more profitable and more prestigious. But, I am getting off the trail. Is that what you say?"

"Close enough." Genevieve bobbed her head, encouraging Delphine to continue.

"The Wangs had just moved into Clos Peyra, so I decided to take a basket of Lizette's pastries, some jams she had made, and, of course, two bottles of wine as a welcome gift."

"What a nice thing to do," Becca said.

"I walked through the headlands and alleyways from Château Beaulieu to Clos Peyra." Two blank faces looked at her. "A headland is the space at the end of a vineyard row and the alleyways are breaks between vineyard blocks, you know, rows of similar vines that are planted together in a block."

"Aha," the two said in unison.

"My point is that because I walked through the vineyard rather than drove, no one heard me coming. When I arrived, I knocked and the front door creaked open, so I eased into the foyer."

"This sounds like a murder mystery," Becca said, eyes wide.

Delphine patted Becca's hand. "I promise, I did not *see* Monsieur Wang actually murder anyone." She bit her lower lip. "But, I did hear an angry conversation, or I should say tirade."

Genevieve shook her head. "Your English is amazing, Delphine." Though Genevieve's French was excellent, she was in awe of Delphine's vast lexicon. "What is the French word for tirade?" she asked.

Delphine's lips twitched. "Why, tirade, of course," she said, which sent the three women into a fit of laughter.

As their hilarity dwindled, Delphine took a deep breath and blew her nose. "Let me finish," she said.

Becca couldn't stop giggling.

"All right, all right." Genevieve tried to look serious. "I want to hear the rest of your story, Delphine."

"And I want to *tell* you the rest of my story, my lady." Her amusement was gone, and she was sober again. "Être-vous prêt?"

Becca gave a thumbs up though she still giggled under her breath.

"Where was I?" Delphine thought for a moment then remembered. "Ah yes," she said, holding up her index finger. "I heard the tirade and had decided I should put the basket of pastries down and leave, when a few words caught my ears. I heard several men in a room. They seemed to be in a hot discussion. I had not met Kim Wang or any of the Wang family so I didn't know their voices, but I could tell that Kim's father was arguing with him."

Genevieve gulped from her water glass. "You don't speak Chinese, do you, Delphine?"

"No, of course not." Delphine shook her head. "They spoke French rather than Chinese, which I thought was odd until I realized there must be men in the room who only spoke French."

"Interesting." Two lines etched between Becca's brows. "What did they say?"

Delphine gazed into the distance, trying to recall what she had heard. "They were arguing about purchasing Château Beaulieu. Kim's father said if Kim couldn't make the deal, he must find another way to use Château Beaulieu's name." With her napkin, she dabbed the perspiration from her upper lip.

"What in the world did he mean by that?" Genevieve scowled then brightened, remembering something. "I may be able to answer my own question. When Daniel came to Paris, he said the Wangs have tried to buy the château several times. According to him, they wanted Château Beaulieu for something their own vineyard didn't have: a prestigious name."

Did you hear anything else," Becca asked.

"I did not. At that moment, Madame Wang appeared in the doorway behind me. She seemed to come from nowhere and I almost dropped the basket. Of course, I was embarrassed that she caught me écoute clandestine, I believe you say eavesdropping." Delphine's breath quickened as she relived the episode. "The madame was tres gentile, very kind, and took me into a beautiful little sitting room. She offered me tea, but I told her I had to get back to Château Beaulieu. I was anxious to leave. I don't know if Madame Wang told le monsieur I had overheard his conversation, but since that time, whenever he sees me he is very cool to me."

Deflated, Genevieve slumped in her chair. She wasn't sure what she had expected, but she thought Delphine's big reveal would be something more dramatic than overhearing a group of disappointed businessmen argue. She shivered and realized her cardigan had slipped off her shoulders and was gathered behind her. She wiggled it up her back and shoved her arms into the sleeves.

"It's chilly in here, isn't it?"

"Un peu, my lady. Would you like some hot coffee? This is cold," Delphine said, cupping her hands around the glass pot. "Or tea, peut être?"

"I think I've had enough. Becca?"

Becca shook her head. "No, thank you. I'm fine. I want to hear the other reason you don't like Kim."

"I need to see if Inspector Boucher has arrived. But, Delphine," Genevieve and Becca leaned forward, eyes riveted on the housekeeper, "before I do, please finish." They had no idea what to expect but hoped for something more exciting.

Going against her rigid standards, Delphine poured cold coffee into her cup and drained it. "This would benefit from a shot of cognac," she mumbled. "What I am about to tell you is rather strange." The gold light streaming through the bank of French doors dimmed as the clouds swept across the sun. Her mood darkened with the fading light. "About six months ago, I took a lunch tray to Daniel. He was not in his office, so I left it on his desk."

"Before going back to the château, I decided to see if Henri needed anything. Knowing there was a new Lord and Lady Crosswick, he was here at the château rather than in Paris. He was going over every automobile to make certain they were all in perfect working order." She hesitated then went on. "I came around the corner of the garage and saw someone I believe to be Kim Wang put a rolled-up Persian carpet in the back of a Clos Peyra Range Rover."

Genevieve's brow furrowed. "Why did you say you saw someone you *believe* to be Kim Wang putting, a carpet in the back of his car?"

"I can't be certain, my lady, because he was wearing a hat and I was quite a distance away."

Becca's eyes narrowed. "I'm sorry, Delphine; how is that significant?"

"That is significant, madame, because what if the carpet had a body rolled up in it?"

TWENTY-EIGHT

THERE WAS A long moment of silence while Genevieve and Becca looked at each other and then at Delphine.

"Delphine, are you suggesting that Kim Wang, a respected international businessman, and our neighbor, rolled a dead body in a carpet and tossed it in his Range Rover? That's what you're telling us?" Becca pressed.

"Oui, madame. A Persian carpet," she emphasized.

Genevieve mirrored Becca's look of disbelief. She was struggling to imagine that the house manager hadn't had a terrible dream. Or perhaps she had eaten magic mushrooms? Or had she been tipsy at the time? In Genevieve's mind, it was impossible that this man could do such a thing. "So, tell us, Delphine, what did you do next?"

Knowing her employer and her employer's friend thought she might be delusional, Delphine proceeded with care. "I can remember my first thought was to take a photograph on my mobile. I reached into my pocket, and it was not there. I could not photograph the man, and I could not call anyone if I got into trouble."

Surprised at the thought, Becca said, "Did you really think you might be in danger?"

Stiffening in her chair, Delphine narrowed her eyes. "Mademoiselle, would you not fear for your life if you were in the company of a man you thought had just murdered a man... or a woman?"

"Well, you weren't actually in his company, were you?"

Delphine rose from her chair, her jaw rigid, and began gathering napkins left on the table, brushing crumbs that had fallen from pastries. "I know what I saw," she said between clenched teeth. She was about to leave when Genevieve caught her arm.

"Delphine, please sit down. Try to understand what a surprise this is for Becca and me. To imagine Kim as a murderer is not easy. He doesn't look like a murderer, does he?" Genevieve flushed.

"And he's very charming," Becca added.

"We're just trying to process a shocking piece of information." Genevieve tugged on Delphine's arm until the house manager sat. "Please tell us what happened next."

Delphine's shoulders softened as she began to relax, but the clock ticked many times before she responded. At last, she said, "As you might imagine, I went straight to Daniel. I looked in his office, but he had not returned."

"Did you ever talk to Daniel?"

With her chin jutting, Delphine said, "Bien sûr, I reached him on his portable in Saint-Émilion and what he told me was surprising. He said the château had sold the carpet to Monsieur Wang. It had been in storage for years and the trustees of the estate wanted everything not in use," she pursed her lips and squinted, thinking, "mmm, liquated?"

Genevieve and Becca grinned at Delphine. "Liquidated," they said together.

"Philip and I know about the 12ᵀᴴ Earl's wishes to ensure his properties were efficient and self-sustaining, and that he ordered anything not in use to be," Genevieve paused and smiled at Delphine, "liquidated. Daniel's explanation about the carpet makes sense. Lord Crosswick and I appreciate what they did because Philip didn't inherit a heap of monetary perils. All the holdings are in sound financial shape." She cocked her head and said, "What did Daniel say about a body in the carpet?"

Delphine studied the border on the tablecloth. She looked up at Genevieve through her lashes. "I did not tell him. I started to, but then I thought he might think I was un peu fou, a little mad." She looked down again. "Perhaps he would have been right. Perhaps we'll never know."

TWENTY-NINE

I NSPECTOR CHARLES BOUCHER of the Bureau of Enquiry and Analysis, the BEA, woke at 5:25 a.m., five minutes before his alarm clock was set to jangle him from sleep. As he showered and dressed his rotund figure more carefully than usual, he felt a tickle of excitement in the pit of his stomach. Since he began investigating the mysterious incident of water in the tank of the 13TH Earl of Crosswick's Bombardier, he was starting every day with a renewed interest in his job.

For the last few years, as retirement loomed, the most important cases had been landing on the desks of younger officers. It didn't matter that he could dance circles around the rookies. They were coming out of universities having mastered mind-blowing technology. They were arrogant, dapper, and too flash. Charles Boucher was a slogger, but he had almost forty years of success under his belt and he was not going to let anyone else have this case. Besides, he had a crush on Lady Crosswick and he liked being around rich people.

By eight o'clock, he was in his wide leather seat, comfortable on the TGV from Paris to Bordeaux. The 340-mile trip would take two hours and twenty minutes. The commute from his home in the Paris suburbs to his office on the opposite side of the city could sometimes take almost that long. With fifteen minutes until departure, he made his way to the café car and indulged in a cappuccino and jambon et fromage croissant, lightly heated. There would be a car waiting for him at the station, and Lord and Lady Crosswick had invited him to stay at their château. He was looking forward to a night on thousand-thread-count sheets.

As the train slid out of Gare Saint-Lazare, Boucher slurped the last of his coffee. When he looked down, a field of flakes from his croissant covered his belly. If the lord and lady invited him to dinner, he'd have to do better.

He glanced at his watch, 8:27. He would be at Gare de Bordeaux-Saint-Jean by 10:45 or so. That would put him at Château Beaulieu around noon, perfect timing for lunch. "I bet they'll have something delicious, something traditional," he said to himself. He hoped there would be foie gras. The Bordelaise loved foie gras, and so did he. He could almost taste the rich, buttery delicacy. He leaned back against the headrest and licked his lips. It was going to be a spectacular twenty-four hours. Perhaps with luck he could stretch it to forty-eight.

"Dad, is this anything?" Duncan held up a copy of an email chain two pages long in French. "It was in this file marked 'Confidentielle'." In his other hand, he waved a blue folder. "Who in the world prints out emails?"

David snorted a laugh. "Wrinklies."

"Is that a shot at people my age, you pipsqueak?" Sitting at the desk, Philip peered between stacks of papers piled high. "What does it say, Duncan?"

"Dad, I can say with confidence that my French is no better today than it was yesterday. David, would you take a look at this?"

"Righto," he said, shoving himself off the floor with a grunt. He skimmed the paper, then scowled and looked at it again, reading slowly this time. "This might be something," he said, not taking his eyes from the page. He reached behind for a chair and sat.

"What is it, David?"

He held up his hand. "Give me a second here," he said, continuing to read.

Behind his desk, Philip stood, straightened his arms over his head, and groaned as he stretched. As he walked around the desk, he and Duncan locked eyes and his son shrugged his shoulders.

Philip sat on the edge of his desk and they waited. He looked at his watch and they waited. "What do you—"

David raised his hand again, demanding silence. Another two minutes dragged by.

Just as Duncan was about to go back to searching the files, David whispered, "Bloody hell. Bloody hell," he said again, louder this time.

"What is it, David?"

"Sit down, you two." His eyes dark as pitch, David looked from the papers in his hands to the two men waiting for his big reveal. "We need to have a French speaker confirm my translation, but this exchange is about a plan to buy Château Beaulieu and the need for another plan if the trustees won't sell."

Reaching for the pages, Philip said, "Let me see that, David. Who's it from?"

"I can't tell who sent or received the correspondence, but someone who knows tech would be able to tell."

Philip's eyes darted back and forth on the page. "What's this?" He pointed to a phrase and turned the page so David could see.

S'ils ne nous vendent pas, nous obtiendrons ce dont nous avons besoin d'une autre manière.

David took the paper. "It says, 'If they won't sell to us, we'll get what we need another way'."

"That's what I thought it said. We'll share this with Boucher when he gets here." He glanced at the 19th-century bronze wall clock just as it pinged the first of twelve chimes. "By the way, shouldn't he be here by now?"

Deep in Philip's pocket, *Les Marseilles* announced a phone call. He fished in his trousers and pulled out his cell phone. Genevieve's picture filled his screen. "Hi, G. What's up?"

"Inspector Boucher just arrived. Delphine is showing him to his room. I told him we'd gather in the salon for drinks at twelve thirty, so you, David, and Duncan need to think about coming back to the house. I assume you're still in the vineyard office. Have you found anything interesting?"

"As a matter of fact, we have." He was still holding the emails. "It's good timing because Boucher might be interested in these."

"These what?" Genevieve's curiosity reached through the line.

"A couple of pages of emails."

"Sounds fascinating." Her sarcasm was hard to ignore.

Philip waved the pages in the air. "You just wait. This might be important."

"Clearly, you three are in a frenzy with your riveting emails and I bet you have a couple of wild texts, too, but you need to come back to the château, now."

"All right, all right. We'll be there. Give us ten minutes to wrap it up here."

"The timer's on, pal." And she was gone.

"Guys, we've got to…"

"We got it, Dad. The general has ordered the troops back to the barracks. Right?"

"Pretty much. Let's roll."

THIRTY

Cozy in an overstuffed chair just close enough to the crackling fire, Charles Boucher closed his eyes and sighed an appreciative "Mmmm," as he sipped his Kir Royale. He was the first to arrive in the salon and was not shy about making himself at home, with Delphine's permission, of course. It would be nice to have a foot stool, he mused, as his feet didn't quite touch the floor. He looked around for an ottoman.

"Inspector Boucher," Philip strode across the sun-kissed room, his hand outstretched.

Boucher scooched his bottom forward in the chair until his feet touched the floor. He popped out of the chair just in time to grab Philip's hand and pump it. "Lord Crosswick, it is un plaisir to be in your beautiful château. Merci pour votre hospitalite."

"It's our pleasure, Inspector. It makes sense for you to stay here. And I'd like you to meet our solicitor, Sir David Weatherington." He motioned for Boucher to be seated. "Lady Crosswick will be down shortly."

With a small tray with Kir Royales for Philip and David in one hand and a tray of hors d'oeuvres in the other, Delphine delivered the drinks, offered the appetizers, and was gone.

Anxious to hear what the inspector had discovered in the last few days, Philip was having difficulty waiting for Genevieve and Duncan, so he focused on small talk. "How was your trip, inspector?"

"It was wonderful, my lord. I love the TGV. I believe they have the best coffee in France."

"Are you serious?" David asked. "It would never have occurred to me that train coffee would be anything special. Good to know. Have you been to Bordeaux before?"

"Ah, oui. I was born in Libourne."

"Libourne! That's just a few miles away."

"So it is. My parents moved to Paris when I was a small boy, but for years I spent my summer holidays in this area with my aunt and uncle. They grew grapes for the wineries in Bordeaux and I would work in the vines."

"What a wonderful way to spend your summers." Images flashed through Philip's mind: of learning to leaf and prune and sucker, and the other important jobs that went into creating the perfect grape.

"I hated it," Boucher deadpanned. "I was miserable every summer. Would rather have stayed in school."

At a loss for words, Philip was grateful to hear Genevieve's voice.

"Inspector Boucher," she said. "How wonderful to see you."

Again, Boucher wiggled out of his chair and stretched to his full five foot three. Genevieve's handshake was firm and her hand silky. He held it a bit too tight and a bit too long and was embarrassed when she had to tug it from his grip.

"It's my pleasure to be here, my lady," he said, feeling heat in the tops of his ears.

"I trust your trip was smooth and uneventful."

"It was. I didn't give my briefcase to a stranger, if that's what you mean." Boucher chuckled and arched his eyebrows at Genevieve in what he thought was a charming flirt.

"You're much too clever for that," she vamped in return. "Duncan is on his way," she said as her son walked into the salon. "Speak of the devil."

"Sorry I'm late. I was on the phone with Julia, trying to solve the crisis of how Ella could stay on the swim team and still take dance and art. So many interests, so little time." The warmth filled his voice as he talked about his daughter. "Inspector Boucher, I'm Duncan Warwick, Lord and Lady Crosswick's son."

Boucher couldn't get out of his chair before Duncan was upon him. He craned his neck looking up at the Warwicks' son, who loomed over him, his hand outstretched. He could do nothing but offer his hand in return and try to meet the strength of the younger man's grasp. He was grateful that the handshake was brief. He admired the easy elegance of the younger Warwick and felt a quiver of jealousy. Why were rich people always attractive, he wondered?

"Have I missed anything?" Before sitting next to his mother on the sofa, Duncan tossed a log on the dwindling fire and the dry wood sparked into flames.

Genevieve patted her son's hand. "We were waiting for you."

"I understand you have news about the water in the Bombardier's fuel tank," Philip said, anxious to get to the point.

Boucher snuggled deep into his chair, happy to have the conversation in his court. He put his glass on the table beside him, hoping Delphine would notice it was empty. He reached into the inside pocket of his jacket and brought out the same small, scuffed notebook he had in Paris, but instead of the gnawed stub of pencil he had used before, he rolled an iconic black Mont Blanc pen lovingly between his fingers.

"First I must say, we in the BEA take incidents such as attempted murder very seriously."

Genevieve looked at Philip to see if the brutality of the words "attempted murder" had startled him. He seemed unphased.

"My team has been working very hard on your case, and we are making progress. We have found several things we would like to share with you, Lord and Lady Crosswick." He nodded at Duncan. "And, you, as well, my lord."

He saw his glass out of the corner of his eye. Somehow Delphine had replaced his empty flute with a fresh Kir Royale without him noticing. "She is stealth. We need her in the BEA," he thought. His observation made him smile.

Turning his thoughts back to business, he flipped his notebook open and studied it for a moment, using his Mont Blanc as a stylus to focus on each line. "Alors," he said, and looked up from the pad, his eyes sparkling. "J'ai trois chose…" He shook his head. "Pardon. En anglais, oui? He apologized and shifted to English. "I have three things of importance to tell you."

"Excellent," Philip said, encouraging the inspector to get on with it.

With his hand fisted, he held up his thumb. "First, we have

information about the mystery of water in the gas tank. With the help of our counterpart in the UK, the AAIB, the Air Accident Investigation Branch and their surveillance cameras, we know who watered your jet fuel."

"They had some decent video?" David asked. "That's a lucky break."

Genevieve shot forward in her chair. "Does that mean you know who did it?" She held her breath.

"Oui," Boucher said.

Philip and Duncan leaned forward, shoulders tense.

"Who did it?" Philip asked through clenched teeth. "Who tried to kill us?"

Looking back at his notebook, Boucher flipped a page forward. "His name is Lee Bowen. He is a minor voyou." He rolled his eyes to the ceiling. "What is the word en anglais?"

"Thug." Delphine had again slipped into the salon to freshen drinks and pass hors d'oeuvres.

The inspector started at her voice. "Merci, madame," he said to her retreating back. "She is quite something, hein?"

"Yes, she's quite something, indeed." Genevieve was anxious to keep Inspector Boucher on track, which was a challenge. "Tell us more about Lee Bowen, the minor thug," she pressed.

Unable to resist his third Kir Royale, he took a drink and then popped a tiny morsel of warm pastry stuffed with goat cheese into his mouth. "Delicieuse," he said, then hummed as he chewed.

Philip stood and walked to the fireplace. He warmed his hands then turned to Boucher. He was finding it difficult to keep his annoyance in check. "If you don't mind, inspector, could you please concentrate on sharing the information you came over three hundred miles to give us. So far, the little you've told us could have been shared in a phone call."

"Mais oui, my lord. I, uh, I apologize for getting off the paths."

"I think you mean track," Philip muttered.

"Hein?"

"Off the track. Getting off the track, man!" Philip almost shouted. He raised both hands in apology. "I'm sorry, Boucher. I'm a little on edge."

"But of course," Boucher smiled. "Who would not be on edge with people trying to kill them and trying to steal their expensive painting and their fine wine poisoning people?" His lips were pursed as he said, "Rohh la la," and shook his hand as if he had burned himself. "Quelle pagaille. Everything is quite a mess, is it not?"

"What do you mean when you say our wine is killing people? Are you talking about Daniel LaGrande?"

"Oui, I am."

Philip squeezed his eyes closed, massaged his neck, then opened his eyes. "How do you know about that? We haven't talked about our suspicions with anyone but the local police."

"Ah, my lord." Boucher's grin revealed deep dimples in his chubby cheeks. "I know everything, everywhere."

David rolled his eyes, impatient.

With a toss of his head, Boucher laughed and waved his hands in the air. His smile faded. "But, sadly, that is not true. If I must tell the truth, I have friends here. When I knew I was coming to see you I called a childhood ami, Frederick Picard, who is le Chef de la police municipal in Saint-Émilion. I wanted to find out if he had any information that could help our investigation. He informed me that Émile de Laudre had been taken to the hospital when he became ill from drinking poisoned wine, the same bottle from which Daniel LaGrande drank just before he died." As if remembering something, he blinked twice, then wrote for a moment in his little book.

He sucked in a breath and let it out, looking over Philip's shoulder with a vacant stare. "There are too many…" he paused, searching for the right word. "Unsettling, is that a word?" He shifted his gaze to Philip, who nodded in confirmation. "There are too many unsettling events to be unrelated."

Duncan slumped back in his chair. "You're suggesting, Inspector Boucher, that there is a thread connecting everything that has happened, from the watered fuel to the poisoned wine?"

"Baahh, oui," Boucher said, again pouting his lips, one brow arched. "It is more sensible than believing that each event is unique, n'est ce pas?"

Genevieve's eyes narrowed as she considered Boucher's theory, and staring into the fire, Philip replayed the inspector's words, wondering if they made sense.

For a while no one spoke, then David said, "But why would anyone be doing these things? Do you think there's a crazed maniac who randomly chose the Warwicks to attack?"

A mischievous smile twisted the inspector's lips. "Non, I do not believe there is a crazed manic stalking the Warwick family, but I do have a theory," he said, but went no further.

Four pairs of eyes stayed riveted on Boucher, waiting for him to go on.

They waited. The crackling of the fire and ticking of the brass pendulum clock bounced off the walls of the salon while the inspector sat in silence. With each tick of the clock, the tension in the room thickened. He rolled his Mont Blanc between his thumb and forefinger, studying the titled trio in front of him.

His nerves fraying with each breath, Philip was willing to wait no longer. He stood, walked to the fireplace, and turned. He drew himself to his full height, looming over Boucher, who sunk back into his overstuffed chair.

Philip's voice was even, but his eyes blazed. "Inspector, what are you playing at?" He stepped toward the officer.

Startled by Philip's sharp tone, Boucher burrowed even further into his cushion. "I promise, my lord, I am not playing at anything," he said and put up both his hands in defense. "I am simply offering a hypothesis."

"Then offer it," Philip snapped. "What do you think is going on?"

Genevieve and Duncan exchanged glances. His family had always known Philip to have an occasional flash of temper, but he was never so quick to anger as when he thought his family was in peril, which seemed to be happening too frequently since inheriting his title and wealth.

Boucher motioned to Philip to sit back down. "My lord, my intention was not to upset you and your family. Rather, my intention was to give you an opportunity to offer any thoughts you might have on all that has happened. It is remarkable how much people recall when they have time to consider events." He spread his hands wide. "Apparently, nothing comes to mind at the moment so I shall tell you my conjecture. Please, my lord, be seated. I promise I am as concerned as you are about the safety and well-being of your family."

"I doubt that very much, inspector." Philip's voice still had a cautionary edge. "But by all means, go on."

Boucher had been hoping that Delphine would appear and offer more of those little salty nibbles. He felt a gnawing in his stomach and worried it would begin rumbling. As if answering his prayers, the house manager appeared in the doorway.

"Excusez-moi, Lady Crosswick, mais le déjeuner est servi."

Genevieve stood, glad for the break in the tension. "Merci, Delphine. Gentlemen," she motioned toward the foyer. "Shall we go into lunch and continue the discussion?"

Boucher salivated at the thought of the delicious lunch to come. He scooched forward in the chair until his feet hit the floor. He drained his glass and set it on the coffee table.

David extended his hand. "Inspector, it has been most interesting. I have another commitment, so I'll say goodbye. Lord Crosswick will keep me informed of your progress."

"It has been mon plaisir, Sir David," Boucher said, then in a gentile gesture he crooked his elbow and offered it to Genevieve. She slipped her arm through his and they ambled across the foyer, into an intimate salon overlooking the vineyard.

As he walked into the beautiful room with a stunning table set for four, Boucher felt both a rush of pleasure and a sense of being out of place. These feelings clashed so loudly in his head, he was sure everyone could hear the clamor.

Genevieve patted the back of an upholstered dining chair.

"Please, inspector, sit here, next to me."

He grinned, held her chair as his mother had taught him years ago, then eased his bulk between the delicate walnut arms of his chair. He watched Genevieve drape her napkin over her lap, snatched his from the table, unfolded it and laid it across his knees.

"Inspector Boucher, did I hear you say you are from Bordeaux?" Genevieve filled the room with small talk until the first course had been served and they could get back to the serious business at hand.

As he responded to Genevieve's query, Boucher leaned toward Lady Crosswick, taking in her elegant scent.

Duncan and Philip exchanged a wordless understanding that they must keep Boucher on track. He seemed distracted by the trappings of Château Beaulieu and by Genevieve herself. Duncan found it annoying that the rumpled police inspector was puppy-dogging his mother. Philip found it amusing.

Chloé placed the first course, smoked salmon, at each person's place and left a tray of small, warm baguettes on the table. When she was finished, she stood by the door.

Deep in conversation about Boucher's childhood in Bordeaux, Genevieve didn't realize Chloé was still in the room. She heard Philip clear his throat, looked up, and saw her lingering in the doorway. "Is there something else, Chloé?" Genevieve said.

"Ah, non, my lady." She dipped into a small curtsy and eased out of the room.

"Let's get back to your thoughts on the case, shall we, inspector?" Philip commanded. He rose, pulled the bottle of white Bordeaux from the cooler and filled each glass.

Boucher gazed lovingly at the wine, pale gold liquid sparkling through the facets. "Si jolie!" he said, eyes filled with delight.

"All right, inspector." Philip was willing to wait no longer. "You were about to tell us your theory that all the events since we arrived in France are connected."

"All except the painting prank. I can say with assurance, Émile de Laudre is not a mastermind in an international ring of art thieves."

Everyone around the table smiled.

"I'm sure we can all agree on that," Duncan said. "But how do you think the fuel and Daniel's poisoning are linked?"

His mouth full of fish, it was a moment before Boucher could answer. He wiped his lips and enjoyed a long drink of the delicate Bordeaux. At last he answered. "First, the AAIB can confirm that Lee Bowen was caught on CCTV watering the fuel. He flew later that day from Leeds Bradford to Paris on a RyanAir flight." He slid another bite of salmon into his mouth.

"Merde," Philip mumbled Genevieve's favorite word under his breath. Here they were again embroiled in a mess, a dangerous mess.

"Dad?" Philip felt Duncan's concerned gaze on him. "I'm all right, Duncan. I just can't imagine why someone would want to kill us in a plane crash. Or kill us at all, for that matter." He leaned back in his chair. "I'm sure there's more to this theory, inspector."

"There is, my lord." Boucher tore an end from a baguette, slathered butter across the moist crumb and bit off a too-big bite. He was the only one eating. The other three were picking at their salmon with little interest and waiting with amazing patience for him to continue. When his mouth was almost empty, he went on. "It is my understanding that, over the years, the Wang family has made several offers to buy Château Beaulieu. Is that correct?"

Philip bobbed his head. "We were unaware of the offers before Daniel told us. As I'm sure you know, the Chinese have been interested in the French wine market for years. They were buying châteaux at a rapid pace for a while, then the pace slowed, but now they're back at it. I'm also sure that you're well aware that Château Beaulieu is not for sale. Not now, and not in the foreseeable future."

Boucher nodded. "Je comprehend. And that makes my point stronger."

Genevieve scowled. "What do you mean?"

Boucher looked around the table. "D'accord, if someone wants to buy your vineyard and you do not want to sell it, how can they get it?"

Duncan sat forward. "You mean if you are a person who doesn't let morality get in the way?"

A light flashed in Philip's eyes. "That would explain the email we found that said if they couldn't buy Château Beaulieu, they would get it another way." Philip couldn't believe what was happening

Surprise jolted Boucher forward in his chair. "Vraiment? You have this email for me?"

"Yes, of course."

Duncan shook his head, skeptical of the idea. "I suppose you kill the people who own it and buy it out of the estate. But wouldn't it be difficult to kill all the heirs?"

"Certainement, but you can frighten enough of the heirs so they might be happy to have a few more euros in their bank account and go home, n'est ce pas?" He narrowed his eyes at Duncan. "If your parents had been killed in a plane crash on their way to France, would you have come here to be the managing director?"

"How do you know about that?" Philip said, startled that Boucher knew of the family's plans for Duncan to take over Château Beaulieu.

Boucher snorted, "My friend on the Saint-Émilion police force told me." He shrugged. "He, how you say, gets about."

"Gets around," Philip said. He stabbed a small piece of salmon and brought it toward his mouth. Halfway there, he froze. His eyes went wide, and he smacked his forehead with his palm. "Of course. Of course. Your friend heads the Saint-Émilion police force. I talked to him yesterday."

Boucher's brows shot up, his Cheshire cat smile stretching from ear to ear.

"I asked him to check the bottle of wine Madame Duveau was drinking when she died."

A smirk had replaced Boucher's broad grin.

"You know, don't you? Tell me. Was Madame Duveau poisoned?"

Boucher shook his head, "No," and opened his mouth to speak, but instead a belch popped from his parted lips. Clutching his napkin, his hand flew to his mouth. He looked down at his plate, then up into Genevieve's eyes, which danced with amusement.

"Oh, my lady, excusez moi."

Stifling a giggle, Genevieve patted his hand. "Please, inspector. It's all right. Quite flattering, really. I'll tell Lizette you loved her salmon." He would carry the embarrassment with him for some time, she was sure.

Disinterested in the inspector's unease, Philip refocused the conversation. "Are you sure her bottle of wine had no traces of poison?"

"The police lab found no traces of poison in the bottle. They have confirmed she died of natural causes."

Genevieve brought her wine glass halfway to her mouth. It hovered there for a moment while she stared out the French doors. "Let's go back further, before Madame Duveau. Why would anyone kill Daniel?" She took a drink and held it in her mouth for a moment before swallowing it. "And you're not suggesting, are you, that someone in the Wang family has set all this in motion?"

Chloé came in and began removing the first course plates from the table.

Using an expression the Warwicks were learning to expect, Inspector Boucher pooched out his lower lip and vibrated a little farty sound, followed by, "Oh la la." He shrugged one shoulder and went on. "I am not yet prepared to say that. It could be many people together, or one person alone. It might be someone in Paris or someone here, or in Bordeaux. There are so many possibilities, but I don't believe it is anyone in Angleterre. We have retrieved Lee Bowen's mobile records. He was not clever enough to use a burner phone, so we know the morning of the fuel incident, he made three calls to an untraceable French number.

With the dishes removed, Chloé set down the tray on the buffet and poured more wine.

Pondering all the possibilities, Genevieve felt as if her head were about to explode. "Who in Paris would be involved? Could it be anything to do with the foundation?"

His glass refilled, Duncan took a swallow and then another. "What sense would that make, Mom? I think the inspector's idea makes the most sense: that all this has to do with wanting the vineyard."

"Look, inspector, this is all speculation, isn't it? No other evidence exists, except for the footage of Lee Bowen messing with the fuel tank and a few phone records, does it?" Philip's patience was wearing thin, and he could feel another headache creeping into his skull. "After lunch, we'll go to the vineyard office, and you can see the email I mentioned."

"Ah, bon." Boucher held up his glass in a salute before he drank.

"And," Philip continued, "since you seem to know everything else that's going on around here, I must ask you. Are you aware an agent from the DREETS is paying us a visit?"

The surprise on Boucher's face was gratifying and Philip smiled. "Aha!" he said and pointed across the table at the inspector. "You didn't know that, did you?"

Boucher could feel a crumb at the corner of his mouth. He scooped it off with his tongue, then said, "Non, my lord. I did not." He cleared his throat and drank from his untouched water glass. "But one must ask, why are they coming to Château Beaulieu?"

"I have no idea. I suppose we'll all find out when they arrive tomorrow."

Chloé picked up the tray of plates and slipped from the petit salon. In the kitchen, she left the tray on a marble counter and slipped out the side door to the courtyard between the château and garage. She needed to make a phone call and she needed to make it now.

THIRTY-ONE

Everything Parisian had style, she thought, even the rain. When it drizzled, it sprinkled with the softness of a gentle caress. When it poured, it raged like a diva, demanding center stage. At the moment, the diva was out of control, pelting the windows at Maison de Laney so hard it was difficult to hear John Coltrane, her favorite, playing softly in the grand salon. Clarisse Morier squinted, looking through the French doors out into the garden, trying to see any signs of spring through the sluicing rain. She sipped her boulevardier cocktail, then ran her tongue over her lips, enjoying the spicey, bitter flavor left behind. Her brows drew together as she thought about the week ahead. Besides all the other things crowding her schedule, she had to direct the event for Cité du Vin at Château Beaulieu. Delphine could manage the mechanics, but only she could bring the style necessary to impress such a prestigious institution.

She felt her phone vibrate, reached into the pocket of her trousers and frowned when she saw the face that filled the screen.

"Oui?" she snapped. "Qu'est-ce que c'est?"

"We might have a problem." The voice on the other end of the line was controlled.

Madame Morier waited.

"As we discussed, it will be chaos here. You need to come to the château earlier than planned."

She noticed the rain was no longer sheeting down the windows and a rainbow had painted itself across the sky.

"There's no need to panic," she said. "This is not the first time I have managed such a situation." She punched *end call* and threw back the two fingers of blood-red boulevardier left in her glass.

THIRTY-TWO

B Y EIGHT O'CLOCK everyone in the household was already up and bustling. Everyone except Inspector Marcel Boucher. He was luxuriating in the guestroom where he hoped to spend several more nights. Why would he want to return to his tiny Paris apartment with its single bed, cramped kitchen and bathroom so small he could sit on the commode and wash his hands in the sink? He stretched, pulled the sheets up to his chin and rubbed the silky linens between his thumb and forefinger. He would love to live like the Warwicks. He thought about the conversation during lunch yesterday and wondered how solid his theory was. He was certain the fuel issue and Daniel LaGrande's death were related, but he was unsure who was responsible or why the events had occurred.

Startled by a gentle knock on the door, he tugged the sheets under his chin and sat up before he said, "Entre."

Chloé nudged the door open with her foot. "Bonjour, inspector," she said, carrying in a tray of coffee, croissants and little pots of jam and butter, which she set on the bedside table. "Voulez-vous quelque chose d'autre?"

He couldn't imagine wanting anything else. "Non, merci. C'est parfait." He remembered her from yesterday. Her face was fresh and pretty and her big eyes were surrounded by thick lashes Boucher thought were fluttering at him. Without any more conversation, she turned and left, pulling the door closed behind her.

He swung his sturdy legs over the edge of the bed and scooted closer to the breakfast tray. Saliva pooled in his mouth as the aroma of the warm pastries wafted into his nostrils. As he poured coffee from the French press into a porcelain cup, an image of Chloé danced in his mind. She was there yesterday pouring wine, pouring water, pouring coffee, removing, serving. Was she ever not in the room? Perhaps they should be more careful to speak only when she wasn't around.

"Perhaps you are getting carried away," he said aloud. "Perhaps you are becoming un peu paranoïaque, eh?" With that, he decided he'd better get moving or he'd miss all the excitement.

Downstairs, David and Becca were ready to leave for London. Henri tucked several bags into the trunk of a deep blue Jaguar XJ, then stood at attention by the open passenger door.

"I'm sorry I won't be here for the meeting today." David and Philip shook hands. "Call me after you talk to the DREETS agent. You know you can always reach me on a video call."

"I'll let you know what this visit's all about. I can't imagine why he's coming, but we'll know soon."

"You're sure you don't want me to stay?" As the Warwicks' attorney, David felt uncomfortable leaving if he might be needed.

"Absolutely not. You need to get back to the firm." Philip slapped him on the back. "Believe me, I'll send up a red flag if we need help on this side of the channel."

"Thank you both for being here this week." Genevieve gave David a peck on the cheek and squeezed Becca.

Becca held Genevieve by both shoulders. "Good luck with the Cité du Vin meeting. Let me know if you want to kick around anymore ideas before then. You're going to have such fun."

Concerned about the time, Henri urged the couple to finish saying their goodbyes. "Sir David, we should go if you don't want to miss your flight."

"Of course. Of course."

Duncan gripped David's hand and pulled him into a hug. "See you soon, mate."

Becca's eyes glistened with tears as she slid into the back seat.

"Why are you crying?" David asked. "Blimey. Women." He shook his head and Genevieve punched him on his arm.

"Ouch." David eased in after Becca, and Henri closed the door behind him.

Genevieve motioned for David to roll down the window. "You be nice to your beautiful bride-to-be." She pinched his cheek. "Or you'll have to deal with me."

"Anything but that," he yelled as they drove off.

The three stood and waved until the car was well down the allée, then trudged up the front steps. Philip pushed open the front door and stood aside to let Genevieve and Duncan enter. He followed them in and stopped short when he saw Inspector Boucher coming down the stairs looking as dashing as his stout body would allow. In navy-wool flannel trousers and a Breton navy-and-white striped sweater, he needed another ten inches to pull off the look. But to his credit, his navy scarf was perfectly draped around his stubby neck.

"Why inspector, how smart you look." Genevieve's smile was genuine. "Are you ready for some breakfast?"

"Ah, oui, my lady. The girl, uh Chloé, brought coffee and croissants, but I would not say non to an omelet." He beamed at his beautiful host.

She took his arm and, wrinkling her nose at his heavy cologne, guided him toward the petit salon where they had lunched the day before. Looking back at Philip, she said, "I assume you and Duncan will be in the office. Did you tell me the agent is coming at ten o'clock?"

"Yes. He sent a text this morning confirming."

"I'll get the inspector settled and be in to help. I won't be long."

"See you in a minute." Grateful that Genevieve was taking care of Boucher, he and Duncan strolled down the hall and back out into the crisp morning. "Do you think the inspector is getting a little bit too comfortable here?" he asked his son as they walked across the terrace.

Duncan smiled and took a beat before answering. "I don't know about that, but I'm pretty sure he's trying to supplant you as lord of the manor."

Philip stopped mid-stride and looked at Duncan before realizing his son was teasing him. "Smartass," he said, giving him a withering look. They chuckled together as they walked through the office door, and braced themselves for what might blindside them next.

THIRTY-THREE

Two people awaited them when Philip, Genevieve and Duncan entered the salon at ten o'clock. A youngish, raw-boned woman of average height stood ramrod straight in front of the fire, holding a coffee cup in one hand and matching saucer in the other. Her hair was pulled into a tight bun at the nape of her neck and her navy suit was severe and well cut, the narrow skirt hitting just below her knees.

A head taller than the woman, the man's posture was less rigid than hers. He seemed more casual, more relaxed. Dressed head to toe in black, he wore his uniform with as much style as one could and held his hat in both hands in front of him.

"Bonjour?" Philip said. Surprised by the fact that there were two people in their living room, not just one as he had expected, his greeting sounded more like a question than a welcome.

"Bonjour, Lord Crosswick."

Philip offered his hand, searched the man's eyes and said, "I assume you are Jules Lambert?"

"Oh, non, my lord. He stepped to the side and swept his hand toward the woman. "Ici, est Agente Lambert."

She set her coffee cup on a small table and moved in to shake

Philip's hand, her lips parting with the beginning of a smile. "It happens all the time," she said in English with just a trace of French accent.

Striding forward with outstretched hand, Genevieve offered a warm greeting. "I'm Genevieve Warwick," she said, "and this is our son, Duncan."

"Lady Crosswick," the fellow said, with a sharp nod. "I am Frederick Picard of the municipal police." He turned to Philip and Duncan and gave another snappy bob of his head. "Lord Crosswick, we spoke on the phone about Madame Duveau."

"Yes, I remember. It's good to put a face to a voice."

The second Boucher hit the doorway, his voice bellowed across the salon. "Freddy! Freddy, mon Dieu! Qu'est-ce qu'on fout ici?"

French zipped back and forth, fast and furious between the two old friends. They bear hugged and slapped each other on the back.

Though Philip and Genevieve didn't catch every word, they knew the razzing was edgy and the sort of banter only two old friends could share.

Just as Agent Lambert was about to break up the reunion, Inspector Boucher backed away from Picard. "Pardon, pardon," he said, and addressed the Warwicks. "As you might have guessed, I had no idea Freddy— er, uh, Directeur Picard, would be coming today. Quelle chance!" His smile stretched from ear to ear.

"What a nice way to begin our meeting," Genevieve said, motioning everyone to be seated. "Please, there is coffee on the sideboard. If you would like anything else, don't hesitate to ask."

"The hospitality here is spectaculaire," Boucher said, flaunting his guest status.

Genevieve arched one brow at Philip, amused how comfortable the inspector was.

"Now, if you don't mind, Lady Crosswick and I are anxious to find out the purpose of this meeting." Philip crossed one leg over the other and straightened the crease in his trouser leg.

"I am certain you are." Agent Lambert took control of the conversation. "My lord, my lady," she nodded at Philip and Genevieve in turn, then flipped open a red leather notebook. "Earlier this year on January 14th, we received an anonymous telephone call from a man who said he believed Château Beaulieu was involved in a counterfeit, uh, shall we say, scheme?" She leaned forward with her elbows on the suede-covered arms of her chair.

"What does that mean?" Philip's brows drew together, and his mouth curved down, not quite certain what to make of what he had just heard.

"I don't understand," Genevieve said, confused. "Are you suggesting we're selling fake wine?"

Lambert raised her palms toward Philip and Genevieve. "Non, non, non," she said. "Let me start again. The person who made the phone call suggested that, without your knowledge, a perpetrator may be using elements of Château Beaulieu's winemaking capability for nefarious purposes."

He shrugged his shoulders. "I don't get it. Who could be using our winery without our knowledge, or the knowledge of our vigneron? And how would they be using it?"

Genevieve pushed out of her chair and walked to the sideboard, her hands shoved in the pockets of her burgundy wool pants. She turned to Agent Lambert and said, "I'm sure you know the story of our recently inherited wealth, which includes this château and its vineyard." She poured a cup of coffee and walked back to her chair. "This is our first experience as owners of a property that's part of such an important industry." She set her coffee on the walnut table next to her chair and sat. "Though we love to drink wine, we are novices in this world of creating a great vintage. One of our strengths as entrepreneurs, is that we always appreciate what we don't know. Assume we know nothing about counterfeit wine, which is true, and start from the beginning."

Lambert's cool blue gaze rested on Genevieve, admiring her composure. "Let me start by telling you that wine fraud is an enormous business. Some estimate it to be a three billion euro gouge in the side of the industry."

Surprised, Genevieve's mouth formed a silent "O" at the enormous number.

"DREETS is a wide-ranging directorate, and I won't bore you with the details of everything it covers. Fraud is our responsibility." Lambert stopped to take a drink of coffee. "There are two challenges when we encounter fraud. The first is, though wine is synonymous with France, its production is a tiny part of our GDP, just one percent."

"Really?" Duncan said, voicing everyone's amazement. "Only one percent?"

"Yes. As a result, wine counterfeiting is a low priority for our directorate and the police have little interest in it. In fact, if we had not had a direct call tipping us off, if Château Beaulieu were not a prominent producer and you were not a titled owner, we would not be here."

"Interesting," Philip said. "And the other challenge?"

"Ah, oui." It was the first French she had used. "The other challenge is that in the illustrious wine regions like Burgundy and Bordeaux, many of the more exclusive châteaux refuse to cooperate."

"Why?" Genevieve couldn't imagine any owner not wanting to root out counterfeiters.

"They don't want anyone to know about the frauds. By telling no one, they feel they are protecting their good name, when, in fact, they are allowing inferior product to reach the marketplace under their label." She threw a smile around the room. "We are grateful that you are allowing us to pursue this." She leaned back and folded her hands in her lap. "And, of course, there was the attempt on your life and the death of Daniel LaGrande, all of which are possibly connected to a wine fraud, so the case becomes quite interesting for departments other than ours."

Though they had talked several times with Inspector Boucher about a connection between all the events, until just now it had all seemed quite far-fetched.

"What a mess," was all Philip could say. "What a fucking mess." He looked at Genevieve, searching her eyes for anything that would tell him what she was thinking. What he saw were questions.

"Okay, Agent Lambert, how is someone using Château Beaulieu to counterfeit wine?" Genevieve said.

"Ah, yes." She nodded. "We see fraud in one of three forms." Her thumb popped up as if she were approving of the ways wine could be counterfeited. "First, counterfeiter's fake bottles and labels. You may have heard of Rudy Kurniawan."

"Rudy Kurniawan! I've heard of this guy." After listening quietly to Agent Lambert, Duncan sparked to life. "A good friend of mine in New York bought some of his Romanee-Conti about a year before he was arrested."

"Which friend?" Philip was curious.

"James Ridgeway. You and Mom met him a couple of times when Julia and I were still living in New York. Now that he knows the wine is fake, he thinks of the bottles as a piece of history. An expensive piece of history, for sure." He looked at Lambert. "Kurniawan's scam was all about creating bottles that looked authentic and filling them with bogus wine, right?"

"Vraiment," Boucher said, anxious to get into the conversation.

"He moved millions of dollars of fake wine before he was caught in 2012."

Duncan was on the edge of his seat now. "Didn't he stupidly forge some Clos Saint-Denis from Domaine Ponsot, labeling them with dates that were way before any recorded production from that domain?"

"I am impressed," Lambert said. "You know a lot about Monsieur Kurniawan. So you understand how faked bottles and labels are used to counterfeit wine?"

Everyone in the room nodded, even Boucher and Picard.

Lambert raised her index finger, so her thumb and pointer looked like a gun. "The second way: counterfeiters use authentic bottles and labels, fill the bottles with inferior wine and sell at the price of the fine vintage. This is more difficult than printing fake labels because genuine bottles and labels are difficult to come by." She took a deep breath, then continued. "That brings us to the last way of counterfeiting wine. If you sell bottles of wine which are authentic but have been damaged by excessive temperatures and you do not disclose the damage, you can be charged with fraud. Under that same category is any wine that is enhanced with chemicals to conceal that it has deteriorated or to increase its sweetness. That kind of fraud can only be detected by analyzing the bottle's contents." She picked up her coffee and drank several sips before putting the gold-rimmed cup back in the saucer. "You now know more than you ever wanted to know about counterfeiting."

"Thank you for the education, Agent Lambert. If you had to guess," Philip said, "what kind of fraud are we involved in?"

She pressed her lips together and shook her head several times. "At the moment, we cannot be certain there *is* counterfeiting involving Château Beaulieu. We must determine that first."

As Genevieve's mind began to wander and her gaze swept around the salon, she smiled at the fire crackling on the hearth and marveled at the view through the windows and beyond the terrace. Grapevines stretched as far as she could see, down the hill and beyond the next rise. She couldn't imagine a more fairytale existence. Everything was perfect—everything except the fact that someone was trying to kill them and steal their wine, maybe their vineyard. She felt her spine stiffen and her jaw clench. It was going to be a cold day in Hell when the Warwicks allowed anyone to take over their lives and harm their family. And according to the forecast, the temperature was not falling. In fact, it was going to get very, very warm.

THIRTY-FOUR

NOBODY DELIVERED A song like Zaz. Her throaty voice blasted "Je Veux" through the speakers, filling the car with energy and making it impossible for Edouard to do anything but join her belting out the lyrics, off key and at the top of his lungs. "Je veux d'l'amour, d'la joie, de la bonne humeur." He slapped time to the beat on the steering wheel and mimicked her kazoo during the chorus. He loved Zaz. Who didn't?

As he turned left off D122 onto Rue du Palat, his pulse revved. He never tired of the approach to Château Beaulieu. After a quarter kilometer, the low, ancient stone walls gave way to row after row of dormant vines, looking like arthritic knuckles. They waited for the earth to warm and the sun to kiss their sleeping buds awake. But before the vines woke, those who cared for them, who nurtured and loved them, would soon begin palissage, the art of trellising the tender shoots. Of the hundreds of tasks necessary every year to bring the perfect grape to its peak, Edouard loved palissage the most. It was an intimate act between the vigneron and his vines. It was the act of spreading the leaves to make certain the sun and the wind could caress every crevice, every surface. If palissage were done well, the vines could flourish and those responsible would be rewarded with a good, perhaps even a great vintage.

After another kilometer, he clicked on his left blinker and pulled into the long driveway that announced Château Beaulieu. Before opening the gates, Edouard sat for a moment savoring the view. Elegant and understated, the château dominated the gentle rise of the earth on which it sat with an undeniable presence. He had been here only three years, but he knew this was where he would be for the rest of his life. This was his vineyard, his château, his soil. He knew how much Daniel had loved Château Beaulieu and in three short years the managing director had infected Edouard with that passion.

He punched in the code. The gates crept open, and he eased the dark green Range Rover under the linden trees. He knew the story about Philip George Winston Laney, the 9TH Earl of Crosswick, inheriting Château Beaulieu from his French wife's family. Lucky bastard. And now this new earl was here to take over. There had to be continuity. The vines knew if their caretakers loved them or if they were just a trophy. Depending on how you cared for them, they would give you everything or they would give you nothing. If the Warwicks didn't give him free rein over the vineyard, the vines would know.

By the time Edouard arrived at the house, he had talked himself into an unpleasant mood, worried that the Warwicks were not going to value him. He was young, but this was his life, his passion. He was already an award-winning vigneron, but his greatest achievement was that Daniel LaGrande had placed the future of Château Beaulieu in his hands. "Dammit," he said, slamming his palm on the dashboard. "The Warwicks better appreciate me." He threw open the car door and jumped down from the seat.

"Edouard," Delphine's voice cut across the courtyard and he turned to see her waving him to come to the house.

"Merde," he said under his breath. He opened the back car door, grabbed his jacket off the seat, and slammed the door harder than he intended.

Delphine's brows shot up and Edouard knew he needed to tuck his irritation into his back pocket.

"Lord et Lady Crosswick sont dans le salon avec l'agente de DREETS. Vas-y tout de suite."

When Delphine commanded, everyone followed her orders, including Edouard. He would join them in the salon, but he wasn't going to be happy about it.

He slumped against the thick molding in the doorway, unnoticed, until Duncan got up to throw a log on the fire and saw him. "Edouard! Great. You're here. Just the man we need."

Surprised by the warmth in Duncan's voice, Edouard's mood lifted ever-so-slightly.

"Come, sit over here." Genevieve patted a spot next to her on the loveseat. "There's coffee on the sideboard."

Again he was taken by surprise. He raised his hand. "Rein, merci. I need nothing."

Introductions were made all around before Edouard sat down on the edge of the loveseat.

"Agent Lambert," Philip said, "would you please fill Edouard in on our conversation? I would imagine you can skip the rudimentary education on wine counterfeiting. As Château Beaulieu's vigneron, I'm sure he has a sophisticated knowledge of such crimes."

Lambert offered a concise recap of the previous hour's conversation and ended with, "Is there anything you can think of that the caller could have been talking about?"

While the agent spoke, Edouard sat with his arms folded across his chest. He stared at the floor, listening for any tone of accusation, but there was none, and his tension began to ease. When she was finished, he relaxed into the loveseat and said to the agent. "First let me ask a couple of questions, if I may."

"But, of course."

"I take it you have no indication who made the phone call or where it was made from."

She shook her head. "Non."

"And there have been no further calls?"

"Non."

"I see," he said, a smug smile tugging at his lips.

"But there is one important piece of information I have yet to share, Monsieur Comte." Agent Lambert flashed a cocky smirk of her own and everyone in the room waited. She reached into her cordovan leather briefcase and pulled out a piece of paper in a plastic folder. "We received this last week." She walked to Philip and handed him the sheathed stationery.

> *A quoi de droit,*
> *Vérifier les commandes de bouteilles*
> *pour Château Beaulieu*
> *rapport aux chiffres de production.*

In an instant, Genevieve was up and looking over Philip's shoulder. "A quoi de droit." She looked at Lambert. "To whom it may concern, right?"

The agent nodded.

"Verify the commands of the bottles?" Confused, Genevieve's brows drew together.

"Allow me." The agent took the paper and read. "To whom it may concern. Check the bottle orders for Château Beaulieu against production figures." She returned to her seat and set the paper on her lap. "What do you think that means?" She looked around the room at four blank faces.

"I don't understand," Duncan said. "Is this suggesting that we might have purchased more bottles than we need?" He screwed up his face. "I mean, wouldn't that be smart to have extra bottles, so if you break some in production, you don't shut down the bottling line?"

Agent Lambert started to reply, but Duncan interrupted her with another thought. "Or are they suggesting we have ordered fewer bottles and we're diverting our wine into someone else's bottles? Why would we do that?" His mind was spinning.

Lambert started again, more forceful this time. "We need to go through all the papers and computer files in the vineyard office. We can either bring in a forensic team or box everything and take it to our headquarters."

"What's your preference?"

"It is best if we stay in the vineyard office and perhaps if we could have a little area where we can organize any evidence we find," Lambert said. "If we are here, we may have ready access to the staff if we have questions, may we not?"

"Everyone will be at your service." Philip looked at their vigneron. "Edouard, will you please tell the vineyard staff that they may be questioned by the DREETS agents and that Lady Crosswick and I would appreciate their cooperation?"

"Of course. I shall make certain everyone is available." Edouard drummed his fingers on the arm of his chair, wondering where this was all going.

"Of course, we shall keep Inspector Boucher and Director Picard informed of our findings." Lambert inclined her head toward her two colleagues. "If you have no objections, the team will come on Monday. And, my lord, please keep the office locked until then."

"Of course. In fact, Edouard, could you go lock it right now? Do you know where the key is?"

Already heading toward the door, Edouard said, "It's in the office, of course."

"Before you go, Monsieur Comte," Agent Lambert called out. "What did you do when you learned that Daniel LaGrande was killed by a poisoned bottle of Château Beaulieu wine? Did you take any precautions to confirm that the methanol wasn't in any other bottles?"

Edouard spun around. "Of course I took precautions. We have strict protocols when there is suspicion that any of our wine is tainted, and we followed all of them. I can say with certainty that the poison was limited to Daniel's bottle." He turned to Philip. "You don't think for a minute that I would allow you, Lady Crosswick, or anyone else to drink our wine if I wasn't sure that it was pure, do you?"

"Of course not, Edouard. I would never question your commitment to Château Beaulieu." Philip walked with him to the French doors. "I know you'll make sure the office is secure." He opened the terrace doors and patted Edouard on the back as he sent him on his way.

Turning back to Lambert, Philip asked, "You'll be heading the task force, won't you?"

"I shall."

"Is that a long commute for you?" Genevieve asked.

"Non," Lambert replied. "I live on the west side of Bordeaux so it's a pleasant drive to Saint-Émilion." She gathered the few things she'd taken from her briefcase and put them back in the exact same place from which they came. When she was finished, she stood and extended her hand. "Thank you for your cooperation."

Philip shook her hand. "Thank you for pursuing this, Agent Lambert. If we have a counterfeiting issue here, we want to get to the bottom of it as quickly as possible." He put his hands in his pockets and gazed out the French doors for a moment before looking back at her. He nodded at Genevieve and Duncan. "We three are out of our element in this situation. We'll do everything we can to be supportive, but I don't believe we're going to be much help in connecting the dots."

"But, my lord, that is our job," Agent Lambert said, and headed for the door.

In the kitchen, Chloé finished polishing the last copper pot and hung it back on its hook on the rack over the island. She plucked the earbuds from her ears and shoved them deep into her apron pocket. The tiny microphone she had stuck under the coffee table in the salon had done its job. She hadn't missed a word and had a lot of information to pass on. She smiled at the thought of the big payday that was about to come her way.

THIRTY-FIVE

ITH THE MORNING gone, Genevieve sat in the petit salon with a bowl of onion soup, a baguette, and a slab of unsalted butter. She combed her fingers through her hair then rested her elbow on the table and cradled her head in her hands. Digging her fingers into the muscles of her neck and shoulders, the tension stored there made her wince. She squeezed the bridge of her nose and decided a quick nap would be the smart strategy. Philip, Duncan and Edouard were reviewing the morning's revelations and plotting plans for Duncan to meet tomorrow with Elise Beaufoy in Bordeaux at Cité du Vin, so now would be the perfect time to sneak away. Exhaustion from stress was the worst, and, since arriving in France, their lives had been packed with one stressful event after another. Small wonder fatigue was about to bury her. She took a last spoonful of her soup and dabbed her chin with her linen napkin.

She dragged herself up the stairs, down the hall to their bedroom, and collapsed onto their bed. Breathing a great sigh, she tugged a celadon cashmere throw up to her chin in one smooth motion before falling into an instant, deep sleep.

When lips nuzzled the back of her neck, she inhaled Philip's warm, woodsy scent.

"Mmm," was all Genevieve could manage.

Looming over her, Philip tugged gently on her shoulder, rolling her from her side to her back. He kissed her softly on her eyelids. "G," he whispered.

"Mmm?" she said again.

"It's almost five o'clock."

"Hum?" She forced her eyes open. "Did you say it's almost five o'clock?" Her voice was hoarse.

"I did." He sat down on the edge of the bed and brushed a wisp of hair from her cheek.

She scrunched her eyes closed, opened them, blew a puff of air from her cheeks and propped herself up on her elbows. "Wow. I just wanted to close my eyes for a minute and four hours later, I'm still comatose. I think I could sleep forever." She leaned into Philip and grazed his lips with hers. "I had a dream about Charlotte," she said, watching his eyes for a reaction.

For a moment Philip was confused, then it dawned on him who Genevieve was talking about. "How is our dear, dead Charlotte?"

"Considering she's almost a hundred and seventy-five, she looks remarkable."

"Did she have any sage counsel for us about all this mess happening here at her venerable château?"

Genevieve shoved herself into a sitting position and rubbed her hands over her face. "I don't know if I'd call it sage counsel, but she did throw a glass of wine in the air, and it evaporated. Then *she* dissolved into a billion tiny stars." She shrugged, smiled and said, "I don't think you can call that advice, do you?"

"I don't think so. Not unless it's some coded message." He stood and ruffled Genevieve's hair. "Listen, cute girl. You need to get your very nice butt out of bed and come talk to Delphine. She needs guidance about what's going to be served to the Cité du Vin Board and when and how much—you know, she has a lot of questions, none of which I could answer. Well," he corrected himself, "I could have given her answers to every question, but they wouldn't have been the right answers." He beamed at his tousled wife.

As he turned to leave, Genevieve whacked him on his bottom with a pillow. At that, he turned, grabbed his wife with one hand and began tickling her with the other until she was screeching and weeping with laughter. "I'm bigger than you are, and you know I'll always win, right?"

"Stop it, Philip! Stop it!" She wheezed.

He gave her one more tickle in the ribs, then stepped back. "Nothing better than a good tickle, is there?" He grinned and he pointed at her as she cocked her arm to heave a small, decorative pillow at him. "I wouldn't if I were you," he said, still grinning.

She lowered the cushion and harrumphed her way off the bed. "You don't play fair."

"Pardon me? As you know, all's fair in love and war."

"Was that love or war?" Genevieve asked as she straightened the bed and slipped into her shoes.

"Both, I guess. Can I tell Delphine you're on your way?"

"Of course, you meanie," she laughed. "I'll be right down."

Genevieve could hear Philip whistling James Brown's "I Feel Good" all the way down the hall.

THIRTY-SIX

T HE MORNING WAS already getting away from him as Duncan gulped the last of his coffee. "I need to get in the shower before I go. Dad, which car do you want me to take?"

"I don't care. Text Henri and ask him. Never mind. You go shower. I'll talk to Henri. Do you want something flashy or something practical?"

Duncan cocked his head. "What do you think, Dad?"

"I'll see what I can do. God, isn't this fun?" Philip said, punching in Henri's number.

"Yup," Duncan said as he jogged off.

"Henri, Duncan has a meeting at Cité du Vin in Bordeaux this morning and needs a car. He wants to drive something exciting. What would you suggest?" Philip was silent, listening to Henri's suggestions. "Whoa. You're kidding. We have that? By all means. That's the car he needs to drive. Thanks, Henri." He listened a moment. "I'd say in about twenty minutes. Perfect." He clicked off and grinned at Genevieve. "This is when I don't mind all the hassle that comes with all of this." He swept his hand around the room."

"I knew you'd come to your senses. I was pretty sure you wouldn't want to give it all up."

"The jury's still out on that, G," he said, worry replacing his smile.

Ignoring his response, Genevieve said, "Sounds as if Henri is bringing something spectacular to the front door." She popped a plump strawberry into her mouth.

His excitement bubbled back. "Wait until you see it. Just wait."

She grinned at her husband, who had turned into a teenager before her eyes.

"You will not believe this car. I've got to go to the garage and have Henri show me everything we own. We've been here almost a week and we haven't had a moment to explore this grownups' amusement park." He sat back and stabbed a piece of quiche.

With his shirt unbuttoned, his shoes in his hand and his hair still dripping, Duncan flew back into the room. "I just checked the traffic. There's an accident on N89. I just called Elise and left a message that I might be late. You know we're meeting to set the schedule for The Art of the Vine."

Philip nodded. "I do."

"According to Elise, the word is getting out and already potential students are requesting applications for the program. Pretty exciting, isn't it?"

"It is, but you need to slow down," Philip warned. "The last thing you need is to get in an accident or get a ticket. Besides, the car you're driving will get you there in a nanosecond."

Duncan sat down to put his shoes on. As he tied his laces, he looked up at his dad with an excited smile. "What does Henri have for me? Something cool?"

"I'm not telling. I'll just let you be surprised when you open the door. We seem to have some amazing cars. Who knew?" Philip snorted a laugh.

Duncan buttoned his shirt, pulled a navy collared sweater over his head, ran his hands through his hair and considered it combed.

When Duncan and Philip opened the front door and walked out onto the terrace, Henri was leaning against a tangerine-colored masterpiece.

A long low whistle announced Philip's pleasure.

"Wow," was all Duncan could manage.

Henri hefted himself off the car and pressed the pop-in handle that opened the driver's door.

For a moment, Duncan had forgotten he was in a rush. "What are we looking at, Henri?" he asked.

A smile stretched across Henri's face, which was unusual, for such a serious man. "You are looking at a Ferrari Purosangue, my lord. Château Beaulieu's name was put on the waiting list when they first began taking orders. It was delivered two weeks ago, just before you got here, Lord Crosswick." He motioned to Duncan to come closer. "I know you don't want to be late for your meeting, but I need to run you through a couple of things."

He pulled on an inch-long plastic fin that appeared to be part of the shoulder line. There was a soft sound of a motor and the back door powered open. "In case someone needs to ride in the back seat, you should know how to open the rear doors."

"Good thinking, Henri. I would never have discovered that

little lever. It could have been embarrassing to shoved Elise Beaufoy through the window." They laughed at the image. He glanced at his watch. "I'm sure there's a lot I need to know to fully appreciate this machine, but the immediate question is, what do I need to know in order to drive to Bordeaux and back?"

Henri took him through the rudimentary operation of the flashy Purosangue and finished with a few cautionary words. "Remember, this car is a V12 and has 725 horsepower. It will not let you forget that it is a thoroughbred. It lives to run fast, so be gentle, be cautious. But above all, have fun."

"Thank you. Thank you for this." He gave Henri a quick smile that said he was ready to get on the road.

"Hurry back," Philip raised his hand. "I mean, come home safely."

Duncan flashed a thumbs up to his dad. He looked on the dash, on the column, on the console, and saw no start button. Henri pointed to the bottom of the steering wheel and Duncan pressed a touch-sensitive spot. The V12 awakened with a sharp bark, then settled into a gravelly purr.

"That was fun," he said.

The door closed with a satisfying thunk and he was ready to go. In the pit of his stomach, a flutter of terror caught his attention. His shallow breathing and sweaty palms confirmed that he was afraid to press on the gas, but pressing on the gas was the only way to make the car go forward. And he had to move forward to get to his meeting. His jaw tightened and the ball of his foot met the firm pedal. He applied the tiniest bit of pressure. Nothing. He pushed more firmly, and the engine whined. Embarrassed, he realized the car was still in park.

Out of the window, he saw his father standing with his arms crossed, and one hand over his mouth. Duncan could tell he was laughing. He could see Henri's shoulders shaking as he chuckled.

"Good god, man, get a grip," Duncan said to himself.

He pushed the switch on the center console from park into drive and, mustering his courage, eased forward. Nothing broke or bent or cracked. He was encouraged and pressed firmer on the gas until he was moving down the driveway at a snappy thirty kilometers an hour. He stopped at the end of the allée. Before moving on to Rue du Palat, he looked both ways several times. At last, he made the turn. Though he had owned several nice cars, they had all been clunkers compared to this. He was driving a dream.

His confidence built and so did his speed. On his right, Clos Peyra flashed past. Duncan smiled knowing he and all his neighbors were anxious for the coming months when the vines would begin to grow, and the châteaux would buzz with activity.

As he approached Château Pitique, he was confused to see a large draft horse charging between the vines, hurtling toward the stone wall that separated the fields from the road. He marveled at the power of the Percheron, hooves pounding against the frozen earth, broad shoulders rippling with each galloping stride. Then, in an instant, awe turned to fear. A man in red ran behind the horse, urging it forward. Shouting and thrashing a crop back and forth above his head, the man's eyes were wide and wild in his crimson face, his mouth distorted with each violent insult he screamed at the stallion.

The horse was now so close, Duncan could see the breath snorting from its nose. His foot hovered over the brake pedal and an image of his crushed Ferrari flashed in his mind.

The horse took two mighty strides and flew over the low wall, landing just in front of the speeding Ferrari. Duncan yanked the steering wheel to the left and the horse thundered in front of the Purosangue, missing it by inches. The motor screamed as the car sped toward the stone wall. He wrenched the wheel to the right, and barely avoided crashing into the barrier before careening back onto the pavement. Slamming on the brakes, he screeched to a halt, his heart roaring in his ears and his breath stuck in his chest.

His head jerked to the right and watched the horse gallop up the vine-covered hill toward Clos Peyra. He flopped back in his seat, gripping the steering wheel with both hands. Out of the corner of his eye, he saw the man in the red barn jacket streak up the hill toward Chateau Pitique.

What in the hell had just happened? Glancing in the rearview mirror, Duncan saw a car approaching. He needed to move. He was unharmed and hoped the Ferrari was as well. Mentally he crossed his fingers and eased his foot on the accelerator. Nothing banged or rattled. The engine still had that exquisite, throaty growl and nothing seemed to be out of alignment. "Thank god for that," he said.

"Turn right in twenty-five meters, onto D122," the GPS lady said in a distinctly British accent, and Duncan laughed out loud. "Well, damn. Why didn't you say, 'Keep calm and carry on?'" he asked his robotic companion, then clicked off the GPS. "Change of plans. Elise Beaufoy and Cité du Vin, you'll have to wait."

His palms were slick with sweat and his heart still beat in his ears. One at a time he wiped his hands on his jeans. He made a U-turn and headed back to Château Beaulieu. As he relived each detail of what had just happened, it seemed clear that someone had tried to kill him, or at the very least, tried to frighten him. If they wanted him dead, they had failed. If frightening him was their goal, their plan was a wild success. The niggling fears that had caused him to delay his family's arrival, had just proven well-founded.

As he turned down down the driveway toward home, his pulse began to quiet. He was anxious to talk to his dad and, for the moment, would keep the bewildering event between the two of them. There was no need to terrify his mother. There'd be time for that later.

THIRTY-SEVEN

ENEVIEVE WAS PUTTING the final special touches on an oversized card she was going to send to Alex and Ella. She had printed several small photographs of the château and pasted them on the inside. One more bright cutout flower between Alex and Ella's names on the front, and it would be perfect. She held up the card, admiring her work. Her fingers, sticky from the glue, picked up everything she touched. She shook her hand, but the tissue on the tip of her finger waved in the air like a flag of surrender. She tried pulling it off with her other hand, but shreds stuck to those fingers. "Soap and water," she thought, and went to the kitchen in search of help.

Normally a hub of activity, today the kitchen was vacant and silent. At the sink, Genevieve shoved the hot water lever with her elbow. She rubbed her hands under the stream. When she depressed the pump on the soap dispenser, she heard a moan and thought it came from the plunger. She hit it again. The moan was louder, followed by a breathy, "Oui! Oui!"

"I don't think that's the soap dispenser," she said under her breath. She grabbed a towel from the rack and wiped her hands as she crept toward the pantry. The door was almost closed. She stood for several seconds, listening to what were decidedly the sounds of sex, trying to decide whether to interrupt the amorous encounter or creep away.

"It's my kitchen," she decided. "If anyone's going to frolic in here, I think it should be Philip and me." She cleared her throat, then cleared it louder. The sounds stopped. "Hello," she said. No reply. "Excuse me. Who's in the pantry? I'd prefer not to come in."

She heard a flurry of startled whispering, then silence, then the rustling of clothes being pulled on or rearranged. "Un moment, s'il vous plaît. Un moment."

Genevieve thought she recognized the voice as Chloé's but wasn't sure. She backed up to the kitchen island, leaned against the wooden countertop, and waited. Finally, the door opened and indeed, Chloé stood between the bright sun streaming into the kitchen and the shadows of the windowless pantry. Rather than embarrassed, she seemed irritated, defiant. Behind her was a man. A young man.

"Excuse-moi, my lady." Chloé jutted her chin. "I suppose I should apologize for being amorous when I should be working, but…" Her voice trailed off. She pouted her lips and shrugged. "Quand l'occasion se presente, when opportunity knocks, one must answer."

Genevieve was more annoyed by Chloé's attitude than her actions. "But, Chloé, did you seize the opportunity, or did you *make* the opportunity?"

Chloé rolled her eyes and sighed.

"At any rate, please introduce me to your opportunity."

Chloé stepped to the side. "Pourquoi pas?" She gestured for the fellow to come forward, and Genevieve could see that he was, in fact, young—and gorgeous. His shirt was misbuttoned, and his pants zipped halfway. Chloé nodded at him. "This is George…" she stopped, realizing she didn't know his last name. "This is George," she said again, but did not go on.

"Well, George George," Genevieve said, "it's interesting to make your acquaintance under these circumstances. I don't recognize you, so I assume you don't work at Château Beaulieu. Where are you from?"

Chloé translated. "He does not speak English," she said. "He works at Château Pitique, the château just beyond Clos Peyra."

"Does he, now?" Genevieve gave them both a withering stare. "Do you invite all your boyfriends to the pantry, Chloé?"

Looking like a frightened rabbit, George stood stone still but his eyes darted back and forth between Chloé and Genevieve.

"How often do you have sex in the kitchen?"

For the first time, color rose in Chloé's cheeks. "Oh, my lady. This is the first time, and I assure you, it won't happen again."

"And I can assure you, if it does, you won't find yourself in this kitchen again, or anywhere else at Château Beaulieu. In the next few weeks, there will be two young children at the château, and I guarantee they are much more precious to me than you are. If I have to worry for one second they might come upon you and old Georgie here," she jerked her thumb toward the boy who was sweating from terror, "in a compromising position in the kitchen, the garden, the garage…" She cocked her head and let the image speak for itself. "I would suggest George leave, and you," she arched her brows at Chloé, "get back to work."

Though he spoke no English, George knew he'd been given his cue to make a run for it. He shoved his arms into his red barn jacket and scurried out the door.

THIRTY-EIGHT

Unsure what Jing Wang would be wearing, Genevieve changed her clothes three times. Dressed and ready to go, Philip sat by the fire in their bedroom, reading a report on this year's anticipated grape yield. Each time Genevieve emerged, Philip glanced up, said, "That's nice," then looked back at his papers as his wife huffed back into the enormous closet to try again.

"G, we've got to go," he said, as he checked his watch. "Fashionably late is one thing, but we're getting close to being rudely tardy."

"I think this is it." He heard her muffled voice from deep in the dressing room.

"Tada." She twirled into the room, the ankle-length skirt of her red cashmere dress billowing out with each turn. The wide bateau neckline swept from shoulder to shoulder and allowed her hair to swish back and forth, grazing her collarbone with each turn of her head. A belt of the same fabric with an ornate gold buckle, nipped in her slender waist. "Worth the wait?" She struck a pose and threw a sultry stare at Philip.

"Always," he said, heaving himself out of the chair and patting her butt as he walked by her to pick up his jacket. He pulled it on, turned to her, and said, "Get your shoes on and let's go. I'll meet you downstairs."

"So much for dazzling the man," Genevieve said. "Not exactly the reaction I was hoping for." She caught a glimpse of the clock on her bedside table. 7:45. "Oh, merde! We were supposed to be there at seven thirty."

When they rang the doorbell at Clos Peyra, they could hear the clock from within gong eight times. A few seconds passed, then a minute. Just as Genevieve was about to press the button again, the door flew wide and there stood Jing, her long, jet-black hair parted in the middle, cut blunt and swaying behind her. An inch shorter than Genevieve, the two were wearing the same color red, but instead of a dress, Jing was wearing a strapless, wide-legged, form-fitting jumpsuit. Around her neck was a thick, eighteen-karat gold collar that hugged her neck like the one-piece suit hugged her slim hips.

"Bonjour! Bonjour!" she said. Her cheeks were flushed, her smile broad, and the smell of vintage red wine whispered on her breath. She pulled Genevieve into the two-story foyer, before giving her la bise. While Genevieve handed her coat to a maid in black, Jing shifted her attention to Philip, bestowing welcoming kisses on him. That done, she linked arms with each of the Warwicks and propelled them into a huge salon with a fireplace crackling at the far end. On either side of the hearth sat a man and a woman, both with flawless porcelain skin glowing from the flames. They were so still and perfect, Genevieve thought for a moment they might be statues. But then they rose together and stood like royalty, waiting for Philip and Genevieve to approach.

"Come, come," Jing laughed, tugging them along. "Meet our friends." They stood in front of the young man who greeted her with a boyish grin. He was more cute than handsome, a bit chubby and shorter than Genevieve, who couldn't resist the mischief in his eyes.

"Han, this is Lord Crosswick." She presented Philip like a prized possession. "And this is Lady Crosswick." She pulled Genevieve forward. "Lord and Lady Crosswick, this is our friend, Han Shou, but we call him Hank. He and his family own Château Pitique, just across the road."

"Hank, we sort of met at our party in Paris. You're a friend of Bernard Reines." Philip extended his hand but didn't mention the scuffle between Bernard and Daniel. "Good to see you."

"Lovely to see you again," Genevieve said, grasping Hank's hand with both of hers.

"I understand the party was quite a success," Hank said. "Bernard told me there were several large donations made that evening."

Jing turned to the beauty standing on the other side of the fireplace. "And this is Hank's wife, Lian."

Her hands folded in front of her, Lian nodded. The corners of her mouth lifted, but the smile didn't quite reach her eyes.

Genevieve grinned at Lian. "I'm sorry you weren't with Hank in Paris, but I'm delighted to meet you now. It's time we start getting to know our neighbors. We've been here just over a week and haven't had a moment to breathe."

"We were at Daniel LaGrande's beautiful celebration but

had to leave the moment it was over." Lian spoke so quietly that Genevieve had to lean forward to hear her. "I'm so sorry I didn't have a chance to introduce myself. Han's parents were here from Hong Kong. They do not like to be left alone, so we had to rush home."

"I thought I saw you in the crowd," Genevieve said, taking Lian's hand in hers. "We'll start our friendship this evening. Shall we?"

This time it was Lian's eyes that smiled when she said, "I would very much like that," and gave Genevieve's hand a squeeze.

"Where's Kim?" Philip turned to Jing.

"I'm right here," he said as he strode into the room carrying two open bottles of Pétrus. He placed them on a sideboard, then made a beeline for Genevieve. He took both her hands in his and said, "Bonjour, ma belle," followed by a kiss on each cheek.

"Philip," he said, offering Philip his hand then giving him a hardy pat on the back as if they were old friends. "Bonjour, mon ami. You met our neighbors?"

"We did." Philip smiled. "We appreciate the invitation this evening. Since we got to Château Beaulieu, we haven't had a second to relax, so this is a real treat."

Kim walked back to the sideboard and began to fuss with the wine glasses. "Well, you two, you can be certain that our mission tonight is for you and Genevieve to enjoy yourselves. To that end, we're going to start the evening by indulging in a couple of bottles of Pétrus. I hope you don't mind that we're drinking this little merlot rather than a divine Château Beaulieu cab." He nodded to Philip as he began to pour.

At the thought of preferring even his château's best wine over a glass of Pétrus, perhaps the most sought-after red wine on the planet, Philip laughed out loud. "I'm offended, Kim, but I'm sure I'll get over it by the time I finish the second glass. Thank you for this," he said, accepting the proffered Conterno glass, its sexy hips tapering into a long neck that captured the exquisite nose of the purplish-ruby ambrosia. Philip swirled the wine, enjoying the beauty of the light peeking through the rich color. He stuck his nose into the neck of the glass and was rewarded with notes of cedar, dark chocolate, blackberries and the richness of leather. As he waited for Kim to propose a toast, he anticipated how the bouquet would translate to the palate. He caught Genevieve's eye and shared an intimate smile.

When everyone held a glass, Kim stood in front of the fireplace looking very much like a master of the universe, dashing in a narrow-cut green velvet dinner jacket, white tieless shirt and sharply creased black pants. "Thank you, dear neighbors, for joining us this evening," he began. As he spoke, he cradled his wine glass between his hands. "We are the lucky ones. We have passion for our work, we have good friends, and we have Pétrus." Polite laughter rippled through the small crowd. "Pétrus in the glass is a beautiful thing, but Pétrus on the palate is heaven. To heaven." He raised his glass, closed his eyes and took a noisy slurping sip. The others followed suit.

"Ganbei," Hank mumbled.

"Santé," Jing offered in a cheerful voice.

Without toasting Lian drank, and Philip and Genevieve said, "Cheers," in unison.

Only once before had Genevieve and Philip enjoyed this legendary wine. Less than six months ago when they arrived in New York City to begin claiming Philip's inheritance, the law firm handling the estate, Holmes Fitch Smythson Morrow, served it upon their arrival. No doubt, the pricey wine was added to their legal bill for that month. The Pétrus was exceptional then, and it was exceptional now.

Genevieve took a second taste, enjoying the silky finish on her tongue. "This is very special, Kim. Thanks for sharing, you two."

"I'm sure you've all heard the stories about how much counterfeit Pétrus there is in the world." Kim remained standing in front of the fire.

"I don't know about this." With her new interest in counterfeit wine, Genevieve leaned forward. "Tell us more."

Kim swirled his glass. "According to reports, there is more Pétrus drunk in Las Vegas every year than their total production. That is to say, there is a lot of counterfeit Pétrus around."

The lines between Genevieve's brows deepened. "Is this true or is it urban legend?" She put her wine glass down and joined Kim at the fireplace. "Are you saying counterfeiting Pétrus is a huge problem or are a lot of wines counterfeited?"

"I would say it is not a big problem at all," Hank said, and drained his glass.

Kim's first glass of wine was almost gone. "You're wrong, Hank. Wine counterfeiting is a massive fraud. Not only does it encompass the most expensive wines," he held up his glass, "but it is a problem all the way down to bodega wines like Yellow Tail, with plenty of fraud in between."

Color rose in Hank's round cheeks and, much to everyone's surprise, he banged his glass down on the table next to him. "If it's such a big problem, why doesn't anyone do anything about it?"

Genevieve's pulse quickened. She had paid attention yesterday, when Agent Lambert lectured them on counterfeit wine, but that had seemed more of an academic discussion. Hearing Kim's story and watching Hank's temperature rise at the introduction of the subject made it more realistic.

"We might have a counterfeit issue at Château Beaulieu." Genevieve started to share their conversation with DREETS, then stopped. She looked at Philip for confirmation that it was all right to continue. He hesitated a second, then nodded. "An agent came from DREETS yesterday. Do you all know what that agency is?"

"Of course," Kim and Jing said. Hank gave a small shrug of his shoulders. Lian said nothing but seemed disinterested.

Genevieve went on. "They received an anonymous note urging them to check our bottle orders against our production. What they're insinuating is that there are more bottles of Château Beaulieu being sold than we are making. They're coming back Monday to start a full forensic investigation."

Kim went from guest to guest, pouring a second glass of wine. "Are you worried?"

"We don't know enough to be worried," Philip said. "If someone is filling our bottles with their wine, where is it being sold? According to Agent Lambert, Hong Kong is the biggest importer of Bordeaux wines followed by mainland China, then the US, but I'm sure you already know that. We, on the other hand, are just coming up to speed."

The woman who had taken their coats stood in the doorway, brows raised at Jing. "Ah, I believe dinner is served," Jing said, sweeping her arm in the direction of the servant. "Florrie will lead the way."

"Please bring your wine. There is more in the dining room, but we don't want to leave any behind." Kim laughed, but his tone was serious.

Kim offered Genevieve his arm. She took it, and they chatted about Clos Peyra as they made their way to dinner. It was an interesting building that had changed and grown over the course of hundreds of years. The front of the house, the salon, dining room, and large library were in the newest wing of the clos, which was only a hundred or so years old. The frescoed walls were a soft, burnished bronze, a stunning background to the many contemporary canvases that hung throughout the first floor.

As they walked into the dining room, Genevieve heard herself gasp. The room was a movie set. The ceiling sparkled with hundreds of tiny lights, muted to a glimmer. A single candelabra with twelve candles lit the intimate round table, set for six. Two identical candleholders sat on the sideboard. The room glowed like a sunset. Flames flickered off faceted glass, and cream-colored porcelain reflected the warmth of the stars in the ceiling.

Kim led Genevieve to a dining chair opposite the sideboard with the candelabras. Above the buffet hung a long Impressionist canvas. While everyone else was being seated and chatting away, Genevieve stared at the painting of green leaves, rippling blue water, pink and yellow lilies, all emerging from the thick brush strokes that defined them. She squinted, hearing none of the conversation. She sensed a joke had been told and people laughed, but still she couldn't drag her attention from the canvas.

"G," Philip said. "G," he said, louder. "Are you okay?"

Genevieve shook her head to break the trance. Her mouth hung open until she could gather herself. Finally, she said, "Kim, Jing, is that really a Monet?"

"You like it?" Jing beamed.

Eyes wide, Genevieve nodded. "Of course."

"It's a fake. A counterfeit, if you like. Good, isn't it?"

She squinted, disbelieving. "It's amazing."

Jing leaned forward. "It's a very good copy, but it's quite dim in here." Everyone but Genevieve laughed. "The mind sees what it wants to see, doesn't it?"

"Hmm," Genevieve hummed. "I suppose it does."

"It's rather like the Pétrus," Kim said. "If you think you are drinking a twenty-thousand-euro bottle of wine, who's to say you're not?"

He squeezed Genevieve's hand. She left it there a moment, then slipped it from his grasp and put it in her lap. Kim was beginning to unnerve her.

Kim didn't notice, and pressed Philip to continue the conversation they were having before dinner was announced. "Tell me more about the counterfeiting at Château Beaulieu. By the way," he interrupted himself, "did your lawyers tell you we've been trying to buy Château Beaulieu for years? My god, your people are tough. They've been unwavering."

Philip's smile dazzled. "That's as it should be, don't you think? They knew that my late cousin, the 12ᵀᴴ Earl of Crosswick loved the château. It has a long family history. Not as long as Clos Peyra's before your family bought it, but long, nonetheless. Of all our properties, Château Beaulieu and Wilmingrove Hall, our family seat in England, are the two estates we'll never part with."

Two servers put small bowls of soup in front of each guest. Kim rose to bring another bottle of wine from the sideboard and refilled his guests' glasses himself. When he finished, he set the bottle on a silver wine coaster at his place.

"Kim, why are you so interested in Château Beaulieu?" Genevieve decided to ask.

"Prestige," he said. "I know. We Chinese have always built for the centuries ahead, but we millennials do not have the patience of our ancestors. And my father has not given me the luxury of patience. Clos Peyra has potential. I believe in another generation it will be a fine vineyard, but my father wants Clos Peyra to be a superior château in the next five years. That will be difficult without adding a property that is already revered. Château Beaulieu is a perfect match. Your château is everything we want ours to be, and it is all of that now."

The words rang in Genevieve's ears. They were almost the exact words Delphine had overheard years ago when Kim and his father were arguing.

"Do you think you can ever make the vintage of your dreams, Kim?" Hank spoke for the first time since they sat down to dinner.

"Of course I do. But I need the time to do it. No amount of money can overcome a lack of time." His words were passionate, then lightened when he said to Hank, "What the hell are you doing over there at Pitique? You seem to be happy growing wine for the corner shop except for the little specialty dessert wine you're fooling around with."

"You're making a dessert wine?" Genevieve asked. "Tell us about it."

"It is wonderful." It was the first thing Lian had said during the entire dinner.

A light sparked in Hank as he started sharing the details of his project. "I have some second wine grapes that—"

"Second wine grapes?" Genevieve interrupted him. "I don't know what those are."

As he spoke, Hank became more and more animated. "These are grapes that will not be used for the Grand vin, or the first label. A second wine is a wine produced with grapes from younger plots, which means they are not as mature. At Château Pitique, we have no great terroir, thus we have no great grape." Eyes dancing, Hank looked at each of the dinner guests. "Unlike Clos Peyra, no amount of time will turn us into a great vineyard. So, I am purchasing second-growth sauternes grapes from a vineyard about an hour from here. Over the last couple of years, I have been experimenting with this grape and at last have created a dessert wine that I believe has a bright future in the Chinese and US markets."

"How can we try this new wine?" Philip said, always anxious to support entrepreneurs, particularly when they were local.

"You're in luck," Jing broke in. "We're serving it this evening with the crème brulée"

"This is our lucky day." Genevieve beamed at Hank, enjoying

his bubbling enthusiasm. "It must be expensive to create a new wine," she commented, "especially when you can't use the grapes from your château."

Hank looked down at his plate, his exuberance dwindling, replaced by discomfort. "As Kim said, we are selling some mediocre Château Pitique wine to the corner shops in the UK and some bodegas in New York, but it has been a challenge. Sometimes, in order to succeed, we must do things we would prefer not to."

When he looked up from his plate, Genevieve saw worry in his eyes. She reached over and patted his hand. "Let's try some of this magical concoction of yours, shall we?"

Jing summoned the servers, who whisked away dinner plates and replaced them with crème brulée, tiny French strawberries piled on the side, topped with a sprig of mint. Servers brought in tulip glasses and set them at each guest's place, next to the glasses left with traces of Pétrus.

With Kim's encouragement and great flourish, Hank held up a long, slender, octagonal bottle. He sliced the sleeve with the foil cutter then inserted the helix off center, pressed in and turned the corkscrew. When he eased the cork out of the mouth of the bottle, there was a satisfying pop. Applause erupted around the table and Hank's lips crept into a self-conscious smile.

"What are you calling this ambrosia?" Genevieve said.

He turned the label toward everyone. On an elegant cream background, the words Château Pitique, La Vie Douce were written in gold, with the burgundy CP logo scrolled at the top of the label.

"Hank, I love the name. The Sweet Life." Genevieve offered her glass, anxious to try the wine.

Hank accommodated by filling hers first, then proceeded around the table. When everyone's glass sparkled with amber liquid, Hank held up his glass. Before he toasted, he held the gaze of each person around the table, then said, "To the sweet life and all my friends who dwell here," he said with tenderness.

Though Philip was not fond of dessert wine, when La Vie Douce hit his palate, he couldn't help but smile. It was like drinking the fragrance of orange blossoms with a soft rose finish. He'd never had anything like it. When he looked across the table at Genevieve, he knew she was having a similar experience.

Genevieve took a tentative sip. She licked her lips, then took a longer draw, grinning as she swallowed. "Hank, this is delicious. Well done. Philip, don't you think we should serve this at the Cité du Vin dinner?"

"Absolutely." Philip set down his empty glass. "Uh, apparently I like it, Hank—very much." He was delighted when Hank poured more La Vie Douce into his glass. "Where are you in production?"

Hank radiated energy as he talked about his plans. "We are about to bottle the first small batch, all of which will go to local restaurants and bars. If we get a good response from this first blend, we will have another ready to go in two months. The next round will go to wider distribution. My father wants us to ship to Hong Kong, then to mainland China, but I want to concentrate on the French market first." His face clouded. "He is pressing me to make a success of the vineyard." He glanced at Kim. "It is no secret that I have botched my life up more than once and the pressure from my father to succeed is enormous. So, I am doing whatever I must." His smile was back, but not as sparkling as before.

"For what it's worth, I think you have a winner here," Philip said.

"How many bottles can we get for a large dinner party next week?" Genevieve shared their plans for creating a work-study program at Cité du Vin, then said, "Hank, this would be a spectacular way to showcase La Vie Douce. This is the board of directors of Cité du Vin. What better group to dazzle?"

"How many people will be at the party?"

"There will be about twenty or twenty-five." She took another drink. "I'm in love with this." A lightbulb went on. "I just remembered. Bernard will be here for the meeting."

"He called yesterday and said he was coming. We're going to spend time together on Sunday after everyone is gone." Hank thought for a moment. "If there are twenty people, I would say two cases should be enough." He looked very young when he said, "I appreciate you serving La Vie Douce to such a prestigious group. It would give my wine a real boost if they like it.

"We're delighted to do it, Hank. The wine is quite special," Philip said. "Two cases should be more than enough, but there's nothing wrong with having some left over. It sounds as if it'll be tough to get for a while, which is a smart strategy."

"That is the plan. We hope to create a big demand for La Vie Douce and keep supply low for a while. That way we can increase production slowly and gradually eliminate the other things we're doing." He studied his hands. "I look forward to that day," he said, as he twisted his napkin.

From somewhere in the house, they heard twelve deep bongs from the longcase clock.

Genevieve shoved her sleeve over her watch. "I can't believe it's midnight." As soon as she knew the time, she realized how tired she was. "Philip, we should be going."

As if the clock signaled the end of the evening, everyone stood and began to move into the foyer and toward the door.

As they stood waiting for their coats, Genevieve and Jing discussed when they could get together again, while Lian looked silently on.

The three men huddled together outside on the front steps in the crisp night air. Seizing the opportunity to speak to them before Genevieve came out, Philip said, "The strangest thing happened earlier today, Hank. Duncan, my son, was driving by your château and a horse jumped from your vineyard, over the stone wall, and almost onto his car. He swore someone in a red jacket was urging the horse over the wall and onto the road. Do you know anything about that?"

"Oh my god, Philip! That was your son? Is he all right?" Hank said, eyes wide with concern. "One of the horses got out this morning and was running through the vines. We have a new, inexperienced stableman who tried to get him back to the barn, and rather than get him under control, the idiot startled the horse and he nearly collided with a car. I am so very sorry."

Philip's eyes narrowed as he studied Hank. "So you knew about this?"

Hank put his hand on Philip's shoulder. "We've been worried all day about what happened but couldn't find out who was driving the car. I am just grateful your son is all right."

"What was that about a horse almost colliding with Duncan?" Genevieve asked as she came out of the front door.

"Nothing, G. I'll tell you about it later." He slid his arm around her waist and nudged her toward the stairs.

Pulling back, Genevieve gave Philip a sidelong glance and was about to ask another question when she saw him shake his head at her. "Thank you for the delightful evening, Kim," she said instead. "And, Hank. We'll have one of our fellows pick up the two cases of La Vie Douce on Monday. Just text us what we owe you and where to pick it up."

"I shall be at a meeting in Bordeaux all day on Monday, so I appreciate your man collecting the cases. They will be ready and waiting."

Genevieve gave him a kiss on each cheek then leaned in to offer the same to Kim.

"Next time we'll do this at Château Beaulieu."

The moment they were in the car, Genevieve turned in her seat to Philip. "What was that all about? What in the world did a horse have to do with Duncan?"

Philip told the story as Duncan had shared it with him earlier in the day, ending with, "Duncan said the Purosangue handled it like a dream."

Stunned, Genevieve had nothing to say for several seconds, then she found her words. "I don't give a crap that Duncan loves the car! First, why am I just hearing that our son was almost killed by a neighbor's horse jumping on his car?"

Philip opened his mouth to speak.

Genevieve held up her hand. "Did you believe Hank when he said the horse was just wandering around in the vines? That's ridiculous!"

Philip kept his eyes on the road but felt the fire of Genevieve's words.

"Don't you think there are too many near-disastrous accidents threatening this family? Why have you kept this a secret all day? Does Julia know?"

He pulled onto the long lane leading to Château Beaulieu, slowed, then stopped the car at the broad front steps. He unclipped his seatbelt and took Genevieve's hand in his. "I should have told you." He turned her wedding band around and around on her finger. "But Duncan and I didn't want to frighten you and Julia." He could just see the outline of her head in the dark but heard her snort at the idea. "We decided to wait until we talked to the local police."

"Did you call them?"

"We did."

"And?"

"They said they would look into it. I asked to speak to Frederick Picard, you know, Boucher's buddy, but he's in Spain until Monday."

"What did you think about Hank's response?"

"He seemed genuinely concerned." Philip held her hand in the dark. "But, he said something that made no sense. He said they've been trying to figure out all day who the driver was so they could contact him and make sure he was all right. I can say with assurance, there is not another tangerine-colored Ferrari Purosangue in the neighborhood, perhaps not in Bordeaux, maybe not even in France. How in the hell did they not know whose car their horse almost crushed?"

Genevieve said nothing, but Philip could hear her breath quicken.

"And the other thing. I've been trying to figure out what the motive would be. What would anyone have to gain by injuring Duncan?"

"Maybe whoever it was isn't trying to injure Duncan but rather frighten our family. Who would like us to give up Château Beaulieu and go back to England or the US?"

They looked at each other through the darkness. "Kim Wang," they said.

THIRTY-NINE

ITH RAIN PELTING the windows and the wind howling through the trees, Sunday morning was made for snuggling deep under the covers.

When Philip, Genevieve and Duncan surfaced, they found the perfect rainy-day breakfast waiting. Lizette's pain perdu, which the three agreed was the best French toast on the planet, was accompanied by fresh orange juice, bloody marys, mimosas, and steaming coffee.

The rest of the day was as lazy as the beginning. Though Philip, Genevieve, and Duncan made several attempts to work on projects, as the sky turned purple then darkened to black, the three were still nestled in Philip's study in front of a dwindling fire where they had been most of the day. Someone needed to toss a log on, but no one had the energy. Genevieve slipped her feet out of her shoes, lifted them into Philip's lap, and gave him a pleading smile, hoping he would massage them.

"I desperately want to go to bed, but I keep thinking about everything that's happened since we got to France, and I'm so exhausted I can't move."

"Ah, ma cherie, let me recount our adventures," Philip grabbed Genevieve's foot, and, began to count. He wiggled her big toe. "On our trip from England to Paris, the engines cut out on the Bombardier, we plummeted, the engines started, and we landed." He moved to her next toe. "A naughty intern at the family art museum tried to extort five million euros from us by stretching a giclee print over an original Jackson Pollock. He was easily found out, but instead of sending him to jail, we took him under our wing and are now employing him here at the vineyard." Genevieve's middle toe was next. "Daniel LaGrande, Château Beaulieu's GM for nearly forty years, is presumed murdered by poisoned wine just before we arrived." Genevieve squealed as Philip tickled the bottom of her foot before moving to her fourth toe. "A close friend of Daniel's warned me that Daniel had told her something very serious before he died, then she died the next day. We thought she was poisoned, but the evidence said no? And last but not least…" He held up Genevieve's foot and wiggled her little toe. "We believe someone tried to make Duncan crash yesterday while he was passing Château Pitique." He raised her foot in victory. "Tada. There you have it, folks. The Warwicks' big French adventure all on one foot."

"Sorry, Dad. We need the other foot."

Philip's brows drew together. "What did I forget?"

"Threatening notes, a stolen briefcase, and the counterfeiting of our wine."

Philip slapped his forehead. "Of course. The counterfeiting may be the one thing that ties all of this together. Except maybe for Émile's five-million euro prank."

"Aah, yes, the one event that may be an isolated incident," Duncan said. "Émile and his prank seems to be unconnected to the other events. He's a chronic screwup who, much to everyone's surprise—"

"And delight," Genevieve added.

"—seems to be finding his way under the firm hand of the staff here." Duncan took a drink of coffee. "I can tell you one thing. That lucky bastard's doing something I'd like to be doing," Duncan said.

"What's that?" Genevieve thought a moment, then clapped her hands. "Oh, I bet I know. He's helping Henri in the garage. That's it, isn't it?"

"It is." Duncan nodded with a sheepish grin.

"But, Duncan, we own all those fabulous cars." Philip pointed out the obvious. "Isn't it better to drive them anytime you like and have someone else take care of them?"

Duncan thought a moment, then aimed his index finger at his father. "You make a good point, Dad. I'm still getting used to our family's ridiculous wealth."

"Good. I'm glad. I'm not interested in anyone in this family becoming one of the entitled rich. We need to do all the good we can with this fortune." Genevieve drained her Cognac glass, put it on the side table and said, "That's the end of my lecture, folks. And now, I'm going to bed. I'll leave this brain trust to solve the problem of who's counterfeiting our wine and why they're trying to kill us all." Genevieve kissed the top of Philip's head and blew a kiss to Duncan.

"I'll be up in a flash," Philip said.

The two watched Genevieve drag herself out the door.

"Duncan," Philip said. We don't need all this money. We struck it rich a long time ago with the women we chose."

FORTY

Bleary-eyed, Duncan sat slump shouldered, head in hands, untouched cold coffee and a croissant in front of him. Just as his mind wandered toward a fuzzy dream, Philip slapped him on the back.

"Good morning," he said. "Rough night?"

"You could say that. I didn't sleep for one second. After your recap of events, I couldn't shut my brain off. I can tell you one thing. I'm glad Julia and the kids aren't coming until all this is over."

"No question. That was the right decision." Philip looked at his watch. "Agent Lambert and the gang are due here any minute. Do you feel up to meeting with them?"

Never one to shirk his duty, Duncan raised an eyebrow. "Of course, Dad. What's your best guess? Do you think they're going to find anything?"

"Beats the hell out of me, but someone's trying to hurt our family and quite possibly Château Beaulieu, so we'll keep at it until we find out who it is. Maybe Lambert's team can unearth something, maybe they can't. After last night, I have my own suspicions."

Duncan leaned forward. "What happened last night?" He gulped his cold coffee and cringed.

As if on cue, Chloé entered the petit salon, a French press in one hand and small tray of croissants straight from the oven in the other.

"Lord Crosswick," Chloé said. "Your guests have arrived and are in the salon. Shall I tell them you will join them when you are finished with breakfast?"

"No, Chloé." Philip was already shoving his chair back. He grabbed a croissant, tore off a piece and shoved it into his mouth. "Come on, Duncan. It's showtime."

When Philip and Duncan arrived, the small army of DREETS agents was milling around, some admiring the salon, some admiring the view. Jules Lambert strode across the room to meet the two Warwick men, hand outstretched.

"Bonjour, my lords," she said, all business and without any preamble. "If you can show us to the vineyard office, we are ready to begin."

"By all means." Philip led the way.

After yesterday's unrelenting rain, today sparkled. The entourage left the salon through the French doors, looking like a little parade as they crossed the courtyard, careful to avoid lingering puddles here and there. Walking three abreast, Philip and Duncan tried to make small talk with the DREETS chief, but Agent Lambert was focused on the task at hand. Her mission was to find any clues to support the accusation that Château Beaulieu was the victim of counterfeiting. When they pushed through the door to the vineyard building, Émile was staggering through the door at the other end of the hall, carrying two cases of wine at a time into the tasting room.

"Émile, why don't you use a hand truck?" Philip yelled to the struggling young man.

He jerked his head in acknowledgment. "It's okay, my lord. There are just a few to bring in. This is what Delphine asked me to pick up from Château Pitique."

Philip flashed a thumbs up and slid the key into the office door. "This door has been locked since you asked us to secure it on Friday," he said to Lambert. As they stepped into the room, a smell filled the air: a combination of leather, red wine and remnants of rose lilies left from Daniel LaGrande's celebration of life a week ago. It was hard for Philip to believe it was just seven days since they had said goodbye to Daniel. So much had happened in a week.

"What do you need from us, Agent Lambert?" Duncan asked.

"I believe we have everything we need," she said, then reconsidered. "Is there a safe?"

Philip thought for a moment, looked around the room then said, "I don't know." He held up one finger. "Give me a second." He tapped in a text, hit send, and kept his eyes on his screen. Almost immediately his phone pinged a response. "Edouard, our vigneron, said there is a safe. He's on his way."

While they waited, Lambert organized her team. Every piece of paper in every file had to be read and cataloged. Every computer file had to be evaluated, and every email read to determine if it was nothing or one of the many brushstrokes that would help to paint the total picture. It was going to be a long, tedious day and Agent Lambert was anxious to get it underway.

Within five minutes, Edouard was through the door, muddy from trellising the vines. As he walked into the room, his dirty boots left perfect tread prints on the brick floors. When he saw what a mess he was making, he winced at Philip and backed up two steps before Philip said, "Don't worry about it, Edouard," and waved it off. "Where's the safe?"

"La bas." He pointed across the room to a still life painting of a bottle of wine, grapes, and a candle.

"Behind the painting?" Philip asked.

"Oui."

Lambert found a latch under the frame on the left. It swung away from the wall on its right-hand hinges. "Et voila," she said. "And the combination?"

Edouard called out the numbers and Lambert rotated the dial as if she had done this many times before. With the final number, Philip and Duncan heard a click and looked at each other, excited to see what would happen next. Lambert pulled the lever and the thick door eased open. She peered into the safe, blocking everyone else's view. She reached in and pulled out a small stack of euros, which she handed to Philip. Next came a few letters and some papers. "And that is all," she said. She rifled through the stack and stopped when she came to a thick cream-colored envelope with *Lord and Lady Crosswick* written in elegant script on the front.

"This appears to be for you, Lord Crosswick."

Confused, Philip took the proffered letter. "Why would there be a letter for me in the safe?" He studied his name on the envelope. "This looks like Daniel's handwriting. He wrote a thank you note to Genevieve and me after he stayed with us in Paris." A lump stuck in his throat as he looked at the script of a dead man.

"If you could open it, it might be helpful. Perhaps there is some useful information, something that will shed light on our investigation."

"Of course." Philip looked around for the best place to sit down. "Uh, yes. I should open it."

Lambert put her hand on Philip's arm. "My lord, why don't you and your son go to the château and read the letter? Call me when you're finished, and we'll go over it together. We'll get on with things here."

"Let's do that, Dad." Duncan put his arm around his father's shoulders and urged him out the door. "Do you want Mom to join us?"

"Yes, of course."

When the three had gathered in the salon, Duncan handed his father a letter opener. Philip slipped it along the fold, slicing it open. He pulled two vellum sheets from the envelope and held them up so Genevieve and Duncan could see Daniel's elegant hand. He pulled his glasses from his sweater pocket and began reading.

My Dearest Lord and Lady Crosswick,

I am not certain how I have come to this moment in my life. I have always treasured honor above all, so the dishonor I have brought upon myself is more than I can bear.

I cannot undo my treachery of the last three years, when I provided bottles and labels to unscrupulous men who stole the prestige of my beloved vineyard and used it to sell their inferior wine as that of Château Beaulieu. I beg your forgiveness.

When I met the two of you in Paris, I realized for the first time that what I was doing was unforgivable. I realized I had not just compromised myself, but I had betrayed your trust and the trust of generations of the House of Crosswick.

My shame is overwhelming and, though there are others involved, I have no one to blame but myself. I cannot return from this dark abyss of shame, so there is nothing for me to do but say adieu.

Please know my love for Château Beaulieu and its soil is in my dying breath.

Daniel LaGrande.

FORTY-ONE

BANK OF ANGRY clouds drifted across the sun and plunged the bright salon into shadows. Philip stared at Daniel's note for a long time before looking at Genevieve. "I don't understand. What's he's saying?"

Genevieve left her chair and walked to Philip. She tugged the letter from his fingers and reread it in silence. When she was finished, she put her hand on his. "I think he's telling us that he's been involved in counterfeiting wine for the last three years." She held the papers up and swallowed hard.

Duncan blew air from his cheeks. "I didn't have the good fortune to meet him, but from everything I've heard, no one would expect this of him, would they?"

"No." Philip shook his head. "No, they wouldn't. The idea that Daniel LaGrande would do something dishonorable and jeopardize Château Beaulieu's reputation is…" Philip searched for the right word. "I guess I'd have to say, shocking." He took the letter back from Genevieve. "Here, where he says, 'I cannot return from this dark abyss of shame, so there is nothing for me to do but say adieu,' is he saying he's going to commit suicide?"

Genevieve blinked and a single tear slid down her cheek. "I don't know any other way to interpret it," she said.

"Ahem," Agent Lambert cleared her throat as she stood in the open door to the terrace. "Excuse me, my lord." She was wearing plastic gloves and holding folders. "We have uncovered a few things I think you should see."

Philip motioned to Lambert. "Come in, come in." He thrust Daniel's letter at the agent. "You think you've discovered something. Wait'll you see what we have." He could feel his bewilderment at Daniel's treachery simmering into anger.

"Is there something interesting in the note?" Lambert pulled her glasses from her pocket and put them on before looking at the pages.

"Oh, I would say so." Philip's mind began to race. "According to Daniel's letter, he's been involved in counterfeiting Château Beaulieu wine for the last three years." He paused, thinking. "Could he have been behind the water in our gas tank? Could he possibly be the one who tried to kill us?" He choked out a laugh. "If we were dead, he'd continue his reign over the château. In fact, it wouldn't surprise me if he and Kim were in cahoots. Together they'd have both properties." As he spoke, he paced back and forth in front of the windows, his fury building. "Kim has made no secret of how much he wants Château Beaulieu." He stopped to stare out at the vineyard, his fists clenched at his sides. "It's a good thing he killed himself. If he hadn't, I might have killed him myself when I found out what he was doing."

"Philip, stop it!" Genevieve pushed herself from her chair and crossed to him in three rapid strides. "What is the matter with you? The man made a terrible mistake and was so fraught with remorse that he didn't feel he should live." She grabbed her husband's shoulders and squeezed them hard. "I don't believe for one minute Daniel had anything to do with the fuel incident. He said there were other people involved in this," she fluttered her hands, "whatever it is."

Agent Lambert had read the note twice. The first time she skimmed it. The second time she read each word, looking for clues. "Lord Crosswick, could you please sit down?" She had the commanding voice of a headmistress and Philip sat. "With Daniel's suicide note and these files, we now have some excellent clues." She laid two folders on the coffee table in front of her. "It is as if Daniel LaGrande laid out a map." She held up one folder. "This is the file of emails you gave me last week, between Daniel and someone receiving Château Beaulieu bottles and labels. When our technical people delved into who was on the email chain besides LaGrande, they found an IP address in Hong Kong—or at least routed through Hong Kong—and one in Paris." She slapped that file closed.

"Paris?" three surprised people said.

"Yes. It appears someone in Paris is a piece of this puzzle." She held up the second folder. "LaGrande kept excellent records of purchase orders and shipping documents. This next piece of information may or may not be important." She shifted in her chair. "When this all started, LaGrande changed bottle manufacturers. For over a hundred years, Château Beaulieu bought bottles from VOA in Albi, about three hundred kilometers from here. Three years ago, he switched that business to a Chinese bottle manufacturer. We just spoke to the managing director of the French factory. He said they did everything they could to save the business, but LaGrande could not be persuaded to stay with them. It is likely his partner pressured him to make the switch because he either owns the Chinese bottling company or they could get a throwback."

"A kickback," Philip corrected.

"You are sure? Kickback?" Lambert's brows drew together.

Philip nodded.

She went on. "For the last three years, he has ordered seventy thousand bottles from the new purveyor. Fifty thousand have been shipped here to Château Beaulieu for your annual production, and twenty thousand shipped to a storage facility just outside Libourne. He did the same thing with your labels. When we did an online search we found that the warehouse holding the bottles and labels is owned by a Chinese mega-corporation with an import-export business as part of their holdings. One of our agents is there now to see if we can find out more information." Agent Lambert sat back in her chair and paused to let the information sink in.

Genevieve was the first to break the silence. She leaned forward and held Lambert's gaze. "You're saying that Daniel was providing bottles to someone who was filling them, probably with an inferior wine, then selling them under our label."

"That's what we've pieced together so far, with LaGrande's help." She waved the second folder, then laid it in her lap. "It seems he wanted to make certain you would be able to solve this riddle. We appreciate his posthumous help."

"But you have no idea who his partner was in all this, do you?" Philip's curiosity was overcoming his anger.

"The evidence is pointing its finger, but we have a few more facts to confirm before we have the total picture." Lambert plucked off her reading glasses and tucked them into her purse. "And one more thing I must tell you. Inspector Boucher called me over the weekend. He discovered that Lee Bowen, the man who put water in your jet fuel, worked for the Wang family until recently."

"I guess that answers the question of who Daniel's partner was, doesn't it?" Duncan said.

"No," Genevieve gasped. "That's not possible. Kim has been so nice to us since we got here. How could anyone try to kill you, then turn around and invite you to dinner?"

Duncan snorted. "Mom, you're not that naïve. There are millions of euros at stake here." He jerked his head at Lambert. "What would you say? How much money is involved in counterfeiting twenty thousand bottles of Château Beaulieu's best wine?"

"It depends on where it is being sold, but if it is shipped to China, the wealthy Chinese business class would pay fifteen hundred euros a bottle for a fine wine. That's thirty million euros a year. The Chinese are just developing their palates, and they are in love with prestigious labels, so it's an easy sell and a huge revenue stream worth protecting at all costs."

A chill shot through the room as Philip, Genevieve and Duncan heard the realities of what was at stake.

"Do you think the threat of being caught and imprisoned

would be reason enough to take drastic action, like maybe causing a Bombardier jet to fall out of the sky?" No one could miss Genevieve's sarcasm. She stood up and walked to the sideboard, poured a glass of lemon-infused water and drank half of it.

"No doubt," the agent said. She stacked the folders on top of each other, picked them up, and tapped the bottoms on the coffee table to align them. When she stood, her lips were pressed together in a grim line.

"What's next?" Philip asked.

"My office needs to double check the evidence we've gathered. We need to wait for a few other pieces of information to be confirmed, then, if everything checks out and it continues to support the Wang family as the counterfeiters, we shall plan a search of Clos Peyra in conjunction with Directeur Picard. That could happen as soon as Wednesday, the day after tomorrow."

"You think you'll have enough evidence for a search warrant," Genevieve said more as a statement than a question.

Confusion flashed across Agent Lambert's face, then, in an instant, disappeared. "Ah, oui, the American search warrant. We do not have such a restriction. If there is belief a law is being broken, we may enter someone's property. Practical, eh? In this case, we have more than enough suspicion to launch a full, what you call, search and seizure."

The Warwicks exchanged mystified looks, trying to understand the whirlwind that was beginning to spin around them.

"Agent Lambert." Duncan shook his head as if to clear his thoughts. "If you find confirmation at Clos Peyra that Kim is the one involved with Daniel in the counterfeiting, what will the charges be?"

Lambert pulled her shoulders back, her eyes dark with concern. "From what we suspect at this moment, the charges will be multiple and serious. Besides the counterfeiting, there will be charges of international fraud, wire fraud, wine fraud, mail fraud, and, of course, conspiracy to commit murder." She walked toward the door. Before leaving, she turned back to the group. "These next few days will be busy here, at Château Beaulieu. I'm sure the Wangs will not cause you any problems. They are aware we are investigating, so they will want to, as you say, keep a low profile. But, Director Picard will have a car and officers at your front gate, and if anything unusual happens here at Château Beaulieu, please let me know immediately. Anything at all." She started to leave, then stopped once more. "Please share this information with no one. Absolutely no one." Finally, she opened the door and dashed across the terrace, leaving three people reeling.

"Wow, that's a lot to digest." Duncan's voice was barely a whisper. "I don't even know where we begin."

A ping announced a text on both Philip's and Genevieve's phones. Genevieve plucked her mobile off the table beside her chair and Philip pulled his from his pocket. "You've got to be shitting me," Philip said.

"What is it?" Duncan asked.

Genevieve looked up from the screen. "It's Kim asking if there's anything he can do to help with the Cité du Vin meeting."

"Yeah, there are two things he can do," Duncan snarled. "He can stop counterfeiting our wine and he can stop trying to kill us."

FORTY-TWO

FOR THE REST of the day, the vineyard office hummed like a beehive. Directeur Picard arrived with a team that fingerprinted everything in sight, but soon abandoned the effort, realizing it would be impossible to identify the many prints on every surface. Phone calls were made. Responses came ringing back. While the officers and agents dug in every crevice for any undiscovered bit that would help support their case, Lambert and Picard set up headquarters in the tasting room. On the massive oak table, where wine lovers often gathered to treat their palates to some of the finest wine in the world, papers were laid out in meticulous order in hopes they would confirm the rapidly evolving theories. All evidence was pointing to the Wang family as the perpetrators of all the crimes that had been committed against Château Beaulieu and its owners.

Lambert massaged her temples. This was a huge case for her. If she wanted to continue her climb up the chain of command, she had to get it right. Just a few more questions to answer before she had an airtight case and would feel confident going ahead with searching Clos Peyra on Wednesday or maybe Thursday.

She leaned her head against the back of her chair, stared at the ceiling, and reviewed the evidence one more time, looking for holes in her theories.

"Agent Lambert." She jumped at Picard's voice, then shook her head as she laughed. "I forgot you were here," she said.

"Deep in thought, hein?"

"Oui."

Picard picked up his pen, ready to write. "If you would, s'il vous plaît, give me the list of loose strings we must tie up. I love that American phrase."

Lambert snickered. "I believe what you meant to say is loose ends we must tie up."

"Ah, oui. That's the phrase." Picard chuckled at himself.

"Allons," she said, and flipped through her notepad. In rapid French, she repeated the list. "We need to know who wrote the note warning Lord Crosswick that there was danger at Château Beaulieu. We need to know how it got into his briefcase. We have to figure out who intercepted the note on the train. How in the world did they know it was there?" she said, and looked at Picard, hoping he would have an explanation. He did not.

She went on. "We have to clarify the Paris connection. You said your people are working on that, oui?"

"Oui. Our tech people are getting close, in fact I expect to hear from them any time. They shouldn't have a problem pinpointing the IP address from the emails." Picard's phone pinged a text and he glanced at the screen. "Tech says another hour and they should have the IP address," he said.

"Ah, bon." Lambert sat back in the wooden chair and tapped

her pen against the edge of the table. "One thing that is bothering me. I want to know what happened to Lee Bowen. He came to France and disappeared. Call Inspector Boucher and see if they have the credit and bank card search results back."

"I'll also ask if they checked video surveillance." He punched in his old friend's number, and it went straight to voice mail. Picard left a message with his questions and ended the call.

"Excuse me." Philip stood in the doorway.

"Lord Crosswick, please come in." Lambert nodded toward a chair. "Join us."

Philip walked to the table and swept his eyes over the pieces of evidence laid out. "You've gathered a lot of information, haven't you?"

She said nothing, but her pride was evident.

Philip held up his phone. "I was just looking through the photos on my phone for something Genevieve wanted and ran across the picture I took of the note that was in my briefcase. Did you two know about that?"

"Yes, of course," Picard said. "Inspector Boucher shared that with us."

"I looked at it closely and I believe it's Daniel LaGrande's handwriting. If you compare it to his suicide note, I think you'll agree. It seems he wanted to warn us of what was going on and wanted us to understand there was more ahead."

"I have the suicide note here." Agent Lambert leaned across the table and picked up the paper sheathed in plastic. She laid it next to Philip's phone. The writing on the photo and Daniel's final note were from the same hand. "I'd say you're right. That would explain how it got into your briefcase. Either he slipped it in there when he was at your home for the party, or he asked someone to do it for him. That would be easy enough." She made a checking off motion. "That's one question answered."

Picard's phone vibrated. "Ah, bon," he said when he saw it was his tech team. He looked at Lambert and Philip and pointed to the screen as he answered. "Picard." He listened. "Oui. Oui. Vraiment? Non." His eyes widened. "Non," he said again, drawing out the word in disbelief. "Vraiment? Eh Bien. Merci. D'accord."

Philip and Lambert waited for Picard to tell them what he had just heard.

"Well?" Philip said.

Picard plopped into his chair, slack jawed. "The IP address was traced to a computer at the Laney Musée des Beaux-Arts."

FORTY-THREE

Philip thought he had misheard. "What did you say, directeur?"

"You heard me correctly, my lord. The IP address is from a computer at the Laney Musée des Beaux-Arts… in Paris… your musée."

Philip looked as if he'd been slapped, his mouth open, his green eyes huge as saucers. "How…" he stopped. "Jesus, how is that possible?"

No one answered.

The sound of wood scraping on brick pierced the silence, as Philip pulled out a chair and crumpled into the seat. His head, cradled in his hands, felt heavy as a stone.

Agent Lambert and Directeur Picard could hear Philip muttering under his breath. They looked at each other, wondering what to do next. As Picard was about to speak, Philip slowly raised his head, his eyes on fire.

"All right," he seethed. "We're going to find out who at the LMBA is involved in this and we're going to make them sorry they ever started this little venture." He stood and leaned on the table. "Directeur, what do we need to do to discover who the Paris link is? Do you want me to call Lillie Langdon and talk to her?"

"Non, non, my lord," Picard cautioned him. "Please leave this to us." He waved his hand between Lambert and himself. "Our people still have papers to go through. Our hope is that there will be a clue somewhere in the file: a name, a reference, something that will tell us who at the musée is involved and what their role is."

With the devastating news about the LMBA connection, Philip was filled with new questions. "You know we're about to host a meeting and dinner for the Cité du Vin Board of Directors. Should we call the meeting off?"

Lambert uncrossed her legs and leaned forward, her elbows on her knees. "I think it's best if everything continues as planned. We want to surprise the Wangs. The moment we discover who the Paris connection is, that's what we'll do."

Picard nodded. "We have looked at who is attending the meeting and see that Mademoiselle Lillie Langdon will be here. She is the directrice of your foundation, oui?"

"Oui."

Philip sat forward and rolled his shoulders, trying to work out a kink between the blades. He hesitated a moment, then asked the question he feared. "You don't think Lillie could be the Paris partner, do you? That would be devastating to Lady Crosswick and me." He felt a lump rising in his throat.

"I'm afraid until we know definitely, we shall remain suspicious of everyone." Picard tapped his pen on his pad. "There are few people in this world who would not be tempted by a part of thirty million euros. Wouldn't you agree, my lord?"

Philip stared through Picard and didn't respond.

"And Bernard Reines will be coming? He is the directeur of the Laney Musée des Beaux-Arts?" Picard continued.

"He is." Philip thought for a moment. "I don't remember if I told you that Bernard is a friend of Hank Shou, who owns Château Pitique. Hank's family hosted Bernard when he was on a fellowship at the China Academy of Art in Hangzhou. They've been friends for at least ten years."

Picard jotted some notes, then looked at Philip. "You had not mentioned this." His brows arched. "Is there anything else you might not have shared with us?" Still clutching his pen and notebook, he laid his hands in his lap and waited.

Philip wasn't sure how to respond. "My apologies, Director Picard. This is all very new to us. Before Agent Lambert brought the counterfeiting to our attention last Friday, we thought we had just two problems: a fuel issue, and a dead managing director." With every word he spoke, Philip felt energy leaking from his body. "We've barely spent any time here at the château. We're just getting to know our staff and we don't know our neighbors or the community. We have no idea what we know or don't know. Please keep asking questions and see if they prompt any answers." He stood and looked down at Picard. "If there's nothing else, I'll excuse myself."

As he left the tasting room, fatigue nearly drowned him. He glanced at his watch and couldn't believe it was only two o'clock. The day felt much older. When his stomach rumbled, he realized, not only was he exhausted, but starving as well, so he trudged to the kitchen. Throughout his sixty-four years, he had found there were very few problems that couldn't be solved with a good sandwich.

FORTY-FOUR

ON WHAT SEEMED to be the longest day of his life, Philip was in bed by nine thirty, propped against piles of pillows with a chocolate-brown duvet tucked under his arms. His eyelids drooped, and a rerun of the day played on a loop in his head as a French game show droned on television in the background. He had yet to tell Genevieve about the LMBA connection. He was dreading that conversation, but it would have to happen soon. Everyone would arrive tomorrow for the Cité du Vin meeting.

His body relaxed into a sleepy freefall, then snapped back to consciousness when he heard Genevieve call goodnight to someone as she opened their bedroom door. Though she was quiet, her energy shouted through his drowse. He could feel her bustling around the room—folding, plumping, straightening—until finally she bent over him and kissed him on his forehead. He reached out, grabbed her by her arms, and swung her across his body onto the bed.

She shrieked with surprise that rolled into laughter. "My god, you startled me," she choked out. "I thought you were asleep."

Free from his covers, Philip loomed over her, no longer tired.

"Aha!" he said. "Thinking I was asleep, you tried to steal a kiss, didn't you, my pretty?" He cackled like the Wicked Witch from Oz.

As she waited to see what her husband would do next, Genevieve giggled, her eyes holding his as the tension mounted.

He lowered his head until their noses were almost touching. She blinked.

He blinked. "I have news," he said.

Still playing their amorous game, she ran her tongue around her lips. "News?" she said, her voice husky. "What kind of news?"

Philip kissed her on the nose, then sat back against his pillows. "News you're not going to want to hear." His playful tone was gone.

Totally confused, Genevieve rolled onto her side and propped herself up on her elbow. "Are we still playing a game, or do you have something serious to tell me?"

"I have something serious to tell you." Philip sighed. "Are you ready for this?"

She shoved herself up and sat cross-legged. "Good god, Philip. You're scaring me. What is it?"

"Picard's people traced the Paris IP address." He stopped.

Genevieve strained forward. "Philip," she said through clenched teeth. "Tell me."

He reached out, took her hand, and squeezed it. "The computer is at the Laney Musée des Beaux-Arts."

Genevieve's face was blank. She sat still as a rock, staring at Philip as if she hadn't heard him.

Then her hand began to fidget in his. He watched her expression as his words began to sink in. A flicker of understanding sparked in her eyes. Her gaze left his and looked over his shoulder at nothing, then came back, locking his eyes with hers.

"Okay," she said at last. "I guess that means someone at our museum is trying to do us harm." She snorted in disgust. "I guess I should say they're trying to kill us and steal our wine. And that someone could be Lillie." She sniffed. "Is that about it?"

Philip raised her hand to his lips and kissed it. "That's about it," he said.

FORTY-FIVE

Tuesday could not have been more chaotic. Madame Morier arrived from Paris to help with the Cité du Vin event. She and Delphine were knee-deep, struggling over who was responsible for what. Genevieve popped in and out of the fray, trying to referee until, at last, she realized that their hostile tone, plentiful hand gestures and endless stream of aggressive French was their way of working together.

Lillie and Bernard would arrive on the TGV this afternoon. They would both stay at the château. Their job was to ensure that at the end of the board meeting everything for The Art of the Vine was in place and the program was ready to roll out.

Though Philip had assured Genevieve Cité du Vin would not turn down the enormous endowment they were offering, she was determined to show the board what an asset the Warwicks would be as partners. Always well-polished, every nook, cranny, doorknob, windowpane, brass hinge, carpet fringe, wood floor, and French door at Château Beaulieu shone with an extra luster. With everyone bustling to create a perfect event, energy bounced from floor to ceiling and back again.

For the next two days, Château Beaulieu was a beehive, buzzing with preparations from morning until well into the evening.

By early afternoon on Thursday, Genevieve's vision was perfectly executed and even she was satisfied.

At Saint-Émilion's elegant Hotel de Pavie, board members were arriving and settling into their rooms before making their way to Château Beaulieu. The invitations waiting for them were not specific about what to expect, but the mystery only served to heighten their excitement.

Please join us at Château Beaulieu,
today at

17:30

AS

The Saint-Émilion Jurade
welcomes the Cité du Vin Foundation Board
with a special tribute.

PHILIP AND GENEVIEVE WARWICK

By five forty-five, everyone had gathered in the salon and a flute of Veuve Clicquot bubbled in each person's hand.

Stunning in a cabernet-red silk jacket and narrow-cut trousers flared from the knee, Elise Beaufoy stepped from the crowd to acknowledge Philip and Genevieve.

"Lord and Lady Crosswick," she gushed, her taut face attempting to smile. "On behalf of the Cité du Vin Foundation Board, I must thank you for your hospitality in hosting our meeting, and for your magnanimous gift to Cité du Vin." Her hands fluttered as she spoke. "By creating The Art of the Vine, you will change the lives of many young people by giving them a place in the magical industry of French wine. Merci beaucoup for allowing our foundation to be a part of this magnificent project." She pulled Genevieve into la bise and blew a kiss across the room to Philip.

Appreciative cheers and claps filled the salon until Philip tapped his Champagne glass to quiet the crowd. "Thank you, thank you," he began. "Présidente Beaufoy and members of le Fondation pour la Culture et les Civilisations du Vin Board of Directors, welcome. Genevieve and I are thrilled you have gathered here at Château Beaulieu as we explore The Art of the Vine and how, together, we'll make this program a reality. But, before we get down to the hard work of creating something from nothing, we have a treat for you. You are all familiar with the Jurade, a group tasked in 1199 by Richard the Lionheart to guard the quality and health of the vines of Saint-Émilion, planted by the Romans and nurtured to this day. This afternoon the Jurade will honor you with their traditional pipe and drum parade, usually seen only twice a year. But today they make an exception just for you, La Cité du Vin Board of Directors. With that introduction, please refill your glasses before Genevieve leads you out to the front steps."

The group followed Genevieve through the foyer, flooded out the front door and onto the wide limestone porch. Those who had seen the parade before buzzed with excitement, thrilled at knowing what awaited them. Those who had not, bubbled with anticipation.

Philip snaked his way through the swarm of bodies and down the stairs to Genevieve's side, where he handed her a faceted flute.

"Ooolala," she said, and sipped, the bubbles tickling her nose.

"Your attention, please," she said, but couldn't be heard over the din. "May I have your attention, please?" She raised her voice, but to no avail. Without warning, Philip let loose an earsplitting whistle that silenced the crowd. "Ah, thank you, Philip." She flashed him a grateful smile. "For the next few minutes, please focus your attention on the far end of the lane and listen carefully."

Even as she spoke, a faint note like thunder rolled in the distance. "Listen," she said, putting her hand to her ear.

The sound grew louder by the second, bass drums booming a rhythmic warning. Then, the whine of the bagpipes began. Twelve pipers, four abreast, turned onto the lane followed by more than a hundred members of the Jurade of Saint-Émilion, their crimson robes swaying to the pipers' music. The haunting tune crescendoed with every step they took toward the château, drones of the bagpipe holding the moaning, low note, the chanter playing the melody.

The bass drums rumbled, and the snare drums trilled their

relentless beat, driving the marching pipers forward. The wail of the bagpipes grew louder and louder until the spectacle was in front of the electrified crowd. As they played the last notes of the melancholy song, the pipers parted and the jurats strode through the aisle.

The first jurat stepped forward. "Lord Crosswick," he bellowed. "I have a decree for the Board of Cité du Vin."

"Of course, Jurat Manoncourt," Philip said. "Présidente Beaufoy, if you please." He motioned for Elise to come forward.

On her four inch stilettos, she teetered down the three broad steps, then, with full pomp and circumstance, the head of the brotherhood began. "Presidente Beaufoy, we wish to extend an invitation for the revered Board of Cité du Vin to join us as our honored guests for the Jurade festival in June and the Ban des Vendanges in September." He handed Elise a rolled-up parchment, tied with a red ribbon, secured with a red wax seal. He kissed both her cheeks. "Now," he said, looking at Philip, "I believe there is wine to drink." And the crowd let out a mighty cheer.

On the other side of Saint-Émilion, at police headquarters, Agent Lambert, Directeur Picard, and Inspector Boucher, who had returned the night before, were in the eye of the storm. While activity swirled around them, they methodically placed the final pieces in the puzzle, the last of which they discovered an hour ago. Stuck to the back of one of the last files they had pulled from the cabinet was a yellow post-it note, written in Daniel's hand. Dated two months ago, the note was a reminder to call his Paris partner, with a name and phone number. Now that they had the last link in the chain, a small team of municipal police prepared for the arrest of a local citizen. They inspected their pepper spray, batons, and handcuffs, bantering back and forth, trying to keep their adrenaline under control.

It was rare in Saint-Émilion for the police to deal with serious crime. A loose dog nosing through an upended garbage bin, the occasional graffiti painted on the side of a house, or a drunk teenager who had to be helped into the back of a police car and driven home was the height of adventure in the pretty, medieval town. For most of the squad, tonight would be the pinnacle of their law enforcement careers, and they could hardly wait for the directeur to give them the order. Their nerves jittered knowing it was mere moments before they were out the door and on their way.

FORTY-SIX

BEAUTIFUL AT ANY time, the tasting room dazzled as the scene of the Cité du Vin opening cocktail party, with the late afternoon sun filtering through the wall of French doors. As the natural light waned, hundreds of candles would cast their glow throughout the room. There were no traces of Lambert, Picard, and their teams. Their boxes and papers had been displaced by sparkling glasses, bottles of fine wine, and a stunning display of hors d'oeuvres.

The Jurade and Cité du Vin guests made their way from the front of the château, across the courtyard and into the vineyard building. As the crowd filtered in, a jazz trio played and the fragrance of lilies and peonies sweetened the air. Spirits were high after the grand introduction to the evening, and the crowd was enjoying themselves as they chatted, nibbled scrumptious morsels, and waited for the wine to flow.

Earlier in the day, Émile had brought in eight cases of Château Beaulieu's best and arranged a case on the table ready to be uncorked. Philip found Jurat Manoncourt in the crowd and caught his eye. He motioned to the portly man with a bushy white mustache and rimless glasses. The Jurat wove his way through the crowd to Philip.

"Oui, my lord. Are we ready to uncork the ambrosia?"

"We are," Philip said, just as his phone vibrated in his pocket. He held up a finger. "Just one minute." He glanced at his screen and saw the text from Directeur Picard.

We are leaving for the search and seizure, it read. *Update soon.*

Philip heard himself gasp and felt blood rush to his head.

"Is everything all right?" Manoncourt asked.

"I'm fine," he said. "Champagne in the afternoon always gets to me." His smile was weak but convincing. "Give me just a couple of minutes and we'll get on with it, shall we?" Before the Jurat could respond, Philip plunged into the crowd in search of Genevieve. When he found her, she, Elise Beaufoy and Lillie were in deep conversation. "G, I need to speak to you for just a minute."

"Hi." Lillie kissed Philip on the cheek. "Find me when your husband's finished with you," she said to Genevieve. Lillie grinned, slid her arm through Elise's and joined a trio of board members who were drooling over the tempura coconut shrimp.

"What's going on?" When she looked at Philip, Genevieve knew something was amiss.

He pulled his phone from his pocket and showed her the screen.

"So, this is happening," she said. "They're on their way to Clos Peyra?"

"It looks that way. I've got to get back to Manoncourt. He needs to uncork this wine and get it flowing." He took her hand. "Come with me," he said, and pulled her with him back to the tasting table. "Are you ready, Monsieur?"

A nod from the jurat assured Philip that he was more than ready. Philip looked at the trio of musicians and motioned for the drummer to give him a flourish. With the room quieting, Philip cleared his throat before he spoke. "Mesdames et Messieurs. We would be fools if we did not impose on Charles Manoncourt, the First Jurat of Saint-Émilion and one of the preeminent wine authorities in Bordeaux, to uncork the first bottle of the evening and pass judgment that it is worthy of this special gathering."

Claps and cheers thundered through the room. With great ceremony, Manoncourt sliced the foil then screwed the worm into the cork until the bootlever was in a perfect position to make the first pull. He twisted it in just a bit further and slid the cork out. Another round of applause erupted from the crowd. Genevieve handed the jurat a sparkling crystal glass with a generous bowl and tapering neck, perfect for their elegant Château Beaulieu grand cru.

As Manoncourt poured then swirled the wine, Genevieve realized she was holding her breath. His nose delved into the glass in search of the beautiful notes created by the marriage of merlot and cabernet franc. It lingered there too long. He lowered the glass, took a breath, exhaled, and again plunged his nose into the goblet. Genevieve and Philip watched as the jurat's eyes darted back and forth. At last, he lowered the glass again, smiled an uncomfortable smile, swirled the wine one more time and took a slurpy sip. In an instant, he turned his back to the crowd and spit the wine back into the glass.

"Monsieur Manoncourt, q'est que c'est? What's the matter?" Philip's eyes bulged. He grabbed a glass and splashed wine into it. What he tasted was a red worthy of Two Buck Chuck.

"Perhaps the bottle was not properly stored, my lord. Shall we try another?" The jurat bit his lower lip.

Philip had already cut the foil on another bottle and handed it to Manoncourt to uncork. "Genevieve, find Émile," he said. She was already texting him.

The second bottle was no better, nor was the third. By the time Émile arrived they had opened five bottles, all of them worthy of a corner shop in a beer-drinking town.

"Émile, where did you get these bottles of wine?"

He shrugged. "These were with the bottles of La Vie Douce Delphine told me to pick up yesterday from Château Pitique. There were two cases of dessert wine. When I was loading them onto the truck, I saw six cases of our grand cru on a pallet in the corner of the warehouse. It seemed odd to me that they would be there." Anxious he had done something wrong, his words tumbled out. "Delphine didn't say to pick up the grand cru, but I assumed they were ours. I asked the guy on the shipping floor and he said to take them. Is there something wrong? What's the matter with it?"

"It's not our wine," Philip said flatly. "They are our bottles, filled with someone else's inexpensive wine."

Sensing something was amiss, Delphine made her way from across the room to Philip and Genevieve. "Bad wine?" she said.

"Looks like it." Philip was unsure how much to reveal. "Until we figure this out, could you get more Champagne from the cellars?"

"Of course, my lord. Consider it done."

"Philip!" Genevieve said, tugging on his sleeve. "You know what this means? This means Kim isn't the counterfeiter, it's Hank. We need to text Picard."

Philip pounded on his phone, then hit send. He and Genevieve watched his screen, but there was no response.

"Call him," she said.

He called, but it went straight to voicemail. He tried Lambert with the same result.

"We need to go to Clos Peyra." Butterflies fluttered in Genevieve's stomach. She wasn't sure if they were from excitement or fear; maybe both.

"We can't let Picard arrest Kim," Philip said. "We need to tell Duncan so he can manage things here and keep the party going." As he and Genevieve shot out of the tasting room, he texted Duncan to meet them at the garage.

Within minutes, they were in a Cotswold-blue Jaguar XKE, waiting for the garage door to open. When Duncan tapped on the window, Philip and Genevieve almost jumped through the roof.

"What's going on?" Duncan said, anticipating the emergency had something to do with the events at the clos.

"We've got to get to Clos Peyra," Philip said, his voice clipped and urgent. "Picard and Lambert are about to raid the Wangs, and they're not the counterfeiters."

Disbelief flashed across Duncan's face. "You're kidding."

Philip brought Duncan up to speed as fast as he could, anxious to get on the road. "Hank must be the counterfeiter. Don't tell anyone. Delphine and Manoncourt are the only people who know what's going on and we want to keep it that way. Get wine from our stock and keep everybody happy. We'll be back as soon as we can."

"But, Dad—"

"We've got to go," Philip interrupted. He put the car in gear and roared out of the garage.

Though their mission was urgent, Philip couldn't keep a smile from his lips. He accelerated and the XKE hugged the road as he banked into the corners. He turned down the narrow lane that led to Clos Peyra, expecting to see police cars and lights flashing, but the only car in front of the house was Kim's BMW.

"That's strange, isn't it?" Genevieve leaned forward, straining against her seatbelt. "Didn't you expect to see cars and lights and lots of police? Where is everybody?"

Philip slowed to a crawl, then stopped twenty yards from the house. He pulled out his phone, scrolled to Picard's text, and read it again, this time aloud. "We are leaving for the search and seizure. Will update you soon."

"He doesn't say they're coming here to Clos Peyra, does he?" Genevieve searched the message for a clue to what was happening.

While he was staring at his screen, Philip's phone vibrated, and a text popped up. "Han Shou in custody. On our way to CB," he read aloud. "What the…" he said as he looked at Genevieve.

She shook her head and held up both palms, confused. "How did they figure that out?"

"If they're on their way to Château Beaulieu, we'd better get moving," he said. He smashed the clutch to the floor and threw the gearshift into first. Gravel spun beneath the wheels as he gave the engine too much gas. They shot around the circular drive and back down the lane. Philip stopped just long enough to see there were no cars coming, then gunned the engine onto the main road. Within three minutes they were racing down their driveway. As they approached the château they noticed three unfamiliar Citroëns.

"Cops," Philip said as he slammed to a stop. "Why in the hell have they come here?" He threw open his door, grabbed the door jamb and grunted as he pulled himself from the low-slung car. By the time he was around to her side, Genevieve was already up the stairs and opening the front door.

In the tasting room, bona fide bottles of Château Beaulieu were being emptied at a rapid clip. Laughter, chatter, and music filled the space, and everyone was having a wonderful time, oblivious to the police drama rumbling nearby.

Lillie's animated conversation captivated two Cité du Vin board members while Bernard smiled at Lillie's ability to engage everyone, from pauper to king. He was about to detail how The Art of the Vin work-study program would fill the void that was growing more critical by the year for vineyard owners, when he felt a vice grip on his left shoulder and an iron grasp on his right wrist. A man's voice was almost a whisper in his ear. "Bernard Reines, you are under arrest," the man on the left said. "Just come quietly. We have Hank Shou in custody and he'd very much like for you to join him."

Fear flooding through him, Bernard looked around for Lillie, but she had eased off into the crowd and left him on his own.

The two officers kept a firm grip on Bernard as they pushed him toward the door. They looked like three friends perhaps going out for a smoke. No one noticed that he was leaving. No one cared.

Realizing that his masterful counterfeiting scheme was about to come crashing down, panic seized him. As they stepped out of the tasting room, Bernard mustered all his strength, broke out of the officers' grips and charged down the hall, head lowered and fists pumping, just as Émile emerged from the storeroom carrying an armful of wine bottles. Bernard smashed into Émile, knocking them both off their feet. Bottles flew into the air and crashed on the brick, spraying shards of glass and splattering wine everywhere.

Terrified that he had injured his former boss, Émile jumped up and pulled on Bernard's arm trying to help him. "M— M— Monsieur Reines, pardon, pardon. Je suis désolé." He pulled his shirttail from his waistband and tried to mop wine from Bernard's face.

Bernard slapped Émile's hands away. "Éloigne-toi de moi espèce, d'idiot," he snarled, fisting his hand, ready to punch Émile. But before he could strike, the two officers pulled his hands behind his back and cuffed him. This time, the officers weren't as polite. They yanked Bernard to stand and held him firmly.

"I wouldn't call Émile an idiot, I'd call him a hero," Duncan said, standing in the doorway. "I came into the hall just in time to see you stop this counterfeiting son-of-a-bitch from getting away. Well done, Émile." He stuck out his hand and pulled the confused young man off the floor.

"Je ne comprends pas. I don't understand." Émile looked at his former boss, who was now wine-soaked, disheveled and handcuffed.

Duncan put his arm around the young man's shoulders. "Émile, for the last three years, Bernard has been the head of a small group that counterfeited millions of euros of Château Beaulieu wine." Duncan felt Émile's body stiffen and a guttural laugh roll from his throat.

"I am not surprised." He glared at Bernard. "From the moment he suggested I cover the Pollock with the giclee, I knew he was full of… I think you say, larceny."

"Wait a minute." Duncan dropped his arm from Émile's shoulders, stood back and studied him. "I thought you got the idea when you read his manuscript."

"That's what he told me to say if I got caught, but I never read his book. He paid me five thousand euros to play the prank on Lord and Lady Crosswick." He shrugged. "It wasn't a lot, just pocket money, but I thought it would be fun. He assured me that even if they traced the joke to me, I would not be in trouble." He smacked his forehead with the heel of his hand. "As he said, I was an idiot to trust him. It wouldn't surprise me if he did other illegal things while heading up the LMBA."

"Well, my friend, Bernard is in custody, and you are the one who stopped him in his tracks." As he gave Émile a pat on the back, he saw his parents at the other end of the hall, his father on the phone and his mother striding toward the strange scene.

Genevieve walked to within inches of Bernard and drilled into his eyes for several seconds. "Thank god it was you." Still staring at him, she shook her head. "I guess the LMBA wasn't enough. Was it just about the money?"

Rather than meet Genevieve's withering gaze, he looked past her.

"Thank god it was you," she said again. "You, we can lose, but we would have been devastated if it had been Lillie." She turned to Émile. "And thank you for saving the day, Émile. You keep surprising us." She stretched up on her tiptoes, kissed his wine-spotted cheek, then licked her lips. "Love the vintage," she said, and beamed at him.

Philip shoved his phone into his pocket as he joined the group. "That was Directeur Picard," he said to Genevieve. "He, Lambert, and Boucher will be here later to brief us, but it seems we have the real prize right here. The mastermind, the puppet master, the genius behind the scheme." He turned to Bernard. "Hank is selling you down the river, my friend, and according to him, you're the one who insisted that Genevieve and I fall out of the sky and die in a French cow pasture. There are so many things I want to say to you, Bernard, but sometimes, a simple gesture says it best." At that, Philip drew back his arm and, for the first time in his life, he punched a man and heard the satisfying crunch of a broken nose.

FORTY-SEVEN

By THE TIME Agent Lambert, Directeur Picard, and Inspector Boucher arrived at Château Beaulieu, the party in the tasting room was over. Where the Jurade had marched en masse and in precision with the pipers to begin the afternoon, they now wandered and wobbled in small groups down the long allée, leaving jollier than when they arrived. The Cité du Vin board members and their entourage piled into hired cars that would return them to Hotel de Pavie, where they would refortify themselves for tomorrow's meeting. Thanks to the discrete handling of events, no one was the wiser about the swirl of police activity just outside the tasting room.

Now the three officers and three Warwicks gathered in Philip's study. The circles around Lambert's eyes suggested sleep had not been her friend over the last few days and judging from Picard's rumpled, spotted shirt, Genevieve was sure he had not been home recently. But Boucher was pert and perky, happy to be at Château Beaulieu and back in Genevieve's company, no matter what the occasion.

"I'm assuming you have a lot to tell us." Philip looked at Lambert and Picard sitting on a sofa, and Boucher by the fire in the down-filled chair he loved.

"We do," Picard said. "Much of it you know, but there are some things that may come as a surprise. Inspector Boucher, would you like to begin?"

Delighted to be the center of attention, the BEA Inspector began. "As you know, we determined some time ago that Lee Bowen was responsible for watering your fuel tank."

"As I recall, Lee Bowen worked for the Wang family. Wasn't that one of the fingers pointing at Kim?" Genevieve said.

"It is true. At one time, he worked for Kim Wang's father in England. According to Hank, he asked Kim to recommend a man in the UK who could help him with a few things. That's how he got Bowen's name. We had no trouble tracking him to France. It got more difficult after that, but through tracing his credit cards we discovered he had rented a car. With that information, we used surveillance camera footage to follow him to Château Pitique. No doubt he came here to receive his payment. The day after he was here, the car was found at the airport parking lot. We think he had access to a new identity, a passport under another name, and left the country." He paused, looked over the top of his glasses and smirked. "He is not worth the resources it would take to find him. He is, as you would say, small onions."

"Small potatoes," Philip corrected. "He's small potatoes." Philip was teeming with questions. "What about Daniel's note in my briefcase? And who were the people who beat you to the train?"

"Ah, oui. A good question," Boucher said. "When LaGrande

was in Paris for the party, he asked Madame Morier to slip the note into your briefcase. He wanted to warn you of the danger that lay ahead. Bernard overheard him ask for Madame Morier's help and arranged for his people to intercept the note."

"But how did—"

Boucher put up his hand, anticipating Philip's next question. "Lord Crosswick, Bernard tapped your phone as soon as he knew you and Lady Crosswick didn't die in a plane crash."

"Holy crap," Philip seethed. He snatched his phone from the side table and threw it into the fireplace. He blew the air from his cheeks and slumped back in his chair.

"Jeeze, Philip. Was that necessary?" Genevieve scowled at her husband.

He mumbled something under his breath.

Taking that as her cue, Lambert picked up the story. "When the Shou family bought Château Pitique three years ago, Bernard convinced Hank that counterfeiting Château Beaulieu wine and shipping it to China would be easy and very profitable."

"That makes sense," Genevieve frowned. "Bernard and Hank were old friends and I imagine Bernard knew Hank was under pressure from his father to make a quick success of Château Pitique. What a perfect opportunity for Bernard, but why he would risk so much—his prestigious position in the art community, his freedom—to be involved in such a thing?"

"Ah," Lambert sighed. "Hank offered some interesting insight. Though Bernard is well educated, he does not come from a wealthy family. According to Hank, he always loved fine things, and as director of the LMBA he was always surrounded by the best of everything, but none of it was his."

"So rather than work hard and earn the lifestyle he lusted after, he decided to steal his way to wealth."

"You are exactly right, Lord Crosswick."

"Take it from someone who knows, it's better to inherit lots of money." Philip laughed at his own joke.

Lambert gave Philip a moment to enjoy himself, then went on. "The other important piece of the puzzle was Daniel LaGrande. They needed Château Beaulieu bottles and labels, which Daniel could easily get for them. The challenge was to get him involved." Agent Lambert looked at the three Warwicks to make sure they were following. They all nodded.

Lambert continued. "You all know about Daniel's nephew, Paul, who borrowed a hundred thousand euros from his uncle." Again, everyone nodded. "Paul told Madam Morier that his uncle had saved him from financial disaster." She looked up from her notes. "Interesting pillow talk, I would say. Later, in one of her gossipy chats with Bernard, she told him Daniel had loaned money to Paul."

Before Lambert could go on, Genevieve jumped in: "So Bernard suggested to Daniel that supplying bottles and labels would be an easy way to refill his coffers…"

"…and it wouldn't do Château Beaulieu any harm," Duncan finished.

Agent Lambert smiled. "Exactly. According to Hank, Daniel was fine with the arrangement until he learned that Bernard had ordered Lee Bowen to water down the gas in your jet. That was too much for him."

Genevieve's eyes flashed. "I would hope so."

"Apparently Daniel found out about Bernard's fuel tank order at your gala in Paris," she went on. "Hank said they had quite a row. Did you know anything about that?"

Genevieve stiffened as she remembered the scene at Maison de Laney. "So that's what their argument was all about!"

Philip and Genevieve gaped at each other.

"When Daniel died, Hank was stunned by his death and feared Bernard had killed him. When he heard it was suicide, he was relieved," Lambert added.

Genevieve thought for a minute, then asked, "Was Madame Morier involved in any of this?"

"No. It appears she knew nothing about Bernard and Daniel's scheme."

"And, just to confirm, Lillie wasn't a part of it, was she?" Genevieve held her breath.

"Non."

She exhaled. "I'm so glad."

"Chloé, however, is another story." Picard spoke for the first time in a long while. "Hank paid her to spy on the household. I doubt that she reported anything important, but, nonetheless, I am certain you will want to address that."

"Won't she be arrested?" Genevieve asked.

"Only if you press charges. And I'm not certain what they would be. Gossiping, perhaps?" Picard chuckled. "There is no indication that she was aware of the criminal activity, however George, her paramour, is a different situation. He has been Hank's bon à tout faire, I believe the English say dogsbody, for the last few months doing all his dirty work. We have him in custody. He was the one who chased the horse through the field and over the wall."

The Warwicks looked at each other, wondering what questions had been left unanswered. After a moment, Philip said, "What happens next?"

"We turn our evidence and our recommendations over to the magistrat de siège, the public prosecutor. That judge will decide whether or not to go forward with prosecution."

Duncan couldn't believe what he was hearing. "You mean it's not a foregone conclusion that Bernard, Hank, and their merry band will be prosecuted?"

"How is that possible?" Genevieve thundered.

"As I told you at our first meeting, it is difficult to entice the law to bring wine counterfeiters to justice." Agent Lambert looked resigned. "I believe, however, that because Bernard tried to murder you, the magistrate will be much keener." She gathered her papers, slipped them into her briefcase, and stood. "We shall keep you posted as the case moves forward. Thank you for everything, all your help and your cooperation. I hope we don't have the opportunity to meet again under the same circumstances."

Philip extended his hand to Agent Lambert. "I assure you, we won't hesitate to call you if we think anyone is fiddling with our wine."

"Directeur Picard." Duncan gave his hand a firm shake. "We now have close ties to our local police. Let's hope we won't need you often, but we know you'll be ready if we do."

Genevieve stepped to where Boucher was standing, waiting

like an eager puppy. "And, last, but certainly not least, Inspector Boucher. You've been with us since we landed in France. We could say you are among our oldest French friends." When she held out her hand, Boucher caressed it in both of his. Duncan grimaced while Philip bit his lower lip, trying not to laugh.

"Lady Crosswick, je suis éternellement à votre service. I am forever at your service. You have but to call, and I shall be here." He brought her hand to his lips, kissed it, then bowed from his waist.

Genevieve looked across Boucher's bent back at Philip, who was stifling a chuckle.

Always gracious, Genevieve nudged Boucher from his bow. "My family and I are in your debt," she said, sliding her hand from Boucher's grip. "It's getting late, and we know you all have many things to do to wrap up this case."

She led them into the foyer and toward the front door where Delphine offered their coats. She gave Picard his jacket and held out Boucher's topcoat and scarf. He took his scarf and swirled it around his short neck, the last loop covering his mouth and nose. He shoved it down, hoping no one had noticed. He took his coat from Delphine and swung it around to drape it over his shoulders. As he took a step toward Genevieve to say a final farewell, his coat slipped off his shoulders, falling to the floor. Trying to look as suave as possible he bent down, scooped it up and slung it over his arm.

Picard and Lambert were already down the stairs and heading toward the police car as Philip stood with the door open. When the inspector realized he was the last one to leave, he grabbed

Genevieve by the shoulders and gave her a final kiss on each cheek. "Au revoir," he said.

"Au revoir, Maurice," Genevieve said, and waved.

Philip closed the door, and they collapsed against it, howling with laughter.

FORTY-EIGHT

HER EYES STILL closed, Genevieve listened to Philip's slow, steady breathing. She thought about the yin and yang of yesterday—a welcoming event and auspicious beginning to their partnership with Cité du Vin amid the turbulent finale to their three-month-long series of mysteries. It was hard to believe that the party guests in the tasting room were oblivious to the capture and arrest of Bernard just yards away, but anyone who heard the crash of bottles as Émile smashed into Bernard would have assumed a server dropped a tray of glasses on the brick floor.

"You have to hand it to the French," Genevieve thought. "They never let anything distract them from superb wine and fine cuisine." In the words of William Shakespeare, "All's well that ends well," she mused. And today everything was going to end perfectly.

She looked at her watch, 7:15. Fifteen more minutes, then she would get up. She rolled toward Philip, slid her hand around his bare chest, kissed his shoulder and snuggled into his back. "It's meeting day," she whispered.

"Hmm," was his response.

She kissed his neck this time. "I said it's meeting day."

He took her hand and kissed the palm. "Go back to sleep. It's the middle of the night."

"It's almost ten o'clock. The board will be here any minute."

Philip pulled her wrist to his eyes and squinted. "It's 7:18. Aren't you exhausted after last night?"

"Like I said, it's meeting day. Lots to do."

He rolled onto his side so they were face to face. "G, you realize *we* are giving millions of euros to the Cité du Vin for a program that, for the next many years, will benefit hundreds of kids and many vineyards. We don't need to impress these people. The Jurade parade kicking everything off and the cocktail party last night were wonderful. You love doing these spectacular events, I know." He put his hand on Genevieve's cheek. "But, shouldn't Cité du Vin be dazzling us?"

Genevieve rolled onto her back and stared at the ceiling. "Let me ask you a question."

"Sure."

Philip saw a tear trickle from the corner of her eye and slide down the side of her face.

"G." Philip traced the damp path with his forefinger.

She turned her head toward him, her eyes sparkling from the tears that were about to overflow.

"What's going on?" Philip searched her face for a sign of what could be wrong.

"Since the jet incident, you've said repeatedly you're going to disinherit yourself," she smiled and sniffed.

He said nothing but remained locked in her gaze.

"With every new revelation, and there were many, you became more emphatic that we should resume our pre-inheritance lives. Now that this crazy mystery is solved, what are you thinking?" She sniffed again.

For what seemed like ages, Philip stared at Genevieve. She could read nothing in his eyes and had no idea what his response was about to be. She caressed the side of his face, but still he said nothing.

Her lips parted as she was about to speak, but before she could, he leaned forward and covered her mouth with his. It was a soft kiss, a gentle kiss, and it said everything. As he pulled back, Genevieve saw the answer in his eyes.

EPILOGUE

SPRING AND SUMMER raced across the calendar in a blur, leaving the chaos and madness of March behind. Now here they were on the edge of fall, watching the September sun streak the sky with yellow and crimson as it dipped toward the horizon.

The view over the vineyard could have been a painting. For miles, green vines waited in tidy rows, heavy with grapes ready for harvest. The red from the sky reflected on the leaves, the grass, the trees. Around a long table covered with a crisp white linen cloth that puddled on the stone floor of the terrace, the Château Beaulieu family lingered over the remnants of a late-summer dinner.

French and English flew around the table non-stop, and laughter pealed across the valley like church bells.

Unusually quiet, Philip and Genevieve sat, shoulders touching, their clasped hands resting on the table. Watching frisky Cooper chase Alex from one end of the terrace to the other, Genevieve couldn't imagine a more perfect tableau. Ella sat on Delphine's lap, frowning in concentration as the house manager showed her the fine art of creative napkin folding. They had turned squares of linen into a parade of whimsey as a rabbit, a swan, a fan, a star, and a bishop's hat marched down the center of the table. Ella was determined to fold a much-crumpled serviette into a unicorn but was having little luck.

Putting a flame to the last unlit candle on the table, Émile paused before moving to the lanterns scattered along the low, stone wall rimming the terrace. "Is this not a perfect evening, Lord Crosswick, Lady Crosswick?" he said, his face bronze and glowing from hours spent in the fields.

This was not the arrogant, lost boy who had attempted to extort money from Philip and Genevieve for their Jackson Pollock a mere seven months ago. Over the summer, he had worked hard under Edouard's keen eye. He was a surprising student, learning quickly and voraciously, and he seemed to be falling in love with Château Beaulieu and vineyard life. At least ten pounds heavier, much of that lean muscle, he was robust and clear-eyed, with an energy and ready smile that confirmed they had made the right decision to bring him to their château. Over the past months, he had become a trusted part of their lives.

At the end of the table, Duncan and Edouard sat in rapt attention while Henri regaled them with stories of the cars in the Château Beaulieu collection. "As interesting as the automobiles in the collection are," he nodded at Duncan, "the stories about, I believe you say, the ones that got away are even more fascinating. One day I shall share them all." He sat back and lit a Gauloise, inhaled, and watched the glow of the cigarette tip as he blew a long stream of smoke into the night.

A cheer went up when David emerged from the house, his

arms filled with reinforcement bottles of mineral water and wine. He and Becca had come for the weekend and rounded out the exuberant group.

"So," Becca said, as David walked around the table filling glasses. "David and I have a rather enormous favor to ask of the Warwick family."

Conversation stopped and everyone on the terrace waited for her to continue. She looked at each expectant face, glowing in the candlelight. Even Alex and Ella leaned forward with anticipation.

She gave David a pleading glance, hoping he would jump in. "Don't look at me, darling. This was your idea."

"You're right," she said. "Philip, Genevieve, Duncan, Julia, and of course Alex and Ella, David and I have decided on our wedding date."

"It's about time," Julia said, raising her goblet.

Genevieve didn't miss a beat. "And you're going to have the wedding here, right?" She pulled her phone from her pocket and brought up her calendar. "What date are you thinking?"

"Oh, boy! Can I be a flower girl?" Ella was off Delphine's lap and at Becca's side in an instant, jumping up and down, curls bouncing around her sweet face.

Stunned that Genevieve knew what she was about to ask, Becca was speechless.

Genevieve scrolled forward through the months, then looked at Becca. "Are you thinking during the holidays?"

"How did you know? We were thinking December 20th. Would that work?"

Genevieve's smile was radiant. "That would be perfect." She leaned into Philip's shoulder. "That's *our* anniversary."

"Really?" Becca's eyes glistened.

"And, The Art of the Vine students will have completed the first half of their program, so we're having a party for them the week before."

"How's the program going?" David asked.

Philip's grin stretched across his face as he thought about what they had created in such a short time. "It's beyond what we could have imagined." He turned to look at Genevieve. "It's amazing what you can accomplish if you throw money at a project."

Genevieve squeezed his hand and smiled into the night.

"It makes all the hassle and mystery and danger worth it, doesn't it, G?" he said. "Didn't I keep telling you it would be crazy to give all this up?"

In response, Genevieve's full-throated laughter rang across the terrace and into the vines.

Philip glanced at his phone, checking the text that had just pinged. It was from Richard Durand, a well-credentialed and fastidious art historian they had hired to replace Bernard as the director of the Laney Musée des Beaux-Arts.

Lord Crosswick, I have found some paperwork that concerns me regarding two paintings that were sold to the Cité du Vin last winter. There is no emergency. Please call Monday. RD

Philip seized on the part of the message that said there was no emergency and drew his attention back to the magical scene whirling around him. For the first time since arriving in France, he was sure he and his family were heading down the right path, and after months of waiting to feel the spirit of his Laney ancestors at Château Beaulieu, tonight their essence surrounded him. The thrill of seeing The Art of the Vin in full operation with the promise of affecting many young lives in the future made everything they had been through worthwhile.

He tapped his wine glass with his knife and a dulcet tone rang out. "Your attention, please. I would like to make a toast to all of you. Everyone around this table is here because Genevieve and I cherish you. You are Château Beaulieu. As Duncan and Julia become the lord and lady of this grand Château, Genevieve and I know they will be successful because of all of you. With many exciting events to look forward to before the end of the year, let's enjoy each and every day in this very special place with you very special people. Santé."

"Santé," everyone responded, including Cooper with a loud bark.

La Fin

KEEP READING FOR A SNEAK PEEK OF

JONATHON WILLIAM WALLACE LANEY

The 12TH Earl of Crosswick

AND SO IT BEGINS

I'M QUITE SURE my first memory is floating in moist darkness, waiting for something extraordinary to happen. And then it did. I remember my surprise at the waves that rhythmically ebbed and flowed. The longer it lasted the more it annoyed me and just when I decided I'd had enough, the biggest wave of all shoved me against an elastic band. Of course, I didn't know at that time what an elastic band was, but in retrospect, that's what it felt like. And then, another big shove through a small hole, and I was blinded by bright lights bouncing off white walls, white uniforms, white sheets, white faces. I think I was upside down, though, again, I have to say, I didn't know what upside down was. I whimpered, but when someone smacked my bottom, I gave them what they were asking for—a big, fat wail. I remember thinking, "What a set of pipes!"

That was 3 August 1921. I've been telling that story since I was four and every time I do, someone pats me on the head, well, not so much anymore, since I'm, well, dead, but they used to, and they would say, "What a funny story, you clever boy." I would roll my eyes knowing, even at four, that they didn't think I could possibly remember my time in the womb and my journey out into the world. But I did.

And I remember my mother. She always smelled of roses. When I was six, she told me that Rose Otto was her favorite perfume because my grandmother Lady Caroline, had given her a vial of the treasured scent on the day she married my father. Our family believes in tradition and Rose Otto was a tradition that began with my great-grandmother, the magnificent Charlotte Chaubert, the toast of Paris and London. According to my mother, who loved to tell a lively story, Charlotte was my grandfather's passion. Lord Philip adored her, denied her nothing, but in the end, the love of his life was taken from him far too soon.

Sometimes I wonder if I had heeded their story as a warning, could I have veered from the events that took my life down a path I did not choose, or want? It's a bit late to ponder these things, but sometimes my mind still goes there.

The London Times, August 6, 1921

THE COUNTESS OF CROSSWICK HAS BEEN DELIVERED OF A SON

The Countess of Crosswick was safely delivered of a son at 05:26, 3 August, at Columbia-Presbyterian Medical Center, New York City, New York. The baby weighed 7lbs 2oz.

The Earl of Crosswick was delighted to greet his first child.

Lord and Lady Crosswick will reside with their son, Jonathon William Wallace Laney, at their home, Margrave House, Kensington, upon their return to London.

And so I was announced to the world. An auspicious beginning, to be sure. A proper English babe wailing his way into the world, not in the serene, shaded lanes of Kensington, London, but into the noisy, brash streets of New York City, surely a harbinger of how I would live my life.

I'm not certain that my parents wanted more children, or actually any children at all. It seemed to me they were delighted with each other and would have been perfectly happy to live their interesting lives surrounded by artists and musicians rather than a brood of young savages. Regardless, I was the only savage they produced, and it suited me that they stopped at one, as long as I was it.

It was said that I was a bonnie baby, but that was my mother and my granny speaking. I doubt if my father said the same. I believe he preferred the attractive swirl of paint on canvas more than the red face of a newborn. He tended to avoid me in my early years until I could ride well enough to join him on The Hunt at Wilmingrove Hall, our family seat in Yorkshire. Or when I could give him a good run for his money on the chessboard. Then he began to take an interest in me and my development.

I had a nanny I loved nearly as much as I adored my mother, but my nanny was my friend and my mother was, well, someone I worshiped. She was a charming, brilliant, and stunning woman who never tired of bringing life and laughter into our home. No matter what I did, she delighted in it. If I colored a picture for her that was nothing more than a few scribbled lines on the paper, she would declare it to be the work of a burgeoning young talent. If I made a mudpie and insisted it was a plum pudding, she would pretend to eat it all and insist it was worthy of a Michelin star. She read to me. She tutored me in the vast and spectacular art collection that was my parents' pride and joy and because she loved it, I loved it.

And she told me stories. The night she told me the tragic tale of my great-grandmother, Charlotte, the wife of the 9th Earl of Crosswick, it was raining and cold. I was six. My mother and I huddled together on a small sofa in my father's study, which would one day be mine. I remember how cozy we were with a lap robe tucked around us and a fire crackling on the hearth. My hands cradled a cup of hot cocoa, and my mother kept stealing sips, smiling at me each time she did, a little cocoa mustache painting her upper lip. The smell of cocoa still reminds me of my mother. The smell of cocoa and Rose Otto.

"Your great-grandmother was a beauty," she began. "Everyone adored her, but no one as much as your great-grandfather." As she spoke, my mother's forehead nearly touched mine. Her voice was so quiet, I watched her lips to make certain I didn't miss any words. "It was your great grandparents' fortieth wedding anniversary, and this house was filled with guests who were here to celebrate with them." My mother's hand was cool on my cheek. "Everyone gathered at the bottom of the staircase, waiting for Charlotte to make her grand entrance. When she appeared, she was stunning in a shimmering silver dress with a train that curved around her feet. Even at sixty-four, she was breathtaking." My mother looked deeper into my eyes. "You have her eyes, darling boy." And she kissed the tip of my nose, then went on. "The 9th Earl raised his Champagne glass and said, 'To my magnificent bride of forty years. No one else has ever walked the earth, whom I could love as I love you.' At the end of the toast, the band struck up Charlotte's favorite song 'Oh You Beautiful Doll' and Charlotte blew a kiss to the Earl." My mother's eyes were glistening with tears. I didn't understand why she was crying. "When she started down the stairs, the toe of her shoe hooked on her gown's silver train. She tried to grab the banister but missed and tumbled head over heels down the stairs. By the time she reached the bottom, she was...." My mother's voice trailed off, but I understood.

"One day, darling boy, I'm sure you'll meet her," she said. I know my mother intended to comfort me, but when she saw my eyes, wide with fear at the idea that I was going to run into an old, dead lady, perhaps in the middle of the night when I got up to go to the loo, I'm certain she realized she had miscalculated. She quickly tried to recover, pulling me close, kissing my forehead, and laughing. "Don't worry darling. I just meant we'll talk about Granny Charlotte again, and the more we talk about her, the more you'll feel you know her."

I didn't believe her, and for the next year, I lived in fear of great granny jumping out of my wardrobe, every evening when I opened the door to get my dressing gown. Other six-year-olds were frightened of monsters or goblins. I was terrified of my beautiful, kind, dead great-grandmother. And then I learned, purely by accident, that Granny Charlotte was a ghost.

YOU ARE CORDIALLY INVITED

to step inside the 12TH Earl's world.

JOIN TANA'S NEWSLETTER TO DOWNLOAD THE WHOLE STORY, FREE:

WWW.TANALHBOERGER.COM

ABOUT TANA

 Though Tana is an unapologetic Anglophile, she also has a passion for France. At fifteen she spent her summer studying French in Villard-de-Lans near Grenoble and fell in love with the French lifestyle. It wasn't long before she realized that her lust for Paris and Bordeaux, where *Art, Wine, and Crime* is set, would keep calling her back. She shares that passion and many others with her husband, Tom. When they aren't in the UK, France or someplace else wonderful, they spend their time in Sanford, NC and New Jersey with their amazing son and daughter-in-law, and their two fabulous grandchildren.

WWW.TANALHBOERGER.COM

f TANALHBOERGER

www.ingramcontent.com/pod-product-compliance
Lightning Source LLC
Chambersburg PA
CBHW070703010826
48975CB00015B/2722